Danny Miller is the author of ... .lk gov uk/libraries or Treadwell novels, the first of which – *Kiss Me Quick* ...s shortlisted for the CWA John Creasey New Blood Award. He started his writing career as a playwright and a scriptwriter, and has written for the BBC, ITV and Channel 4.

After a successful career writing for radio, **R. D. Wingfield** turned his attention to fiction, creating the character of Jack Frost. The series has been adapted for television as the perennially popular *A Touch of Frost*, starring David Jason. R. D. Wingfield died in 2007.

www.penguin.co.uk

Have you read all the books in the acclaimed Frost prequel series?

FIRST FROST

Denton, 1981. Britain is in recession, the IRA is becoming increasingly active and the country's on alert for an outbreak of rabies.

Detective Sergeant Jack Frost is working under his mentor and inspiration DI Bert Williams, and coping badly with his increasingly strained marriage.

But DI Williams is nowhere to be seen. So when a 12-year-old girl goes missing from a department store changing room, DS Frost is put in charge of the investigation . . .

FATAL FROST

May, 1982. Britain celebrates the sinking of the Belgrano, Princess Diana prepares for the birth of her first child and Denton Police Division welcomes its first black policeman, DS Waters – recently relocated from East London.

While the force is busy dealing with a spate of local burglaries, the body of fifteen-year-old Samantha Ellis is discovered in woodland next to the nearby railway track. Then a fifteen-year-old boy is found dead on Denton's golf course, his organs removed.

Detective Sergeant Jack Frost is sent to investigate – a welcome distraction from troubles at home. And when the murdered boy's sister goes missing, Frost and Waters must work together to find her . . . before it's too late.

MORNING FROST

November 1982. It's been one of the worst days of **DS Jack Frost**'s life.

He has buried his wife Mary, and must now endure the wake, attended by all of Denton's finest.

All, that is, apart from DC Sue Clarke, who has been summoned to the discovery of a human foot in a farmer's field. And things get worse. Local entrepreneur Harry Baskin is shot inside his club and a valuable painting goes missing.

As the week goes on, a cyclist is found dead in suspicious circumstances. Frost is on the case, but another disaster – one he is entirely unprepared for – is about to strike . . .

FROST AT MIDNIGHT

August, 1983. Denton is preparing for a wedding, with less than a week to go until Detective Sergeant Waters marries Kim Myles. But the Sunday before the big day, the body of a young woman is found in the churchyard. Their idyllic wedding venue has become a crime scene.

As best man to Waters, **Detective Inspector Jack Frost** has a responsibility to solve the mystery before the wedding. But with nowhere to live since his wife's family sold his matrimonial home, Frost's got other things on his mind.

Can he put his own troubles aside and step up to be the detective they need him to be?

A LETHAL FROST

Denton, 1984. After a morning's betting at the races, bookmaker George Price is found in his car, barely alive with a bullet in his head. As he's rushed to hospital, **Detective Inspector Jack Frost** and the Denton police force start their hunt for the would-be murderer.

But with a long list of enemies who might want the bookie dead, the team have got their work cut out for them. And with a slew of other crimes hitting the area, from counterfeit goods to a violent drugs gang swamping Denton with cheap heroin, the stakes have never been higher.

Will Frost find the answers he's looking for before things go from bad to worse?

A LETHAL FROST

DANNY MILLER

CORGI BOOKS

TRANSWORLD PUBLISHERS
61–63 Uxbridge Road, London W5 5SA
www.penguin.co.uk

Transworld is part of the Penguin Random House group of companies
whose addresses can be found at global.penguinrandomhouse.com

 Penguin
Random House
UK

First published in Great Britain in 2018 by Bantam Press
an imprint of Transworld Publishers
Corgi edition published 2018

Written for the Estate of R. D. Wingfield by Danny Miller
Copyright © The Estate of R. D. Wingfield 2018

Danny Miller has asserted his right under the Copyright,
Designs and Patents Act 1988 to be identified as the author of this work.

Quotation on p.185 from *Monty Python's Flying Circus* written by
John Cleese and Graham Chapman.
Quotation on p.354 from *Apocalypse Now* written by John Milius
and Francis Ford Coppola.

Every effort has been made to obtain the necessary permissions with
reference to copyright material, both illustrative and quoted. We apologize
for any omissions in this respect and will be pleased to make the
appropriate acknowledgements in any future edition.

A CIP catalogue record for this book
is available from the British Library.

ISBN
9780552175050

Typeset in 11.5/15pt Caslon 540 by Jouve (UK), Milton Keynes
Printed and bound in Great Britain by Clays Ltd, Elcograf S.p.A.

Penguin Random House is committed to a sustainable
future for our business, our readers and our planet. This book
is made from Forest Stewardship Council® certified paper.

 MIX
Paper from
responsible sources
FSC
www.fsc.org FSC® C018179

1 3 5 7 9 10 8 6 4 2

A LETHAL FROST

Prologue

As the horses rounded the last turn and came into the home straight the crowd roared. The favourite, a locally trained thoroughbred, thundered past the winning post after leading the field from the off.

But he wasn't watching the race; he was watching *them*. He watched as she kissed him goodbye. It seemed obscene to him: the man was old enough to be her father. He was over sixty and she was only thirty-two. Her birthday was next month. He knew all about her. She was everything to him. She was everything he desired in a woman.

And he knew he had to be with her and he was sure she felt the same. They were meant to be together, whatever the cost. There was only one thing standing in his way. He'd reconciled himself to that fact. It was a hoary old cliché, but one that had been proven time and time again. *The course of true love never did run smooth.*

There was always an obstacle to overcome. Perhaps that's what made the prize so tantalizing, the thrill of the chase. It was the stuff of all great love stories, and at this stage, with the constant ache that he felt for her pulsing through his body, he was sure he was a character in one of those stories, maybe the greatest one of all, he told himself.

As he watched the big lump of an obstacle make his way to his car, with his disgusting wrinkled liver-spotted hand gripping the leather bag, a bag stuffed full of money, he knew what had to be done. There was only going to be one winner in this race.

He followed the old man to the car park, which was little more than a roped-off field with two geriatric stewards guiding the traffic in and out. He could do it right here, he thought. A bullet, up close, and if he timed it properly the roar of the crowd for the last race would cover the shot. It would take bottle to pull the trigger up close like that; you'd hear the man gasp, see his face contort with shock, maybe get blood on you. It wasn't like shooting game, some target in the distance. It would take stealth, guile and a firm hand. But he had all those qualities, he was sure. He'd convinced himself that killing the old bastard would be easy. And his hatred for the man was such that he'd dehumanized him a long time ago – as far as he was concerned, the old man was dead already. All he had to do was keep his nerve, get up nice and close and squeeze the trigger to make what had been playing over and over in his head a reality.

As his target lowered his considerable bulk into the

little Mercedes, he got into his own car. Yes, the car park was a distinct possibility, but he knew the route the old man would be taking today, and for the next two days. And from Radleigh Park Racecourse to North Denton, where the old man lived, there were also plenty of opportunities to kill him. He turned the key in the ignition, pressed down the accelerator and felt the power of the engine revving behind him, all the time keeping his eye on the prize in front of him.

He followed the Mercedes at a safe distance, but not too far behind. He knew the old man's eyesight wasn't that great, but he was too vain to wear glasses even when driving on his own. So he wouldn't recognize who was following him, it would just be a red blur in the rear-view mirror.

Out on the open road, he almost started to feel sorry for the old bastard. He was no longer the enemy, the obstacle. He was his quarry, his victim. He was as good as dead already.

Friday (1)

Frost was standing in Paradise and looking out over Eden and Utopia.

He pulled a pack of Rothmans from the inside pocket of his leather jacket and sparked one up. He took a long thoughtful pull on the cigarette, blew out a plume of smoke in the direction of Utopia and in a weary voice said, 'Not much of a view. To be honest, I was expecting more.'

'But as you can see there's plenty of parking space. Do you have a car, Mr Frost?'

'A company car, and I can park that anywhere. It's one of the perks of the job. But I do have a motorbike. Very temperamental, only likes the hot weather. Currently it's leaking oil all over the mechanic's garage floor.'

'The building does have a gym, Mr Frost. Great for that after-work workout.'

'Pulling the ring off a can of Hofmeister is about all the exercise I can manage after work.' Frost had to laugh at the sheer cheek of these property developers; the boxy little 'apartments' were hardly anyone's idea of paradise, no matter how hot the property market was right now.

'As I was saying, Mr Frost—'

'Jack, call me Jack.'

Jack. *Jack* Frost?

Frost tore his gaze away from the vista of the new four-storey developments, whimsically named Eden Gardens, Utopia Tower and Paradise Lodge, and turned his attention towards the young estate agent. 'What's so funny about that?' he asked with a straight face.

'Nothing, Mr Frost ... just ...' The young man cleared his throat and changed the subject. 'If this isn't to your liking, on the other side of the building with its north-facing aspect you get an oblique view of the Three Elms Forest.'

'Never heard of it.'

'It's not been planted yet, but the land has been approved for forestation.'

'Well, son,' said Frost, 'looking out at some little trees growing is something to look forward to in my dotage.'

The estate agent was a bit of a young sapling himself, not long out of his teens. With a head full of hair gel and a top lip furred with bum-fluff, all eight stone of him was slotted into a shiny double-breasted suit that really looked like it was wearing him. His striped shirt was obviously fresh out of the cellophane and still had unsightly creases, but with the addition of thick red braces and a tightly knotted nylon tie that was pilling mercilessly, he probably thought he looked the business.

Frost wasn't in the mood to shatter the lad's delusions or confidence, so he threw him an avuncular smile and said, 'Just the three of them, is there?'

'Eh?'

'Elms, just the three of them.'

'Er, I'll have to check with the office, Mr Frost.'

'You best do that, son, because three trees does not a forest make. And along with Paradise, Utopia and Eden, you could get nicked under the Trades Description Act for talking utter cobblers.' Frost gave him a friendly wink, and had another quick recce around the flat, which consisted of three rooms of roughly the same size all painted in magnolia.

The brand-new one-bedroom apartment was the polar opposite of his present accommodation, a furnished studio flat above the Jade Rabbit Chinese restaurant in the High Street. But as characterful as that place was, it had taken its toll. And Frost had come to the conclusion that man cannot live on Kung Po and lager alone, no matter how hard he tried, or even how much he wanted to.

There was also the case of the missing bird. Frost had been put in charge of looking after Monty the parrot, which had once graced the takeaway counter, but after a visit from the health inspector had been moved to share the upstairs flat with Frost. And as much as Frost had forged a career out of locking up the bad guys, the sight

7

of the innocent Monty confined to its cage, literally doing bird for a crime it hadn't committed, depressed the detective. So every now and then Frost would grant it parole and let it fly around the flat. The lure of cuttlefish and Trill always brought it back to the cage. However, so frequent had these flights become, that Frost had forgotten to check if Monty was back in its cage that particular night before flinging open the window to air the place of its inevitable sweet and sour odours. The minute he'd opened it, Frost felt a flurry of feathers against his cheek as Monty flapped past. And he was sure it squawked 'See ya' in his ear as it made its heroic escape.

This had been last week. Old Mrs Fong lost her famed inscrutability and let out a tirade in Cantonese that wasn't entirely lost in translation on Frost. Monty was in fact Monty II: a recent, much flashier and more expensive replacement for the African Grey that had died a few months earlier (Frost suspected continued exposure to monosodium glutamate had done for it). Which made Monty II's flight for freedom even more keenly felt by the Fongs. The detective inspector was issued with an ultimatum: unless the bird was back in situ and banged up in its cage within the month, Frost could consider that as his notice period.

Frost said he couldn't promise anything, and held out little hope of finding Monty. He really couldn't envisage Superintendent Mullett releasing the necessary manpower that would be required to make such a search successful. But for the last few days Frost had found

8

himself looking up to the heavens more often than usual. He had effectively been homeless since his in-laws had sold the semi that he'd once lived in with his late wife, and he didn't relish the prospect of finding new digs yet again. But needs must, hence his sneaking out of the CID office on a slow Friday afternoon to visit Paradise.

'What's your name again, son?'

'Jason.'

'How much is it, Jason?'

'It's on the market for twenty-two thousand.'

Bleedin' daylight robbery, Frost thought to himself. He weighed this up. It did seem like a lot to him. Then again, everything did compared to the large home he'd once shared with Mary, lost to him eighteen months ago. It was a three-bedroom house, which the in-laws had hoped and expected would be filled with grandchildren. It had never happened.

'What's it like for grub around here – any good places to eat?'

'There's the Chinese on the High Street.'

'I'm banned.'

Jason's brow furrowed. Frost's pager bleeped into action, helping him avoid the lengthy explanation.

George Price was sixty-two years old, according to his driving licence, well over six feet tall, and to Detective Sue Clarke he looked like he tipped the scales at around eighteen stone. So she fully appreciated the effort involved for the four paramedics to remove him from the car, a compact silver Mercedes-Benz 380SL. Thankfully they'd managed to get the top of the convertible down, but to Clarke's eyes he still resembled a whale jammed into a sardine can. She watched pensively as they eventually secured him to the gurney and put him into the back of the ambulance. She had wanted to help, and felt rather useless standing on the sidelines watching them struggle with the big man, but getting him out of the car and into the ambulance was a job best left to the professionals.

The bullet in George Price's head had rendered all eighteen stone of him lifeless – but not technically dead. The young couple who had found him had come to the conclusion that he was dead, and had said so quite categorically when they rang 999. Hence the presence of Dr Maltby, the police doctor, who didn't as a rule court the living, but who had discerned a pulse, and had spotted that the prone man's barrel chest was moving ever so slightly. Time was now of the essence if George Price's life was to be saved.

The siren wailed into action and the ambulance pulled out of the lay-by at speed, just as Frost's Metro was pulling in. The detective inspector announced himself on the scene with a screech of tyres as he braked just in time to avoid a collision. Frost parked the Metro next to a light-blue Ford Fiesta that belonged to the young couple, who were now being questioned by Detective Sergeant John Waters.

Clarke acknowledged Frost with a nod, and saw that he was still shaking his head and muttering obscenities in the direction of the departing ambulance.

10

'His name is George Price, shot in the back of the head,' Clarke informed him.

'Mm. Name rings a bell. I take it it's not a murder case just yet, the way they were driving. Unless they crash on the way to the hospital, which is a distinct possibility.'

'He's a bookmaker. Got the shop in the High Street, and one in Rimmington, I think. How was it?'

'What?'

'The flat?'

'Wonderful. Paradise on Earth. And I'm not joking, that's the name of the block.' A thought struck him. 'Radleigh races are on today – does George Price ply his trade there as well?'

Clarke shrugged and changed the subject to something she did know about. 'He was shot just behind the ear, close range. Just the one shot fired. No exit wound. And yes, he's still alive.'

'One shot behind the ear at close range. Very professional.'

'Only if he dies.'

'Very true, Susan, very true.' Frost peered into the car as he patted himself down and located his pack of Rothmans, then repeated the process until he'd found his orange Bic lighter. He took a long drag, the nicotine calming his jangled nerves after almost ending up in the back of the ambulance with the gunshot victim. He took in the scene. It was a lay-by off a B-road that, if you were coming from Radleigh Park Racecourse, would lead you to North Denton, which, until he heard otherwise, was Frost's assumption for Price's destination.

The lay-by was deeper than normal, and was partially obscured from the road by the thick hedgerow that grew around it. The surface wasn't tarmacked, just a mixture of gravel, grass and weeds. It was the perfect place to arrange to meet someone and kill them, and then make a quick getaway.

Frost blew out a jet of smoke in the direction of the young couple talking to John Waters, only to have his view obscured by the figure of Maltby. He made his way over.

'Jack. We can't find any shell casings. I did get a quick peek at the entry wound before they took him off, and the bullet looks like it went in at an angle, not head on, as it were, suggesting the victim moved. That might well have saved his life. Of course, we won't really know until we get the X-rays, or they dig the bullet out. Or, worst-case scenario, he dies ... then Drysdale at the path lab will only be too glad to get his hands on him.'

Frost gestured towards the couple. 'I take it those two found him?'

'Unless they shot him.'

'Good point. Got any gloves?'

Maltby took a pair of surgical gloves out of his pocket and handed them to Frost, then went over to join the Forensics boys crouched over what looked like a small pile of litter.

Frost stretched the latex over his right hand, made his way around to the passenger side of the Merc and popped open the glove compartment. Its gaping mouth

12

revealed a folded AA map, a half-eaten tube of Polo mints, a pair of expensive sunglasses and a metal comb.

His focus of attention then turned to the young couple. The girl was sat in the passenger seat of the light-blue Ford Fiesta; the door was open and her feet, shod in white stilettos, rested on the gravel. Rather optimistically for early spring, her legs were bare, but they were long and tanned, although on closer inspection the skin looked an unhealthy mottled carroty colour. Her arms were folded protectively in front of her and she was hunched over, looking exhausted by the whole episode. The man, in his early twenties, was at the side of the car, his hands buried in the pockets of his stonewashed jeans and rocking from heel to toe in his blue suede trainers. He looked rather excited by what was happening around him. Not every day you find someone who's been shot in the head. And no two people will react the same way to it.

Detective Sergeant Waters was a picture of denim today: jeans, jean jacket *and* jean shirt. The only thing missing was a waistcoat courtesy of Status Quo, and he'd have the full ensemble. Waters tested the police dress code, and Superintendent Mullett's patience, with his choice of clobber every day. Frost just laughed – he knew his friend's favourite film was *Serpico*, and Waters had openly admitted to being a fan of Pacino's wardrobe.

'Jack, this is Derek Reece and Karen Walden,' said Waters. 'This is Inspector Frost.'

Frost gave them both encouraging smiles. Derek started to say something, but Waters cut him off and

13

filled Frost in on the main points of their statement. Reece and Walden had just come from the Feathers pub half a mile down the road, when they'd had to pull in so Derek could relieve himself in the bushes.

At this point, Reece spoke up: 'I'd only had a pint and a half of Foster's top. I wasn't over the limit or anything.'

'Relax, Derek,' said Waters, 'we've got bigger fish to fry. Why don't you tell Inspector Frost what you saw.'

Reece got animated, pulled his hands out of his pockets and gesticulated his way through his account. 'Well, it must have been about three o'clock. Me and Kas drove in just as some bloke was pulling out. He was going fast, I only managed to stop because I heard the skidding on the gravel before I saw him. Just like happened to you, Inspector Frost, on the way in here.'

'Go on, Derek,' prompted Waters.

'Anyway, this bloke wasn't looking at all where he was going, and he only just missed us. I slammed on the brakes. Then he had to back up to pull out again.'

'So you got a good look at him and his car?' asked Frost.

Derek gave a big toothy grin that exposed a mouth of crooked teeth and said, 'I did. I got a *really* good look. He was driving a red Porsche 924. I'd know that car anywhere. It's my favourite motor of all time, I'd love one of those.'

'Magnum,' came a timid voice from the passenger seat.

'Sorry, love?' said Frost, glancing down at Karen.

14

She repeated, 'Magnum. He looked like Magnum. You know, the TV show.'

Waters attempted to explain. 'Yeah, Tom Selleck, in that Hawaiian cop show?'

Frost looked puzzled. 'Not "Book 'em, Danno" from *Hawaii Five-O*? I know him.'

Karen shook her head and said solemnly, 'No, definitely Magnum.'

Derek backed her up. 'Yeah, he did. Dead ringer for Magnum PI. Thick brown hair and a big moustache. A proper one.'

Frost's mind immediately and inexplicably scrolled back to Jason the estate agent, and his bum-fluffed top lip. No doubt Derek would consider that a very 'unproper' moustache. Still, at least it put the young estate agent out of the frame.

'And then what happened?'

'I hopped out of the motor and went over to the Merc.' Reece winced at the recollection. 'I thought the bloke was dead – he looked terrible. Never occurred to me that he might still be alive. I said to Karen, we've got to ring the rozzers.'

'Derek!' scolded Karen.

'I mean ring the police, sorry.'

'Relax, son, been called a lot worse,' assured Frost. 'Go on.'

'So we drove back to the Feathers pronto, and I rang from the phone box outside. Then we drove back here and waited.'

The DI surveyed the lay-by again. Seeing Forensics

15

crawling all over the scene, Frost made a growly sound that perfectly expressed two things: he could kill for a cup of tea and bacon sarnie, and there was nothing more to be gleaned from hanging about here. He told the young couple they were to accompany Waters down to Eagle Lane, so they could make formal statements, but, more importantly, work with a police sketch artist to come up with a picture of the Porsche driver. Still caught up in the excitement, they were happy to do so.

Frost then turned to Waters and issued his next instructions in a faux American accent: 'Right then, Serpico, get on to Control to put out an APB to all cars on Magnum!' He then headed back to the Metro for the drive to Eagle Lane, wondering if he had time to slip in that brown-sauce-smothered bacon sarnie before events overtook him.

Friday (2)

As Billy 'Bomber' Harris walked along Hillside Road on the Southern Housing Estate he took a quick glance over his shoulder and spotted the black BMW 7 series purring its way behind him. It was the same one he'd seen out of his bedroom window hours ago, when the internal alarm clock of his belly grumbling got him out of bed at around midday for his full English. Old Bill, he suspected. As he quickly recounted the litany of petty larcenies and small-time dope-dealing he'd participated in lately, nothing much sprang to mind that would warrant more than a good knock on the door from one of Denton's finest. It would probably be a call from that black copper, Waters was his name – he usually kept pretty close tabs on what was going on on the estate. Harris always thought Waters was capable; he looked like he could handle himself, and was one of the few coppers he wouldn't get too lippy with. But as for

17

following him in a Bimmer, well, it was all a bit over the top, wasn't it?

Bomber usually walked around the Southern Housing Estate at a leisurely pace, knowing he didn't have to move fast for anyone, or even be anywhere on time. He could do exactly as he pleased, when he pleased, no one would mess with him. He carried himself with a broad-shouldered swagger, looked like he had an invisible football tucked under each arm. Harris enjoyed watching people move out of his way as he went about his business, or seeing them cowering when he approached, even when he had a big smile on his face. Outside of his little gang, no one on the estate wanted Bomber Harris coming up to them, smiling or otherwise.

But not today. Today the swagger had left him and his pace had picked up, as he looked nervously about him for an escape route. All the while the thrum of the car's engine behind him seemed to be getting louder and louder, matching him step for step. He could sprint down a side road and bolt up some stairs and disappear along one of the tower-block walkways. He knew the estate better than anyone, certainly better than these interlopers.

He made his move. But so did they. The screech of tyres as he pulled away alerted him to the fact that the chase was on. He could feel his heart hammering in his chest as he legged it down the road and the adrenalin kicked in. Then he heard a noise, a strange noise. It sounded like a finger flicking a crisp sheet of paper.

Then came a searing pain in his right leg that alerted him to the fact that the chase was over.

Harris stopped in his tracks and quickly crumpled to the ground. He gripped his calf, bulky with hard muscle, the result of playing football for the county in his youth, and of working out thrice weekly in the gym. It was bleeding profusely, and hurt unbearably. He looked at the red hole oozing blood and still couldn't believe what it was.

He then felt the warm tip of a just-fired gun touch his chin and guide his terrified and pained gaze upwards. It was met by the cold smiles of the two men standing over him. Harris refocused on the gun still at his chin. Its barrel protruded like a small rifle. Harris liked guns, had seen a few in his time, yet he'd never seen one like this before. Then he realized the gun had a silencer attached to it, hence the muted discharge. Was this the gun that was going to kill him? It all seemed a bit elaborate ... and strangely exceptional for a toe-rag like him. Even Bomber would admit to that. It was an assassin's gun. This is mad, he thought, looking up at the two very proficient-looking men, their poker faces giving nothing away, certainly not his fate.

One had short and thick black hair, a slab of a face and a scar running across his chin, a thin white line cutting through his five-o'clock shadow. The other had a crop of fine blond hair, which looked almost downy, like a baby's. But there any affinity with innocence ended. His bony face held a pair of flinty eyes that looked like

19

pulling the trigger of the gun he was holding wouldn't even elicit a blink from them. These two really were in a different league.

Maybe they've got the wrong bloke? That must be it, he thought, *they've got the wrong bloke.*

'How are you, Billy boy?'

Billy's heart sank.

'Inspector Frost and DC Clarke to see Mrs Price,' announced Sue into the intercom. There was a muffled reply and the high wrought-iron gates slid sedately open.

'Fort Knox,' said Frost, spying the security camera positioned by the gates. 'And a fat lot of good it's done him.'

As the Metro crunched along the imposing gravel drive, Clarke ruminated on her resentment of chauffeuring Frost about. He'd pulled his usual trick and tossed her the keys to the Metro to drive them to the hospital from the lay-by. At Denton General they'd discovered George Price was still in emergency surgery, and the doctor told them it was too early to tell if he'd pull through.

And now they were in leafy and expensive North Denton, approaching George Price's mock-Tudor mansion. As Clarke parked up next to another convertible (the Prices seemed to have gone for a 'his and hers' in Mercs) she concluded that as much as she resented ferrying Frost about, she feared his erratic driving more. He was always complaining about other drivers, though he himself drove one-handed, with the car invariably

20

swerving perilously across the dual carriageway as he fumbled for a stick of Juicy Fruit chewing gum in the glove compartment, then freeing it from its paper sleeve and foil wrapper with his free hand and mouth, then squeezing his eyes shut, wincing as a molar bit down on the silver paper, reminding him why he should be chewing Dentyne. And her, all the time, gripping the dashboard in front of her.

'Can I get you something to drink? No? Not even a cup of tea?' asked Melody Price.

'We're fine, thank you, Mrs Price,' said Frost.

'Melody. Please, call me Melody,' she said with a warm smile, as her bejewelled hand gestured them to take a seat on the big cream-coloured sofa.

If the exterior of the house was all olde worlde traditional with its dark brick, black timber, climbing ivy and a couple of fearsome stone lions either side of the front door, the inside was in stark contrast. Everything was white or just off-white, from the modern furniture to the thick-pile carpets. A twinge of jealousy came over Sue Clarke as she sat down on the boat-like sofa. How she would love to bring her son up in a place like this, instead of her cramped little flat on the London Road. She quickly realized, however, that with little Philip now mastering walking, nothing would stay this pristinely white for long. His grubby little paw prints would be over everything.

Then there was Melody Price herself. She was in her early thirties, and was something of a stunner. Sue Clarke would concede that point. Melody had blonde-streaked

21

hair that looked like it had just been attacked by a crack team of top hairdressers, not a lock out of place. With her pouty glossed-pink lips, long-lashed big blue eyes, and out-of-season tan, she looked like she'd stepped out of a pop video, shot in Rio, on a yacht. Clarke would have bet a month's pay there was a sunbed lurking somewhere in the six-bedroomed house, probably had a room all of its own. And that figure, it was the kind of figure that men craved, curving in and out in all the right places. Melody was wearing a turquoise T-shirt with the words *Pineapple Dance Studios* emblazoned across it in sequins and a pair of matching leggings that accentuated her toned body. On the top shelf of a bookcase Clarke spied some professionally taken photos of Melody in various 'glamour' model poses.

Mrs Price hadn't noticed Clarke's sideways glances; she was too busy lavishing all her attention on Frost. She was the type of woman who was programmed to flirt with men, she just couldn't help it – even the offer of a cup of tea had sounded like a proposition.

Clarke saw that Frost had a lascivious smirk on his face. His eyes were lit up like those of a puppy accepting a treat, and he was obviously lapping up the attention.

'We're very sorry about what's happened to your husband,' said Frost, with uncharacteristic sincerity.

'Thank you, Inspector. I've just come off the phone from the hospital. There's no more news at the moment. I'm going to go up there as soon as they say I can see him.'

'It must have all come as a terrible shock to you,'

Clarke added, though she herself thought that Melody looked remarkably chipper, given the circumstances. 'But you do feel up to answering some questions?'

Mrs Price nodded.

'Do you normally go to the races with your husband?' Frost asked.

'Oh Mr Frost, you don't understand, I'm not just a . . . what do they call them? A trophy wife? I *work* with George at the races. I love the racing game and the gambling world. It's so exciting, it's a real buzz, on a good day it's better than . . . well, no, not quite, but you get my drift.'

Frost got her drift and smiled back. Clarke got it too, but didn't smile back.

Melody Price continued, 'I reckon I know the bookmaking business as well as any man at the track. Apart from George, that is.'

'That is impressive,' declared Frost. 'I've always had an aversion to betting on the nags, if I'm honest. I'd rather spend my money wisely down the pub.'

She laughed and uttered conspiratorially, 'Very wise. The bookies always win. They'll get your money eventually.'

'So tell me, Mrs Price—'

'*Melody*, please.'

'Melody. Your husband left Radleigh races early, before the last race. Is that normal?'

'It is. And he usually has the day's takings with him. I'm given a lift home by Jimmy – Jimmy Drake, he's our clerk.'

'Clerk?'

'Yes, there's usually three of us working the pitch.'

'The pitch is where the bookies take bets from the punters?' clarified Frost.

'That's right. George takes bets at eight racetracks, mainly in the south. The pitches work the same way a fruit and veg stall does at a market – except we earn more money.'

'No kidding,' muttered Clarke, unable to disguise the envy in her voice as her eyes did another quick sweep of the huge living room and settled on the view from the French windows: the patio leading to a kidney-shaped swimming pool, the long manicured lawn and the wooded grounds beyond. Back in the room, Clarke wondered what Frost was playing at. He was usually the first to try to ruffle an interviewee's feathers, and as far as she was concerned, if anyone needed their feathers ruffling, it was Melody Price.

The lady of the house continued without even registering Clarke's attempted intrusion into the conversation. 'George has the best pitches at all the courses.' She smiled again; it was obviously a source of some pride.

'Is there any reason your husband leaves the races early? I'd have thought he'd want to accompany you home.'

'My safety. A lot of bookmakers have been robbed on the way home from the races over the years. Bookies are an easy target. It's a cash business. A bag full of money, no security as such. Some of the bookmakers carry coshes in their cars, but no one really wants to carry a gun. The thieves are at the races, watching you, probably have a bet with you, then follow you home, pull you over and . . . George was robbed a few years ago, he put up a fight and chased them off.' There was a palpable quake in her voice now and she suddenly seemed visibly upset. 'George always said he'd never let anyone take his money. That's why he thought it safer for me . . . He didn't want anything happening with me in the car.'

'How much was in the bag?'

'I believe there was over . . . over . . . over a thousand pounds . . .'

Melody Price's head dipped and she plucked some tissues from a box on the glass-topped coffee table to dry her tears. When she emerged from the wad of tissues, she took a deep breath.

'It's OK, Melody,' said Frost gently. 'In your own time.'

Sue Clarke was losing patience. 'What time did your husband leave the races exactly?'

Mrs Price, regaining her composure, addressed her answer to the inspector: 'It must have been shortly before three.'

'That's quite a bit before the last race, isn't it?' Frost ventured.

'It is. George said he was feeling tired today, so I said he should go home. And anyway, the main race of the day, the Bennington's Bank stakes, was long over. The crowd was thinning out.'

'I know this is hard, and at this time robbery does seem like the obvious motive for your husband's assault, but does George have any enemies, anyone who might do this?'

Melody Price arched her perfectly plucked eyebrows, seemingly surprised by the question. 'No. Everyone loves George.' She sighed. 'He has a wonderful sense of humour. He's the funniest man in the world. Generous to a fault, he'll help anyone out. I fell in love with him the minute I met him, that's almost two years ago now.' She looked down at the large diamond ring she was twisting around on her finger. 'We've not been married long.'

'How long is that exactly?' asked Clarke.

Mrs Price looked up sharply towards the DC and snapped back, 'Is that really relevant?'

Clarke let it hang.

Melody eventually answered, 'Six months. Married and honeymooned in Marbella, where we first met. It was lovely.'

Frost drew the interview to a close with a covert little wink at Clarke, who snapped her notebook shut. The inspector went through the drill of informing Melody that they would of course keep in touch as the case progressed, and if she thought of anything that might be of help, no matter how small, to call them right away. He plucked a card from his inside jacket pocket and handed it to her, which she accepted with a show of exaggerated delight. She then escorted them to the door.

'Oh, one thing, you reported a break-in on . . . on the . . .' Frost frisked himself in search of his notebook, but came up empty-handed.

Clarke came to his rescue. 'February fifth, I believe.'

Melody Price's perfect eyebrows dipped and flicked up again as she looked quizzical and tried to recall the event. 'Oh, that, no, it was nothing.'

It was Frost's turn to do some eyebrow play now. 'Nothing?'

'Yes, it was a mistake. The maid reported a burglary, but she made a mistake, nothing was taken, we weren't broken into. I spoke to one of your officers about it, I forget his name. He was . . . fat?'

'DC Arthur Hanlon. He still is . . . fat.'

'Is it relevant? I'm surprised you're mentioning it, with all that's happened.'

'When we checked your address it came up on our database. These things usually stay on there for a month or two.'

'Oh well, you can take it off your database now.'

Melody Price opened the door. Frost received a lavish 'thank you' from her, Clarke barely a nod.

In the confines of the Metro, once Frost had obliterated the smell of pine from the little green tree hanging from the rear-view mirror with the first blast of his Rothmans, he announced, 'Methinks she doth protest too much. I wouldn't mind talking to that maid, without Mrs Price about. That said, I didn't even see a maid. What do you reckon? Susan? *What?*'

Clarke waited until the Metro was out of the gates before she delivered her fulsome opinion on Melody Price's obvious flirting with him, and how, rendered useless, he had sat there on the cream-coloured couch like a schoolboy with a crush.

Frost set out his defence. 'I saw your claws were out so I just played to our strengths. No point both of us going in strong. You know as well as I do, she's the type of woman who likes men. You won't get anything out of her. You're the competition, me, I'm the—'

'Infatuated copper who doesn't get anything out of her? There could still be a lot more to this robbery than meets the eye.' She paused before adding, 'You didn't even mention Magnum.'

Frost looked blank.

'The bloke the couple ID'd coming out of the lay-by in the red Porsche.'

'No, I didn't. And here's why: you sit there giving a verbal description of a suspect, and it just gives them plenty of time to say "No". I want to wait until we get the sketch of him and shove it right under her nose. See what her reaction is.'

Clarke conceded the point. 'So, outside of her Page Three charms, what do you reckon on her?'

'Page Three? I *thought* I recognized her—'

'*Unbelievable*, Jack—'

'All right, don't get narked, and don't get sarky either, even though it suits you. I'm the first to admit I'm not immune to her . . . her ample attributes, shall we say, but I won't let it cloud my judgement. My first thought is, I think George Price provides her with a very nice lifestyle, one she looks like she wouldn't want to jeopardize.'

'Younger woman, older man. I bet there's a big fat insurance claim to be had.'

28

'I'm sure there is. But not every attractive blonde is Barbara Stanwyck.'

'Who?'

'She was in a film about a woman who has her husband bumped off to claim the insur—'

'I get it.'

'What's your problem with her? Don't tell me, outside of her husband getting one in the head, she looks like she hasn't got a problem in the world: big house, big diamonds, big shoulder pads, big hair.'

Clarke let out a sigh. 'Sorry. That obvious, is it?'

'Don't let it cloud *your* judgement. And for all you know, Melody Price might like nothing more than a toddler crawling about the place. The grass is always greener, and all that.'

Frost didn't have to be a mind reader, or even that astute, it was written all over her face. Even with her mum helping out, raising a child on her own while putting in her full quota of shifts, and overtime when she could, it was all taking its toll – and it showed.

'I know you've got a lot on your plate, what with the nipper. Maybe one night, if you need, need a . . . Ah, nothing.'

Clarke, hardly believing what she was hearing, had no intention of letting him off the hook. 'If I need *what*, Jack? Go on, you were about to say something?'

'If you need any help with the nipper one night, or something, I'm around. All I ask for is some of your shepherd's pie.'

'Is that a euphemism?'

29

'I've been on the Kung Po the last three months solid. Much as I love it, it's losing its exotic oriental charm. I'd kill for some decent homemade grub. I'd even babysit an ankle-biter. That's how bloody desperate I am!'

Friday (3)

George Price had just come out of surgery, but the bullet was still lodged in his head. It had entered at an angle and travelled to just above his temple and settled there. What had stopped it killing him was the fact that George Price had moved a fraction just in time, so it hadn't penetrated his skull. At this stage it was deemed too dangerous to remove the bullet. Price was on a ventilator and had not regained consciousness. The next forty-eight hours were going to prove critical for the big bookmaker.

Frost had stationed PC David Simms at Denton General to watch over Price. Not that the inspector thought that Price was in any immediate danger – currently there was no reason to believe the robber or robbers would return to finish the job off. Frost had also had Dr Maltby examine the comatose Price to see if there were any markings on his body to indicate a struggle with his assailant, but there were none.

Simms was instructed to contact Frost immediately should anyone of interest turn up. And someone did.

'Hello, Harry.'

Harry Baskin, holding a bunch of grapes and a tin of Quality Street, spun round sharply, or as sharply as a man of his heft could, to see Frost approaching.

'Well, well, well. As I live and breathe, Inspector Frost of Eagle Lane,' replied Baskin, deadpan and as dry as you like.

The owner of Denton's pre-eminent nightclub, strip club, and scene of many dodgy dealings, the Coconut Grove, was stood in the corridor and had been peering through the window of Intensive Care, where he himself had been less than two years ago, also with a bullet wound.

'Must bring back painful memories for you, Harry.'

Harry Baskin shrugged: water off a duck's back. 'George is a fighter like me. I got through it, I'm sure he will too. Pity he can't have no visitors yet.'

Frost nodded in agreement, then gestured for Harry Baskin to sit with him on one of the orange plastic chairs that lined the corridor. The two men then proceeded to lay waste to George Price's grapes. 'It doesn't surprise me, Harry, that you know George Price, but how well?'

'We grew up together, Stepney, East London. When I moved out to this neck of the woods, George followed. It was nice to get out of the Big Smoke, all that crime and violence.'

Frost checked Baskin for irony, but saw only sincerity.

32

'Well, at least you won't get homesick, since you seem to have brought it with you.'

Baskin ignored Frost's barb and busied himself with opening the tin of Quality Street, which he then offered to the detective and asked, 'Any clues as to who might have done it?'

Frost took a green triangle. 'I was hoping you could tell me.'

Baskin took an orange cream and then a strawberry cream. 'Dunno.'

'Well, it looks like robbery. The bag with his day's takings was gone. He was found parked up in a lay-by, about half a mile down from the Feathers pub.'

'I know the one. A well-known beauty spot for young lovers to get better acquainted, shall we say?'

'And two of them found George.'

'Yeah?'

Frost picked a toffee cup this time, but kept an eye on Baskin's reaction as he said, 'They gave us a very good description of a fella leaving the scene. I'll show you the picture when we get it.'

Baskin dipped his meaty hand into the tin again and grabbed two toffee fingers, an almond octagon and some blue ones that always seemed to be the last to go. 'I'll stick it up in the club, see if any of the punters recognize him.'

'Unless Melody Price decides to offer a significant reward for information, with all those topless birds dancing around in your establishment, Harry, I doubt anyone will bother looking at it.'

33

'Dunno. We could put her on the poster too. She could take up her old profession and get out those lovely big—'

'Harry! That's no way to talk about your mate's missus.'

'What he can't hear won't hurt him. Anyway, you don't marry a bird like Melody without expecting the occasional ogle, know what I mean?'

Frost knew what he meant, but wasn't interested. 'What concerns me is what was he doing parked up in a lay-by so near home. Any ideas?'

Baskin shrugged. 'Stopped off for a leak?'

'Like you said, a meeting spot for young lovers, maybe it was for a bit of how's-your-father – he got a secret girlfriend on the go, a bit on the side?'

Harry Baskin almost choked on his toffee fingers. 'Jesus! Do me a favour! I know he has a penchant for Angie Dickinson and Raquel Welch, but this is Denton. No, with a woman like Melody waiting for you at home, you don't need a bit on the side – you need a day off! She's got it covered, front, back and every side imaginable. And anyway, take it from me, he was in love with her. Do anything for her, *anything*.'

'But robbery aside, does George have any enemies?'

Baskin screwed up his face so it resembled the toffee he was chewing. It was patently the most ridiculous thing he'd ever heard. 'Enemies? Are you kidding me? I can attest to the fact that George Price has more enemies than you could shake several sticks at, he has thousands of them!' Frost was surprised at Baskin's candour. 'In the

34

gambling world,' continued the club-owner, 'the book-makers are the enemy. They're the ones you have to beat. Everyone lost money to George, that makes for a lot of enemies.'

'How about you, Harry?'

'How about me what?'

'Are you one of them?'

Baskin's cheery façade melted away and a dark and serious cast took its place. 'No. Not me. And I take offence at the insinuation. He's a dear, dear pal of mine. It pains me to see anything happen to him.'

Frost saw that for all his bluster, Harry Baskin was indeed very fond of his dear pal George Price.

Baskin then pulled a face, as if he'd bitten into a Quality Street he particularly disliked, and said, 'We've got a timeshare business in Tenerife on the go, and without George, I stand to lose a bloody fortune.'

The tender moment was over and normal business in Harry Baskin's world had resumed. Frost spotted DS Waters at the end of the corridor looking intently at the drinks dispenser. He told Baskin he'd be in touch and then made his way over to the DS, who was now punching the machine.

'I've dealt with this bandit before – you've got to finesse it.'

Frost took over, put the money in the slot, carefully pressed the requisite buttons and procured them a coffee and a hot chocolate.

Waters explained why he was at the hospital: 'Billy "Bomber" Harris, they've just pulled a bullet out of his

35

right peg. Still, at least it's not in the head like George Price.'

'Bomber would be all right with one in the head, odds-on it would still miss his brain by a country mile.'

They laughed, and sipped from the wobbly plastic cups that the piping-hot water had practically melted. Luckily the machine was right next to Accident and Emergency, to deal with all those scalded lips.

'So what's Bomber got to say about playing target practice for someone?'

'He's not saying a word,' said Waters, blowing on his coffee.

'Have you put the fear of God up him? Proper jail time for . . .'

'What? For getting shot?'

Frost conceded the point.

'I've told him it's serious. He's had a beef with Tommy Wilkins for a couple of years now. They both fancy themselves as the number-one boy on the Southern Housing Estate. You know, strictly petty stuff. Collecting their dole whilst dealing some hash, nicking car stereos, robbing telephone boxes and fighting at football.'

'What did these two captains of industry fall out over?'

'Billy was having it off with Wilkins' sister, who was also having it off with—'

'Spare me the details, John, it sounds like meet the cast of *Deliverance*.'

Waters laughed. 'You're not wrong. The thing is, if Wilkins did somehow manage to get his hands on a gun,

36

and then work out how to use it, Harris would be the first one to grass him up.'

Frost shook his head at the ineptitude. 'The code of *omertà*'s not reached the Southern Housing Estate yet, then?'

'This lot grass each other up with abandon. That's what half the feud is about. But Harris isn't saying a word this time.' Waters looked over to the ward they had taken Harris into. 'All joking aside, he's genuinely scared.'

'Inspector Frost?'

They both turned to see a smiling young blonde nurse holding up a thick A4 Jiffy bag. 'Doctor Gillard told me to give you these, Mr Price's possessions.'

'Ah, yes, thank you.'

'I know who you are, Inspector, but he said I needed to see some ID.'

'Very wise.' Frost showed her his warrant card. The nurse handed over the envelope and ambled off. Frost opened it. The first thing he pulled out was a gold Rolex Day-Date watch with a diamond-encrusted bezel. Waters whistled in recognition of the dazzling timepiece.

'So, if it was robbery, they only got the day's takings, about a thousand pounds, according to his missus. They didn't get what was on his wrist, and this Rollie's got to be worth over five grand,' said Frost, dropping it back in the bag and next pulling out a heavy engine-turned gold money clip that was holding together a thick wad of notes of high denomination. 'And they didn't ask him to empty his pockets. There's about five hundred here, plus the gold money clip, the scrap value on that's about the same again.'

Waters weighed up the possible scenarios and suggested, 'Maybe they did ask him for the watch and what was inside his pockets, but hot-headed George Price told them to go fuck themselves, so they shot him?'

It was a compelling theory, but somehow Frost wasn't convinced. And he'd already dipped back into the Jiffy bag and was pulling a big grin that suggested he'd got lucky. It was a little black notebook. Frost opened up the leatherette cover and saw it was crammed full of potential information. 'These always make interesting reading.'

Stanley Mullett eased himself into the button-backed Chesterfield chair. It had been an unsatisfactory afternoon so far. The four county divisional superintendents had arranged to meet up once a month at the Denton and Rimmington Golf Club, for what they'd designated as a 'working lunch'. It was to involve a short round of golf, seven holes, preceded by said lunch, then retiring to the bar for a round (or four) of drinks. All under the ruse of building closer relationships between the county's stations, pooling information and brainstorming strategies to lower crime in the area.

Mullett felt good that he had been chosen to chair the event. But to his mind it was only befitting a man of his stature. After all, it was he who'd suggested the monthly meet-ups. And it was he who had offered the hospitality of the Denton golf club. After the resignation of the previous incumbent over the misappropriation of club funds, the board had decided to elect Mullett as their new chairman. Despite the debacle of the previous year when he'd missed out on the top spot, Mullett didn't let pride get in the way and gleefully accepted the post. Because if ever there was an opportunity for social advancement in the district, being the chairman of the golf club was it. Mullett knew that membership of the Masons was only a nod and funny handshake away; and maybe even the mayoral mace and chain further down the road. Mullett's ambition was unbounded.

So it always rankled when one of the three other supers was late for the event, or had to cut his visit short, or worse, didn't turn up at all. Mullett had never been late or cancelled, and he felt it a personal slight when one of the others did. It somehow undermined his authority, even though they were all of the same rank; at his golf club Mullett always felt like a first amongst equals.

'Sorry I was late earlier on, Stanley, Roger,' said Peter Kelsey, setting down three brimming tumblers of Johnnie Walker Red Label on the table. 'Still no sign of Martin?'

Roger Bradley shook his head. 'Looks like he's not going to make it, after all. He's appearing on County Radio. Recent spate of counterfeit goods – perfumes, designer clothing, videos and the like – hitting the area, what to look out for and what not.'

Mullett nodded in recognition. 'Indeed, got a memo about that this morning. Some expert from London's West End Central is briefing us tomorrow. Lot of it coming from around here, apparently. Must say, we haven't noticed, or even heard of any complaints.'

Roger Bradley said, 'Public won't complain, they're more concerned with having their video players stolen, rather than buying cheap cassettes for them.'

Mullett agreed. 'Buying cheap tat off a market stall is a national pastime, isn't it?'

They all laughed. Peter Kelsey said, 'Martin does have a face for radio.'

'Pity about his speaking voice, bit of a stutter, hasn't he?' ventured Mullett.

'Only when he's drunk,' said Kelsey.

'Like I said, he stutters most of the time.'

The supers laughed some more. Mullett re-appraised the afternoon; it wasn't turning out so badly after all. It looked like they might be settling in for a convivial evening. He picked up his tumbler, held it aloft and inspected the volume. 'Good heavens, Peter, what are these?'

'They're very large ones, by way of apology,' said Kelsey, easing himself further into the Chesterfield armchair.

Mullett beamed. 'Very kind of you, Peter, all is forgiven.'

Superintendent Roger Bradley did the same. 'Indeed. Taxis home, I fear.'

'Or, alternatively, turn up the siren, put your foot down and hope for the best!' said Mullett, supremely satisfied as the laughter rebounded around the table.

He raised his glass to his cohorts, dressed in their

40

Pringle golfing finery, and true to form, he and Bradley were in various shades of conservative blue. By contrast, the younger man, Kelsey, looked particularly flashy, sporting a bright-pink polo shirt, a multicoloured argyle jumper and garish plaid trousers. Despite their attire, they hadn't actually ventured on to the greens at all.

The three supers didn't seem to mind the lack of exercise. They were perfectly content to drink deeply, laugh loudly and watch the day slip by.

Friday (4)

The world looked different from up here, and from this angle. He could have said it looked rosy, but that was due to the blood from his mouth and nose seeping into his eyes and giving everything a hazy red glaze. Tommy Wilkins would have shouted out for help once more, but every time he'd done so, the two men holding his legs loosened their grip and threatened to let go of him altogether and let gravity take its course. That would entail a ten-storey drop on to the pavement from the roof of Wilshaw House, a high-rise block on the Southern Housing Estate.

'Please . . . please . . .'

Wilkins stopped pleading and made a rasping sound that emanated from the back of his throat. He'd just located the front tooth the men had knocked out earlier, and he now elected to spit it out rather than swallow it. The upside-down Wilkins tried to propel the tooth from his mouth but it didn't get very far, as his swollen nose immediately broke its fall. The two men laughed, and then remarked that the view from their angle was bloody disgusting, what with the bloodied tooth resting on Tommy's bloodied septum.

'Jaysus, maybe we should just drop you now, Tommy, and be done with it,' said one of the men in a voice shot through with repulsion. 'Because you're making us feel sick, so you are.'

Wilkins felt their grip weaken and his legs slide from knees to ankles through their hands.

'No! Please, *no*!' His eyes widened and focused in the growing twilight on the faces of the two men leaning over the parapet. One was tall and wiry with a scar on his chin; the other was squat and muscly. But both had cold grey and pitiless eyes. They seemed unstoppable. They'd been following him for a couple of days now. At first he'd thought they were with Bomber Harris, his only real competition on the estate, and whose ugly sister he was . . . Well, this was no time to open that can of worms. But he soon realized these two were the real deal. Even with their heavy Irish brogue, they were easy to understand and had made it very clear what they wanted.

This latest jolt did the trick, and the broken tooth slid from the ledge of his upturned nose and plummeted away to the ground. If Wilkins had been in any doubt about his likely fate, now he knew. And as attached to the tooth as he was, or had been, he had no desire to join it. Then came the final humiliation as Tommy

43

Wilkins felt a warm sensation creeping its way towards his mouth. He realized he'd wet himself.

'P . . . p . . . please . . . I'll do anything . . . anything you want!'

'We know you will, Tommy.'

'Evening,' greeted Night Sergeant Johnny Johnson as Frost entered Eagle Lane station.

'Just got on?'

Johnson, immersed in the back pages of the *Sun*, didn't look up. 'About twenty minutes ago. You had a message, from one Jason Kingly.'

'Who?'

Johnson folded the newspaper and put it under the counter, then looked at the notepad in front of him. 'He said it's about a flat, wants to know if you've made up your mind, or want to look at some more.' Johnson tapped a stubby forefinger on the notepad. 'You moving on, Jack?'

'I am, but never far enough away for my liking. Is our beloved leader about?'

'He's at his monthly meeting of the supers. Won't be back this evening.'

Frost rolled his eyes at this. 'Otherwise known as a very long booze-up spoilt by a very short game of golf.'

On that note, Frost made his way through to the main incident room of CID. The strip lighting hummed, the phones still rang, and calls of 'goodnight' and 'see you in the morning' were being bandied about.

DC Sue Clarke was at her desk, looking through a

44

thick file. She could have been busy, or she could have been doing what Frost had done on more than one occasion: buried his head in paperwork and counted down the minutes until the end of a shift so he could wrap his laughing-gear around a nice cold pint, all the time hoping there wasn't an inconvenient call to investigate something that someone might have seen somewhere.

'Busy?'

Clarke looked up. 'How's George Price?'

'Stable. That's the best we can say. He had a visitor when I was there – one Harold Baskin.'

She closed the file, sat back in her swivel chair and laced her hands together in front of her. 'Why doesn't that surprise me?'

'Me neither. They were old muckers from the East End, apparently. Probably knocking around with the Kray twins, Jack the Ripper and Dick Van Dyke from *Mary Poppins*. But it does open up a whole new world of potential inquiries with Harry in the frame.'

'Is he?'

'In the frame? Gut feeling, no. Funnily enough, I think he's rather fond of George Price. You know what he's like, got more front and bluster than Great Yarmouth, but this time he seemed genuinely upset.' Frost pulled up a chair and sat opposite Clarke. 'How about you?'

Sue Clarke gave a triumphant smile. On leaving the Prices' mini-mansion, Clarke had dropped Frost off at the hospital and then gone back to Eagle Lane to collect copies of the police artist's sketch that the witnesses, Derek and Karen, had helped create. On seeing the image,

Clarke thought the Magnum PI reference had influenced the starry-eyed young couple a little too much. The only thing missing was the red Hawaiian shirt.

She then went to see Jimmy Drake, George Price's clerk. Drake ID'd the man immediately, said he'd known him well for years, and his late father. He even went out to his garden shed where he kept his photo albums and provided a picture. Sue Clarke reached into another file open on her desk and handed Frost the photo Drake had given her.

Frost's brow furrowed. 'If he's Magnum, me and you are Starsky and Hutch!'

'I should be grateful, at least we're not in *McMillan and Wife*.'

Frost dropped the photo back in the file. 'Who is he, then?'

'His name's Terry Langdon, thirty-five years of age, and a bookmaker who has pitches next to George Price at the races. And he drives a red Porsche 924. He may not be the spit of Tom Selleck, but if you're a betting man, who would you put your money on? And according to Jimmy Drake, he has a motive. Or, at least, a burning hatred of George Price. Terry Langdon believes that George was responsible for his father's death.'

'Go on,' urged Frost.

'George and Bert Langdon, Terry's father, went into business together, opening betting shops in the area. George believed that Bert Langdon was ripping him off. They got into a fight, an actual fistfight, and George got the better of him. Bert Langdon walked away from

46

the business. Four years later he died, brain haemorrhage. Langdon believed the haemorrhage was a result of the beating he took from George Price. Not quite the picture Melody Price painted, of big friendly George.'

'Then again, she did say that he'd rather die than let anyone take his money. Which looks like he did.' He paused. 'Is any of this on file, anyone press any charges? Did you check with Records?'

'I did. No. And to be honest, Jimmy seemed reluctant to tell me much.'

'Probably hedging his bets, waiting to see if George Price comes out of his coma. Doesn't want to talk out of turn about his boss. Well, let's find Terry first. We have an address?'

'Langdon lives near Parkview Woods, at the Billings Stables,' Clarke read off her notebook.

'The riding school?'

'That's the one. I sent PC Mills and Drayton round there, no one in. No red Porsche. Langdon's divorced, his ex-wife lives in Kent with her new husband. We've faxed all the info and his ID over to Transport. And we'll get a search warrant first thing tomorrow.'

Frost gave a nod of approval for all the procedural, and scratched an imaginary itch on his chin as he pondered, 'Jimmy Drake, he's been working with George Price for how long?'

'Over thirty years, he said.'

'He must know him better than anyone?'

'You'd think so. But if he does, he was staying tight-lipped about it. Don't get me wrong, he was helpful,

47

answered all the questions I put to him, just a bit cagey. When I mentioned Melody Price's assertions that her husband was the happiest man in the world and everyone loved him, Jimmy just nodded in agreement. But I could tell he didn't believe it.'

'Harry Baskin says George has plenty of enemies. It's the nature of the business he's in. And let's face it, everyone has enemies and no one is that happy.'

'Cynical.'

'Realistic. Not even with the delightful Melody Price's ample charms to cushion the blows that life throws at you.'

Clarke narrowed her eyes and shook a disapproving head.

Frost ignored her and carried on. 'You won't get much from Jimmy Drake, he's a betting man and he's playing the odds. I'm sure he knows all about George Price, the secrets, where the bodies are buried, as they say. But George isn't dead, yet. So he's not going to give them away.'

'So what you're saying is, we'd be better off if George Price was dead?'

'What I'm saying is—'

'Here we go, guv, Doreen Trafford's statement,' called out Arthur Hanlon as he came over with a file in his hand.

'Who the hell is Doreen?'

'The Prices' cleaner,' Clarke reminded him.

'Go on then, Arthur, give us the "skinny", as they say in America.'

Clarke suppressed a laugh as Frost patted Hanlon's belly.

Undeterred, the DC made some unsavoury throat-clearing noises and proceeded to read solemnly from the file. 'On February fifth 1984, at precisely ten thirty-five a.m., I was called to number 24 Gable Close in North Denton on a suspected break-in of the property. There I was met by Mrs Doreen Trafford, forty-eight years of age, profession: cleaning lady. I ascertained it was the home of Mr and Mrs Price at—'

'Oh, stop tarting around, Arthur, and just give us the bloody facts!'

Sue Clarke laughed openly this time.

Arthur Hanlon dumped the file on the desk and stopped talking like an automaton. 'OK, guv. Doreen said she came into work that morning and thought someone had been in the house – there were items out of place, nothing much, just details a cleaning woman would pick up on. She said she had a forensic eye for these things, everything correctly in its place. But she did see that some tapes were missing and—'

'Tapes?'

'Videotapes. The Prices had a shelf full of them. Both films and blank ones for recording. They were all gone, she said, about twenty of them. Funny thing was, if it was a burglary, they didn't take the hardware. You know – the video player or the cameras.'

'What cameras?'

'She showed me, there were some video cameras in the bedroom. Very expensive-looking kit it was, very professional. Makes you wonder,' said Hanlon, delivered with enough of a wink and a nudge-nudge to elicit groans from Clarke – and pique Frost's interest.

'Does indeed.'

'With your mucky little minds it does,' added Clarke.

'And the Prices denied it all?'

Hanlon gave a solid nod to this. 'I followed it up a week later, because the Prices were on holiday at the time of the so-called break-in. But Doreen used to come in every day and air the place, feed the fish, keep an eye on it. She swore blind someone had broken in.'

'So, if some tapes were stolen, what was on them?'

'Some real salacious X-rated goings-on at the Price household, if you ask me.'

'All right, Arthur, we know, I was just thinking out loud. But it does make you wonder, though.'

'Wonder what?' asked Clarke.

Frost sprang up from his chair and rubbed his hands together gleefully. 'Get your jackets on, I'll tell you over a pint.'

'Frank Trafford,' said Arthur Hanlon, 'Doreen Trafford's husband. I nicked him about a year or so ago, pub fight, that dump on the Wilton Road. He's quite a handful when he gets a drink in him. Ex-army.'

'Tell us all about it over a pint.'

Clarke lifted her jacket off the back of the chair and slipped it over her shoulders. 'Did I tell you about Michael Price – George Price's son from his first marriage?'

'Tell us over a pint.'

Sue Clarke made that at least three pints already – it was going to be a long night. Thank goodness her mother was staying with her and would put Philip to bed.

He clocked them for what they were the minute the trio walked into the pub. No matter how much they tried to blend in. There was one who was on the lardy side. He went straight up to the bar and helped himself to a pickled egg and a handful of nuts. The other bloke had sandy-coloured hair, looked like it needed a cut badly, and stubble. Stubble seemed to be popular these days, although this one looked like he just couldn't be bothered to shave. He was wearing a leather bomber jacket, grey Farah trousers and a red Slazenger V-neck jumper with a grubby-looking white polo shirt underneath. The bird looked good, in her smart black jacket cinched in at the waist and black boots. She had a short Lady Di-style haircut and was pretty, but not in a flashy way like Melody. They looked like a normal couple, but he could tell they were coppers. What on earth was his name again ... Fred ... Fred ... *Fred* Flintstone?

He laughed. It was loud enough for the couple next to him to glance nervously around, probably curious as to what the man stood at the bar on his own, with his half-drained pint of strong German lager and whisky chaser, could possibly be laughing about. He threw the couple a look that quickly made them turn round and mind their own naffing business. He had that aura of

51

danger about him. He'd inherited his father's height and heft, and the ability to intimidate people, to go from smiling joker to grimacing menace in a heartbeat. But he'd always known that though he had the bark, he lacked his father's bite. He laughed again. The couple collected their drinks off the bar and moved further away from him. It wasn't Fred . . . it was Jack, *Jack Frost*. He knew it was something stupid.

Were they looking for him? There was a good chance they were, he thought. He downed his lager in two noisy gulps, then knocked back the chaser without it even touching the sides. But as the whisky hit the spot, he felt that warm glow in the pit of his stomach; a welcome respite from the fear that had been residing there for the last few days. But he also knew that the booze just wasn't cutting it these days. He needed something more, always something more.

He pulled up the collar of his jacket and made his way out of the saloon bar, keeping his head down to ensure that Frost and the woman wouldn't see him. There was a phone box opposite the pub – he could make a call, see if he could get his hands on what he was after, and what he knew he'd soon be needing. It was after nine, it shouldn't be a problem.

As he made his way across the road a black car pulled up sharply in front of him. The back door opened, if not by magic, then certainly with a practised and fluid stealth. He recognized the man driving, the white scar standing out on his black-bristled chin, like lightning cutting through the night sky.

And when the man offered in that lilting but commanding voice, 'We'll give you a lift home, Michael. We don't want anything to happen to you now, do we?', Michael Price knew better than to argue the point, and folded his large frame into the back seat of the black car.

Saturday (1)

Frost and Clarke were admiring the view from Billings Stables. It was a wonderfully picturesque spot. It was hard to believe that they were only five miles outside of Denton. There was a swirling morning mist around the trees and wild spring foliage, and the undulating green fields stretched as far as you could see, with no unsightly modern buildings that made up the 'New Town' to blight the vista.

'I think I'd like to bring Philip up here when he's old enough to appreciate it,' Clarke said as they got out of the car.

'I'll pay for the little nipper's riding lessons, when the time comes, if that's what he wants,' offered Frost, inhaling a Rothmans and the clean country air at the same time.

'Really?'

'Well, don't look so bloody surprised. Least I can do, after all the nights I spent on your sofa.'

'Thanks, Jack, I don't know what to say. That's very generous of you.'

Frost pulled a wicked grin. 'I don't think your mum will ever get over the fright I gave her that night, the poor mare.'

Thankfully, any further reminiscing about that unfortunate incident was cut short by the appearance of Peter Billings, who walked over from an outbuilding to greet them.

Billings was a thickset man with a ruddy weathered face. In his battered blue cords tucked into green wellingtons, and with his reddish curly hair topped off with a tweed flat cap, he looked every inch the country sportsman.

After an exchange of pleasantries about the beautiful setting of the stables, Clarke showed Billings the photograph they'd brought with them.

'That's Terry all right,' the stable owner confirmed. 'But he's not around – I tried him just after you called. There was no answer. I don't think I've seen him since yesterday morning. But let me show you the way.'

As he walked Frost and Clarke towards the bungalow that he rented out to Terry Langdon, Billings explained that he and Terry went back a long way. They'd bonded over their shared love of all things equine. Billings had taken over his father's stables, and Terry had taken over his father's bookmaking business; stepping into their fathers' shoes was something else they had in common. When Terry's wife left him, Peter was happy to let him rent the small bungalow he had on his property.

55

'Do you know George Price too?' asked Frost.

'I don't have much truck with the bookies at the races – more the owners and the jockeys. But Terry was an old schoolfriend. We were at a very minor public school together, both academic dunces, but as I say, both loved horses. He was a lot different at school. He was quiet, a shy boy as I remember.'

'Oh, and how would you describe him now?'

'Well, you know, drives a red Porsche, bit of a Jack the lad. I suppose he was trying to fit in with the image of a bookie, to emulate his father. If so, it didn't work out.'

'How do you mean?'

'Terry's just gone bust. I think last week was his final race meeting. Held on for as long as he could, but he just couldn't make a go of it.'

'So he had financial troubles?'

Billings shook his head in a gesture of pity for his old friend. 'He never went into detail, but with the horse racing and gambling you need a fair dollop of luck on your side, even the bookies. And it seems Terry never had that. I was never sure he was cut out for it anyway. All the big bookmakers have something of the buccaneering spirit about them, like the top City traders. Men like George Price have it, and so did Terry's dad. But not Terry, I'm afraid.'

'So the acorn fell far from the tree, in this case.'

'Eloquently put, Inspector. Terry's a good man, just not as shrewd as his father.'

'Was that why his wife left him?'

'Money? No, Allison wasn't like that. She's a sweet

56

girl, really. And Terry always fancied himself as a bit of a ladies' man, so I wasn't surprised his marriage didn't stick. But when she left him I knew it shook him to the core. I think he thought he'd always be with her, that he could rely on her and she'd forgive him his dalliances. I did warn him. She left him for a *gas fitter*.' Billings gave a derisive snort. 'Do you really suspect him of the shooting? He's not good with guns.'

'Well, we don't suspect the *gas fitter*.'

'Touché, Inspector.'

'You said he's not good with guns. Did you ever know him to have any sort of firearm in his possession?'

'Not to my knowledge, no. But I do remember a weekend a few years ago, we stayed at a rather grand hotel in Yorkshire with our wives and tried our hand at clay pigeon shooting. Terry was a lousy shot, couldn't hit a barn door, never mind a disc spinning through the air. So we stuck to the fishing instead.' Billings smiled at the memory. 'Poor sod wasn't much better at that.'

'Well, you've been very helpful, and I'm sure you realize the sooner we can talk to him, the better it will be for him.'

Billings, who struck them as a practical man, agreed.

'And it's no secret he didn't like George Price,' added Frost, 'because of what happened to his father.'

'I don't think he ever got over it. Not really.'

'But there's the other matter ...' Frost left it hanging.

Billings was about to say something then stopped himself.

Frost prompted, 'There's always another matter, Mr Billings, and I'll find that one out just as fast.'

'Underneath all the Jack-the-lad bravado, he's a good man, you know?'

'Who just happens to be in love with Melody Price?'

Sue Clarke, who had been momentarily distracted by the riders and horses just coming into the adjacent field, turned sharply towards Frost, a look of surprise on her face.

Peter Billings' pensive look disappeared. 'Ah, you know about that,' he said in a voice that sounded relieved.

Frost smiled. 'Not until now. It was a hunch, but an educated one. I *have* met Melody Price. And I suspect crimes of passion sort of come with the territory.'

'And to make things worse, I don't think it was reciprocated, not in the way he wanted.' Billings let out a sigh.

'You said that the end of his marriage shook him to his core.'

'That's right.'

'How would you describe his state of mind lately?'

Billings puffed out his ruddy cheeks. 'Tell you the truth, not that I'm a shrink or anything, but he did seem a bit shaky. He wanted to be left on his own most of the time. I'd invite him up to the house, and we'd occasionally sit in front of the fire, chatting away, depleting a decanter of port. But in the end he always got so bloody maudlin about everything. Going on about missing his father, and how he'd let him down by ruining the business; his wife leaving him and the family they'd never have now; and then, of course, the Price woman. His one real chance at love, he reckoned. Convinced of it, he was: it was her or nothing.' Billings shook his head, as if the very memory of it was simultaneously too much to bear and, frankly, ridiculous. 'After the third drink, it always ended in tears – and that's not a turn of phrase, Inspector, I mean real ones. Bloody great tears streaming down his cheeks. Well, I stopped inviting him up in the end. I can't say I agree with all that.'

'All what?' asked Clarke.

'Well, it's different for us chaps. I know you chapesses are very good at it, talking about everything, feelings and such like, all the time. But I think there's a lot to be said for stiffening your resolve and just bloody getting on with it. Blubbering like a baby won't get you anywhere, will it?'

Frost didn't dare look round at the 'chapess' next to him.

'Thank you, Miss Smith, if you can make sure everyone who needs to be gathered in the briefing room is gathered, I'll be right out to meet her.'

Stanley Mullett put the receiver back in its cradle as if one wrong move and the thing would explode. Such was his fragility this morning that he was sure he could hear dust settle. Mullett was hosting the hangover from hell. All the other hangovers he'd endured over the years were impostors compared to this one; this one was the real deal. He was also hosting DI Eve Hayward from West End Central. She was to do a presentation on the evils of knock-off goods, which had increasingly been turning

59

up of late at Denton markets and car-boot fairs. The memo he'd received from County was very firm, it was a three-line whip, and all of Denton CID and a good representation of uniform were to be present, despite it being a Saturday morning.

Mullett picked up his mug of tepid coffee with its three heaped teaspoons of Nescafé; it was his third mug and it still hadn't done the trick. He was barely conscious. He gripped the arms of his leather-upholstered executive chair and lifted himself out of it. Once up, he took a sonorous breath, straightened his tie and headed for the conference room.

Ten minutes later and Mullett was in the front row of the large briefing room, smiling, his hangover a distant memory as he listened intently, and watched closely, totally immersed in DI Eve Hayward's presentation.

'The idea that counterfeit goods are a victimless crime is as big a fraud as the goods themselves that make it on to the market. And this idea is often perpetuated as much by law enforcement as by the general public,' asserted DI Hayward to her audience of some fifteen Eagle Lane officers of varying rank. 'From Sergio Tacchini tracksuits to Sony Trinitron TVs to TDK videotapes with *Footloose* recorded on them before the film's even come out in this country. Branded designer goods have never been more important to consumers, and equally never have they been bigger business for the counterfeiters. But not only can the goods themselves be dangerous – for instance, fake perfume that causes serious skin damage, faulty electrical goods that cause fires and loss of

60

life – but the profits are often reinvested into other criminal activities, such as the funding of large-scale drugs deals.'

Mullett approved of DI Eve Hayward on many levels. One being the way she delivered her message, with firm authority. Mullett's monster of a hangover had been vanquished more or less the very second he'd clapped his rheumy red eyes on the London inspector. She was in her mid to late thirties, he'd surmised, with auburn hair worn in a short bob that had a lustre as satisfying as his toecaps, and plucked eyebrows that were as expressive as a cracked whip. And with her full lips and a voice that was husky and warm, with the hint of an accent, Irish perhaps, she was making quite an impression.

She turned round to switch on the TV and video player for the training film. As she bent over to insert the video in the machine, Mullett had to avert his eyes, and instead turned his attention towards the audience behind him. He wasn't happy with what he saw. There was David Simms and some other young PCs nudging each other the minute she'd turned her back, licentious grins stretching their pimply faces. Then he caught sight of John Waters, married less than a year, and yet Mullett was sure he heard him make an obscene noise, like someone sucking their teeth. Arthur Hanlon was as usual not paying attention, his gaze drifting aimlessly around the room and finally floating out of the window, probably down to the canteen as he pondered the lunch menu.

No Frost. *Typical*. And no DC Clarke either. He'd

61

heard the rumours about Frost and Clarke; there was even talk of the DI being the father of her child. And as unpalatable and unbelievable as it seemed, he knew that women found the widowed Frost attractive. His late wife had been a good-looking woman from a well-connected local family. Mullett had even once courted her father with a view to joining the Masons. But as for the troublesome inspector, that whole rumpled maverick look obviously had some traction with the opposite sex.

DI Eve Hayward would need someone to show her around Denton and the surrounding area, and knowing that with his other duties it couldn't be him, Mullett had just the right person in mind. As Hayward turned to address her audience again, Mullett emitted a satisfied sigh. For once he was happy that Frost had ignored his instructions. He was happy Frost wasn't—

'*Excuse me, sir.*'

Mullett turned sharply to his left to find DS John Waters crouched at his shoulder, whispering in his ear.

'What is it?'

'I've got to go, community outreach at the Southern Housing Estate?'

This was news to Mullett, and his frown expressed as much.

'Some of the mothers are concerned about drugs on the estate. Inspector Frost said I should follow it up. I've had some experience, and we thought I would—'

'Yes, yes,' interrupted an impatient Mullett, almost shooing him away. He watched Waters leave, mouthing an apology to Eve Hayward, which she graciously accepted with a smile. Again, it vexed him that Frost had suggested Waters for community outreach on the estate. It was a good idea. Damn good idea. Again, corroborating the super's theory that the men respected Frost, that he had their ear. Mullett was determined to stem this pernicious influence. Frost would slip up, men like him always did. And when he did . . .

Saturday (2)

Radleigh Park Racecourse was situated some eight miles north of Denton town centre. It was best known as an all-weather racecourse, and it was one and a half miles in length, with a finishing straight of four furlongs to the winning post. Opened in 1949, it went into a steep decline and was then closed for almost five years in the 1970s, when everything seemed to be closing down, going on strike or just taking it easy with the three-day week. The punters were no longer turning up as they didn't have the money to throw away. But now it was boom time again, and 1984 was doing a good job of harking back to the golden age of the 1950s, when the nation was told they'd never had it so good, and the great Sir Gordon Richards won the Radleigh Classic in 1953 on the Queen Mother's horse in front of a crowd of some 30,000. There weren't quite that many here today when Frost took his place in the grandstand to survey the scene. But the bars were busy and the bookies in the betting ring looked like they were doing a roaring business.

Frost, always keen to learn something new about the patch he'd lived and worked in all his life, perused his race programme to discover that what made the reinvigorated Radleigh Park a course of interest was that it was now composed of Polytrack, a mixture of silica sand and synthetic fibres, as opposed to good old-fashioned turf. In many ways the course mirrored large parts of the ever-expanding town of Denton itself: modern, new and supposedly efficient, but also unpredictable.

He looked up from his programme, and even from the distance of the main stand, you couldn't miss her. Melody Price was standing on two upturned crates at her bookie's pitch, chalking up the runners for the next race on the betting board which bore the legend 'George Price & Son, Turf Accountants'. Frost wondered where the 'Son' was, and why he hadn't come up on his radar yet. Hadn't Clarke mentioned something about a son?

Melody Price was wearing a full-length fur coat with a matching Russian-style hat, and patent-leather boots with a heel that made standing on the crates a feat in itself. Amongst the rows of camel-coated, trilby-hatted and cigar-chomping bookies, she struck a glamorous figure, and certainly drew to her flocks of male punters eager to fritter away their hard-earned cash in return for a moment of her attention.

The detective then made his way down to the betting ring and picked his way through the crowds; he

65

could tell that a lot of these were the real hard-nosed gamblers who weren't interested in taking in the scenery or enjoying a pleasant day out at the races. They were there to wage war on the bookies and try to beat the odds, and had started to gather around the boards to see the starting prices. Frost was soon in Melody Price's eyeline. She welcomed him with the sort of big smile and wave normally reserved for dear old friends, not coppers investigating a husband's attempted murder. Frost would have liked to put money on how long she would keep up this charade – not long, if he was doing his job right.

'Ah, Jack, how lovely to see you, but I thought you weren't a betting man?'

'Still not, I'm afraid, but I'm always on the lookout for a hot tip. And I do need to talk to you, Mrs Price—'

'*Melody*, Jack, please, how many more times?'

'Well, Melody, there have been some further developments.'

'I am rather busy, Jack.'

'And this is very important.'

Melody Price stopped smiling and turned towards a man posted at what looked like a music stand, but instead of a score there was a large open ledger, in the columns of which he was adding figures with a worn-down pencil. Frost took him to be Jimmy Drake, the clerk. He was in his sixties, short, around five four, with a thickset build and an appearance that would best be described as dapper, in a beige covert coat with a dark-brown felt collar, topped off with a Lincoln green fedora. On the tip of

66

his hawkish nose a pair of half-moon spectacles rested precariously. Perhaps to ensure they remained in place, Jimmy Drake didn't look up from his bookkeeping duties to acknowledge Frost's presence, and he replied to Melody's instructions with barely a grunt.

Frost and Mrs Price made their way out of the betting ring towards the hospitality tents and refreshment stalls, and soon found themselves at a table in the Champagne & Oyster Marquee. The DI had fancied a bacon sarnie and piping-hot tea from one of the many vans offering such fast-food delights, but Melody had insisted otherwise. She was drinking a Buck's Fizz in a flute. Frost was pacing himself for what he thought would be a long day by drinking what he assumed to be a Buck's without the Fizz. He wasn't used to anything quite as healthy as plain orange juice and it left an unpleasant tang in his mouth, which he quickly countered by sparking up a Rothmans.

'To be honest, I'm surprised to see you here today.'

'George would go mad if I missed a day's racing.'

'All things considered, I'm sure he'd understand.'

'No, if I know my George, and I think I do, it's not just about the money we'd be missing out on today, it's the principle of the thing. George would view it as surrendering, letting them win. No, I had to fly the flag today.'

He looked confused. 'I'm sorry, Melody, let who win, exactly?'

'The bad guys, the robbers, the ones that put George in the hospital.'

67

Frost gave a cautious smile of acknowledgement, but didn't altogether agree with the logic, and suspected that Melody's stoicism in turning up at the races today had as much, if not more, to do with the money than anything else. He watched as she raised her tall glass to her glossy lips and sipped her drink, seemingly without a care in the world, as if turning up at the races and 'flying the flag' for George Price really was fulfilling her wifely duties.

To be fair, the tent was packed with people who looked like they didn't have a care in the world. There were groups of young men in double-breasted suits, candy-striped shirts, floral ties and red braces; and girls with big hair to match their big shoulder pads. As the champagne flowed, there were off-colour jokes to scare the horses followed by raucous laughter from the flash young men, and tittering giggles from the pliable girls. Frost had them pegged as City boys, or the new breed of estate agents who, like that Jason, seemed to be cropping up like toadstools all over the place. Denton and the surrounding area were on the up, with the council freeing up green-belt and brown-belt land, and old properties were being bought up and quickly converted and redeveloped. Frost got back to the business in hand.

'Terry Langdon used to have the pitch next to yours, I believe.' Melody took the opportunity to wave to someone at the bar. Frost wasn't so easily distracted. 'Tall fella, drives a Porsche 924, bears a passing resemblance to Magnum PI?'

68

Her head rolled back and she let out a peal of laughter. 'My God, Terry would love to hear you say that! He'll be selling the Porsche, too, I hear he owes the taxman.' She stopped laughing. 'Are you suggesting Terry Langdon might . . . ?'

'We have two eyewitnesses who saw a man leaving the scene of the crime in a red Porsche 924. Apparently he looked like some actor called Tom Selleck in one of these American cop shows, or at least they thought so. As you know, Terry does own a 924.'

'Makes sense. He's broke so he robbed George. What do you think?'

He took a moment, then leaned in closer to her. 'I think there's another motive that makes a lot more sense to me. A lot more.'

Frost's hushed tones and seeming tactfulness must have appealed to her vanity, because she didn't deny it or even question it. She took in a dramatic breath and said, 'I don't take you for an idiot, Jack. And I assume you've been doing your job since I saw you yesterday, namely, trying to find out who did this to my husband.'

'I have.'

'And you've spoken to some people and found out that Terry . . . shall we say, has feelings for me?'

'Correct. More than just feelings, I'd say – allegedly, he's in love with you.'

'I'd say, *allegedly*, that's about right.'

'Were you having an affair with him?'

Melody Price was about to raise her glass again but stopped. Her glossy red lips were pursed in an almost perfect O. She held the position longer than was necessary, as if posing on a photoshoot.

'Please, Melody, don't look so shocked. It's not the most outrageous suggestion in the world, considering the circumstances. And it does require a truthful answer, because I will find out.'

She put her glass back down on the table, stopped pouting and adopted a very formal and businesslike tone. 'No, I wasn't having an affair. That was simply out of the question because I love George and I would never cheat on him, never mind with someone like Terry Langdon. And talk about doing a doo-doo on your own doorstep, so no, it would never happen. But yes, Terry had made it clear how he felt about me.'

'Did George know about it, or suspect anything?'

'No, and I made sure George didn't. George would have killed him if he'd found out – not literally, you understand, but he'd have given him a thump . . .' Melody looked like a fresh and frightening idea had struck her. 'Something Terry said, I didn't give it much thought because he'd said so many stupid things. He said he was sure that without George around, things would be different.'

'And what did you say?'

'I didn't take any notice of it – like I said, he said lots of things. I certainly didn't encourage it. To be honest, Jack, men drooling over you like that is never very appealing. Trust me, it's not an attractive look.'

'I'll bear it in mind.'

Melody Price straightened her back and pursed her lips again. Frost realized they were the most animated

70

part of her. She then executed a look of intense contemplation. 'But now I think about it, I do remember feeling sorry for him. He'd left his wife, or she'd left him?'

'For a gas fitter, apparently.'

'Sort of says it all.'

'Does it?'

'Well, I don't recall an episode of *Magnum* where he's given the heave-ho for a bloke in a boiler suit with a spanner hanging out of his back pocket, do you?'

'I've never watched it, so I couldn't say, but it doesn't sound likely to me, no. So, the reality of Terry's life didn't quite match up to the fantasy of it, or how he saw himself?'

Melody made a low humming sound that signified she was impressed by his deduction. 'Very good, Jack. You have a real insight into the human condition.'

'Most blokes walk through life thinking they're Richard Gere, until a reflective surface tells them otherwise.'

She laughed. 'The male ego is a fragile thing, and Terry's was more fragile than most, I reckon. I could tell that deep down he wasn't happy. He was lonely, seemed sort of sad, really. I didn't have the heart to tell him, to possibly send him over the edge. I remember I said something like . . . maybe another time, in another life, without George around. So he said something like, let's run away together, get away from it all, go wherever we want. Spain, maybe. I told him I wasn't running anywhere. Maybe he thought . . .'

'George should go? Get rid of him, and then it would be different between you two?'

71

Melody's eyes widened around this thought, and she shook her head in disbelief. 'It was a throwaway comment, but now I come to think about it . . . he had been acting so weird lately.'

'How so?'

'Like I said, Terry always used to flirt and say silly things when it was safe and George wasn't around, of course, but the last few times I've seen him he'd stopped. He seemed more serious. Resolute. Determined. Now I know why. I reckon he'd made up his mind to do something about it. Do you know where he is?'

'If we did, we might be having a different conversation,' said Frost. 'How about you, could you throw any light on where he might be?'

'Why would I know?'

'He wanted to take you to Spain, you said – does he have contacts there?'

Mrs Price insisted she didn't know, then got nervous about her own safety. She asked if she needed twenty-four-hour police protection. Frost joked there would be no shortage of volunteers amongst the male members of the force for that job, but assured her she was safe as there was a full alert out for Langdon. He told her that if Terry did make contact, she should call him immediately.

As they left the tent and she was beginning to relax, content in the knowledge that the questioning was over, Frost pulled one more out of the bag. 'I know about the tapes.'

On hearing this, she arched one of her perfectly plucked eyebrows so it resembled the rounded top of a

72

question mark, and kept it there for an inordinate amount of time, without so much as a quiver. If Frost thought he could stare her down into a withering submission of some sort, he was wrong. He could feel the seconds dragging slowly by – he counted twenty of them – before he realized he was in the hands of a stone-cold professional.

Frost broke first. 'I read DC Arthur Hanlon's statement.'

'Who's he?'

'The *rotund* detective you spoke to about the missing tapes from the break-in.'

'There were no missing tapes.'

'Mrs Doreen Trafford, she reported the break-in—'

'Yes, I'm aware who she is and what she said.'

'She swore blind some videotapes had been stolen, adamant she was.'

Melody sighed, and a weary smile broke across her face. 'Jack, please. I've held off because I don't like to speak ill of people. Not in my nature. But I actually fired her shortly after the incident. I don't know what she told your . . . *rotund* detective, but she is a vindictive, bitter woman. This wasn't the first time she'd tried to cause trouble, cast aspersions. The minute I stepped into that house she was looking daggers at me. I inherited her, you see, and she made it very clear that George's first wife was a complete angel, and I was dirt on her J Cloth. I tried my best, really I did. I was very good to her, and her layabout husband. He used to do odd jobs around the place, which were generally botched, and he

73

used to steal the booze. George had it out with him. Frank got nasty. So George sacked him, and I sacked her. If anything had been stolen, tapes or otherwise, I'd have known. So it's my word against hers.'

Melody pointedly checked her watch, which was the ladies' version of her husband's, and said she needed to get back as the first race would be starting soon.

The watch was a timely reminder for Frost too. And he had one last gambit. 'By the way, your husband's personal possessions – a gold Rolex, like yours, I see, just bigger; a gold money clip with, if memory serves, five hundred quid in it; some loose change and keys – are ready and waiting to be picked up at Eagle Lane station. I would have brought them with me, but you need to sign for them in person. I'd hate anything to happen to them. Which makes you wonder why they weren't stolen in the robbery?'

Melody ignored that last comment and smiled appreciatively. 'Was that all he had on him?'

By most people's standards that would be a hell of a lot to have on you, thought Frost, but he kept his counsel, and let the question hang in the air for a bit, looking for something in her eyes, or a twitch from that very expressive mouth of hers. But nothing came, so he lied, 'Yes, that's all.'

Saturday (3)

'That was an excellent briefing. Clear, concise and informative. Everything one could hope for. I feel secure that Denton CID understands the pervasiveness of this crime, from Trinitrons to trannies to T-shirts, and what to look out for and how to tackle it. Well done, Detective Inspector . . . May I call you Eve?'

'You may indeed, Superintendent Mullett.'

'And you must call me Stanley.'

DI Eve Hayward demurred with a polite smile. She was sitting on the opposite side of the Denton superintendent's desk, a desk that was spotless, not a sheet of paper askew, nor a paperclip out of place. She took the opportunity to survey the office, mainly to avoid the lascivious gaze that Mullett was fixing her with. One of the dark wood-panelled walls was adorned with a portrait of the Queen, circa 1964, which, alongside a map of the area with coloured thumbtacks stuck seemingly arbitrarily in it, was pretty much standard in a super's office out in the provinces. In her time of going station to station in her war against the counterfeiters she'd seen portraits of Wellington, Churchill, even Nelson, and lots of Spitfires going over the white cliffs of Dover.

'Well, I must say, the reaction and questions I got from your team were very intelligent and pertinent. Sometimes they just sit there and pretend to take notes and can't wait to get out.'

'They are an inquisitive lot,' said Mullett, 'and making the most of a good briefing and expert opinion is something I've tried to instil in them over the years.'

'Some can be a little suspicious of outsiders coming on to their patch, especially from London.'

Mullett smiled, sat back in his chair, and laced his hands together over his stomach, which still felt delicate and more distended than usual due to the kebab he'd drunkenly devoured on the way home from the golf club last night. 'It wasn't always thus, I've had to work on them, they can be a narrow-minded provincial lot. But I believe modern policing is built on networks and the sharing of information.'

'I fully agree, Superintendent.'

'Stanley, please.'

'Cooperation across the lines is the only way modern policing works. And I'm looking forward to sharing my database with you.'

Mullett's brow furrowed at this before total blankness set in.

Eve Hayward prompted, 'Computer database?'

'Ah, yes, of course. You know, only yesterday I chaired a meeting with some fellow top brass from the surrounding districts in the county at the Denton and Rimmington Golf Club, of which I'm chairman, incidentally.'

The London DI was getting the measure of Stanley Mullett. 'That's very, *very* impressive. I can see you run a tight ship here at Eagle Lane. I've had lots of offers to show me around. PC Simms, DC Hanlon, DC Perks, DS Waters, someone called Pete. All said they'd received information on counterfeit goods in the area.'

Mullett stopped smiling and leaned forward on his desk and placed his hand on the phone receiver. 'All capable men, though I'm not sure who "Pete" is, but I've already taken the liberty of assigning someone to show you around.' Mullett picked up his phone and asked Miss Smith to get DC Clarke in his office immediately.

'Clarke? I don't think I met him.'

'An excellent DC with extensive knowledge of the area. I'm sure you'll be more than satisfied.' Mullett relaxed back in his chair again, then removed his horn-rimmed glasses and rubbed at the lenses vigorously, as if keen to ensure that nothing would hinder his view of Eve Hayward, not a speck of dust or the slightest smudge. 'I was thinking, Eve, it might be good for us to liaise later today, maybe this evening, to assess what progress you've made in your investigations and for you to fill me in. I do like to be kept abreast of what's going on.'

'Yes, of course.'

'How about dinner tonight? I know a nice little bistro not far—'

77

'You wanted to see me, sir?' said DC Sue Clarke, managing to knock, enter and talk all at the same time, much to the chagrin of Mullett.

'Yes, Clarke, take a seat.'

Clarke and Hayward exchanged smiles and the DC sat down. Mullett made the introductions and told Clarke she would now be helping DI Hayward with her inquiries into the glut of counterfeit merchandise in the area.

Clarke couldn't conceal her disappointment. 'I'm still working on the George Price shooting, sir. DI Frost believes there are further avenues to look into other than just Terry Langdon – hence me not being at the briefing earlier on.'

'From what I know about the case, in Langdon you already have a prime suspect who's been identified by eyewitnesses as leaving the scene of the crime in great haste. You've received corroboration from others that he has more than sufficient motive for the shooting. And he's missing. Whilst I never say a case is closed until the judge pronounces his sentence, I think we can spare you.'

Eve Hayward gave a clandestine little roll of her eyes at this. Sue Clarke clocked it and suppressed a smirk. This little exchange seemed to make them immediate allies.

As they got up to leave, Mullett said, 'Oh, about our meeting later, Eve—'

Hayward cut him off. 'I don't believe I've met DI

Frost yet, but I seem to be hearing about him a lot. Shame he wasn't at the briefing, too.'

Mullett frowned. 'Indeed. Where is he, Susan?'

'Gordon bleeding Bennett! You useless bloody nag!'

Frost tore up his betting slip and threw it in the air in disgust. It was the third race in a row where he'd backed a loser. He was using the Tote in the grandstand, away from Melody Price and her fellow bookies in the betting ring. On leaving the Champagne & Oyster Marquee, they'd said their goodbyes with Melody's ringing endorsement of Terry Langdon's guilt reverberating in his ears.

But Frost didn't leave the races, and it certainly wasn't his luck on the horses that was making him stay. His wallet was taking a vicious beating and flattening out fast. One of the reasons he stayed was propped up against the counter at the public bar, a bar that was rapidly filling up as the punters poured in for their race-interval drink. It was thirsty work throwing money away. And Frank Trafford looked like he'd been working harder at it than most; grim-faced but seemingly undeterred, he was supping a pint and looking attentively at his copy of the *Racing Post* for his next investment.

Frost pulled out the copy of the mugshot that Arthur Hanlon had given him. It had piqued his interest that Trafford, like Terry Langdon, was the proud possessor of a moustache. Not quite in Magnum PI's league, or so Hanlon said – less flamboyant, more trimmed and

79

utilitarian. Frank was a big block of a man, with a square-shaped head and close-cropped iron-grey hair. His charge sheet put his age at fifty-two, and he looked like he'd gone through the years hard.

'How's your luck, Frank?'

Trafford looked up from his paper at the man who had just sidled up to him at the bar. His mouth torqued into a grimace, and his eyes, grey as his hair, narrowed menacingly.

Frost didn't waste any more time and pulled out his warrant card. 'Detective Inspector Frost. Your wife reported a robbery at the Prices' place in February? George Price, I believe your—'

'I know who he is.' He folded the paper over a few times and held it gripped in his hand like a cosh. Frost hadn't ever seen a more threatening-looking newspaper. 'My wife worked for him for fifteen years. What do you want to know: who shot him?'

'You know about that?'

'I see he's not here today. Word gets around fast at the races, down there in the betting ring. What's it got to do with me?'

'Just wondering if you had any information on the robbery at the house, as your wife reported some video-tapes had been stolen.'

'How'd you know I was here?'

Frost shrugged. 'I didn't. There's a lot of people here I know. It's a popular, if unprofitable, place to be on a Saturday afternoon.' That was a lie. Arthur Hanlon had given Frost the tip that he might well find Frank

80

Trafford at the races today. 'But from what I hear, you and George Price had a falling-out?'

Trafford's scowl intensified. He balled his free fist and looked like he wanted to hammer it down on the bar, where his pint sat. 'He's a welsher. In more ways than one. He owed me money for work I did for him – and bets I had with him.' Trafford took a glug of the pint. 'All that money, big house, and they treat Doreen like dirt, don't pay what they owe. Scum!'

Frost weighed him up. He stank of alcohol like he was infused with the stuff, that sort of long-term boozing that kept him perpetually topped up. There was probably an army pension paying for the gambling and drinking, with his wife working her fingers to the bone to pay for everything else. Or maybe he was drummed out of the army, dishonourable discharge, thought Frost. Had he been in the Falklands? No, too old. Somewhere along the line he'd lost it, but he looked like he still had further to go.

'Makes you wonder what was on those tapes, right?'

'Her with her kit off, probably!'

'Who?'

'The wife, little Lady Muck, Melody Price.'

'You watched the tapes?'

'No, didn't have to. Doreen reckoned that's what they got up to. You know that's what she did, Page Three? She can put on airs and graces, but once a tart, always a tart.'

'Sounds interesting, I'd like to talk to Doreen about it.'

'Ha! Then buy a ticket to Manchester, that's where she is. She's staying with her sister.'

'How long for?'

Frank Trafford's thick shoulders gave a heavy shrug. Frost now realized it wasn't a fleeting visit to the sister, and what Trafford had lost. And it wasn't hard to imagine what had driven Doreen away from her husband.

'Where were you yesterday, Frank?'

At this he straightened up from his slump across the bar, as if being called to attention, and like the well-drilled soldier he once was, he didn't want to be caught off guard. 'I was here, doing my money. Bloody book-makers, they always win.'

'What time did you leave?'

'Soon as I ran out of bloody money – no point being here otherwise.'

'What time?'

'What is this, what are you accusing me of?'

'A simple question. Got nothing to hide, have you?'

'No. Maybe after the fourth race. I didn't even have my fare home, so I walked.'

'Long walk. You live on Langley Road, right?'

'Through the woods it's quick enough. I'm used to marching, put in longer stretches than that. And I'll do it again today, the way things are going.'

'I think we're going to have to talk further, down at the station,' said Frost, delivering this with a smile and as much informality as he could muster. 'Just to eliminate you from our inquiries.'

Frank Trafford picked up his pint glass, and sucked down the final dregs. Frost saw that running out of booze

82

was Frank's biggest problem right now, rather than being a possible suspect in an attempted murder.

'Buy us a whisky and I'll talk now, I'll talk to your heart's content, me old flower!'

'Best not, think you've had enough.'

Trafford attempted to pull a jovial grin. It trembled precariously on his lips, and certainly didn't match his eyes that were now brimming with anger. 'Buy us a drink, go on, tight bastard, what's wrong with you!'

'No.'

Frank Trafford lifted himself off his stool and took himself up to his full height, over six foot; under a grubby donkey jacket he was barrel-chested and a very capable-looking unit. Frost kept one eye on the glass in the ex-soldier's hand that was now brandished like a weapon, and the other was drawn to the spittle-flecked moustache twitching above his scowling mouth.

Don't do it, Frank ... Don't do it, uttered Frost to himself, keeping his lips sealed and his eyes trained on the glass that looked like it might shatter under the pressure of Trafford's white-knuckled fist. The ex-soldier was now so close to Frost's face that he could feel his booze-laden breath beating down on him.

'You can come for me, copper ... I'll be ready for you.'

It was said with enough menace for Frost to leave it at that – he wasn't there for whatever Trafford could throw at him, which at that point looked like the pint glass. So he let the drunken man glare at him for a moment or

83

two longer, before Frank put the glass on the bar counter with a thud and stalked off.

Frank shouldered and elbowed his way through the crowd, just looking to provoke a fight. Luckily there were no takers and he was soon gone, to begin another long march home through the woods, if his story was to be believed.

Frost blew out a noisy gust of air in relief that the ex-soldier had left, not only because most men who'd suffered the intimidating attentions of Frank Trafford would have done the same, but because he wasn't interested in wasting any more time on him today.

However, two pints of lager, three packs of salt and vinegar, five more quid blown on one more losing horse later, and his reason for being there finally presented himself.

Frost followed Jimmy Drake as he picked his way through the packed bar and took his place at the counter, a pound note fluttering in his hand to attract the barmaid. The DI was soon at his side. 'Buy you a drink, Mr Drake?'

Jimmy Drake looked round at Frost, the half-moon gold-rimmed specs still balancing perilously on the tip of his nose. 'Inspector Frost, isn't it?'

'Not for long if I get caught in here – no one will believe I'm on police business.'

'Like a flutter, do you?'

'Not particularly. I've never understood the lure of the betting shop. But the roar of the crowd is infectious, I'll give you that. I've already lost fifteen quid.'

84

'That's what we like to hear. I suppose you want to talk about George, what else? Terrible business. I already spoke to a colleague of yours, nice girl, told her everything I know.'

'Yes, DC Clarke said you'd known George longer than anyone.'

'It's nose and nose between me and Harry Baskin, who I take it you know rather well.'

'Our paths have crossed.'

'I've worked with George for over thirty years.' Drake shook his head and looked pained at the thought. 'I've not been to the hospital. Can't bear to see him like that. Lying there . . . tubes running in and out of him. Horrible. But as soon as he wakes up, as I know he will, I'll be there.'

Frost couldn't share his confidence but luckily the barmaid distracted them. He ordered half a Double Diamond for the clerk and a pint of Hofmeister for himself. Cheers! They took their drinks over to a table that had just become available.

Jimmy Drake picked up his pale ale and downed it in two noisy glugs, followed by a throaty 'Ah'. 'Thirsty work, racing. The Melster tells me Terry Langdon is the odds-on favourite.'

'The Melster?'

'My little nickname for her. She hates it.' He smiled mischievously. 'But I can tell you now, Mr Frost, if you've put your money on him, you'll lose it. I've known Terry Langdon since he was a kid, and he couldn't fight his way out of a paper bag with a water pistol. Hasn't got the bottle for that type of caper. And now he's blown his father's business, he'll swap the Porsche for a Cortina and get a job selling double-glazing and be very happy, probably. But you haven't cornered me to ask me that, so what's really on your mind?'

'We found this on George.' Frost reached inside his leather jacket and pulled out the little black book, all the time keeping his eye on Drake, watching for the gambler's 'tell', the involuntary reaction which could be anything from a slight twitch to a near-imperceptible smile, that would tell Frost he had a winning hand.

He needn't have bothered, because Jimmy came right out and said it: 'If that's what I think it is, I'll wager that whoever took a shot at George might well be in that black book.'

Frost couldn't help but give a victorious grin on hearing this. 'That's what I was hoping you'd say. Trouble is, there's no discernible names in it, just initials and columns of numbers. Bets, I assume.'

The clerk looked at the notebook like it had just been retrieved from a toilet bowl, and a particularly unsanitary one at that. Frost raised a questioning eyebrow, and Jimmy eventually snatched the book out of his hand and flicked through it, running a quick calculating gaze over the figures and letters.

Frost smiled. 'Another Double Diamond, Jimmy?'

'I'll have another half. Oh, and a Hamlet cigar.'

When Frost returned from the bar, Drake laid out the whole deal. George Price ran an off-course betting service for prized customers. The type of men who didn't like

86

going into betting shops and mixing with the hoi polloi there, and whose reputations might suffer if they were seen in such places – or were indeed seen gambling at all. Trusted gold-star customers could call up George on his private number and have a bet. This entailed the bookie extending them credit as and when. Jimmy said that George could keep all the bets in his head, and knew who owed him and how much, and the little black book was just back-up.

Frost pieced the rest together himself: with both George and the notebook gone there would be no record of how much they owed, or even who they were. And as some of the large sums listed in the book showed, killing George Price made good financial sense. Jimmy Drake said that running a betting credit business is always risky, because transactions between the punters and bookies are unenforceable by law. 'It's a gentleman's agreement, always has been.'

So who collects for George if someone decides to be un-gentlemanly and not honour the bet? Frost asked himself. And as quickly he came back with the answer: Harry Baskin.

'Recognize any of the initials?'

Drake shook his head and handed the book back to Frost. 'Nothing stands out. But to be honest, I had nothing to do with this part of the business; like I said, George ran it all himself. I just clerk for him at the races.'

'You don't seem to approve.'

'Well, if I'm right, look where it got him. Running a betting shop and working at the races where you see the

87

colour of people's money is a perfectly respectable business. But when it comes to letting them gamble without seeing their money, it's like betting on tomorrow, and who knows what tomorrow brings.'

'Very philosophical, Jimmy,' said Frost, straining to get it, as betting generally seemed to him like throwing money into the great void of the unknowable anyway. 'How about these two, you know what these mean?' Frost pointed at the two most prominent entries in the book, the only ones that weren't just initials. They were in capitals and underlined: <u>SOCKS</u> and <u>WINSTON</u>. They also had the biggest amounts next to them.

Drake muttered 'Socks and Winston' to himself a few times, then his face crumpled in bafflement as he tried to make sense of the names and the numbers. 'Well, whoever they are, they're into George for a bloody fortune, unless those are their telephone numbers. Have you tried ringing them?'

'Socks and Winston,' Frost ruminated. 'Nicknames, I'm assuming . . . or names of horses?'

Jimmy shook his head at the last suggestion. 'Horses don't gamble, too clever by half. George likes giving people nicknames. Plus it's more discreet, just in case the book fell into the wrong hands. Like yours.' He smiled.

The DI returned the smile. 'I know all about nicknames – mine's stuck so much most people think it's my real name.'

'Jack – it makes sense to me. What's your real one?'

'I was christened William. But only my mother-in-law used to call me that, and then just to wind me up.'

88

'As Shakespeare once said, "What's in a name?"'

'In this case, Jimmy, quite a bit.' Jack Frost closed the book and slipped it back into his jacket pocket. 'It said "George Price and Son" on the board – tell me about the son, Michael?'

The clerk shook his head again and let out a gloomy sigh. 'Michael's a good lad. The trouble with him and George is that the boy just wasn't cut out for the racing world. Wasn't quick enough, wasn't good with the numbers. In this game, at the height of the betting, the betting ring is like the floor of the London Stock Exchange. Money passes from hand to hand real fast, the odds are always changing, and you have to keep your wits about you, think fast on your feet. George was always shouting at Michael, and eventually it just did for the kid's confidence. Then when Melody came along, that was it. Michael was out of the business, and she was in.'

'You don't sound too happy about it.'

'It's a family thing, none of my concern. When George's first wife passed away he was heartbroken, devastated. Then Melody came along and changed all that, got him smiling again.'

Frost noted a cool reserve in Drake's tone. He seemed disapproving of Price's newfound happiness, or at least suspicious of it. 'How did George seem to you, Jimmy? Did he have other problems, like money problems, personal problems, enemies?'

'Bookmakers are the—'

'Bookmakers are the enemy, I've heard,' said Frost. 'But I'm talking about real enemies who would want him dead. Recently, was George happy, unhappy, moody, nervous, anything?'

'George always prided himself on being the life and soul, always cracking jokes, larger than life, you know the type. But these last few weeks he seemed out of sorts. Short-tempered, sullen. I can't really say any more, because George wasn't the type to talk about things.'

Jimmy shrugged and added, 'Me neither, really. Her indoors says it's like getting blood out of a stone, getting me to natter.' He then muttered his complaints about 'her indoors' into his glass of Double Diamond.

Drake wiped away the froth from his mouth with the back of his hand, and checked his watch whilst doing it. 'Right, I need to get back to work,' he said, before clamping his Hamlet between his teeth and rising to his feet.

Frost stood up with him, took out his wallet and handed the clerk his card. 'If you think of anything that might help, day or night.'

Jimmy took the card. 'Thanks for the drinks,' he said, giving a tug on the brim of his fedora and starting to make his way out of the bar.

'Oh, Jimmy. One last thing.'

Drake wheeled round.

'You haven't got any tips for the next race?'

Jimmy took the cigar out of his mouth, had a quick glance around him to make sure no one was listening, then said in a conspiratorial stage whisper, 'You want me to tell you the secret of how to make a small fortune from betting on the horses?'

90

Frost's eyes widened, his ears pricked up. 'Yes, please.'

'You start with a *large* fortune.'

'Go on, my beauty! Go on, my son! Ride him home! That's it! . . . That's it! . . . YES!'

Frost jumped up in the air, pumped his fist and kissed his betting slip. It was his fourth winner in a row, more than making up for the three losing tickets before Drake had literally 'marked his card', and given him four tips for the following races. Jimmy had asked only one thing, that he didn't place his bets with the Prices.

Frost went to the Tote window to collect his winnings off an unsmiling and brittle blonde who counted out his money as if it was coming out of her own purse. He now had four hundred quid and some loose change burning a hole in his pocket. Money for nothing, he thought, and now Frost could fully understand the lure of gambling.

The DI shouldered his way back into the bar, feeling ten feet tall and parched. Standing at the winning post cheering on your winning horse really was thirsty work. He'd already had four . . . maybe five pints? So he did the sensible thing and ordered half a Double Diamond and a Hamlet in honour of Jimmy Drake and his tips. He stood at the bar lighting the cigar and thinking about the funny TV adverts for the brand. They always featured some poor loser having terrible luck in some way or other, then lighting up the cigar to take away the pain, a consolation prize of sorts. Well, not today, Saatchi & Saatchi, thought Frost as he stood

91

triumphant at the bar, puffing out perfectly formed smoke rings.

The magic was only broken when he glanced down at his watch. He was very late for something – he was pretty sure Mullett had arranged a briefing of some description, something about counterfeit goods?

Frost made his way out of the racecourse to the car park, which was no more than a series of roped-off fields, and began looking for his Metro. He thought he'd beat the traffic leaving before the last race, and he also didn't trust himself not to have a final bet; and as he stood gently swaying in the muddy field, he didn't trust himself with another drink inside him, either. And whilst he didn't plan on getting much more work done today, he thought he should at least put in an appearance at Eagle Lane, hoping he wouldn't bump into Mullett, before sloping off again. More by luck than effort, he spotted the yellow Metro boxed in amongst the tight rows of cars. A taxi was looking like the best option, or maybe radioing for a uniform, getting Simms to come and pick him up, urgent police business. He'd see how he felt when he got behind the wheel.

He put both hands in his trouser pockets to locate his keys, then yanked them out to lean on the roof of the car – like a tightrope walker teetering on his feet he did feel rather wobbly. And he really didn't stand much of a chance when he heard the loud thwack that reverberated around his skull, followed by a searing all-consuming pain. Almost immediately the yellow Metro started to fade from view as blurry insensibility took

92

hold of him . . . He just managed to raise his right hand to the crown of his head and feel a warm ooze of blood. Everything seemed to move in slow motion as he swayed helplessly . . . Then the fist connected with his face and all went black.

Saturday (4)

'If we see anyone dealing drugs, we should chop their bloody hands off!'

'Drag 'em up to the fifteenth floor and throw 'em off the roof!'

'Better idea, lean out the window and pour boiling water over the bastards, that way we don't have to look at their ugly faces!'

'Now, now, ladies,' pleaded the Reverend James Tutt, trying to cut through the raucous laughter. 'Please can we be constructive and try and keep within the limits of the law with what we can do. DS Waters has kindly come along to help us with this matter, it would be wise to hear him out.'

John Waters sat in front of a semi-circle of concerned residents of the Southern Housing Estate, about twenty in total, predominantly young mothers with a vested interest in keeping hard drugs away from their children.

94

They didn't want Denton's largest estate to become a drug-infested no-go area for decent citizens, the fate that had hit so many up and down the country. Drugs, especially heroin, were cheap, addictive and deadly. It was the new scourge, bumping football hooliganism and Arthur Scargill off the front pages of the tabloids and making the nightly news, feeding the fear, as it spread and tightened its pernicious grip on the impoverished sink estates of England.

The Reverend James Tutt, the vicar of the parish, was present to chair the meeting, and to keep the more vociferous, if not downright ferocious, of the mothers at bay. They were in the Rainbow Room, the community hall that abutted one of the blocks on the west side of the sprawling estate. The windowless space was lit up with fizzing strip lighting that revealed the brightly coloured murals of rolling green hills, blue skies, fluffy white clouds, a smiling sun and, of course, a rainbow; a country idyll, and a view that in reality wasn't available anywhere on the estate. The room doubled as a play centre and an after-school club, and toys and footballs that hadn't been put away littered the grass-green carpeted floor.

Waters had got involved with the community outreach programme through the urging of Frost, who thought the London-born DS could bring some of his big-city nous and experience to bear. The first thing Waters did was target the kids; he got to know them, learned their first names, and soon won their trust – some of them at least. He organized a minibus and took

95

groups of the kids to play football, and he even considered starting a boxing club. Red tape tied everything up and stopped it happening. But his efforts hadn't gone unnoticed, and he had the trust of the parents as a good copper who wasn't interested just in nicking them.

'Sorry, vicar, but I still think, anyone we see dealing drugs on the estate, we should kill them on sight.'

'Oh please, Natasha,' implored the vicar. 'Listen to DS Waters.'

'Come on, girls, let the man speak,' said Cathy Bartlett.

'That's right, he has experience with this stuff, he's not just a pretty face,' said Jackie.

Ella Ross agreed. 'Yes, we'll listen to what John has to say.'

Natasha insisted, 'And if we don't agree, then we can still kill them on sight.'

They all cheered. Ella quietened them down. 'Go on, John, we're listening. We are, really.'

Not big on public speaking, and suitably cowed by the passion of his audience, Waters was grateful for the words of encouragement that were now coming his way.

'My experience is that the ones who finally decide if drugs are welcome in an area are the potential customers and those who live in that area – not the gangsters and thugs who push the merchandise, no matter how threatening they are. So we get to the kids before the dealers do. Where I grew up, around Stoke Newington, the local residents, mainly the women, I have to say, got together and did something about it. They formed an action

96

group, took to the streets, made banners and placards and marched in the so-called no-go areas, and made their presence felt. But it was all very peaceful, all very orderly, all very . . . serene and dignified. And that's what gave them their power.'

On hearing this, a deep hush fell over the room. The Reverend James Tutt breathed easy. Waters, his public-speaking nerves quelled, paused to let his words sink in, and all the women's rowdy bravado slipped away as they realized, probably for the first time, the full potential of what they could do. They glanced around at each other and exchanged little nods of agreement.

'I don't know if you know too many Baptist West Indian mothers, but I can tell you, they scared the hell out of the roughest and toughest gangsters on the block.' There were howls of laughter and cheers at this. The women gathered there probably hadn't met any West Indian mums from Hackney, but the sisterhood was resilient enough to cut through the divide. 'As a group, together, we're strong. We don't just warn kids of the dangers, we bring in people whose lives have been affected . . . Me, for instance . . .'

Two hours later (the community meeting ran over by a full hour) and DS Waters was finally released from the Rainbow Room with its cartoon primary colours, and was back out in the harsh realities of the estate itself, with its looming grey tower blocks casting ominous shadows on what green space there was. Before he headed back to Eagle Lane, he drove past the home of Tommy Wilkins, sworn enemy of Billy 'Bomber' Harris, and prime suspect in his shooting. Waters had resolved to have one last cruise around the Southern Housing Estate before heading back into Denton town centre and checking the other known haunts of Wilkins, such as the Three Cherries amusement arcade, the YMCA leisure centre, the Life in the Fast Lane bowling alley, Silver's gym and any number of fast-food outlets. For Wilkins and Harris these were all the hang-outs of a misspent youth they had never grown out of as they dossed their way into their mid-twenties.

Waters had exhausted every other possible source of information for locating Wilkins. His mother hadn't seen him in days, but that wasn't a rare occurrence, and his girlfriend, the mother of his infant son, told the same tale of woe. Then Waters caught a break. In his rear-view mirror he spotted a figure in a postbox-red tracksuit with a matching bucket hat and a pair of pristine white trainers. It was Tommy Wilkins. If he was supposed to be lying low, in his flashy 'casual' clobber he was sticking out like a sore thumb.

Tommy had obviously recognized Waters or his motor; the local villains pretty much had every unmarked Eagle Lane car clocked either by licence plate or just colour and type. And the DS's Nissan Maxima was well known to Wilkins, of that Waters was sure. The young man froze, obviously hoping that Waters hadn't spotted him. But in that eye-ripping outfit Tommy didn't stand a hope in hell of going unnoticed.

The DS kept a steady eye on his rear-view mirror and watched as Wilkins began a slow backwards retreat.

Then he twirled the key in the ignition, put her into reverse, lowered the handbrake, floored the accelerator and screeched after him. Tommy turned tail and raced off around the corner. As Waters approached the junction he let out a mighty yell of pleasure as he sensed that this was his moment, and he executed a perfect handbrake turn; the handbrake turn he'd been dreaming of ever since he got the keys of his first area car; the handbrake turn that had been running through his head ever since he saw Steve McQueen execute one in *Bullitt*. And whilst the Southern Housing Estate couldn't match the undulating mean streets of San Francisco, and Tommy Wilkins really wasn't worthy of it, it had worked a treat and the conspicuous target was clearly in his sights as he straightened up down Hillside Road.

The elation was short-lived as the red figure disappeared over a garden wall. Waters pulled up sharply, got out of the car and gave chase. Tommy slipped into an alley backing on to a row of houses. Waters heard a crashing sound up ahead, and as he turned into the alley he stumbled over the first obstacles that Wilkins had put in his path. All the dustbins had been overturned. And face down in the spilt rubbish Waters smelt some bad things. His left hand was now covered in some noxious green matter that was obviously some sort of degraded food. However, that was Angel Delight compared to what was now wrapped around his right arm – a wad of baby's nappies. Waters suddenly had a self-righteous loathing of people who didn't know how to dispose of their rubbish properly, and promised himself that when he was made superintendent he would ruthlessly enforce any relevant laws he could find. They deserved nothing less than the death penalty.

Waters retched, swore loudly and then got to his feet and carried on the chase, swerving around and jumping over the rolling bins and their contents. He spotted a flash of white trainer making its way into the entrance of Tideway House.

'Come on, Tommy, that's enough running about for one day!' the DS called as he followed him.

Tommy stopped, three floors up. Waters caught up with him on the walkway. The DS was right, that was more than enough running around for one day, and Wilkins was bent over on his haunches, doubled up in exhaustion, wheezing and sweating in his new bright-red tracksuit. He might have been dressed like an athlete, but the daily diet of JPS Black King Size cigarettes and snakebite and black had taken a significant toll over the years. Tommy took on board some laboured breaths that sounded like sheets of coarse sandpaper being rubbed together, and then straightened up.

Waters smiled and gave him the headline: 'Gotcha.'

Then Tommy did the strangest thing. He jumped over the balcony.

'I can tell you're not really up for this.'

'I'm just a humble DC and I'm happy to work on whatever case I'm assigned,' said Sue Clarke as she and DI Eve Hayward stepped out of Eagle Lane station and made their way to her car.

100

'But you can't beat a nice juicy attempted murder case, can you?' Hayward didn't wait for an answer. 'Of course you can't – unless it's an actual murder case. Working round the clock on one of those really gets the adrenalin running. Do you get a lot of shootings around here?'

'Normally I'd say, not really. But there were a couple last year and, of course, we've just had two in one day. Whilst it's not West End Central, for a town like Denton it's a bit like the Wild West at the moment.'

'Those would be George Price, a sixty-two-year-old bookmaker from North Denton, and one Billy Harris, twenty-five, otherwise known as Bomber, an unemployed resident of the Southern Housing Estate.'

Sue Clarke nodded her approval. 'Wow, I'm impressed. And I thought you were just here for the dodgy designer T-shirts.'

Eve Hayward laughed. 'And I appreciate your frankness. I see I'm going to have to give you one of my scintillating lectures on the evils of dodgy designer T-shirts.'

'I'm sorry, Inspector Hayward, I didn't mean to be disrespectful, I know that counterfeit—'

'Relax. And please, call me Eve.'

'Sue.'

They shook hands and crossed the road to Clarke's green Datsun Cherry. As the DC searched her handbag for her key, she noticed Eve Hayward peering inside the car, and saw what she saw: the grubby child seat in the back, next to a big furry purple elephant, some

101

half-chewed Farley's Rusks, a banana skin and a naked Action Man. In the front seats, where the grown-ups sat, it was even worse – there was the collection of empty Styrofoam containers, from takeaway burgers and curries, along with countless empty crisp bags and Frost's old fag packets and Wrigley's Juicy Fruit wrappers. Sue Clarke winced in embarrassment; she'd bet a month's wages that Eve Hayward's car didn't look like this tip on wheels.

'Tell you what, Sue, why don't we take my car, it's just up the road. I've got all my stuff in it, which I think I'll be needing.'

Clarke said it was a good idea and started to explain away the mess, but the DI simply strode off. Hayward completely changed the subject and seemingly couldn't care less about the state of the debris-strewn Datsun, a lack of interest which suited Clarke down to the ground.

'I fully understand, a couple of shootings does seem more like the business end of what we do,' the DI was saying. 'But what I've noticed since we set up the counterfeit-goods unit is that one thing tends to lead to another. I've covered all sorts of cases where you think there's no connection, but when there's a high volume of counterfeit goods suddenly turning up in an area, it's usually something highly organized and leads to other crimes. Just out of interest, how's it going with the George Price case, anyway?'

'We have a couple of eyewitnesses who gave us a good description of someone leaving the scene whom we've been able to identify, but not yet been able to eliminate from our inquiries,' said Clarke, aware she was sounding stiff and formal, but also realizing she was trying to make up for the sloppy and unprofessional interior of her car.

'So, Terry Langdon is away on his toes?'

Is there anything this woman doesn't know? thought Clarke. 'So for me to become a DI, like you, I really do have to be smarter than everyone else?'

'Just all the blokes. Not that hard.'

'Jack thinks there's potentially too many people with too many motives to focus all our attention on Terry Langdon so quickly.'

'Jack is DI William Frost, I take it. That's not me being clever, that's just obvious.'

'Are videos on your list of counterfeit items?'

Eve Hayward nodded. 'We call it piracy, you know, like with bootlegging music cassettes. And they're right at the top of it. It's fast turning into a multi-million-pound industry.'

'Well, maybe we can kill two birds with one stone. I was going to talk to George Price's son, and he works at Video Stars on the High Street.'

'Perfect. Multi-tasking, that's what the men think we're good at, apparently. I just call it getting stuff done.'

Hayward stopped at a highly polished red MG MGB GT. 'This is me.'

Clarke couldn't help but exclaim, 'Yes, it is!' Then she explained, 'I've always wanted one of these. Ever since I was a kid. The closest I got is the car my Barbie had.'

'Funny you should say that, Barbie dolls are probably the most counterfeited toy on the market.'

Hayward turned the key in the lock and let Sue in. She took in the interior with its polished burr-walnut dashboard and shiny chrome-framed dials, like the binnacles on luxury yachts. Not so much as a stray Ferrero Rocher wrapper in the ashtray. Clarke bit her lip, hard, because right now she felt like crying. She couldn't precisely say why . . . or maybe she could: she was tired, little Philip hadn't been sleeping, and with all her overtime, and her mother staying at the flat, life was proving to be hard work and chaotic at the moment. But she knew that now wasn't the time for tears. She concentrated on her breathing, so she wouldn't get all juddering and emotional.

The DI started the engine and revved it up. She then turned on the radio, tuned it to Radio 1 and turned up the volume. Status Quo were rocking out with their customary raucous three chords, which shook her out of her funk. Clarke suspected Eve Hayward knew exactly what she was doing and she was grateful for it. She was making the inside of her immaculately kept car as noisy and distracting as possible, and giving Sue time to regain her composure.

'Right, Video Stars it is then. I think I know where I'm going, I had a good drive around earlier.' The London inspector turned to Clarke and gave her a big warm smile. 'But I have a tendency to drive stupidly fast, so give us a shout, Sue, if I take a wrong turn.'

Eve Hayward was as good as her word and drove off fast – very fast.

Saturday (5)

Tommy Wilkins was now on the same ward at Denton General as his arch-enemy, Billy 'Bomber' Harris. In fact, their beds were next to each other. This wasn't bad luck on their behalf; it was smart strategic thinking by DS John Waters, who had contrived the cosy arrangement.

When Waters had peered down from the third-floor balcony of Tideway House, he'd seen the red-tracksuited figure of Tommy Wilkins splayed out on the ground like a starfish. There was some blood (a crack on the back of the head had made a pool of it) but not as much as Waters initially thought, because a good deal of it was in fact Tommy's red Fila bucket hat. And there was a broken arm and wrist where Tommy had tried to break his fall. But he'd got lucky. What had actually been more effective in breaking his fall was the big green plastic wheelie bin that he'd bounced off before he hit the deck. Still, there was also the issue of a missing tooth and a broken nose, which Waters had spotted before Tommy jumped. It looked like he'd been in the wars before he'd leapt off the balcony in an attempt to escape the law.

John Waters sat between the two wannabe gangsters with what, even he would admit, was a smug grin on his face.

'So, tell me, boys, who's gonna break first? Billy, how about you? Anything you want to say to Tommy? Maybe compliment him on his marksmanship?'

Bomber didn't flinch. He lay in his hospital bed, stiff as its starched sheets, staring straight ahead of him.

Waters turned his attention to Wilkins. 'How about you, Tommy? You wanna tell Bomber what a son of a bitch he is for knocking out your front toothy-peg, and breaking that beautiful, noble-looking nose of yours?'

Tommy was mimicking Bomber in his indefatigable pursuit of staring ahead of him, keeping his mouth shut and not giving anything away. He also appeared strangely serene, and didn't even look in pain any more, like he was practising some sort of Zen meditation. Or maybe it was just his normal empty-headed stare, thought Waters.

'OK, you two. Let me run this by you. I'm assuming it's tit for tat between you, as usual. Something happened, maybe it was over a girl, maybe it was over a couple of quid, some hash, some amphetamines, a football match – or maybe it was some deep philosophical point you two just couldn't agree on. But either way, you know me, boys, and you know I'm going to find out what's it all about.'

106

There was a sizeable pause, and then the two men, almost in unison, looked at each other. John Waters watched them closely – who would be the first to talk, who would be the first to grass and drop the other one right in it. Waters' eyes narrowed as another glance passed between them and they silently communed; but for the life of him, the DS couldn't get a read on it.

Then Billy 'Bomber' Harris broke the silence: 'Tommy didn't shoot me. I shot myself. I was playing with a mate's gun, and the thing went off. End of.'

'And Bomber didn't break my nose, or knock my tooth out. I fell down some stairs in our flats. Nothing more to it.'

They both now aimed their gaze at Waters, and grinned, Tommy perhaps a little more gap-toothed than Bomber. DS Waters would have been the first to admit it: their declarations of innocence and unity had managed to wipe the smug smile right off his face.

'Sugar?'

'Two for me, please,' said DC Sue Clarke.

'None for me,' said DI Eve Hayward.

'Actually, sorry, no, none for me either.' Clarke then turned to Hayward and said, 'Keep forgetting I'm trying to give up.'

Michael Price disappeared behind the counter to make the coffees. As they waited for him to return, they busied themselves by looking at the latest releases. The shop was small, a one-man operation at the best of times, but it still had a wall-to-wall offering of all the latest releases. Ignoring these, Clarke picked up a copy of *The French Connection* and read the blurry synopsis. She remembered what a great film it was, with its gritty realism and the enigmatic ending of Gene Hackman's detective, Popeye Doyle, stepping into the darkened warehouse after the main villain, and the single gunshot. Did he, didn't he? Was he, wasn't he? In complete contrast, Eve Hayward picked up a copy of *Octopussy* and tested the box by running her thumb under the clear plastic cover to feel the quality of the printed paper. Clarke raised an eyebrow at this, and Hayward returned her questioning glance with a little side-to-side wobble of her head as she weighed up the possibilities of it being pirated.

'I've not been to the hospital yet. How is he?' asked Michael Price as he put down three mugs of coffee, each bearing a *Star Wars* theme and several chips.

The women both put the videos back on the shelf and also returned to the counter. Michael Price sat on his stool behind it, but still managed to look far too big for the small space. Clarke was struck by just how much he resembled his father. Not yet as heavy, and with a fuller head of short curly black hair, but a chip off the old block nonetheless.

'He's stable,' said Clarke.

'Always knew it would happen.'

The two detectives exchanged surreptitious glances. 'Why's that?' asked Clarke.

Michael shrugged as if it was the most obvious thing in

108

the world. 'It's just the sort of bloke he is. You know, what goes around comes around.'

Clarke didn't attempt to catch Hayward's eye this time; there was no need to. *What goes around comes around* – these were not the guarded words you'd expect to hear from a potential suspect. And at this point, attempted patricide was a distinct possibility.

'Where were you yesterday afternoon, Michael?'

Michael Price laughed, and it was loud and seemed to fill the whole shop. 'Jesus, you think *I* did it?'

'We need to eliminate as many people as possible from our inquiries as quickly as possible.'

'I was at home.'

'All day?'

'All day.'

'Was anyone with you?'

'No.'

'Do you have anyone at all to corroborate that you were at home all day?'

'No. It was my day off. I just got a stack of films and spent the day on the couch watching them and playing Chuckie Egg.'

'What's Chuckie—'

Eve Hayward interjected, 'Chuckie Egg is the latest ZX Spectrum game, right, Michael?'

Michael Price's eyes widened in approval at a potential fellow game-player. 'You play it?'

'No. But I've heard good things.'

That obviously counted for nothing in his world, and

he quickly dropped the smile of camaraderie he was wearing.

'What else did you do yesterday, Michael?' asked Clarke.

'Went for a pint, had a couple, actually.'

'What pub?'

'The Spread Eagle on Eagle Lane.'

'What time?'

'About eightish.'

'You use that pub a lot?'

'Not as much as you coppers. I know it's a coppers' pub. Maybe that's why there's never any trouble in there. Apart from the coppers getting drunk, that is.'

Eve Hayward laughed. Sue felt the need to defend Eagle Lane. 'We're not that bad, except on birthdays, promotions, solving cases, and any day with a Y in it. Tell me, did you talk to any coppers in there?'

He gave what Clarke considered a sly smile. 'I don't *know* any coppers, apart from you two now. I've never been in trouble in my life. Like I say, a couple of pints, then home. Not much of a productive day – in fact it was the kind of day that my father would look down his nose at. George has a picture of Maggie Thatcher up in his office, she's his pin-up. He divides people into strivers and shirkers and always considered me to be a shirker. That's why we never got on. Did Terry Langdon do it? I heard you're looking for him.'

'How'd you hear that?'

'Uncle Jim told me.'

'Jimmy Drake?'

110

Michael Price nodded. 'He's not my real uncle, but I've called him that since I was a kid. I know Terry Langdon too. He always seemed like a nice bloke. I suppose you know all about him?'

'We know your father was in business with Terry Langdon's father and there was a dispute. Michael, did your father know the rumours about—'

'Terry shagging Melody?'

Sue Clarke wouldn't have chosen those exact words, but couldn't argue with their immediacy.

But on blurting them out, Michael Price's expression suddenly changed as his eyes widened, and he looked startled, shocked by his own words.

'Did he?' pressed Clarke.

'Did he what?'

'Did Terry Langdon, as you said, "shag" Melody, and did your dad know about it?'

'I don't know. I shouldn't have said that. Sometimes I just . . . I just say things.'

'You don't get on with your new step-mum then?'

'She's all right. She's . . . she's nice to me.'

'That's quite a thing to say, that she was having an affair with another man.'

'You won't tell her, will you?' Michael Price's wide-eyed gaze flitted from Clarke to Eve Hayward again and again, as if he was looking for a glint of sympathy in the detectives' eyes, a way out. 'I didn't . . . I didn't say she *was* having an affair with Terry Langdon. I just used to see them together at the races, when my dad wasn't around, and I could tell he liked her, and that she liked

111

him . . . a bit . . . maybe . . . They were about the same age . . . and stuff . . . I don't know. And anyway, I make it my business to stay out of Dad's business since he sacked me. I used to work at the races, you know that?' Clarke nodded. 'Ever since I was a kid it was George Price and Son. My mum wanted me to go to college. I don't know, maybe become a vet or something. I wouldn't have minded that, I like animals. But my dad wanted me to go into the business with him. I liked watching the horses, but that was about it. I'm not good at maths or anything like that, you have to be good with numbers to be a bookie. But he wasn't interested in what I wanted, couldn't give a toss. And once Mum died, well, he sort of lost interest altogether.'

'Lost interest in what?'

'Well, in me, I guess.'

Sue Clarke considered Michael Price, now sipping coffee from his chipped *Return of the Jedi* mug. Despite his height and bulk and resemblance to his father, he managed to look small and vulnerable, like a kid. But without an alibi or anyone to corroborate his movements on the previous day, he was very much a suspect in his father's shooting.

When Clarke wound up her questioning, she was satisfied that it had been a fruitful exchange. She had learned that Terry Langdon and Melody Price might well have taken their relationship beyond the bounds of flirtation and actually consummated it. And if Michael Price knew about it, a man who struck Clarke, even by his own admission, as not the sharpest knife in the drawer, maybe

112

his father knew about it too. And maybe George and Terry Langdon had arranged to meet up yesterday to settle it once and for all. This combustive scenario wasn't hard to imagine: the older cuckolded husband and the younger lover; they argued and one thing led to another, and Langdon shot Price. And with Langdon 'away on his toes', as Hayward would say, it really was looking like case solved, or certainly an abundance of motive and evidence was closing in around Terry Langdon.

And as Clarke sat in the lounge bar of Denton's premier hotel, the Prince Albert, drinking her filtered coffee, Eve Hayward agreed with her.

'From what you've told me,' said Eve, 'all fingers are pointing at Terry Langdon. Spotted leaving the scene, motive, opportunity and—'

'Away on his toes.'

'Precisely. It seems a better fit than Michael Price, even though you can't verify his whereabouts yesterday afternoon.'

'I was in the Spread Eagle with Jack last night after work, must have been around the same time he claims to have been there, bit later, and I didn't see him. And I believe him when he says he spent the day on his own playing video games. He just doesn't strike me as a good liar, seems rather guileless. And if I'm totally honest, maybe a little odd. It's almost like he *wanted* to get himself in trouble. Like a trip down the station wouldn't be a bad day out, maybe a bit of excitement for him. And yet, he didn't want to drop Melody Price in it?'

'His step-monster?'

'Yeah. She effectively ousted him from his birthright. "George Price and Son" is now "George Price and Sexy New Young Wife". You'd think he'd have a bit more to say about her. Instead he was apologizing for saying anything he did say about her. Like she was his real mum, and he was a bit scared of her.'

'Tell me really, why doesn't DI Frost fancy Terry Langdon for the shooting?' wondered Hayward.

'Well, it's like I said before. He thinks it's too early to tie it all up and not scout about for other suspects and motives. Mind you, I have my suspicions that he just enjoys kicking against the super, who likes to tie everything up as quickly as possible. It's good for the clear-up stats, you see . . .' Sue Clarke mopped up the mess she'd made of the fancy Rombouts plastic filter to cover up her confusion – she rather suspected she'd said too much. 'I'm sorry, I shouldn't be speaking out of turn about Superintendent—'

'Relax, Sue. I get it! He's a real piece of work, your Stanley Mullett, I got that when I first met him. And I smelt booze on him, too.'

'In all fairness to him, I think he had a big day and night out yesterday with the other superintendents from the county.'

'And this is Eagle Lane, and you like a drink, or five – sounds like my kind of station.' They laughed.

'I'm sorry about earlier, in the car,' said Clarke.

'I didn't notice anything.'

'Yeah, you did, you just didn't say anything. I appreciated it. I'm not usually so—'

114

'How old is he? I'm assuming he's a boy, from the Action Man on the back seat.'

'He's just one.'

Eve Hayward smiled. 'What's his name?'

'Philip. It was my grandad's name.' Sue Clarke took another sip of her coffee. 'I don't know, you just seem to have it all together, and I'm running around in a car that looks like . . . looks like how I feel most of the time . . .'

'I don't have kids, Sue. It may happen, but it hasn't happened yet. And if I'm really honest with myself, maybe I'm just too selfish, or too ambitious and wrapped up in my own career. But my mum brought me up on her own, so I know the challenges.'

'I didn't say I was on my own.'

'Oh, I'm sorry, I didn't mean . . .' Eve Hayward then glanced over to the clock on the marble mantelpiece.

'We should get going, I suppose,' said Clarke, taking that as her cue and finishing off her coffee.

'Relax, I don't think we're going to get much serious work done in the next twenty minutes. Fancy something a bit stronger than coffee?'

Clarke picked up her handbag. 'I think I'll need to go to the cashpoint—'

'Again, relax, we can put it on my tab. This is where I'm staying for the next week.'

Sue Clarke looked around the impossibly posh hotel, with its chandeliered lounge bar decorated like a Georgian drawing room. 'You sure?'

'Expenses, taxpayers' money well spent.'

115

Saturday (6)

They'd arranged to meet at midnight. It was his idea to meet here. The damned fool had wanted to meet in a pub. There was no way that was going to happen – he didn't even want to meet in the car park of a pub, much less the public bar, as the little man was an arch criminal, a thief, a burglar of repute and, to his credit, great skill. And that's why he used him, his skill as a burglar. But the little man's reputation went before him, and with a record as long as his arm, he was the last person he wanted to be seen with. But then again, it wouldn't have done much for the other bloke to be seen with *him*, either.

'Fancy bumping into you here,' joked the grinning little thief, Stevie Wooder, on approaching him. 'You got my money?'

'Very funny. You've been paid very handsomely already and failed to come up with the goods. Why should I pay you more now?'

116

The swaggering thief reached into the inside pocket of his overcoat and pulled out the little black book, the little black book that had for a short while been in the possession of Jack Frost. 'Is this perhaps of any interest to you? It should be, it's got your name in it.'

'Where did you find it?'

'I didn't find it, mate, I took it, I stole it. I risked my liberty to get it.'

He reached over to take the book, but the little thief whipped it away and put it back in his pocket. He eyed Wooder, looking down at him with barely disguised contempt, like he was something that could slither off into the undergrowth at any moment. But it was that slipperiness that made him such a good thief. Little Stevie Wooder barely scraped five foot three, was whip thin and had the physique of an eel, which all made him perfect for his profession.

'I was at the races. And who do I see there, but none other than Inspector Jack Frost. He's up at the bar talking to Jimmy Drake. And what do we know about Jimmy Drake? He's a good man, honest as the day's long, keeps his head down and gets on with his work. I'm a betting man, and I'd bet pound notes for pennies that he's not involved in anything that George and Melody are up to. But when Jack Frost bought him a drink, sat him down and started questioning him, he looked like he had plenty to say.'

'What did he say?'

'I'm not a lip-reader, mate . . .'

He didn't like Stevie Wooder calling him 'mate', and

117

that was the second time. But then again, it was preferable to him using his actual name. It had a catch-all anonymity to it. So, all things considered, he'd take 'mate'. And anyway, their business relationship would be over soon. Terminated.

'. . . And I don't want Jack Frost to spot me,' continued the thief, 'so I keep my distance. But I did see Frost get this little black book out of his pocket and show it to Jimmy. And from where I was stood, it looked like Jimmy was a mine of information for the copper. He looked like he was telling him things about the book, and Frost was taking note of what he was saying, nodding away like he was glad to hear it.'

'OK, I get the picture. But how did you get it?'

'You've not heard?'

'Heard what?'

'I thought—'

'Never mind what you thought, just tell me.'

He could feel himself tense up just listening to the little thief. He buried his hands deep in the pockets of his expensive mac. He was wearing his driving gloves, finest calfskin leather. He'd purchased them on a weekend trip to Paris. Funny the things you remembered, at the oddest times. But when you were on edge, like he was, it was comforting to remember the little things that gave you pleasure. He'd always appreciated the finer things in life. He liked that his wife went out in designer clothes, that he himself sported a Rolex watch; after all, the opposition did, they spent their money as they pleased, so why shouldn't he? And if you couldn't flash

118

the cash in this day and age, then when could you? But now he was here, bargaining with a lowlife thief like little Stevie Wooder in the shadow of the Southern Housing Estate, its brutal towers looming in the distance, ugly reminders of the human and social blight that scarred the landscape. Of course, his wife didn't know about any of this. Did Mrs Jekyll know about Mr Hyde? Not until it was too late, and he was determined that wouldn't happen. He'd sort out this mess, finish it once and for all and get back on track. Take back control of his life.

'Well, cut a long story short, Jimmy must have given Frost some racing tips as well, because he starts betting and wins a few quid. Which, incidentally, I do too, because I know Jimmy Drake knows how to sniff out a winner, so I just bet on the horses Frost does. Which is easy, because by now, Frost has had a few beers and he's got the gambling fever on him, so I can get close enough to hear what he's betting on . . .'

He was getting sick of his voice now, the chirpy little cockney thief boasting and mouthing off. How they liked to stand in their pubs, their pool halls, their card clubs and their betting offices and boast about their criminal exploits – no wonder they always got nicked. Couldn't keep their vainglorious braggart mouths shut.

'. . . So I just follow him out of the races. Luckily I'm tooled up, got a jemmy in the poacher's pocket of my lucky Crombie that I always wear to the gee-gees and the dogs. Lovely it is, mixed fibre, blue velvet collar. So I look around, no one about, just me and Frost. Be rude not to, so I hit him over the head with the tool . . .'

119

He watched intently as Wooder laughed. Then he thought about his gloves again. The little thief and his cheap 'mixed fibre'. Crombie wouldn't appreciate their sublime quality. They didn't feel like gloves at all, rather like an extra layer of skin, a gossamer sensation, the finger on the trigger without any bulk or loss of control . . . control . . . control . . .

Little Stevie Wooder stopped laughing the moment he saw the gun. His eyes almost crossed as the barrel of the shooter rested just inches from the bridge of his nose. He looked confused, but just for a second. Then he fell backwards with a hole in his forehead, a single bullet right between the eyes. The assassin, because that's what he was now, bent down to take a look, to check if by some miracle the thief was still alive, and if he was, put another bullet in him. He then went to his car to retrieve the length of tarpaulin in which he would roll the dead man and carry him to the boot. And then he would drive to the spot and make him disappear for good. He knew how to make someone disappear. It's amazing what you pick up over the years, he thought.

Sunday (1)

When Frost's eyes eventually ratcheted open and the blur of unconsciousness gradually dissipated, his vision was filled with the concerned, and then smiling, visage of DS John Waters.

'Man, we thought you were never going to wake up. How you feeling?'

'How do I look?'

'You look terrible.'

'That's how I'm feeling.'

Frost glanced around at the unfamiliar surroundings. 'I'm in hospital, right?'

'Yeah. VIP suite. Managed to swing a private room for you.'

'I'm looking for a new place and this could do nicely. Food's probably not too good, but the bed baths from the nurses will be welcome.'

'You know what happened, right?'

121

'Yeah . . .' A thought struck him. 'Where's my clothes, John?'

'They're hanging up, but your wallet and keys are in the bedside table.'

Frost lifted himself up in bed, then paused and winced as he suffered the full extent of the damage with each move he made. His ribs hurt, his left eye felt hugely swollen, and the back of his head throbbed hot. He did a quick recce with his tongue around his mouth searching for gaps left by knocked-out teeth, but he felt none and was grateful they were all still in situ. All he noticed was the tang of blood and broken flesh from a cut lip.

Waters said, 'They gave you a good working-over, but not the worst. You've got some stitches at the back of your head, bruised ribs, but not broken. And a real beauty of a shiner, and that's about it.'

'Thank you, Dr Feelgood, that's enough to be getting on with.'

Frost reached over to the side table and opened the drawer. Inside were his Casio watch, some loose change and his wallet – empty. The day's winnings were gone, no real surprise there. But most importantly, George Price's little black book wasn't there either.

'The doctor said you were muttering something about winning big at the races. How much was in the wallet?'

'About four hundred quid.'

John Waters whistled, impressed, and then shook his head like the loss of the cash was more painful than getting coshed over the bonce.

'Pass me my jacket.'

Waters responded to the urgency in Frost's voice and collected his brown leather jacket off the hanger and handed it to him. Frost checked the inside pocket first, then the side pockets.

'The book too. The black book's gone!'

'Did you have a lot to drink?'

'A few.'

'How many?'

'I don't know.'

'Three, four . . . ?'

'Three, maybe five, and a chaser or two . . .' Frost stopped thinking about the missing black book and staring into the empty drawer and turned his attention to Waters, who was sat with his arms folded, looking every inch the inquisitive and unconvinced copper. 'Are you *questioning* me?'

The DS shifted in his seat before answering. 'Yeah, I suppose I am. You were the victim of a crime, Jack. You were mugged. I checked – a couple of years ago Radleigh races had a spate of drunks being rolled in the car park. It's easy pickings, they've got a wad of cash on them, their guard is down, and they're followed out of the bar and then coshed over the canister and relieved of their winnings. Easy money for the muggers.'

'I wasn't drunk, I was *working*. Very productive, should go to the races more often, most of the villains in Denton are there. Bumped into Frank Trafford.'

Waters looked blank, as he wasn't working the case now, and the name meant nothing to him.

'Long story, but he's got a moustache, a vicious temper and a weak alibi.'

Waters nodded along, then let out another long plangent whistle for the plight of Frost's formerly cash-packed wallet. 'Wow, man, four hundred quid, that's a lot of bread to win . . . and then lose.'

'And the book, the little black book, Jimmy Drake reckoned whoever took a potshot at George Price might very well be in that book. Gambling debts. Makes you think, eh?'

'It makes me think that you might have lost a valuable piece of evidence that doesn't belong to you. If, or when, George Price wakes up, he's going to want his book back. And if Mullett finds out—'

'Cheers, John! Are you trying to bloody cheer me up or what?'

'Just saying.'

'Sod Mullett, Hornrim Harry's the least of my worries.' Frost took a moment to think about his situation. Then he let out a plaintive groan and went to shake his head, but it hurt too much. 'Where's my Hamlet cigar now, when I need it?'

'Uh?'

'Nothing. Did his nibs send you down here?'

'No, I was already in here last night. I saw them bring you in so I stayed.'

'You've been here all night?'

'Slept in this very chair.'

'Your new missus won't believe that.'

'You can back me up.'

'I know I can – and that's why Kim won't believe a word, she's a copper too!' Joking aside, Frost gave Waters an appreciative smile, as the denim-clad DS rubbed the sleep out of his eyes and indulged in some noisy yawns. As grateful to his friend as Frost was, Waters' actions also sent a wave of despondency through him as he pondered his present predicament, and it dawned on him just how alone he was. As much as he liked the affable DS, he'd have much preferred to have woken up and seen someone who wasn't a copper, and who definitely wasn't a bloke, with a concerned expression on her face as she lovingly unwrapped him a strawberry soft centre from the big tin of Quality Street she'd brought him. In that split second, Frost realized it was time to get back out there again. Make a concerted effort to bag himself another Mrs Frost, or at least get himself a few dates. If only to have someone to watch over him when he got banged on the head, which was an occupational hazard.

'Who were you here for, Bomber Harris?'

'No, Tommy Wilkins,' said Waters. 'I caught up with him on the SHE.'

'Did he confess to shooting Bomber?'

Waters laid out the story to Frost, and the whole weird Pax Romana that seemed to be taking place between the two feuding factions. And also the fact that they had both discharged themselves from hospital that morning, together, and then both had been picked up in a black BMW 733i. Waters said that as well as absolving each other of their crimes, they did it all with the minimum of fuss or verbals. They were so uncharacteristically cool and well-behaved about the whole thing that Waters suspected that they'd undergone a frontal lobotomy whilst in hospital.

'Nah, you have to have a brain in the first place to have one of them,' said Frost. He then threw back the sheets, sat upright and swung his legs round.

'Where you going?'

'First off, I'm going to check on George Price. Then I'm getting a uniform posted outside his room, twenty-four/seven.'

'Mullett won't like that. And he wasn't best pleased you didn't make the briefing yesterday morning.'

'Briefing? Oh yeah, I do remember a memo about it, and I also remember filing it under a-sodding-waste-of-my-time,' said Frost as he ran his fingertips over his bruised ribs like he was gently strumming a guitar. Despite expert medical opinion, they felt broken to him. Whoever had robbed him had taken the opportunity to give him a good kicking too. Which led Frost to believe that he might have previously encountered the perpetrator in a professional capacity.

'It was a three-line whip, all CID were expected to attend,' said Waters. 'It was quite a presentation.'

'I was busy at the races, doing my job.'

'That's the problem – Mullett thinks it's a waste of time. Case closed, Terry Langdon did it. Uniform can take over from here.'

'Well, experience has taught me that doing the exact opposite of what our great leader thinks is bound to get results.'

126

'Tell you what, though.' A lubricious smile spread across Waters' face. 'That DI Eve Hayward from the counterfeit unit, she's quite a looker.'

Frost, with fresh determination, said, 'Right, let's get out of here,' and pointed in the direction of his clothes. 'Pass us those.'

Waters turned round and saw the Y-fronts that may or may not have been white at one time or another draped over the arm of a chair, and grimaced. 'Not without surgical gloves. You can get them yourself.'

Stanley Mullett was at home, in the garden, powering the electric mower across the lawn with athleticism and precision. He was aiming for the perfect finish, the manicured criss-cross of the hallowed Wembley turf. Not that he was a fan of football, as it seemed to be the preserve of hooligans and took up far too much of his men's time and resources with policing the wretched games, but the work of the groundsmen had always impressed him.

He was feeling so much better than yesterday, the hangover now a distant memory. Today there would be some sherry before dinner, and maybe a pint at their favourite country pub on the usual Sunday drive with his wife, Grace, but nothing like the session he had endured with his fellow superintendents.

And yet, the image of Eve Hayward in her crisp white shirt and black pencil skirt, with her shiny auburn bob and striking features, had not left him. And somehow, a whole Sunday at home with Mrs Mullett seemed like a

127

life sentence. He wanted to be at Eagle Lane; he knew that DI Hayward would be going about her duties today, visiting markets, boot fairs and local suppliers in her search for counterfeit goods.

As buttoned up as he was about his emotions, he recognized the impropriety of his thoughts about Eve. And maybe that's why he was doing such a thorough and vigorous job mowing the lawn. He was really putting his back into it, trying to exhaust himself, to take his mind off her, expunge all thoughts of her.

'Darling?'

He didn't hear his wife, calling to him from the French windows. His mind was on other things, going through the throes of a romantic tryst with Eve Hayward. There she was standing before him, just as she had been at the briefing, but now it was just the two of them. Everything that had been so damned enticing about her yesterday was even more so now: the lips were redder, the fitted shirt was tighter, the skirt was shorter, the heels were higher, the pointer she had in her hand now resembled a rider's crop, and she was—

'What on earth is wrong with you?'

He felt the sudden jab on his arm. He turned and saw Grace, his sour-faced wife, with an especially curdled expression on her now. His disappointment was palpable.

'Sorry,' he uttered, 'I was . . .'

'You were *what*?' She was slowly looking him up and down with a scowl of disgust. 'Just as well it's the rear lawn, I suppose, where the neighbours can't see you! It's the phone, for you,' she barked before turning her back on him and stalking up to the house.

Mrs Mullett hadn't had to read his mind to know what he was thinking out there in the back garden – his train of lust-filled thought was very pronouncedly made flesh – and she was most definitely going to give him the cold shoulder for the rest of the day.

Two hours later, and Stanley Mullett was at the Denton and Rimmington Golf Club, teeing off for a quick seven holes with Peter Kelsey. Mullett was delighted at the call from Rimmington's superintendent. It had facilitated his escape from Grace, and it should break him out of his immoral thoughts of Eve Hayward; it was Sunday, after all. Though even out here on the greens, every now and again images of the delectable DI were popping up when he least expected or needed them – he was pretty sure he'd sliced the ball on his last shot because of her.

And there was the added bonus that he enjoyed Kelsey's company. He was younger than Mullett, and full of ambition. Which would normally be grounds for the Denton super to take an instant dislike to the man. But a pleasing rapport had prevailed between the two, especially recently, when the older officer had rather taken on a mentoring role to the young superintendent. And Mullett was happy to help. If he could give Kelsey one piece of advice, it would be about his dress sense, especially on the greens. Mullett, who largely based his golf on Gary Player, with his steady determination and unfussy game, heartily approved of the Black Knight's predilection for wearing sober black on the course, and was himself never seen in anything racier than dark blue. He considered Peter Kelsey to be a bit flash. The younger superintendent was again wearing the most lurid of golfing attire: as on Friday afternoon, he was a riot of colour and argyle patterns. Mullett thought he would take this opportunity to steer him in the right sartorial direction, as it was not the sort of thing he wanted to encourage at the golf club; probably around the fifth hole would be the time to broach the subject.

'Good shot, Stanley. You've avoided the rough.'

It *was* a good shot, Mullett thought, one of his better ones, but still plenty of room for improvement. 'Too close to the trees for my liking.'

'Have you ever played the links up in Scotland? I still have a place back home, near Fort William. It's little more than a croft, but it's comfortable enough and there's always a few wee drams to keep the cold out. The wife doesn't like it much, too far away from the shops.'

'I can imagine. I hope I'm not speaking out of turn, Peter, but you certainly have a very attractive wife. You're a lucky man. The few times I've seen her, she's looked like she's stepped off the set of *Dynasty*. Must cost you a fortune.'

'I am lucky. And it's an expense I'm happy to live with – if Patricia's happy, I'm happy.'

'Yes, I'm glad to say I'm not encumbered with such an expense . . .' said Mullett, starting off cheerily, then trailing off gloomily as the dowdy Mrs Mullett came to mind.

'But do give it some thought. If we could get a week off work, just the two of us, we could go up there and play the links. St Andrews, best course in the world. I think you would love it.'

'Very generous of you, yes, I think I could wangle that. You Scotsmen certainly know your golf, I'll give you that!'

With that, Peter Kelsey hit his ball straight down the middle. The Scotsman smiled wryly, uttered something about getting lucky on that one, and they strode off to join the queue. The course was unsurprisingly busy, which was just how Mullett liked it. As the club chairman, he enjoyed soaking up the adulation and respect that came with the role, in the form of deferential nods and greetings from the great and the good of the area.

'So, how's the shooting of the bookmaker going, Stanley? What's the chap's name again . . . ?'

'Price, George Price.'

'Of course, it's not a murder case yet, is it?'

'No, he's still in a coma. I believe he is to have a second operation soon. But even if he pulls through, with a bullet in the brain, who knows the damage it will have done? He may never be able to function properly again.'

Mullett and Kelsey waved at two men heading in the opposite direction in a golf buggy – Sir Robert Elmore, Denton and Rimmington MP, and local Tory councillor Edward Havilland.

The Denton super said, 'They say a game of golf is a good walk spoilt, and I can't say I approve of buggies. Don't get that on the links, I bet.'

Kelsey smiled. 'It's not as if Councillor Havilland couldn't do with a good walk, either.'

'Too true, Peter. I'm surprised he can fit into a buggy.'

Kelsey laughed and complimented Mullett on his wicked sense of humour before asking, 'Have you narrowed down the field?'

'How do you mean?'

'Suspects for the Price shooting?'

'Pretty much case closed. Looked like a robbery gone wrong at first, but now it looks like a fellow bookmaker did it. Long-standing feud, apparently. He was also, allegedly, having an affair with Price's wife.'

'Surely it should have been the other way around then, and Price should have shot Langdon?'

'Langdon?'

'You said the other bookmaker?'

'So I did. Yes, Langdon. Well, we all know how ridiculously stupid and irrational things can get when love enters the frame. Logic goes straight out of the window.'

'Sounds pretty cut and dried to me. And you have witnesses, I believe?'

'That's right. Gave a good description of Langdon, and his car, leaving the scene at speed. A minute earlier, and they'd probably have been in danger of getting shot themselves.'

'You consider him that dangerous?'

'Like I said, crimes of passion, unpredictable; when a

132

man kills for money there's less emotion involved. We're warning the public not to approach him. But it's the type of clear-up I like, solve the crime within forty-eight hours. Even if we don't yet have him in custody, it's still job done.'

'It does sound like it. Sounds indeed like job done, and makes you wonder why your man Frost thinks otherwise.'

'Frost?'

'You've not heard? About Jack Frost spending most of the day at the Radleigh races yesterday?'

No, no one had told him. But that didn't come as too much of a surprise; he'd long suspected that others in CID, and lower in the ranks, habitually covered for Frost. Frost could be as bad-tempered and cutting as the worst of them. He could work his team into the ground to get results, and hardly set a good example as far as discipline and propriety were concerned – and yet he had their respect, and they had his back. It was unfathomable and it rankled.

And it rankled even more when hearing it from a fellow superintendent from another area; it made him look inefficient and not in full mastery of his brief. He knew Kelsey was trying to help, but still Mullett's mood blackened. He was pretty sure he'd raise Kelsey's dress sense at the very next hole.

Sunday (2) ───────────────

'This is a hell of a place they've got here. George Price has done very well for himself,' whispered DS Waters.

'Men like him and Harry Baskin know where the money is: sex and gambling. Talking of which, she's not bad either,' muttered Frost, in the same hushed tones as Waters, as he gestured towards the cluster of framed 'glamour' pictures of Melody Price. They were perched on the top shelf of the smoked-glass and steel entertainment centre that also housed the top-of-the-range Bang & Olufsen stereo equipment.

The two detectives sat on the cream sofa, waiting for Melody to arrive with a pot of fresh coffee. Both men were grateful for it; it had been a long night for Waters, and Frost was still groggy.

The first thing the DI had done once he'd discharged himself was to call Sue Clarke. Her mother, with the customary cold edge that ran through her voice

134

whenever she spoke to him, said that Sue wasn't at home as she had stayed the night at the Prince Albert Hotel. She then hung up briskly before he could ask any more. Frost, rather intrigued, called the Prince Albert, and eventually got hold of Clarke, who briefed him on the details of her visit the previous day to Michael Price.

Frost then asked her what on earth she was doing at the posh hotel. The DC sighed, then made some noises that sounded like giggling, but equally they could have just been her clearing her throat. She said it had been a long night and then rang off almost as fast as her mother. She sounded hung-over. Frost recognized a hung-over female voice when he heard one: invariably husky and sexy. But what the blazes was she doing there? And who was she with, more to the point?

With Frost unable to drive due to doctor's orders, and Clarke seemingly unavailable to 'chauffeur' him about, Frost had seconded DS Waters for the duty.

'Wow, Jack, you certainly do look like you've been in the wars, you poor thing,' said Melody Price, in a voice that billed and cooed like she was addressing a three-year-old. She was carrying a tray with three bone-china cups and saucers, a silver milk jug and sugar bowl, and a big cafetière full of pitch-black coffee.

Waters sprang to his feet and in three energetic bounds was at her side, relieving her of the tray and putting it on the coffee table.

'Oh, thank you, John – you don't mind me calling you John?'

'Not at all, Melody, not at all,' said Waters with an eager-to-please smile plastered across his face.

Frost sat there, looking just as Melody had described, with his black eye and a big bandage wrapped around his head. No longer the recipient of Melody's attention, Frost watched on as she worked her magic on Waters. He couldn't help but smile. Sue Clarke, with her female intuition and competitiveness, had sussed her out right from the start. There was no sisterhood with Melody Price. She knew where her power lay; like with Maggie Thatcher and her all-male Cabinet, wrapped around her perfectly manicured little finger.

Once all the coffees were poured, Melody asked, 'So, Jack, tell me, how was George this morning? I'm seeing him after the races tonight.' Without waiting for an answer, she turned to Waters. 'Being in a coma, John, I know he doesn't see me, but I sense he senses my presence, my physical presence. My aura, if you will. He breathes easier when I'm there.' She then turned her gaze back to Frost, and winced at the sight of him. 'You're always better just handing over your money, instead of putting up a fight . . . and losing.'

'I'm a policeman, it's sort of my job to put up a fight.' Frost ran a thumbnail across his throbbing cheekbone that prickled with heat. 'Although in fairness, I don't actually remember putting up much of a fight. I think they just cracked me over the back of the head and I was out like a light. But some good did come out of it. It opened up other lines of inquiry into George's shooting.'

'Robbery, you mean? Punters as well as bookies

136

getting done over? I thought you were looking for Terry Langdon?'

'Oh, we are. We need to question him so we can formally eliminate him from our inquiries.'

'But I thought you said Terry was . . .'

'Innocent until proven otherwise, I think is what we say.'

'Well, nice as it is to see you, I'm not sure how I can help. I've told you all I can.'

'That's interesting. But we believe your relationship with Terry Langdon went a bit further than just an infatuation on his part.'

'What are you insinuating?'

'I'm saying, quite openly, that you and Terry Langdon consummated the relationship, had an affair.'

Frost watched as she palpably consumed this information with a noisy swallow of her coffee. She straightened up in her chair, bristling, eyes full of hot indignation, mouth snarling like it could spit venom. 'How dare you! I'm a happily married woman, my beloved husband is in hospital, *I* am the injured party here—'

'We have it on good authority.'

'Who from?'

Frost matched her high-octane outrage with a blank-eyed indifference. 'When we find Langdon, and we will, no doubt he'll tell us himself all about it. Bound to. So why don't you give us your side of the story first.'

Melody dropped her act as quickly as she'd taken it up. 'It was a drunken fumble, nothing more. A mistake on my part. George was away for a few days. Terry had

137

been pestering me. I went out with some friends, to Blazes nightclub in Rimmington, and he turned up. Now I think about it, I think he must have been following me. I'd had too much to drink, he kept saying he worshipped me, and one thing led to another.'

'Did George know about it?'

'He suspected it.'

'What was his reaction?'

'Not best pleased. But I denied it, and kept on denying it.'

'Do you think Terry might have told George?'

'I told Terry that if he did, I'd never forgive him. And anyway, it was his word against mine. I had nothing to worry about, or to hide. I'm an open book, as they say.'

'We all have our little secrets, Melody.'

Mrs Price gestured towards the top shelf of the glass-and-steel unit. Both Waters and Frost gladly took the opportunity to have yet another look at her in various stages of undress, posed artfully, and not so artfully, against a studio backdrop, or draped across a Harley-Davidson.

She proceeded to explain herself: 'I've been a glamour model. Done some Page Threes back in the day. If Terry said to George, I know your wife has three moles on her bum, he'd just look like he knew about as much as the average *Sun* reader, because there's very little of me that hasn't been on public display at one time or another.'

DS Waters couldn't help but smirk. And Frost probably would have joined him, but his swollen lip was

138

prohibiting anything remotely expressive; every time he spoke he felt like a ventriloquist without his dummy.

Melody Price placed her cup and saucer on the coffee table, and drew the meeting to a close by rising to her feet and saying, 'Now, gentlemen, you'll have to excuse me. I have a lot of things to do today, including visiting my husband in the hospital again this afternoon.'

On that cue, Waters and Frost also stood up. Frost then suddenly barked out, 'Socks and Winston!'

Mrs Price, who had been heading towards the lounge door, came to an abrupt standstill, took a moment, and then spun round in a perfectly executed catwalk turn. 'Sex . . . and winking?'

'Socks and Winston,' Frost repeated slowly.

Her usually lineless forehead crinkled in a frown of confusion at this.

The DI put her out of her misery: 'Those were the only two full names in a black notebook that we found on George. There were also lists of initials in there with numbers beside them. Bets, we assume. But just two names, Socks and Winston, and they were in capitals and underlined. They had the biggest numbers beside them. Jimmy told us—'

'Jimmy, Jimmy Drake?'

'Yes, Jimmy Drake, your clerk, I spoke to him at the races yesterday after I spoke to you.'

'Oh yes, Jimmy said he'd given you some tips.' Melody smiled and then pursed her lips and made a little tutting sound. 'You were right, Jack, betting's not your

139

game. Even when you do win you manage to lose it in the car park.'

Cut lip permitting, Frost attempted to return the smile. 'He told us about George's betting service for special customers.'

'I'm sorry, I can't help you, I don't know anything about this. I don't know about a black notebook. Even so, why is it important?'

'Because I don't think whoever coshed me in the car park was after my money, they were after the book. And I think the same person who shot George was after it, too.'

'They didn't get it then. How about now?'

'They did this time. With George dead the book would become irrelevant – all bets would be off, as they say. And maybe that was their intention all along, to kill him.'

'But they failed. Thank God.'

'But with him in a coma, and the possibility of him yet making a recovery, the book still holds a lethal power. Don't you think?' Frost asked pointedly.

Melody stalked over to the living-room door, swung it open and announced in glacial tones, 'I think next time you need to speak to me, it will have to be with my lawyer present.' She then bellowed out into the hallway, 'Keith!'

Frost was about to ask who 'Keith' was, when he appeared in the doorway. Frost recognized him immediately. He was one of Harry Baskin's bouncers from the Coconut Grove. He wasn't one of Harry's biggest

140

bouncers, but togged up in a black Puma tracksuit and white boxing boots, he looked like a capable and fast middleweight.

'Keith will see you out.'

'I hope he's not going to try and lift us up by the collar and sling us out like he does at the strip club.'

Keith swivelled his heavily muscled neck and rolled his bulked-out shoulders like he was limbering up for round one.

'Harry is a great friend of George's, as you know, and whilst Terry Langdon remains at large, and you're here harassing me when you should be out looking for him, Harry thought I might need a man about the house.' She must have seen something akin to amusement in the two detectives' eyes, as she emphasized angrily, '*Protection* – for my protection!'

'Come on, don't be a wuss, it's brilliant,' said Gavin Ross to his best mate, Dean Bartlett. Dean was unsure, but Gavin was an old hand at it by now, he'd done it three or four times. It was the latest thing; all the lads on the estate were trying it. The first time he did it, he didn't feel so brilliant. In fact, he puked all over his new Fred Perry shirt. The second time was OK, the last couple of times were just as promised. And it definitely felt better than sniffing glue or smoking hash. Not that he did those things much, but this was different. It opened up a whole new world – Gavin felt enveloped in this warm glow of ease and comfort where everything just felt good.

When Gavin asked Tommy Wilkins if he'd get

addicted to it, Tommy and his mates laughed in his face. They said he'd watched too many films. Only idiots got addicted to it. They told him to think about it: if it was so bad why would so many people be doing it, why would the biggest rock and roll stars in the world do it? Tommy said that all the bad stuff you heard and read about it was government propaganda, what the police wanted you to think, because they didn't want people having a good time. Plus the fact they weren't making money from it, and anything they couldn't make money from they didn't want people to do. Gavin couldn't argue with that, it all made perfect sense. And his experiences with his teachers and occasional run-ins with the police would pretty much back up what Tommy said. There was fuck all to do on the Southern Housing Estate, so why not?

Gavin took the tin foil and folded it over to form a gully to sprinkle the brown powder in. He'd upped the dose this time. After all, the last two had been brilliant, but even now, whilst hardly a seasoned user, and certainly not hooked on the stuff – he was sure of that – he suspected the roller-coaster ride could be better with more stuff. And it was so cheap, cheaper than the hash they'd been smoking, so why not take advantage?

Dean did as he was instructed and took out the ink tube of the clear plastic biro. Gavin then took the silver foil and lit up the underside with his Bic lighter, and sucked up the heavy smoke through the empty biro like a milkshake through a straw. This little ritual had a name, and the name sounded exciting to Gavin. It sounded dangerous to Dean. And maybe this was the difference between the two sixteen-year-old lads. They'd grown up together on the SHE, had known each other as long as they could remember. But Gavin had always led the way. Gavin had been the first to dive off the high board at the local swimming baths; the first to get vertical on the ramp they'd built when the skateboarding craze hit; the first to do what he did with Sally Webber; the first to drink, smoke, sniff all sorts: and now the first to Chase the Dragon. That was what they called it, and it sounded exciting or dangerous, depending on whether you were Gavin or Dean. But Dean knew that he'd follow his mate. He always had.

Sunday (3) ⸻

'Jesus wept!' cried out PC David Simms, after taking his first tentative sip of scalding coffee from the machine in the corridor of Denton General. The burning liquid had blistered his top lip and turned his mouth nuclear, or that's how it felt. He thought he must look like one of the Ready Brek kids, with a disturbing orange glow around him.

'Are you OK?'

Simms spun round to see a pretty nurse with big blue eyes and a little upturned nose. He'd seen her before, the last time Frost had put him on duty to watch over George Price. She'd made hanging around the place bearable, with him hoping she would stop on her way past so he could engage her in conversation. But she never did, she was probably too busy.

He felt a hot wave of embarrassment come over him, almost as hot as the coffee – she must have seen him puffing away and furiously fanning his mouth with his hand whilst doing a little jig on the spot. Simms tried to recover some poise before saying, 'Your coffee machine is a major health hazard.'

'I know. I keep telling the management they should put it by the Burns unit.'

Simms laughed, she laughed. The PC introduced himself and said he was on duty, watching over George Price, the shooting victim on C-Ward.

'I'm sure I can make you a cuppa next time I'm passing.'

He was about to thank her and was trying to muster the courage to ask her out for a drink after work when she queried, 'Are you expecting trouble?'

'In this job you always expect trouble, and if there is any I'm ready!' Even he cringed at this. What the hell was he thinking? *I'm ready?* I'm a bloody Ready Brek kid! The nurse just gave a polite smile, the standard one she probably gave to all babbling and incoherent patients just before they went under the anaesthetic, he reckoned.

'Well, it's nice to know we're in safe hands,' she said, turning her back on him and sashaying down the gleaming tiled hallway.

Simms concluded that he was already probably hopelessly in love with her. He made his way to C-Ward, pondering how he could extricate himself from the status of complete dickhead. He was determined to ask her out by the end of the day, but he now had his work cut out to make that happen. Maybe some flowers, chocolates?

145

What took his mind off the task at hand was the rapidly approaching man. He was around six foot six in height, and probably that again in width. He had a bald head that was as smooth and shiny as the just-polished tiles of the corridor. The man was wearing a sheepskin coat that looked way too small for his seam-popping frame. His big fists were bunched up and he was making his way directly to George Price's private room.

'Just a minute, sir. Where are you going?'

The big bald bruiser spun round to face his challenger, faster than a man of that bulk has any right to do, thought Simms. The Neanderthal then slipped his right hand into his coat – which was bulging alarmingly with something.

The young PC could swear he saw a glint of metal under the bruiser's coat and repeated with more urgency this time, 'Where are you going?'

'To sort George out,' came the gruff reply.

'*Excuse me?*'

Simms turned in the direction of the woman's voice he'd instantly recognized: it was the nurse, the nurse he was pretty sure he was in love with. Maybe this was his chance to redeem himself in her eyes by being a real-life hero. He quickly swung back towards the bruiser, who was now just feet away from George Price's door. The PC ran at him and rugby-tackled him, which sent them both crashing through the door. Simms heard a gasp and a faint 'Oh no!' from the nurse behind him, and then a very loud 'Oh yeah!' from the huge assassin he was now in fact straddling. With his left arm he

146

pressed down on the bruiser's neck, an area that seemed pretty indistinguishable from his head and shoulders, while reaching down with his right hand to retrieve his truncheon. But before he could, he felt himself rise up involuntarily. It was like he'd been lying on top of a large pachyderm that had just stirred and was about to shake him off like a pesky oxpecker. Simms soon realized that he wasn't actually pinioning anyone, and the big man proved it with a swinging arm that sent him crashing into the wall.

Simms groaned, but not for long, as he was prevented from doing even this by the thick fingers tightening around his throat. A moment later his whole body was lifted off the floor and he was dangling in the air, whilst his feet desperately sought terra firma like those of a man at the scaffold. The young PC was now face to face with his would-be killer, and as his eyes widened and bulged in terror, the killer's own narrowed to black soulless slits.

'Wherever he is, he can't have got very far.'

DC Clarke turned slowly; the white-wine hangover she was suffering from made taking things nice and slow a necessity today. Arthur Hanlon was holding up a passport. Sue, accompanied by Hanlon, had entered the home of Terry Langdon at ten thirty that morning, armed with a search warrant that they'd had to present to Peter Billings, his landlord. Since last year's fiasco, when Frost had been reprimanded for entering a property without a search warrant (even though everyone agreed it had been justified), almost jeopardizing a case,

147

all procedures had to be followed to the letter and all evidence gathered had to be properly documented. Frost blamed the ruthless efficiency of the newfangled Eagle Lane computer system. But the DI was blaming everything on the new computers these days – to him, 1984 really did feel like *1984*.

Still, Clarke could have done without Arthur Hanlon this morning. He'd picked her up at the Prince Albert Hotel where she'd crashed last night, after sharing a bottle too many with her new best friend, Eve Hayward. Hanlon seemed intrigued by the scenario. He, like every male who had attended her presentation on the evils of counterfeit goods, had fallen for the DI from West End Central. As he pumped her for information, Clarke, instead of providing a simple explanation, first toyed with him and then tetchily told him to mind his own business; it would now be left to Hanlon's fevered imagination.

As they went through the sparse little bungalow, bagging up anything they thought could be of interest, something familiar caught Sue Clarke's eye. On the kitchen table, under a pile of the *Sporting Life* and *Racing News*, was a glossy brochure for some new developments on the edge of town. The cover showed a triptych of modern apartment blocks that went by the unlikely names of Eden Gardens, Utopia Tower and Paradise Lodge. Wasn't that where Frost was considering buying a place? Sue had to smile: if things had turned out differently, Frost and Terry Langdon could have been neighbours.

It was clear to Clarke that Langdon had grabbed

whatever he could and made his escape as quickly as possible without much forethought or planning. The bungalow was littered with incriminating evidence. There were two gun publications under the bed, and Sue had searched enough bachelor pads in her time to know that literature kept under the bed was usually of the porn variety. But for the obsessed Terry Langdon, it was publications on how to use handguns properly that were his reading of choice at night, not fantasizing about centrefolds and grappling with unfortunately placed staples. He'd been learning all about pulling the trigger and ending George Price's life so he could be with his own real-life pin-up – Melody, presumably.

As Clarke sat on the corner of the single bed, flicking through the pages, she saw there was one revolver in particular that had been circled in both magazines. It was the Webley Mk IV .38/200 Service Revolver. The article about the popular handgun told her that the Webley had been widely in service during the last war and could be picked up second-hand very easily. Decommissioned guns could readily be put back into use with just a few tweaks and were changing hands for as little as sixty pounds.

'*I've found something!*' came a muffled cry from outside.

Clarke put down the magazines and went out to Arthur Hanlon, who was searching the grounds. Past the overgrown garden and further out towards the wooded area that abutted the fields, Hanlon was standing by a pile of logs on top of which perched a collection of empty bottles. There were beer bottles, wine bottles, vodka bottles, and lots more in reserve on the ground. Clarke could hear broken glass crunching underfoot as she made her way over. It was clear that someone had been doing target practice out here. She remembered that Peter Billings had said that Langdon was a lousy shot. At the time she'd wondered if Billings had been lying to protect his friend, but she was now certain he hadn't – any proficient marksman wouldn't have had to put in this much practice, surely. And maybe George Price would be dead by now if he'd had more of it.

'I can't see any shells, he must have collected them up.'

'I don't know why he'd bother. The bottles are still here, so it's obvious what he's been doing, and I found two well-thumbed gun magazines under his bed. All the same, it would have been useful to find one – to see if they match up with the one fired at Price.'

Clarke looked around, not really knowing what else she expected to see. But just beyond this small clearing where the trees had been felled for logs, the woodland was dense. She traced the supposed direction of Terry Langdon's aim and some way off found what she was looking for – the white flesh wound of split bark where a stray bullet had hit a tree.

She pointed at it. 'See over there?'

Hanlon followed her directions and eventually clocked it. 'You've got eagle eyes.'

'You got a penknife or something to dig it out with?'

Hanlon pulled out a thick red Huntsman Swiss Army Knife with everything apart from the kitchen sink attached to it. He offered it to Clarke.

150

She pointedly ignored it and headed back to the bungalow. 'What did your last slave die of, Arthur? The exercise will do you good.'

'I think she's hot.'

'What?'

'You asked me what I thought and I'm telling you,' said DS John Waters.

The two detectives were in Waters' Nissan Maxima, making their way along the scenic B-roads around Denton with Bob Marley's *Exodus* playing on the cassette player. Waters usually played his music loud, with the bass turned up as far as it could go so you could see the windows wobble. But bearing in mind the fragility of his passenger, he kept the volume nice and low, which suited the sedate pace they were travelling at. Mainly because they hadn't actually decided where they were going.

'To be honest, DS Waters, married man of barely six months, I don't need your opinion on the delights of Mrs George Price, as they're on display for the whole world to see. I'm talking about the book, the little black book.'

'Oh, the book. You really think that's why you were mugged?'

'I do. Now, do you think Melody knew about the black book? When I said the names, Socks and Winston, she reacted to it.'

'I couldn't see her face – she had her back to us. Anyway, you shouted it out so loud she was bound to react.' Waters smirked. 'She thought you said *sex*, but I have a feeling that's never far from her mind. That aside, I'm thinking there's very little George Price does without her knowing about it. She wears the trousers in that house.'

'What gives you that impression? He's a formidable bloke, George Price. Not to be messed with, right out of the Harry Baskin charm school.'

'You can just tell. For example, the way the house is decorated, very feminine, and would you have pictures of your wife with her kit off in the living room for all to drool over?'

'I would if she looked like that!'

'No, man, that's her idea, and she gets what she wants. She's the younger woman, she's got the whip hand in that relationship.'

Frost pulled out his crumpled box of Rothmans from his jacket, and managed to find one that was only badly bent out of shape but not completely broken. He cracked open the window, sparked up the coffin nail and enjoyed a long thoughtful drag. He thought about his late wife, Mary. He really couldn't remember any more – had he worn the trousers at home or had she? She may well have decorated the house the way she wanted it, but that was because it belonged to her parents and, frankly, he trusted her taste and couldn't be bothered how it was done up. Maybe he should have bothered, and invested far more energy in their relationship and spent less time obsessing over work. Their marriage was over with a whimper, not a bang, and long before the cancer took

152

her. She'd been a seriously good-looking woman, and there must have once been a spark between them for her to leave behind her stolidly middle-class family and take up with a policeman from the wrong part of town, but at some point it had all simply fizzled out.

The radio crackling into action broke his melancholic train of thought. The message came over: a man down in Denton General, PC Simms. Frost and Waters exchanged grave looks. Then came gales of static-filled laughter as everyone in the area with access to a radio got the story of what had happened to PC Simms. It involved a nurse, a bedpan and an assailant armed with a box of chocolates.

When Frost and Waters had recovered their composure and absorbed the finer details of the Denton General debacle, they finally decided on a destination. Twenty minutes later they reached it.

'*Denton's pre-eminent nightclub for the discerning gentleman with a taste for exotic glamour and an appreciation for the female form of the highest order.*' That was how the Coconut Grove described itself and its entertainment offerings on the flyers distributed around the pubs and other clubs of Denton. And the place was packed. Because on Sunday afternoons, they always had the strippers in, as opposed to just the scantily dressed hostesses and dancers they had every other afternoon.

And as the detectives made their way through the dimly lit club, the first performer, 'X-rated Sister Sledge', as she was billed on the board at the entrance, had just

153

taken to the stage and had started to peel off her highly modified PVC nun's habit.

'Is nothing sacred?' asked Waters.

'Well, it is Sunday, at least she's made the effort,' said Frost, distracted as he recognized Michael Hudson, the manager of Bennington's Bank, sitting at the front nursing a drink. The DI made a mental note to make sure he said hello to him on his way out. It would make an interesting topic of conversation when they talked through the small print on his impending mortgage application in Hudson's office.

The two men had to go through the kitchen to get to Baskin's lair. The serving of food was all part of the licensing agreement. There weren't too many chefs in the kitchen – it was a given that you didn't *really* come to the Coconut Grove to eat – just a couple of bouncers in monkey suits eating fish and chips out of newspaper and watching *Ski Sunday* on the portable. They glanced lazily around at the two coppers and recognized them immediately.

'All right, Jack?'

'All right, Taff. How's your mum?'

'Oh you know, up and down, now she's got her new Stannah stairlift. What happened to your bonce? Looks nasty.'

'I fell off my Stannah stairlift. You want to tell your mum to be careful. Need a word with Harry.' Frost approached the door marked PRIVATE and knocked three times in quick succession, then entered without waiting for a reply.

154

Baskin was sitting at his desk, fully absorbed in cooking the books. He didn't look up as he invited Frost and Waters to take a seat.

In a moderate and measured voice Frost said, 'Socks and Winston.'

The club-owner stopped running his pencil down a column of figures, and his lips, which usually twitched as he totted up the numbers, stopped twitching. Harry looked up at the two men across from him. He tore off his delicate gold-framed reading spectacles that were perched incongruously on a nose that had been flattened more than once in the boxing rings of Bethnal Green in his youth. His thick brow creased and dipped.

Frost smiled, he knew he was on to something. Nothing much rattled Harry Baskin, and he looked rattled.

'Tell us about them, Harry, we know you know who they are.'

'Well, I know what socks are, they're what you put on your feet before you put your shoes on.'

'I'm not leaving here till I get some answers.'

'You better make yourself comfortable, then, because I haven't got a bleedin' clue what you're talking about.'

'Socks and Winston.'

'Muppets?'

'Easy, Harry,' warned Waters.

'I wasn't being rude, but they've got a frog called Kermit, so just wondering if they added a Socks and Winston to the line-up of characters. Or maybe it's those two old duffers who sit up in the box. You know, the ones who—'

'Hurry up, Harry, we wanna get down the pub.'

'Nothing stopping you, Inspector.'

'You're lying – I can see it in your beady little black eyes.'

Harry Baskin leaned forward across his desk for emphasis and said, 'My missus says my eyes are my best feature, blue as an azure sky, she says. Now, one last time: I haven't got a bloody clue who they are. Never heard of them!'

Frost met his challenging glare and also leaned across the desk from his side until they were practically nose to nose. You could barely fit a cigarette paper between the two men. 'And I'm telling you, Harold, I don't bloody believe you!'

'OK, OK, gentlemen, time out, time out,' said Waters, rising to his feet and raising his hands like a boxing referee to separate the two contenders. Both retreated to their respective corners and sat back in their seats.

Frost appreciated the intervention and knew that his colleague was right. It was pointless raising your voice, getting angry or attempting to intimidate a hardened criminal like Baskin. Threats to press charges for not cooperating with an investigation or obstructing the pursuit of justice simply didn't bother him. Water off a duck's back . . . If Harry Baskin didn't want to talk, he wouldn't. He didn't grass. Baskin wasn't old school – he was the school they knocked down to build the old school.

The DI tried a different tack. 'OK, Harry. But it strikes me as strange that I come in here, black eye, fat lip and a turban, and you don't so much as bat an eyelid.'

'That's the difference between me and you: if you told me a pigeon fell out of the sky and hit you on the head, I'd leave it at that. None of my business.'

'Bloody big pigeon.'

'Like I say, none of my business.'

'Some things, Harry, you don't have to say. When I said, "Socks and Winston", your face was a picture, told its own story.'

'All right, all right. Stop going on. You're giving me earache. I'll tell you what I know. George mentioned them once, but he wouldn't tell me who they really were. That's why he used nicknames for them, so no one found out.'

'Not even his best mate and business partner?'

'Only in certain things. I stay out of the gambling business, and he stays out of show business.'

Frost and Waters laughed derisively at Harry Baskin's description of his establishment.

'Those girls out there show it all every day of the week and twice on Sundays, and they look the business – that's what I call show business!' Baskin protested.

They laughed again, and it managed to dispel some of the tension in the room.

'All George said was that they were a couple of big-wigs that he had on the hook,' continued the club-owner. 'They owed him money, a lot of money. More money than a bookie would normally allow on credit. But it wasn't the money with George, not really.' Baskin shook his head and looked reflective, as if, like Frost and Waters, he couldn't quite believe this.

'Come on, with men like George Price, and you for that matter, it's *always* about the money.'

Baskin flipped open the lid of a wooden box to reveal a row of Cuban cigars as big as coppers' truncheons. He clipped the end of one with a silver cigar-cutter and lit it with a Ronson table-lighter. His fat red cheeks were going in and out like a pair of leather bellows as he puffed away at the Montecristo to maintain its glowing red tip. The whole process took so long that the two detectives exchanged a look of exasperation, and Frost sparked up a Rothmans, his last unbroken one in the pack.

The club-owner then exhaled a heavy plume of smoke in the direction of the yellowed overhead light shade, which looked like it was a frequent target.

'Granted, with me it's all about the money, but not so with George. He likes the power. Now, I'm not averse to a bit of that myself, because invariably the money quickly follows. But George likes to hold it over you. When I was doing a five-stretch in the Scrubs many years ago, I did a fair bit of reading. You know, you have to keep your mind active in the slammer. Anyway, one book George recommended to me was *The Prince* by Machiavelli. Which, of course, is where the phrase—'

'Come on, Harry!' demanded Frost, getting impatient again as he watched Baskin relaxing in his chair. 'Spare us the Bamber Gascoigne routine and get to the point. It's not bleedin' *University Challenge.*'

Baskin smiled. 'George told me that Socks and Winston could be useful to me and him in the future. But he wouldn't say how. And he wouldn't say what they did or

158

who they were. They were his ace in the hole. Yet again, typical George – by not telling me, he had one over me. He had the power. After a while I just thought he was talking bollocks, you know, giving it large, the big one, being flash. So how come you know about them? Wouldn't have anything to do with you getting a crack on the head, would it?'

'Didn't think you were interested in such things.' Frost stubbed out his barely smoked cigarette in the big crystal ashtray on the desk; his split lip hurt too much and took all the fun out of it. 'One last thing: how come you've got one of your men watching over Melody and another posted at George's door at the hospital?'

Harry's big bellowing cheeks had filled the small windowless room with smoke, and with the pine panelling covering the walls, the place now resembled a sauna. 'Melody asked me, and I thought it was a good idea.'

'*She* asked *you*? It wasn't your idea?'

Baskin shrugged. 'Makes sense, happy to help. George is a mate and if Her Majesty's Constabulary doesn't have anyone there, what harm can it do?'

'Yeah, well, the poor sod at the hospital is now in a hospital bed.'

Harry laughed incredulously and shook his head like it was the most ridiculous thing he'd ever heard. 'Bad Manners Bob? He's as strong as an ox.'

'A nurse hit him over the head with a metal bedpan. He got in a fight with one of my uniform lads, PC Simms, who *was* on duty watching over and protecting George Price, and stopped' – Frost raised his eyes to the heavens

159

at the bruiser's moniker – 'Bad Manners Bob from going into George's room. PC Simms thought he had a gun under his jacket; turned out to be a tin of Quality Street.'

'That's right, I told him to take George some for when he wakes up, which' – Baskin rapped his knuckles on the wooden desk – 'I'm confident he will. We ate all the good ones, remember?' He then addressed a confused-looking John Waters. 'There was only the nut cracknel and the horrible blue ones left; criminal waste of space, they are.'

Baskin blew out a puff of smoke as if sickened at the very thought, and Frost and Waters bestowed little nods of assent to this universally accepted truth.

Sunday (4)

The weekly Denton boot fair and market was packed as usual. Situated on a large plot of land behind the railway station, it had grown in recent times due to the demolition of a small shopping precinct, an early sixties brutalist affair in drab concrete, which had proved so unpopular and so poorly constructed that it had been torn down (or had fallen down) some five years ago. Nothing had replaced it, just car parking, and the boot fair that was held every Sunday.

Over a hundred stalls were offering an impossibly wide range of goods, everything from discounted dishtowels to antique Meissen china. It was a frenzy of tax-free trading. And it was the perfect hunting ground for Detective Inspector Eve Hayward. Dressed in faded jeans, cowboy boots and an olive-green MA-1 bomber jacket, her hair tucked under a black baseball cap with 'BOY' emblazoned across it, she was walking the aisles and perusing the stalls for that elusive bargain, just like everyone else.

When Eve Hayward woke up that morning, Sue Clarke was still fast asleep in her hotel room. She didn't bother waking her and just left a note. Because unlike Superintendent Mullett, she didn't believe she needed someone from Eagle Lane station escorting her around and showing her the lay of the land, and generally informing the populace, criminal or otherwise, that she was a copper. In fact, being seen with anyone from Denton CID was the last thing she needed or wanted. But, of course, she couldn't tell Mullett or any of Denton CID that because, as far as she was concerned, they were under investigation as much as anyone else.

'See anything you fancy, darling?'

She kept walking and didn't even spare a glance for the man who had just sidled up to her. She knew all about him: he was a tall, handsome, flash-looking sod with a blow-dried George Michael haircut replete with blond highlights, and a square jaw that was sprinkled with designer stubble.

Eve Hayward said, 'No, it's all cheap tat or knock-off gear, and that goes for the blokes too.'

The man smiled. Even his teeth were fakes, very white and capped to within an inch of their lives. But in all fairness to him, the extensive and expensive dental work he'd undertaken was because he'd had them practically all knocked out with the butt of a sawn-off shotgun whilst trying to stop an armed robbery. 'That's what we're here for, Eve. I've been doing a little shopping myself.'

162

Hayward turned to DI Tony Norton, her colleague from West End Central, and saw that he had a plastic carrier bag with about ten videos in it.

'All the latest releases,' said Tony Norton, 'not on sale yet. Not officially, anyway. And some of them not even released in this country. And I was also offered cartons of cigarettes and crates of booze, all with no British tax on them.'

'There's a local bookmaker, George Price, on the critical list in Denton General,' said Hayward. 'He was shot on Friday. I've got a hunch it might all be connected.'

Tony Norton weighed this up. 'So we've got the gee-gees and gambling, a glut of counterfeit goods hitting town, and our two men from Dublin spotted in the area. It sounds like our intelligence is right: they've spread their wings and are on the mainland. Which is a shrewd move, more money over here. Plus the fact things are getting too hot for them over there. They've made too many enemies, on both sides of the law. You know what comes next, don't you?'

Eve Hayward did indeed know what came next. They carried on walking, no longer interested in what was on the stalls. This was little more than a sideline, only one part of the impending crime wave that would soon engulf Denton and the surrounding area if their intelligence proved correct. Her job on the inside was now to connect all the dots.

'Any bad apples at Eagle Lane who might be on the payroll?' asked Norton.

'It's only my second day. Start going in too hard and

heavy about personalities and they'll smell a rat and think I'm investigating them. But I've heard some interesting things about a DI Frost. Seems to like doing things his own way, and we know how that usually turns out.'

They made their way out of the market to the privacy of DI Norton's car, where he filled her in on a robbery that had happened last night in nearby Rimmington.

At 7 a.m. that morning a white Transit van was reported to the police because it had been parked all night next to a jewellery shop. On checking the plates, the investigating PCs discovered the van was stolen. It was actually flush against the wall of the jeweller's, so with the side door open the thieves had been able to use their drills and sledgehammers, muffled with blankets, to make a hole big enough to crawl through. Only the door and window grilles of the shop were alarmed, and so they had effectively bypassed the security system. The old cast-iron safe that held most of the stock was a doddle for the thieves to open. The shop's owner, a Mr Raymond Handler, said that there was over twenty thousand pounds' worth of jewels, precious coins and gold missing. The sum might have been rather inflated for insurance purposes, but it was nonetheless a significant haul.

And for Eve Hayward and her colleague, the crime had all the professional and daring modus operandi of one gang in particular, from over the water in Dublin: the Hogan Gang.

As they drove away from the Coconut Grove, Frost and Waters discussed the case. They agreed that whilst

164

Baskin was largely keeping up the criminal code of conduct by keeping his mouth mostly shut, he was also on edge. And they both felt that Melody had lied about Harry Baskin volunteering to provide protection for both her and George – Keith had been all her idea. She was alone in that big house and she was rattled.

For Frost, it was becoming clear that there were darker forces at play than just Terry Langdon, who, according to everyone who knew him, was no cold-blooded killer likely to come back to finish off the job. Baskin was proving to be a loyal friend to George Price, but he was also a pragmatist and a businessman who wanted to protect his investments and the nefarious ventures they shared, and he wouldn't bother posting Bad Manners Bob outside Price's hospital room, or indeed providing Keith's services to Melody, if the threat was solely from a playboy chancer like Langdon. As far as the DI was concerned, and Waters agreed, all these little facts blew the whole case wide open again.

DS Waters dropped off a very reluctant Frost at the Jade Rabbit. Frost had wanted to go back to Eagle Lane to get stuck in. He was keen to liaise with Sue Clarke on what she'd discovered at Langdon's place; she'd hinted over the radio that it could be of interest, and that she was just waiting for an urgent ballistics report (she'd called in a favour and ruined a technician's Sunday lie-in). But Waters was having none of it, and insisted that for once Frost should follow orders, and go home to get some rest.

On entering the Jade Rabbit, and being hit with the

165

powerful aroma of sweet and sour emanating from Kenny Fong's wok, Frost decided to get a Kung Po to take away. He was still *persona non grata* with Old Mrs Fong, and it was probably the safer option to eat upstairs in the flat. So he quickly put in his order with Kenny before his mother appeared, and went upstairs. Frost knew the only way to make peace with her was either to find Monty the parrot, an impossible task, or to replace it, a not-so-impossible task, though likely to be an expensive one; due to their longevity he was sure they didn't come cheap.

As he lay on his futon, an all-the-rage Japanese form of bed that was about as comfortable as lying on a griddle, he glanced through the brochure for Paradise Lodge. The three identical blocks with their colourful Lego brickwork and cladding didn't look like they would age well, but he was pretty sure he was going to pull the trigger on one of the flats anyway.

His lodgings upstairs at the Jade Rabbit were ruining his love life, or attempts at a love life. He'd come to the conclusion that he couldn't bring birds back here any more than he could keep them from flying out of here. And futons, as far as he could tell, were the preserve of students and not of grown men in respectable professions ... or coppers. No, he'd made up his mind – tomorrow he would contact young Jason Kingly, the estate agent, and have one last look around Paradise, Eden and Utopia, and make an offer. There was a knock on the door: his Kung Po with extra Po and an ice-cold can of Harp lager had arrived. He smiled. This was Jack Frost's idea of Paradise, Eden and Utopia right here.

166

Monday (1)

The cold morning still managed to be luminously bright and filled Frost with optimism. He was happy to be in the Metro, with Art Pepper playing on the cassette deck, as he drove northwest, foot down, with a renewed vigour and purpose, to purchase himself a flat. A new home, somewhere he could call his own. And he was determined to be in his new place as quickly as possible. This fresh resolve to be out of the Jade Rabbit pronto was brought about by him getting his timing terribly wrong, and bumping into the venerable Mrs Fong.

He didn't have a clue what she was saying, but in all honesty it didn't take an interpreter of Cantonese for Jack Frost to get the message: she wanted him out. At 8.30 a.m. Frost had slipped ninja-like out of his room, along the hallway and down the creaking stairs, which he managed to make *not creak* due to his stocking-footed stealth – he was holding his old suede slip-ons in his

167

hands. The front door of the restaurant was in sight, but as he got to the bottom of the stairs, she was coming out of the kitchen. Her inscrutable features screwed up in distaste when she caught sight of him. He still had the bandage, now rather grubby, around his head; the shiner was in full florid bloom; and his lip was swollen and curled like that of a bad Elvis impersonator. Frost attempted a smile through a face that was still puffy and tight with pain and said good morning. To no avail; seemingly his condition didn't elicit any sympathy from the Fong matriarch. She just looked at him as you would an overflowing toilet, and fixed him with a baleful glare. She pinched her nose with one hand, then pointed at his feet with the other, and let loose a burst of loud Cantonese. Hearing the commotion, Kenny Fong quickly appeared on the scene, coming out of the kitchen.

'Frost, you must put your shoes on!'

'I thought it was a Chinese custom to take them off.'

'No, Frost! Shoes *on*. Mum reckons that's why her beloved parrot Monty flew off, because of your feet, they stink!'

Frost thought about it; Monty did used to let out a mighty and sustained squawk and flap about in his cage whenever Frost slipped off his shoes.

'I never knew parrots had such a highly developed sense of smell, I thought that was dogs.'

'Frost, you don't need that much of a developed sense of smell with your feet, no offence. Pen and ink! Pen and ink!'

'Eh?'

168

'Pen and ink! Pen and ink!'

Frost had momentarily forgotten that Kenny and his family were fans of Chas & Dave, and when they weren't listening to their records they were reading through their book of rhyming slang, inexplicably, to improve their Queen's English.

'Pen and ink – stink?' questioned Frost.

'Yeah, stink! Even up the apples and pears, can still smell your plates of meat!'

'Well, Kenny, you know what they say about coppers' feet – that's why they call us the Plod. Spend all day on them, bound to hum a little. But it's the start of the day, no pong now?'

Kenny Fong looked as furious as his mother. 'No pong now? *No pong now?* You taking mickey?'

Frost held up the brochure for his potential new home, said he wouldn't be here much longer and made his escape. He went straight to the phone box at the corner of the road and phoned Jason Kingly.

As he pulled the Metro into the car park of Paradise Lodge, Frost was met by Kingly. The young estate agent was looking keen and today was wearing a Prince of Wales double-breasted suit that looked far too big for him. In fact, it looked like he was wearing a sandwich board advertising Prince of Wales check.

'Morning, Mr Frost, beautiful day to be purchasing a luxury yet very affordable home,' he said in his best patter. But as Frost got out of the car, Jason stopped smiling and looked concerned. 'You been in the wars?'

'Eh? Oh, yeah, all part of the job.' They shook hands.

'I've got an appointment with the bank manager later today, should sort out all the paperwork for the mortgage this week.'

They made their way towards the entrance of Paradise Lodge.

'Should go through OK, will it, Mr Frost?'

Frost smiled. 'I don't think I'll have any problems, I saw the bank manager only yesterday, in fact. In church.'

'If you don't mind me saying so, you don't strike me as a church-goer, Mr Frost.'

'Well, I say a church. There was a woman of the cloth there. And then she took it off.'

Jason looked confused. Then worried. 'Just out of curiosity, how did you get . . . ?'

'A good kicking?'

The estate agent nodded.

'Have a guess.'

Kingly guessed and shrugged as he answered, 'Playing rugby?'

'Sports were involved, but not rugby. It was horse racing. And I didn't fall off a horse. It's a long story, Jason, but I was at the races and I'd had a few drinks, and I was . . .' Frost stopped in his tracks as something caught his eye. 'I thought you said all these flats were empty, no one had moved in yet.'

'I did. They haven't. By the way, the office didn't tell me, what did you say you did for a living? Your job?'

Frost ignored his question and went over to the flat on the ground floor that had piqued his interest. He peered through the window. The flat was expensively decorated

170

and furnished. In the living room was a black leather and chrome-framed three-piece suite arranged around a deco-style coffee table. All very swanky and tasteful, thought Frost, getting ideas for maybe how his own place could look with a bit of effort. But what really grabbed his attention was what was on the sleek coffee table. There was an empty bottle of wine and some scrunched-up cans of Castlemaine XXXX, and a big box of fried chicken that someone had laid waste to. Frost grinned; *now* he could really imagine what his place would look like. He pulled himself away from the window to be confronted with Jason, who was looking concerned.

'Well, Mr Frost?'

'Well what?'

'What is it you do, professionally, for a living?'

Frost understood: the cuts and bruises, they didn't give a very good impression, and the estate agent obviously didn't want hooligans moving in to the newly built properties and lowering the tone – and future asking prices. Frost, to put Jason's mind at rest, pulled out his wallet and warrant card. 'I'm a detective inspector with Denton CID. So, who's moved in there, then?'

Kingly should never commit a crime, thought Frost, as he looked quizzically at the young man – his mouth was wide open, his eyes were rounded in terror, and his bum-fluffed pasty face was colouring up a treat.

'Jason, you all right, lad, something you want to tell me?'

'It's a show flat. We show it to people so they can see what it would look like furnished. We usually have some flowers in there, a bowl of fruit on the side table, maybe some books on the shelf. That sort of thing.'

'So how do you account for an empty bottle of plonk, some tins of Aussie lager and a chicken dinner?'

'Err, yeah, well, between me and you, Mr—'

'*Inspector* Frost.'

'Yes, of course, Inspector Frost. I've been using it for . . . for entertaining. I've got a new girlfriend, you see. We use it sometimes for—'

'All right, I get the picture. I take it you're not supposed to entertain birds in here, right?'

'They'd go mad if they found out, I'd be sacked immediately.'

Frost gave him a nudge and a wink. 'Don't worry, son, your secret's safe with me. I'd do the same in your shoes. So why didn't you show me this show flat? Looks nice, and it's on the ground floor.'

'It was a bit out of the price range you were looking at, Inspector.'

'Don't worry about that, the mortgage is not a problem. My bank manager is putty in my hands. It's the bank that likes to say "Yes".' Frost then muttered to himself, 'Anything so I don't tell his wife.'

'It's a two-bedroom flat with an extra boxroom, for a growing family, that type of thing.'

Frost considered the show flat again – it looked enticing. Maybe young Jason was on to something, maybe he had to expand his horizons, plan for the future. The bump on the head had woken him up to new ideas and possibilities, mainly that he didn't want to end up

172

on his own, come the day of reckoning. And if he did meet the right woman and a kid came along, Frost would be ready now, he felt.

'Inspector Frost?'

Frost glanced round to discover Jason marching off ahead towards Paradise Lodge. Frost called out to him to hold his horses. 'I want to have a look *in here.*'

The estate agent stopped and reluctantly made his way back over to Frost, who was again peering in at the window of his potential future home.

'You can't. I don't have the keys.'

'You don't need them,' said Frost.

'I do, how else are we going—'

'What caught my eye, Jason, was the window – it's not properly closed.' Frost slipped his fingers in the gap and pulled it open. 'I'm a copper, we're trained to spot things like this. Crime prevention is half the work.'

Kingly froze, with that soppy wide-eyed look on his face that was beginning to annoy Frost.

'We can't . . . we can't go in . . . I don't have permission.' Jason quickly looked around. 'People might think we're breaking in . . .'

'What people? There's no one around, they're empty flats. And relax, I'm a policeman. Plus, I don't think your superiors will mind me having a nose around if I decide to spend more money, do you?'

'We can't go in, we're not supposed to, I don't have permission,' repeated Kingly.

With a hint of blackmail in his voice, Frost reminded

him, 'That's never stopped you in the past, eh? You and your bird?'

Frost climbed through the window and was soon standing in the living room. Jason followed him in. And as he did so, he called out to the DI in a very loud and incongruous fashion, 'No, Inspector, I don't suppose they will mind you coming in . . . what with you being a policeman!'

Terry Langdon's heart was pounding in his chest, so loudly was his panic reverberating around his body that he was sure they could hear the thumping racket. Cold sweat prickled his spine. He tried to slow his breathing, to calm himself. The gun felt heavy in his hand now. He'd been carrying it about with him, just in case, just in case something like this should happen. But now it felt real, it didn't feel like a toy, a prop, it felt like something he was going to use, a tool to deploy. To kill if need be. And he would.

But first he'd kill Jason. That little idiot – letting someone into the flat – what the hell was he thinking of? Though in all fairness to him, it did sound like the other man's idea. In fact, from what he'd heard, the fella sounded like a pushy bugger. Insisting on taking a look, not taking no for an answer. He could hear Jason trying to usher him out. And in all fairness to the kid, he did try to warn him, by shouting out that he was coming in.

Langdon could hear them getting closer. The man had insisted on a tour of the flat, and after obviously starting in the lounge, Jason had taken him to the

174

bathroom, the kitchen and the two smaller bedrooms, and now they were fast approaching the master bedroom – where he was hiding.

As they entered it, Terry could just make out their figures as he peered through the slatted door of the fitted wardrobe he was standing in. The gun was fully loaded, and cocked. He could hear them perfectly now. The man had a strong voice, sounded commanding.

'Not bad, not bad at all. Tell me, Jason, does the bed come with it?'

He saw the man bouncing up and down on it, trying it out.

'I bet this has seen some action, eh? You and your girlfriend, what's her name? I want some discount on it, seeing as it's been used. One young enthusiastic owner, lots of spins around the block but not a lot of mileage on the . . . Are you all right, son?'

'Yes. I . . . I was just thinking I've got another appointment . . . I should really be going.'

'That's not the attitude.'

'Sorry?'

'Well, far be it for me to tell you your business, but you're looking at it all wrong. Are you sure you're OK? You're looking a bit peaky.'

'I'm all right, Mr Frost.'

Frost. He had a name for him now. He wished he hadn't heard it – it made it just that bit more personal. Terry Langdon watched as the man got up from the bed and moved around the room, opening the door to the en suite and peering in. Langdon heard the shower curtain

175

being swished aside, and he congratulated himself for not hiding in there.

Frost came out of the bathroom and stood by Jason. There were some shuffling sounds. A quick burst of flame and then the familiar aroma of cigarette smoke.

'What I mean by your attitude is, well, I'm here, and I'm ready to buy. You might rush out of here to your next appointment and discover they're messing you about. They just like spending their time looking around properties. Me, I'm a live one. I'm hot to trot. I'm a goer. Get my meaning, Jason?'

'I . . . I think so.'

The man, Frost, was moving again. Footfalls drawing closer. He was now inches away from the wardrobe. It was bound to be his next port of call after the bathroom. That's what people do with doors – they open them, natural reaction. Frost would take a look to see if he could fit all his clobber in there. You always check the wardrobe space. It was the next logical move, no matter how much Terry Langdon wanted it to be otherwise, and it was going to happen. It was his destiny. His fate. To kill, to be a murderer.

Langdon raised the gun to chest height. He was pressed into the corner of the wardrobe now. Maybe if Frost only opened one door he wouldn't see him. But he knew that wasn't going to happen. Frost was going to open both doors to take a proper look. And when he did, Terry was going to shoot him. Put a bullet right in his head. After all, he had to. He knew they were looking for him, prime suspect, and he was done for. What difference would one more make?

176

'No, if you want to succeed in this game, think of it this way, son. It's a bit like you having one of your birds back here – they're sitting on the flash couch, you've had your pizza, your bottle of vino, then you decide to go to the local nightclub to see if you can pull a better-looking bird. That's where the expression "A bird in the hand is worth two in the bush" comes from.'

'Does it?'

'Of course it does, what else can it be?'

Frost's hand was on the doorknob now. It creaked, it edged open. Langdon stopped breathing. He didn't want to see his face. He would shoot the bastard through the door. He had a good silhouette of the man against the light from outside. He aimed the gun at his head. Nothing mattered now, just getting away. Getting away as far as he could, then who knows, send for Melody to join him once he'd got fixed up in another country, maybe Spain. Canada, yes, that was better, somewhere far away from Denton, a fresh start for them both. But to do that he had to get away first, and for that to happen he had to kill this man now. Frost. The door opened further and Terry Langdon's forefinger squeezed itself around the trigger . . .

'Bloody hell!' shrieked Jason.

'What?'

'A parrot! Look!'

'I'll be damned . . . It's . . . it's . . . Monty!'

Both men rushed from the room. With their footsteps fading into the distance, Terry Langdon gave a huge sigh of relief, and then eased his finger off the trigger. As

177

he carefully nudged the wardrobe door ajar, he heard Jason and the man called Frost noisily scrambling out of the lounge window . . . Frost seemed to be whistling and calling out the name of something . . . a name Terry couldn't make out. Then he heard Frost swearing. He swore like a trooper. Then more muttered voices from outside before he heard someone clamber back in through the window.

The wardrobe door was quickly opened and Langdon took aim again.

'Don't shoot!'

Langdon lowered the barrel from Jason's forehead.

'Bloody hell, Terry, why didn't you just hide under the bed?'

'Where's . . . Frost?'

'Gone back to the station, probably.'

'What station?'

'The police-bloody-station! He's a *copper*! Didn't you hear me? I shouted it out when we came in, said the word "policeman" really loudly.'

Langdon shook his head, stunned by his narrow escape. 'No, I was too busy looking for somewhere to hide.'

The fugitive stepped out of his hiding place and now stood in the middle of the master bedroom. A pale-looking Jason sat on the bed, loosening his tie and undoing the top button of his shirt; not that it made much difference, as his scrawny neck barely touched the sides of his fifteen-inch collar anyway. It was more an expression of despair than a necessity. Because

178

Kingly now realized that he was way out of his depth and was drowning in panic.

Langdon wasn't doing much better. He was pacing up and down, and every now and again taking a peek out of the bedroom window just to make sure that Frost wasn't attempting a re-entry. The gun was hanging loosely from his hand and looking lethally dangerous and out of control, like it could slip from his sweaty palm at any minute, rebound on the thick nap of the carpet and let off a shot. Jason kept one eye on the revolver, and the other eye on his erratic cousin.

Kingly had always admired his cousin Terry. He was older, richer, better-looking and it was sort of taken for granted that he was smarter – though Jason was swiftly re-evaluating that. So he was happy to help him, give him some time to sort this mess out, and Terry assured him that he was innocent and all would be OK. But Jason could see that Langdon was disintegrating before his very eyes: he looked sallow and gaunt. It had only been a few days, but Kingly could tell that he was a nervous wreck. Right on the edge. And Jason feared he was going to take him over it with him.

'That was close.'

'Yeah. Then I really would have been a murderer.'

The word *murderer* freaked Jason out some more, and he began to scratch maniacally at the heel of his left hand, where there was a livid patch of itchy eczema that flared up at times of stress and crisis. 'I knew it was a mistake letting you stay here . . .' he started to say, thinking out loud, and not considering his cousin. 'If they find out you're here I'll lose my job . . . Sod that, I'll lose my freedom too, probably . . . I don't want to go to—'

'Calm down, Jace, for God's sake! It's only for another day or so. I've got a passport and some money coming to me. Soon as they're delivered I'm out of here, out of Denton, out of the country.'

'Bloody hell, why didn't you bring your passport and your money with you?'

'Same reason I didn't hide under the bed! Heat of the moment.'

'Maybe you should hide somewhere else? I'm not trying to get rid of you, it just might be safer now the flats are on the market. People will start coming around to take a look, you'll be seen—'

'No. This place is even more perfect now. Frost's been here and seen it's empty. He won't look again, it's perfect.' Terry smiled a satisfied smile at his young cousin. 'And all thanks to your quick thinking. What did you tell him? You brought birds back here? Though to be honest, Jace, I don't know how he swallowed that. Let's face it, you couldn't bring chewing gum back here if it got stuck to your shoe, never mind a bird!' Terry laughed and ruffled his cousin's hair. He then looked at his hand, grimaced, and rubbed the residue of hair gel on Kingly's Prince of Wales shoulder.

Jason didn't appreciate it. 'Cheers!'

Terry pinched his cheek and winked. 'I've got a nice burgundy leather box jacket you can have, looks the business, Italian. Alberto Armani, Giorgio's more talented brother, said the fella on the stall.'

Langdon laughed, but it was hollow, and certainly didn't entice Jason to join him.

'I won't need it where I'm going,' continued Terry, stepping up the bravado. 'Down to Spain, it's lovely in Marbella this time of year. Then off to Canada, maybe Australia, the world is my lobster, as they say. Yeah, that could be just the ticket, Australia, a new country, a new life. The Gold Coast, full of good-looking birds down there, mate. You can come and visit, I'll see you right.'

Kingly watched as Terry resumed pacing up and down. He was grinning at the prospect of Australia, but Jason could hear the trepidation tugging at the edges of his cousin's voice, like he knew, at heart, that it was all just a pipe dream.

'Maybe I could talk to Frost,' offered the younger man. 'He likes me.'

'What on earth are you talking about?'

'Well, if you tell him the truth, he'll listen.'

'No, no, no! Look, it's not as simple as just handing myself in.'

Terry sat down on the bed next to Jason. With the gun resting across his lap, it was now pointed at the young man. It may not have been aimed at him intentionally, but Jason still tensed up.

'But I reckon he's all right,' said Kingly. 'He seems like a good bloke, a fair bloke. Maybe I could have a word.'

Terry turned sharply towards his cousin. Now the gun was aimed at him on purpose. 'Are you fucking mad? Don't you dare! Don't you even think about it! This isn't kids' games we're playing here!'

181

Jason raised his hands in surrender.

Terry looked bemused at this reaction. 'What the hell are you doing now?'

'You've . . . you've got a gun pointed at me . . . a gun.'

Terry glanced down at the shooter in his hand, and seemed almost as shocked and distressed as Jason to see it aimed at him. He stood up, went over to the side table and put the gun in the drawer. He then stood over Jason and put his hand on his shoulder and gave it a reassuring squeeze.

'I'm sorry, Jace, I wouldn't hurt you – don't be silly, you're family. But don't talk about calling the Old Bill again, not Frost, not anyone.'

'But you didn't do it! You're innocent. You told me that you didn't kill George Price.'

'Kill? What have you heard? Is he dead?'

Kingly shrugged. 'I don't know. I haven't heard anything.'

Terry sighed. Jason couldn't tell if he was relieved that he wasn't dead, or upset.

'If he's gone, then so be it. I'm not shedding any tears over him. You know what he did to my dad, to your uncle, don't you? You know how upset your mum was when he died.'

Jason knew, but in fact he was sick of hearing it from Terry. The way he went on about what had happened all those years ago made Kingly believe that Terry had in fact shot George Price. Then there was the wife, Melody. Jason had seen her in the flesh at the races, and in some old Page Threes where there was even more of her on show. She was a cross between Sam Fox and Linda Lusardi, Jason reckoned, though she had never quite hit the heights, the twin peaks, if you will, of those two *Sun* 'scorchers'. What broke Jason out of his soft-core reverie was Terry's hand on his shoulder, but its grip was hard this time, not comforting.

'Jason?'

Kingly glanced up at him. Langdon's large brown eyes – bedroom eyes, as they had been described by more than one of his conquests – now just looked dark with foreboding. He looked a lot harder without his moustache. The distinctive 'tache was the first thing to go in an effort to distinguish himself from his wanted poster. And his lips were thin, and prickled with tension.

'You do believe me, don't you?'

Jason nodded. Too scared to actually say yes, just in case Terry caught the doubt in his voice.

'Good. But I'll tell you something, I do know who did shoot George Price, and that's why I can't go to the police, Frost or anyone else.'

'I understand. You don't want to grass. So who shot him?'

Terry looked grim and shook his head. 'You don't want to know. But it's not just about being a grass, it's about being believed. You don't know what goes on in this town, corruption right to the top. I'll be glad to get out of this place. So trust me, and no more talk about telling Jack Frost anything – you swear?'

Jason swore on his mother's life, no more talk of Jack Frost. 'You wouldn't have shot him, would you?'

183

'Who?'

'Inspector Frost?'

Langdon didn't answer, and Kingly took that to mean that he would have. And by the look in his eyes, the desperation etched on his face, Jason believed that he would have, too.

'Poor sod,' said Jason. 'He doesn't know how close he came. A parrot saved his life.'

'What are you talking about?'

'There was a parrot, an actual parrot. He was sitting on the windowsill.'

'You're joking!'

'Nah.' Jason started laughing, like he'd never seen a parrot before – much less a wild one in Denton.

'I thought you'd just said that to distract him?'

'No, the parrot looked like he wanted to come into the flat. Frost started calling out to him. Then he flew off, out of sight. Frost kept shouting out his name, though.'

Monday (2)

'Monty!'

'Monty who?'

'The parrot. Monty the parrot. Or Monty the Second, to give him his full title. But as his home was a Chinese restaurant, he was more commonly referred to as Monty Number Two.'

'And you saw him flying about, out in the wild?'

'I did, Johnny. He flew down and sat on the windowsill – it was like he was waiting for me, or had come to tell me he wanted to go home.'

'He wasn't nailed to his perch, then?' said Desk Sergeant Bill Wells.

'Eh?'

Wells started to channel John Cleese: 'This parrot is dead, deceased, this parrot is a—'

Frost groaned.

185

'Cut it out, you muppet. Not even funny,' said Johnny Johnson.

Frost had come into Eagle Lane to find that Night Sergeant Johnson was lingering long after the end of his shift, to discuss with Bill Wells some of the finer points of the new computer system neither of them could master but that they both hated. They were always good value for some banter, but Frost wasn't in the mood for it. He wanted results, he wanted action, he wanted dogged detective work, and he wanted Monty banged up behind bars by the end of the day. Although the parrot had looked in good health, Frost was sure he could do with the creature comforts of home, the Trill, the cuttlefish, the swing and the plush newspaper carpet.

'He saw me coming through the window and he took off, headed towards town. I got in the car and was able to follow him for a bit – then I lost him.'

Wells asked, 'This window ledge he was on, where was it, Jack?'

'The flats I'm looking to move into. Paradise Lodge.'

'Perhaps he lives there. Paradise Lodge,' said Johnson. 'Perfect place for a bird of paradise.'

'You're not taking this seriously, are you?'

'So what do you want us to do about it?' asked Johnson. 'Call the flying squad?'

'Maybe he's nesting in there,' said Wells, gesturing towards the DI's heavily bandaged head.

The two sergeants laughed uproariously at the gag. Frost remained impervious to their desk-bound double act.

186

'Funnily enough,' said Wells, 'you're not the only one having bird trouble. Got a call on Saturday and one late on Friday from Joe Kelso. His farm's missing some chickens.'

'They've probably joined the parrot, migrated for the spring,' posited Johnson.

'Chickens don't fly.'

'That's penguins.'

'And you're gonna end up like a couple of dodos if you don't start making some calls to find my parrot!'

'RSPCA,' said Johnny Johnson.

'RSP*B*,' corrected Bill Wells.

'RSVP, whichever it bloody is! Just call them, tell them what I saw, give them a description . . . He's mainly blue, with a bit of green and yellow around the collar.'

'If they see a parrot flying around Market Square, Jack, I'll tell them to assume it's yours,' said Bill Wells, looking up the number for the RSPB.

'I'll see you later, chaps, and good luck,' said Johnson, making his way out of the door. Before he left he warned Frost, 'Talking about swooping birds of prey, Hornrim Harry's gunning for you.'

'Feather-brained peckerhead, more like,' muttered Frost, pushing through the swing doors into the main CID incident room, just as a beleaguered Detective Constable Arthur Hanlon was making his way into reception.

'Calm down, Debbie, *calm down*,' pleaded Hanlon to the fierce Debbie Wooder, who was with him.

187

'And I'm telling you, *Officer*, I've got as much right to be here as anyone!'

'No one is saying you haven't. Just a surprise to see you here, that's all.'

Stevie Wooder's missus was with three of her brood, aged from five to seven. There were two more children, but they, worryingly for Hanlon and Eagle Lane, had disappeared from view the second they'd stepped into the station. Debbie was a vision with her shiny pink shellsuit, fluffy slippers, bleached and backcombed hair, and a face so slathered in slap that she looked like a Rimmel make-up counter had been dropped on her. She had more gold chains around her neck than Mr T, and a sovereign ring on every available finger. And every item was probably plunder from someone else's jewellery box. Hanlon wondered how she had the nerve to come into a police station wearing so much stolen swag, and all a gift from her loving husband, Little Stevie Wooder, who, although he had a record as long as a pickpocket's arm, was renowned as a very successful burglar due to his agility and diminutive size.

'I just said . . . maybe he's off . . . working somewhere.'

'What are you implying?'

'Listen, Debbie, I could say a lot – we've known Little Stevie almost as long as you have. In fact, the first person to nick him, when Little Stevie was even smaller than he is now, retired two years ago. He was his first nick, and his last. He was going to invite him to his leaving-drinks do, but Little Stevie was banged up in

Brixton at the time. But we know Little Stevie doesn't work locally, prefers big houses out in the shires, that's his game, right, Debbie?'

'PUT IT DOWN!' Debbie had just located one of her brood trying to detach a fire extinguisher from the wall. Arthur Hanlon rolled his eyes. Debbie continued, 'So what are you going to do about it?'

'Have you thought that he might not want us looking for him? I'm just saying. I mean, it will be a first, you wanting us to go looking for him.'

Debbie considered this and thrummed her fingers on Wells' desk. Hanlon looked at her bejewelled hands and gold-laden neck. Jack Frost had told him he once saw Little Stevie with his family and friends in the pub, and he took off a couple of chains from around Debbie's neck and gave them to the landlord to pay for the night's drinks. She was his walking, talking cashpoint.

Debbie said, 'Even if Stevie was away working he still always calls me. Lets me know he's all right. Always. He never came home on Saturday night. I think he slipped out real late, but he didn't come back. He's been missing for more than a day now. I'm going mental, I am, wondering where he is.'

Hanlon wanted to tell her he was probably shacked up with some girlfriend, but didn't. He saw that beneath the brassy carapace and tough-as-nails criminal self-sufficiency, Debbie was genuinely concerned. She wouldn't be standing in Eagle Lane station of her own volition if she wasn't.

189

'OK, let me get you a form to fill out and we'll put out a missing-persons on Stevie.'

Debbie pulled a big beaming smile that showed she had almost as much gold on her teeth as she had about her neck and fingers. 'Thanks, love, that's all I ask as a tax-paying citizen.'

Hanlon suppressed a crack of laughter at that one – she'd never paid tax on anything in her life. 'Do you have a recent photo of Stevie? I'm sure we have some, but they're mugshots.'

Debbie glared at him. 'I'll find one.'

On entering the incident room where the team were gathered for what was known as the 'scrum' – the morning progress briefing covering the cases CID were dealing with – Frost was met with a barrage of mickey-taking. There were Egyptian-mummy gags and references to turbans and tea cosies. No possibly offensive remark was left unused. Knowing that banter was all part of the job, Frost was ready and countered with some choice insults himself.

The clack of the digital clock on the wall told them it was now precisely 11 a.m., and the fun and games of the weekend were over.

'All right, all right, shut up, everybody, and let's have your attention!' he eventually called out as he stepped up to the incident board.

The board had all the known information about the George Price shooting pinned up on it, with the most urgent or significant facts, names and dates underlined

190

with a red marker pen. 'Progress report, what do we think, what do we know.' Frost laid out what he believed to be the significance of Price's little black book. He turned towards the board and picked up a red pen, and in big bold letters wrote SOCKS and WINSTON.

He then addressed the team: 'Nicknames, or code names; either way, I suspect they owe George Price a lot of money. Enough to kill him? We've seen people killed for a lot less than these two owe. Let's try and find out who they are. Use all your available sources. They could be nicknames used by other people as well, not just Price. They're gamblers, obviously, but they're high-rollers, they have money. Who knows, maybe they also owe other people money? Maybe there's people out there who are angry with them, and wouldn't mind telling us about it.'

'Are they the ones who hit you on the head and nicked your dosh, sir?' asked PC Simms. 'That's not me trying to be funny . . . sir.'

'You couldn't if you tried, son. I only wish I had a nurse and a bedpan to save *me*.' More laughter. 'As Simms correctly pointed out, whoever it was went through my pockets and took the money out of my wallet and the black book. This may sound counter-intuitive, but I reckon it was the book they were after and not the dosh. The money was just a bonus, they couldn't resist that. So, was it Socks and Winston who did it? Did they see me at the races with the book? Is it someone we've already spoken to?'

Frost spotted Arthur Hanlon slip through the door and make his way to the desks.

191

'Nice of you to join us, Arthur.'

'Sorry, guv, got waylaid. Debbie Wooder's lost her husband.'

'She can go shoplift herself another one!' someone shouted out.

'Any luck with Frank Trafford?' asked Hanlon.

'Thank you, Arthur, I was just getting to him.' Frost wrote up the name on the board along with 'Moustache 2'.

The DI filled in the rest of the team on his meeting with Frank Trafford at the races. 'He's got plenty of motive. After his wife got sacked she left him, so he's definitely got a beef with the Prices. He drinks too much and gambles too much, so it's no surprise he has money troubles, and he's got a temper on him and a record for violence. And as an ex-squaddie with two Northern Ireland tours under his belt, he's no stranger to firearms. And from what I've heard he doesn't have a solid alibi.'

'Could he be Socks or Winston?' asked Simms.

Frost considered the young PC. Simms was just like his late older brother, Derek, at his age. He had a knack for asking the right questions, and he'd be making CID like his brother in no time, Frost would make sure of that. 'Frank Trafford isn't in that league.'

'He's got the violence about him, though,' suggested Hanlon. 'He might be the one who hit you over the head?'

'That's what you're going to find out, Arthur. Bring him in, and let's see if we can organize a line-up for our

192

two eyewitnesses who saw' – Frost wrote 'Moustache 1' on the board – 'Terry Langdon leaving the scene in a red Porsche.'

'Don't think Frank Trafford's got a Porsche, though,' said Arthur Hanlon.

'How do you know? He might have Chitty Chitty Bang Bang in his garage.' Frost turned his attention back to the team. 'We also got some insights from his landlord into the state of Terry Langdon's mind at the time of the Price shooting – fragile at best—' Just then DC Clarke entered looking pleased with herself and holding a ring binder. 'What you got for us, Sue?'

Clarke explained she'd just returned from the ballistics lab. She then ran through what she and DC Hanlon had discovered in and around Terry Langdon's bungalow: his passport, which would suggest that he was still in the country, some recent gun magazines and an improvised firing range out in the woods, where they had recovered a bullet.

'However,' she continued, 'the bullet in George Price's head, from what Dr Maltby could ascertain from the entry wound and X-rays, indicates a 9mm handgun, maybe something like a Beretta. The bullet we dug out of the tree was from a .38, which matches the reading material Langdon had about the Webley Mk IV.'

'So, the big question is, if you were doing firing practice – you'd use the same gun, surely?' Frost's question was rhetorical. 'A semi-automatic and revolver have a completely different action and kick. Why would you change guns?'

193

'And why leave your passport behind if you've planned in advance on killing someone and then going on the run?' asked Hanlon.

'You're on a roll. But I'm surprised to see you still here, I thought you'd be knocking on Frank Trafford's door by now.'

DC Hanlon stopped grinning and leaning back in his chair with his hands laced across his ample belly like he'd single-handedly cracked the case, and made his way out.

Clarke suggested, 'Might want to put another name up there. Michael Price.'

Frost wrote it up. 'He's got motive. Doesn't get on with his father, as George ousted him from the business in favour of his new wife.'

'And he hasn't got an alibi. He spent the day at home playing Chuckie Egg. It's a video game. And I sort of believe him, he strikes me as the type who spends a lot of time on his own, bit of a misfit.'

'That's hardly a defence. But then again, you lot could hardly claim to be well adjusted either, could you?' joked Frost.

Clarke joined in the laughter. Someone then asked if they were to give any assistance to the investigation into the jewel robbery in Rimmington over the weekend. Frost said only if they were asked to or if they came across some pertinent facts, intimating that Superintendent Kelsey and his team were more than capable, and even more territorial. There was always competition between Eagle Lane and the Rimmington nick:

194

the last five-a-side regional tournament they'd played in had had more than a whiff of an 'Auld Firm' game about it, with shins getting whacked more than the ball.

Satisfied that everyone was fired up and there was enough to be getting on with, Frost drew the 'scrum' to a close, then went over to Sue Clarke's desk and propped himself on the corner of it. She winced at the sight of him.

'Looks nasty, Jack.'

'What does?'

'Your head.'

'Not all of it, surely?'

'No, not all of it. The bit that's covered with a bandage looks OK.'

'Ha-bloody-ha. Sounds like we might need to pay another visit to Michael Price, though from what I've heard he's not—'

'Hiya!' said Clarke, bursting into a big smile.

Frost turned round towards the object of Sue's interest, certainly of greater interest than him, and performed a perfectly executed comedy double-take as he saw DI Eve Hayward approaching. She was everything that John Waters had said she was. Frost did a smooth dismount from Clarke's desk. As Hayward drew closer, he swore he could detect a little shimmy in her hips, a faint smile on her red lips, and a glint in her eyes as she looked at him. Maybe it was wishful thinking, or the bump on the head messing with his wiring, but Frost went with it anyway.

'DI Eve Hayward, meet DI Jack Frost.'

'Thank you, Sue,' said Frost, extending a hand. 'Nice to meet you, Eve.'

She took his hand. 'Likewise, Jack.'

'I'm sorry I missed your briefing on Saturday, must have got the times mixed up.'

'I hope that wasn't due to you getting dropped on your head.'

Frost laughed. 'You know how it is, all in the line of duty.'

Eve Hayward nodded. She then glanced down. Frost followed her gaze and realized he was still holding her hand, a hand that was heating up.

He let go, nervously cleared his throat and said, 'So then, counterfeit goods cropping up in the area? I can't say that I've noticed.'

'Because you haven't been looking. But I think it will be a real eye-opener when you see just how far it goes.'

'Put like that, how can I refuse?' Frost glanced down at his watch. 'How about I buy you a cup of tea and a bacon butty and you can tell me all about it? I like to keep abreast of things, Eve.'

'I'm sure. And put like that, how can I refuse?'

Frost looked on as Hayward's smile suddenly soured and dropped from her face altogether. Frost could feel jets of hot air beating down on the back of his neck. He turned to find Superintendent Stanley Mullett: his heavily magnified eyes behind his horn-rim spectacles were glaring down at him.

Frost never made it down to the canteen for the superior repast he'd promised Eve. He couldn't help but suspect that the very prospect of he and DI Hayward sharing anything, much less the delights of the canteen, exasperated Mullett to his very core. It was clear to Frost that she had caught the super's attention, and captured his imagination too, just as she had with everyone else in Eagle Lane who was male and had a pulse.

So there Frost stood, in Mullett's office, whilst the superintendent sat at his desk in his top-of-the-range black leather, height-adjustable executive chair. He hadn't invited Frost to sit down. Mullett's back was straight and his hands were laced together in front of him with purpose – he looked like a newsreader, about to read him the riot act.

'Your behaviour has been a disgrace, no other word for it.'

'I beg to differ, Superintendent Mullett.'

'Drinking, gambling, brawling, and then ending up in Denton General. Can you deny it? Unless that bandage around your head is the latest in fashion statements . . . Mr Adam and his Ants, perhaps?'

Frost raised an amused eye to the heavens at Mullett's botched pop-culture reference; they usually stopped just short of Gilbert and Sullivan. 'I can account for my actions.'

'What you do at the weekends, Frost, is your business, but when it's done under the guise of police work, then it becomes my business.'

Frost wanted to laugh good and hard as Hornrim Harry sat there stiff in his starched collar; his perfectly pressed uniform as black as boot polish; and the boots themselves, buffed to within an inch of their lives for a mirrored finish. Who was he kidding? He was so out of

197

touch with the nitty-gritty, the gut instinct, and sometimes, when needs be, the down-and-dirty of real police work that he'd have to call a copper if he lost his keys. Everything came down to columns of figures – statistics and clear-up rates – for Mullett these days. All so that his desk could remain as empty as his head. It took a certain type to sit at that empty desk, and Frost thanked his lucky stars he'd never make it. Mullett could swivel on his top-of-the-range office chair to his heart's content as far as he was concerned.

'George Price, the victim,' said Frost in a measured tone, 'is a bookmaker who has a pitch at Radleigh races, so it made sense to me that anyone who knows anything about George Price would be at Radleigh races. And to do that, I had to blend in with the surroundings, win people's trust, get them talking and try not to stick out like a sore thumb.' Frost gently tapped a forefinger on the bandage. 'Hence the sore head, not planned or intended, just some collateral damage. All part of the job, I'm afraid, and worth it for what I found out.'

Mullett drew his brows together above his glasses and examined Frost with a beady-eyed intent. 'We have the name of the culprit, Terrence Langdon. There are eyewitnesses who saw him leave the scene of the crime, and from what I've read on the case, from what you've bothered to put in your report, he has plenty of motive: a long-standing feud with Price, and designs on his wife. We have Traffic and Transport Police looking for him, we've frozen his assets, and this week he'll feature on Shaw Taylor's *Police 5*. I don't want Denton's CID wasting any more time or resources on this.'

'With all due respect, further information has turned up that leads me to believe there may be other suspects.'

'Don't take your eye off the ball, man, it's Langdon we need to find.'

'The first few days of any investigation are vital, and I already have DS Waters off the case because of the Bomber Harris shooting and unrest on the SHE, and now you want to take away DC Clarke for some bloody old nonsense no one gives a monkey's about!'

'I'm warning you—'

'And I'm just trying to do my job!'

Mullett rose up from his seat with such force that Frost rocked back on his heels.

'I didn't come to see you just because of your dissolute behaviour in public—'

'All in the line of duty—'

'Concerns on the Southern Housing Estate have taken a turn—'

'I'm not arguing against Waters being taken off the Price case, the Harris shooting is just as important – it's Clarke that I'm angry—'

'A young lad on the estate has died of a heroin overdose. Sixteen years old. He was found this morning.'

Frost rocked back on his heels again. Both men stood there, fixed in their positions, but without the heart to debate them any more. Something much bigger had just entered the frame. Of course, in reality, it was no great surprise, it had just been a matter of when. This was their first fatality in the drugs war, and *sixteen* years of age, just a kid. The drugs epidemic, as the media had labelled it, had already hit all the major cities. But still he felt a surge of indignant rage for the forces out there that would allow this to happen. Heroin was like a disease, and it was now on *his* patch, and he would do whatever it took to stop it, stop it spreading. He let out a heavy sigh, and Mullett did the same. For all the differences between the two men, when push came to shove, as it so often did, they had probably more in common than not. And right now, Frost wasn't about to question the super's authority any further. The death of the boy put it all into perspective – somehow a rich bookmaker getting shot, and still being alive, lost ground, and the new tragedy elicited the only possible response from Frost.

'I'll give it my full attention.'

Monday (3)

'It's a bad business, George, I'm telling you that. We've had the offer before, but we've always played with a straight bat. But I'm telling you, this is the end for me.'

Jimmy Drake sat in the wooden-framed armchair with its bobbling orange nylon upholstery. He was eating grapes, the grapes that he'd got for George Price. He was chatting to his old friend as if George was lying on a sun-lounger in the garden, by his swimming pool, as he liked to do on a hot summer's day.

But of course Jimmy knew that wasn't the reality as he watched George's big barrel chest going up and down in time with the life-support system that pumped air into his lungs, kept his heart beating and the blood sloshing around; and all the tubes going in and out of him, and the steady bleeps and bouncing little lights of the machines telling him that George was still alive.

Jimmy had promised himself, and everyone else, that

he wouldn't visit his old friend until he was out of hospital. In his bed or in his garden at home, where he was sure he would be soon, with George immediately contravening doctor's orders and smoking one of his big cigars and enjoying three fingers of Johnnie Walker Blue Label, if Jimmy knew George. But he'd come here today to tell him something. And he was just about to say it when—

'Jimmy?'

Drake turned round and saw Melody Price framed in the doorway. She was dressed in her full-length fur coat, the finest Russian sable. God knows how many of the poor little sods have copped it to keep her in style like Lady Muck, thought the clerk, as she stepped into the room.

Melody looked at her husband, sort of peering over at him, almost as you would peer into a coffin. She had an expression of blank impassiveness that could, at a push, charitably pass as some sort of wifely stoicism. But then again, Jimmy couldn't quite fully condemn her, either, as he wasn't big on emotional displays himself.

She took a deep breath and shook her head. Almost as if she was disappointed in George, for having the temerity to get himself shot and then just lie about in bed all day; like those lazy scroungers he was always railing against on the news when the unemployment figures hit new record highs.

She eventually backed up what Jimmy was thinking by saying, 'It seems strange seeing him like this. It's just . . . it's just not George, is it?'

Drake felt compelled to agree with her. He'd never known George to miss a day's racing through illness. He couldn't even remember him having a cold, never mind a hospital stay.

'He's so full of life,' she continued. 'I didn't think anything would stop him.'

'He'll soon be up and about.'

She lifted her eyes from the plight of her husband and focused them on Jimmy. 'I'm surprised to find you here. I called your house and your wife said you were visiting George. I thought it was another George, what with you saying you'd never visit him in hospital.'

'You know my wife's name, it's Maureen, always has been ever since you've known her, but you never call her it.' Jimmy went to get up. 'I'll leave you and your *husband* to it.'

'Don't go, Jimmy, it's you I've come to see.'

There was another chair for Melody to sit in, but she chose not to. She stood on the other side of the bed, her hands buried in the fur-coat pockets. Unsmiling, in fact, with a practised expression of withering contempt on her face. It was somehow fitting that they were on opposite sides, with George in the middle. Jimmy had felt this way for some time, ever since he'd found out what Melody was really up to.

'Traitor!'

'What are you bloody talking about?'

'You were spotted,' said Melody. 'Talking to the police.'

'Saturday?'

She nodded bleakly.

'The same one you were talking to earlier – Inspector Frost. Nice fella, terrible luck with the horses. I gave him some tips.'

'I don't think he'll thank you for it. Someone coshed him over the head in the car park and stole all his winnings.'

Jimmy Drake glanced towards George Price, and wondered for a moment if he could hear this conversation. He'd been talking to him earlier, convinced that he could.

'Going to the races is turning into a dangerous business, Melody.'

'Maybe you should retire, find quieter pursuits.'

Drake returned the cold smile, with interest on top.

'What did Frost ask you, Jimmy, and what did you say?'

'What's it got to do with you?'

Melody bristled at this. 'I'm George's wife and a partner in the business. Your *boss*.'

Jimmy let out a contemptuous crack of laughter at that one.

Her eyes blazed. 'If you said anything to the police, I need to know.'

He offered up an insouciant shrug, and pulled another grape from the stem, a stem that was now looking as depleted as a late-autumn oak.

'Did Frost mention a notebook?'

'A little black book? Might have.' Jimmy watched her closely. He knew when a thoroughbred filly was spooked, and Melody was all those things. 'What's that got to do with you?'

'I'm a concerned wife, who just wants to know—'

'Oh, is that what you are—'

'Don't talk to me like that. I'm running the show now, and you'd do well to remember that.'

Jimmy took out his box of Hamlet cigars and peeled the cellophane off one.

'You can't smoke in here.'

'I'm not staying,' said Drake. 'I know what's got your knickers in a twist. You're worried in case I mentioned something to Inspector Frost about horse fixing.'

'What are you talking about?'

He laughed again incredulously, but it quickly subsided, leaving nothing but rancour in his voice. 'Don't take me for a mug, Melody. I've been in the game too long. I know when the fix is on. I'm the one who writes down the numbers, remember. I know when a horse goes from short to long for no good reason other than it's been fixed. I hear things. And I know that's what you've been up to with your . . . *friends*.'

'You're slandering me, and you're slandering George. How dare you!'

'I've known George longer than anyone, apart from Harry Baskin maybe, and I know that whatever George is and George isn't, he's not a cheat. Not when it comes to horse racing. There's no way that George would have anything to do with fixed races. Because he loves the game, and if he gets caught he's finished, it's over, they'll ban him from every racecourse in the country – for life.

205

And that's why he's been so unhappy this last month or so, with that hanging over his head.'

'You're fired! I'm retiring you.'

'Too late, love. That's why I've come here today, to tell George I'm handing in my notice, as they say. I quit. The George Price I know wouldn't have got involved with horse fixing, because he knows that we can beat the punters fair and square, so we don't have to rob them!'

Jimmy stood up so fast that he felt light-headed, and it took a moment for the blood to catch up and fill his cheeks again.

'No, now I'm even more worried, Jimmy, and not about what you've already told Frost, but about what you're going to tell him. But it will be my word against yours. And the way I see it, it's just a vicious rumour spread by a bitter ex-employee. Jack will believe me, not you.'

Drake gave her a breezy couldn't-care-less smile. 'Don't worry, I didn't tell him anything, and I wouldn't. Because I know that when George wakes up, he'll come to his senses and he'll have nothing to with it, or your pals.'

The dapper clerk stuck the cigar in his mouth and lit up; his rosy cheeks ventilated the stogie as efficiently as the machine George Price was on, until he had a mouthful of smoke that he was able to expertly dispatch in the direction of the patient. The pungent cloud seemed to hang in the air and settle under George's nose. Jimmy swore he could see his old friend's nostrils twitch and an imperceptible smile flicker across his lips. George loved his cigars, even the cheap ones that Jimmy favoured.

206

Jimmy took up his green snapbrim fedora, fixed it to his head and said defiantly, 'Top of the morning to you.'

Melody Price got the message, and matched his defiant look. Out in the corridor, Jimmy gave a nod to Harry Baskin's man watching over George. Bad Manners Bob now had a bandage around his bald head, but the burly bouncer still looked more than capable of protecting his charge.

'I don't know what to say, Cathy . . . I'm so sorry.'

On seeing DS John Waters, Cathy Bartlett collapsed in his arms and sobbed. It was mid-afternoon and she was standing in the corridor of the County morgue. Her sixteen-year-old son, Dean, had been pronounced dead that morning, and she now faced the terrible task of identifying his body. Dr Maltby suspected that Dean had succumbed to catastrophic organ failure after a heroin overdose. It was likely that there was a bad batch of the narcotic in the area – either too strong, too pure, or cut with something deadly. The post-mortem and the toxicology reports would tell them.

Waters, with the help of a WPC and an orderly, got Cathy to the relatives' room. The orderly ferried in some hot teas for them, and Cathy, after a while, appeared to regain her composure. In fact, Waters was surprised by just how determined she became not to cry any more, or fall to pieces, as was surely her right.

Cathy Bartlett was thirty-four years old, petite and slim, with her long crinkly brown hair pulled back off her face in a bun. She was wearing a blue uniform tunic from the supermarket she worked in as a cashier. A life of hard work and struggling against a tide of bad luck had done its best to diminish her good looks, but had failed. The supermarket job she had was only half the story; she was in her final year of a part-time degree at the local poly.

In his time with the residents of the Southern Housing Estate, Waters had got to know two lads in particular, Gavin Ross and Dean Bartlett. They were both only children from single-parent homes, and had mums who made every effort to keep their kids on track for a better future. In this respect, the two boys reminded Waters of his own background; his mother was also a single parent who had worked hard not to lose her son to the streets. It was seeing his friends and family fall into that life of crime that had deepened the resolve his mother had instilled in him, that had made him choose his path.

So when he'd first seen Cathy he'd also had tears in his eyes. But now he would take his cue from her.

'Did you find him, John?' she asked, using his first name without hesitation.

'Yes.'

He'd been in his car early that morning, at the end of a night's surveillance of the tower block that Tommy Wilkins lived in, when there was a sharp rap of little knuckles on the window. He turned to see three kids on BMXs, and they looked scared or excited, he couldn't tell which. Waters got out and followed them to the top floor of one of the nearby blocks; there was a young lad slumped in the stairwell. It was presumably the first time the kids had seen a dead body, hence their mixture of emotions.

There was the usual drug paraphernalia: the bent teaspoon, the syringe. Dean Bartlett was on his knees, doubled over, his arms spread out in front of him. There was blood on the floor, and blood on his fingertips. It looked like he was trying to claw his way through the concrete floor, tunnel his way out of the pain and misery he'd just condemned himself to.

'I had no idea he was on anything, no idea at all.'

'I know, Cathy.' John Waters took a deep breath, as right now it was the last thing he wanted to ask, but it was also the most necessary: 'But I need to know, do you know who's dealing it?'

She gave a weary shake of her head, as if that was all she'd been thinking about. 'If I knew, if I had names, I would have told you the other day. I could suggest a load of people who *might* be dealing it, but you probably know them too, right?'

Waters matched her weary gesture.

'But none for sure. I've got no proof, haven't actually seen anyone, heard no definite names. It was just a rumour that heroin was on the estate. To be honest, even at the meeting I didn't think it would . . .' her voice trembled, '. . . it would affect us. I thought maybe it was just people panicking because it's been on the TV so much. And I certainly didn't think Dean would ever . . . would ever try it. He wasn't like that. He'd never been interested in drugs, especially anything like heroin, it would have scared the life out of him.'

'How about Gavin?'

Cathy Bartlett drew in a deep steady breath as she considered this, as if wanting to phrase what she thought very carefully. 'If it would be anyone, it would be Gavin. He was always the one to try things first. The more outgoing kid . . . but . . . but you know as well as I do, where Gavin went, Dean followed. Eventually.'

Waters did know that: the pair had been best mates, for all of their young lives. They were always together; they'd even planned on going to college together, to do the same course, to train as electricians. Dean may very well have injected it for the first time, but, considering the result, that seemed irrelevant. Waters suspected that Dean's best friend had been present, or certainly knew about it. Shooting heroin, for a first-timer like Dean, would be a two-man job, and would involve someone who had done it before. Did Gavin lead the way – did he give Dean the lethal fix?

Cathy Bartlett wrapped her arms around herself as if a cold gust had just blown into the room. She began a slow rocking motion on the edge of her chair, then grabbed at the tissues sprouting out of the box on the table. She lost the battle to contain the pain she was feeling, and from her red-rimmed eyes the tears began to fall again.

'My baby boy . . . such a waste . . . such a . . .'

Tuesday (1)

Jimmy Drake took his tea and plate of Bourbon biscuits into the living room for his elevenses and set them down on the side table next to his favourite chintz-covered armchair. He was still in his woollen striped dressing gown, and at this time of day it felt totally decadent. He could hear his wife upstairs, fussing about, as he liked to call it.

Usually when he opened his copy of the *Daily Express* his hands automatically went to the racing section – but not today, he thought; today, instead of finding who's the favourite for the three-thirty at Doncaster, I'll find out what's actually happening in the world, and not just in the hermetically sealed one of racing. Jimmy and all his friends were 'racing men', and all racing men ever talked about was the little world they inhabited: horses, horse racing, the dogs, football results, cricket scores, snooker games, egg and spoon races, in fact, just about any activity you could gamble on.

211

But no more, Jimmy promised himself. Now he'd . . . *retired* . . . he was determined that life would open up to him. He would read books, see more films, go to the theatre, get into London more, take his grandkids places, the Natural History Museum for starters, watch their faces light up in awe as they set eyes on the Diplodocus in the entrance hall. Today's the first day of the rest of my life, he told himself.

'Here, sign this,' said his wife, entering the living room with a birthday card in her hand.

'Who's it for?'

'Malcolm.'

Jimmy took the card, and saw it had a picture of an old 1930s Bentley racing car on it. He really didn't know the significance that held for his son-in-law, who was thirty-six today, drove a Volvo, and worked in insurance. Jimmy signed the card without much enthusiasm and handed it back to his wife, Maureen.

'What are you going to do today?' she prompted.

'Sit here.'

'All day?'

'No, not all day. I'll probably go down the Winchester later.'

She pursed her lips, gave a hollow laugh, and then shook her head. It was a medley of reactions that Jimmy took as criticism.

'Well, it is my day off.'

He hadn't told his wife that he had . . . *retired*. He would, sometime this week, but he just couldn't face broaching the subject with Maureen today. She wasn't stupid, she knew that Jimmy couldn't retire. That was another thing about racing men, they all died on the racecourse. Popped their clogs with heart attacks in the excitement of seeing their horse sprinting for the winning post, or keeled over with despair when they lost, or sometimes burst their livers in the bar – win, lose or draw. But racing men didn't retire.

So Jimmy said that they were taking the day off, out of respect for George, knowing that Maureen would smell a rat, and that rat would be Melody Price. Maureen despised Melody. She had the younger woman pegged as a gold-digger the moment she clapped eyes on her, and Melody's behaviour over the intervening couple of years or so had not assuaged that opinion. So Jimmy would tell Maureen later – right now he just wanted to relax, and enjoy the first day of the rest of his life, as he kept telling himself.

'All right, love, I'm off, and remember, Janice and the kids are popping around later.'

Jimmy smiled – his grandkids, now that was something to look forward to.

'So don't eat all the biscuits.'

'I won't. See you later.'

She bent down and kissed the top of his head and left. As the front door closed behind her, the newspaper fell open at the racing section. And Jimmy's eye automatically lit on the runners and riders at Catterick, and one horse in particular that he fancied. And he knew that it would be a day in front of the telly, watching the racing, probably having a bet or three, if he could be bothered to drag himself to the local bookie's. His feet stretched out and landed on the pouffe with a practised ease, and he let out a satisfied sigh. *The first day of the rest of my life.*

The phone rang. Jimmy groaned and hauled himself out of his armchair and padded into the hallway. Each trill of the phone was met with a muttered curse, at the sheer inconvenience of having to get up when he didn't want to.

He picked the receiver off the cradle and barked, 'Hello.'

He heard the pips go, then the voice: 'Jimmy? It's me. I need to talk to you.'

There was a long pause.

'It's me—'

'Yes, I know who it is. What do you want?'

'Can we meet up, Jimmy?'

'Most irregular, don't you think?'

'I just need a quick word, in private?'

'It's really none of my business. In fact, I don't want anything to do with it.'

'You don't think—'

'I don't know what I think. All I know is, I'm out. And whatever will happen, will happen. The big fella, George, he's still with us. And I'm expecting a full recovery.'

'Please, Jimmy, I need to see you.'

There was another long pause.

'Her indoors has just gone out, be gone most of the day. Give it an hour or two. I'll meet you in the Winchester.'

'Perfect.'

'I'll see you then. *Socks*.'

There was some laboured breathing.

'How do you know?'

'I didn't know, it's a guess. But I know George, and I know his sense of humour. You just want to hope Jack Frost doesn't have the same one.'

The voice on the end started to formulate a reply, but the pips went and the line was dead.

'You all right, John?' Frost asked his friend and colleague, knowing of DS Waters' close association with Cathy and Dean Bartlett.

'I'm OK.'

'And now the most stupid bloody question in the world – how's Cathy?'

'I asked it myself. She's got her mates around, her sister's there.'

Waters was hovering in Frost's office. The two men hadn't sat down, because outside in the incident room the team were hard at it, and that's where they would soon be. Sitting down just didn't seem appropriate at the moment. Pacing around and thinking, keeping up the sense of urgency, now that did seem appropriate. Who had supplied the heroin? That was the question, the headline written up in big red capitals on the new incident board. Every known drug dealer, however low-key and whatever his merchandise, would be 'spun around' and made to know just how serious this was.

The name of Gavin Ross, also sixteen, was written up on the board – he hadn't been seen since Sunday night, and his mother was worried sick. Because of his age and vulnerability, there was a search party out looking for him.

'Guv?'

Frost lifted his eyes up from the stained carpet tiles to find Arthur Hanlon framed in the doorway.

'Don't you ever knock?'

Hanlon looked confused. 'It was open?'

'So find a bit of wood and knock! What?'

'I've got Frank Trafford down in Interview Room Two. He's with his brief, Sarah Hollis; she's a Legal Aid one. D'you want to see him?'

Frost blew out an exasperated breath – never enough time, never enough resources. 'You can handle it, take Clarke with you if she's available – but don't be all day about it.'

Hanlon gave a nod and disappeared from view. Waters looked surprised that Frost wasn't doing the interview – he delegated as little as possible and always liked to hear things first-hand. The DI clocked his colleague's reaction and explained, 'It's a three-line whip from Hornrim Harry, all eyes on this case. I'm seen anywhere near the George Price shooting, guts for garters.'

'Never bothered you in the past.'

'Kid dead on drugs, and if it's a bad batch on the estate, there could well be more to follow him. For once I can see his point. Anyway, Arthur's a big boy, he can handle it.'

'And getting bigger every day.'

A knock on the doorframe broke through their much-needed laughter.

216

'What the bloody hell is it now, Arthur?' Frost glanced over to the doorway and saw the curvaceous and far more appealing figure of Eve Hayward standing there.

'Jack, is there any chance of that word now?'

Frost turned to Waters and muttered, 'The second most stupid question in the world.'

'I'm really sorry, but I'd like to discuss the counterfeit-goods operation in your area.'

'Now's not the time.'

'I understand. But I think I can—'

'Sorry, Inspector Hayward, I know you have a job to do, but I've got a kid dead from a heroin overdose, and I can tell you straight off that I'm not remotely interested in knock-off copies of *Risky Business* or Gucci baseball caps.'

Eve Hayward shot back, 'And what if I told you I could prove a link between the two – the heroin and the knock-off goods?'

'I'd probably say something along the lines of . . . *prove it.*'

Tuesday (2)

'I went round to see Cathy . . . but her sister said she wasn't seeing anyone. I was relieved. I'm her best friend and I was relieved she didn't want to see me. Does that sound terrible?'

John Waters gave an understanding shake of his head – it didn't sound terrible at all to him. The raw grief of a mother who's just lost her child is overwhelming for anyone. He was in the living room of Ella Ross, the mother of Gavin. The room was compact and perfectly kept. There were lots of ferns and rubber plants in bright pots that Ella had decorated herself, and what looked like modern art framed up on the walls, in bold primary colours, but on closer inspection they'd been painted by Gavin, with his name and age, $7\frac{1}{2}$, in the corner. There were photos dotted around the room, and some of them showed Gavin with Dean, and in some Cathy was present too, like one big, happy extended family.

218

Waters reached into his jacket pocket and took out his notebook and pen. Ella Ross took a measured breath, as if the notebook and pen represented a frightening new reality. Her son Gavin was missing, he hadn't returned home since Sunday night. On Monday morning first thing, Ella hadn't thought to report Gavin missing as he often stayed over with a friend. Then at lunchtime she heard about Dean. And by the end of Monday, she knew something was definitely wrong. Gavin hadn't turned up at school. So she'd phoned the police.

She was about to call them again when the phone rang – it was John Waters, to tell her he was on his way to see her.

'Sunday afternoon. It was about five-thirty.'

Waters gave her a questioning look.

'Sorry, I thought you were going to ask when I last saw Gavin. That's usually the first question, isn't it?'

'Usually, yeah. So where was that?'

'Here. I'd just got in. Gavin rushed out when he saw me. He's been doing that a lot lately.'

'Where did he say he was going?'

'To play football.'

'You don't sound convinced that he was.'

'If he was, it was just in the streets, because he didn't have his football kit or boots with him. One thing is for sure, if Dean was messing with drugs, Gavin was too.' She gave a heartbreaking sigh. 'That's why Cathy doesn't want to see me. She knows the pair of them as well as I do. That's why, if anything like this was going to happen, I'd have sworn it would be Gavin.'

219

Waters heard the quake in Ella's voice. He couldn't tell whether it was grief, fear, or relief that it wasn't Gavin who'd been found in the stairwell. It was probably a combination of all three, with some guilt thrown into the mix as well.

'Had you noticed any changes in him?'

'He'd snapped at me a couple of times, a bit short-tempered lately, but I just put that down to him being sixteen. But when he wasn't out he was spending more time in his room. Which wasn't like him, there's only one TV in the flat . . . maybe he was listening to his Walkman. Apart from that, he seemed normal enough. He's got exams coming up soon. Wants to go to college. Determined, he is.'

John Waters smiled. 'I bet.'

There was a pause, and Ella's gaze turned towards the window, where there were brightly coloured drapes that let in the light but made the view of the grey blocks of the Southern Housing Estate just a little more agreeable.

'I've heard the rumours that it's out there . . . on the estate. I asked Gavin about it, but he said he hadn't heard anything.'

'You know who?'

Ella shook her head. 'Usually you hear things, but I haven't heard who's actually dealing it. It's like everyone's too scared to talk. And someone is making them scared.'

John Waters wrote that down verbatim and under-lined it.

*

220

'How was the flight?'

'Short and sweet,' said Eamon 'The Hook' Hogan, as he eased himself into the back of the black BMW. Eamon had got the nickname 'The Hook' from his early years as a boxer: as a handy middleweight in his youth he could soak up punishment for the first few rounds, and then get them with the one left hook. The left hook became legendary. But he'd been cultivating it for years – long before he'd stepped into a boxing ring, he was exploiting its formidable power on the streets of Dublin, and on the Finglas estates in particular, ever since he first knocked out another boy at the age of eleven. The boy he knocked out was four years older, about five stone heavier and a good foot taller than young Eamon. From that day on, Hogan never took another backward step and his reputation soared.

There were lots of apocryphal stories out there about him that he hadn't denied or corroborated; let them talk, let them exaggerate, it all added to the myths and the legend that men in his line of work needed to cement their position.

Eamon Hogan retired from the ring aged twenty-one with some silverware and some prize money. And although he'd been considered a real contender, there just wasn't enough cold hard cash in it for his liking. He was always drawing a lot of publicity, publicity he began to feel he could well do without. As other 'opportunities' presented themselves he didn't like seeing his face in the papers; it just wasn't good for business.

But even though he hadn't laced a pair of boxing

221

gloves in anger for twenty years, the moniker of The Hook had stuck; it had just taken on a new meaning, and a darker purpose. But then he dropped it. Though it's seldom within the recipient's power to drop a nickname, he never heard anyone call him that again to his face once he'd let it be known that he didn't like it. But every now and again it cropped up in newspaper headlines, when a rival was found slumped over his steering wheel with a bullet in the back of the head, or a body was dredged from the Liffey, or a dismembered corpse was discovered in the boot of a car at Dublin airport's long-stay car park. Then The Hook was summoned up as part of an ongoing gangland feud.

Eamon was happy to see Colm and Shane: they were two of his most trusted lieutenants. They'd grown up together in Finglas and been with him from the start. And now that he was 'expanding', as he preferred to call it, and moving part of his business over to England, they were perfect for the work of setting up the operation. Infiltrating the existing provincial underworld and showing them what real gangsters looked like. And Denton was perfect for Hogan's purposes.

Colm reached into his jacket pocket, pulled out a small velvet bag and handed it to Eamon. He took a peek inside and saw fifteen brilliant-cut diamonds sparkling away.

'This is from the jewellery job.'

Eamon grinned and handed him back the bag. 'Nice. *Very* nice.'

'And there's more of that where it came from,' said Colm.

Eamon nodded his approval. 'Sounds good to me, lads, as long as it doesn't interfere with the main event. How's it going?'

'We made our presence felt, told them what we expected of them, and now it's up and running. As far as punters are concerned, we've had a single casualty. The gear we sold was too strong, so we're gonna make some adjustments.'

Eamon shrugged. 'Mess with drugs, that's what happens. They're the ones buying it, not me.'

It was said with a coldness that left a deep silence in the car. Colm and Shane nodded along to their boss's sentiments. Not just because he was the boss, but because it's what they wanted to hear. His words absolved them. They were in a supply-and-demand business, they told themselves. But all three of them knew that by selling the drugs dirt cheap, they were the ones creating the demand. And when the 'demand' rose, so would the price of the heroin. That's how it worked. A fail-safe business model.

'It's Melody I'm worried about,' said Eamon. 'She thinks we did it, you know that?'

Shane said, 'The minute I heard what had happened, I contacted her, said it wasn't us.'

Eamon weighed this up. 'Well, it doesn't matter what you said, she doesn't believe us. I know George Price was a flash bastard, proved difficult in the past, but he was playing along now, thanks to Melody. So I'll ask this only once: did you twose shoot him?'

Almost in unison both men said no and swore their

223

innocence. Colm added, 'Melody had him wrapped around her little finger, he'd have done anything for her. There was no profit in us doing anything to harm him.'

Shane said, 'We're looking for whoever did it, and when we find him, we'll take his head off.'

'Any clues?' asked Eamon.

'The police reckon it was some rival bookie.'

Colm agreed. 'He was in love with Melody apparently, crime of passion, they're calling it.'

Eamon gave a knowing laugh; fellas falling in love with Melody was no surprise to him. He cautioned, 'OK, well, if that's what it is, there's no need for us to get involved. Leave it to the police. I need to sort this out with Melody as soon as possible. Hell hath no fury like a woman scorned, right, lads?'

The lads agreed.

Tuesday (3)

Frost and Sue Clarke eased themselves into one of the six red vinyl-covered booths that lined the walls of the Pellerocco Café. The menus on the light-blue speckled Formica tables informed them that breakfast was still being served, before the dishes listed got all Italian. Frost's favourite of these was the spaghetti with meatballs in a rich 'secret sauce', but it was no secret that it had plenty of strong vino in it. Angelo, the owner, full of Mediterranean bonhomie and chatting away in broken English, would grate the fresh Parmesan over your bowl at the table, to try to staunch the alcohol fumes rising up from the food. Very little work was ever achieved after a spag and meatball lunch at the Pellerocco.

It was Angelo's unsmiling wife who took their orders: two bacon sandwiches and teas.

'Why here, the canteen's cheaper?' Clarke wondered.

Frost said, 'I prefer the levels of grease in here. The

new salad bar at the canteen is having a negative effect, corrupting everything, all the grub is getting so disgustingly fat-free and healthy. I suspect it's another of Hornrim Harry's stupider initiatives. By the way, good work on getting that bullet.'

'It was just there. No big deal.'

Frost tutted. 'Take credit for your work, or someone else will. Look at young DC Kevin Perks in Robbery, he takes credit for everything and makes sure I hear about it. Sometimes I think he thinks I'm deaf, the way he repeats everything to me, and very loudly. But as unsubtle and annoying as it is, it gets him noticed. He doesn't hide his light under a bushel. There's no profit in being humble, not if you want to make sergeant.'

Sue Clarke considered this. 'Thanks for the heads-up, Jack.'

'I want you to stay with the George Price case – we switch off and we'll lose him.'

'Unfortunate turn of phrase.'

'Eh? Oh, yeah. You know what I mean. Maybe that's the problem, if the poor sod was switched off it would probably get higher priority. But stick with Socks and Winston, see what you find.'

The bacon sarnies and teas arrived. Frost asked for ketchup as there was none on the table. Angelo's still unsmiling wife reluctantly obliged with a squeezy plastic tomato, but gave them disapproving looks like they were committing some culinary crime.

'Eve Hayward, she seems very proficient. What do you know about her?'

226

Clarke smiled. 'This is why we're here, away from the prying ears of the rest of Eagle Lane. What have you heard?'

'I'm asking you?'

'If it's about what I told Arthur, then I was only joking—'

'What did you tell Arthur?'

'Nothing, just a stupid joke. I know Eve Hayward is single, if that's what you want to know.'

Frost stayed deadly serious. 'No, it isn't. I want to know what she's up to.'

'She's with the counterfeit-goods unit—'

'So she says.'

Clarke was about to take a bite of her sarnie, then stopped. 'What's that supposed to mean?'

'How about she's part of an anti-corruption team out to nail coppers? I don't know for sure, you never do with those slippery sods – until it's too late. But she seems to be asking a lot of questions about everyone in our unit. I know you've spent time with her, what has she asked you?'

Clarke put her bacon sandwich back on her plate, and looked like she was giving it some serious thought, as her mind scrolled back over the time she'd spent with Eve Hayward. 'Yeah, you're right, she does ask a lot of questions. She also knows a lot of stuff.'

'Thought so. About what?'

'Stuff she asks about, or stuff she knows?'

'Both.'

She shrugged. 'About everything, you can't really put

227

your finger on it. She just comes across as dead confident. Seems to know everything we're up to, makes it all seem like simple deduction.'

'That's probably because she does know everything, has a big file on all of us and the cases we're working.'

'I don't doubt she's with the counterfeit-goods unit, though.'

'I do. I've never heard of anything like that.'

'They're based at West End Central.'

'Yeah? Good for them. Handy for the shops, I suppose.' Frost's voice dripped cynicism the way his bacon sarnie was dripping grease. 'Let's face it, the only time we ever hear about counterfeit goods is when something danger-ous turns up. You know the sort of thing: a kid's toy with a ruddy great metal spike sticking out of it, aftershave that burns your skin off. And even then they usually just send a memo around. But with this one, Eve Hayward, I smell a rat. Has she been asking things about me?'

'You think she's running a check on Eagle Lane?'

'Could be, we've not had a visit for a while – a good ten years.'

'Even if she is, we've got nothing to hide, and we're all on the same side, right?'

'Don't kid yourself, sweetheart, they're after results like the rest of us.'

Clarke pushed her plate away. Frost repeated his question about whether Hayward had been asking about him.

'Not really, not directly. But I'll be honest, we have spoken about you.'

'What did you say?'

'How handsome and clever you are.'

'Funny.'

'I don't know, Jack . . . nothing bad. All good. If she is PSD she's very clever and good at what she does. Because she'll talk around a subject, get you to open up about things. I've told her everything about the George Price case. She seemed interested, especially in the horse-racing angle. And what with Michael Price working in the video shop, she was looking for a connection there with pirated videos.'

'Oh yes, she's looking for connections everywhere, and she might well be right,' said Frost as he soaked up the rust-coloured pool of grease on his plate with the crust of his sandwich and snaffled it down. 'OK. Well, no one's done anything wrong or got anything to hide. So, we don't have anything to worry about.'

'Who else knows?'

'No one. Because it's not a rock-solid fact yet, just a hunch, a gut feeling. Talking about gut feelings' – Frost aimed a nicotine-stained forefinger at Clarke's barely dented bacon sarnie – 'you finished with that?'

She made a face like the stained forefinger was enough to put her off food for life. 'Be my guest,' she said, over her mug of tea. 'Oh, Frank Trafford, you read his statement?'

'I had a quick peruse. Says at the time of the shooting he was walking home from Radleigh races. Which would have taken him in the opposite direction from the shooting, through the woods and over the hills, leaving him up shit creek without an alibi or witnesses to his whereabouts. Right?'

'That's about it. You still want me to set up an ID parade with him?'

'If we can get enough blokes with dodgy 'taches to join him.'

'Tell you what, though, since his wife left him, he's really gone downhill, I reckon. Arthur said the house was a real mess, beer bottles all over the place, chicken shit all over the carpet, and what with her being a cleaner—'

'*Chicken* shit?'

'Yeah, he keeps chickens in his back garden. He must have left the back door open. Place stank, Arthur said, it was all over the carpet, the sofa . . .'

Frost laughed. 'Don't bother with the ID parade.'

'Why?'

'Aye, aye! Fancy seeing you here, Signor Jack Frost, the *capo di tutti capi* of crime solving!'

Frost glanced around to locate the owner of the voice he'd recognized. It was Sandy Lane, the chief crime reporter at the *Denton Echo*. Sandy had a nose for sniffing out a good story, as good as any of the sleaziest red-top hacks. And he had a red nose to prove it, where the booze had fired up his face with a beaming display of burst capillaries. He firmly believed that hanging around pubs was more profitable than hanging around newsrooms waiting for the phone to ring – that's where good stories lurked, and so did Sandy, nursing his three fingers of Scotch with just the lightest of touches of soda water.

230

Before Sandy Lane could take a seat, Frost winked at Clarke and muttered that he'd tell her why later. Sue got the message and sidled out of the booth. 'I'll leave you two, err, um, gentlemen to it. I've work to do.'

Sandy Lane upped the broadness of his Italian accent. '*Bella donna*, don't leave on my behalf, love, I'm always looking for the woman's side of the story.'

'Thank God we're not in an Indian restaurant, Sandy, or you'd be doing your best *It Ain't Half Hot Mum*.' She left the café.

The hack took her seat opposite Frost.

The DI glanced at his watch. 'Shouldn't you be queuing up outside a pub door by now?'

Sandy Lane dropped the accent and got serious. 'Any more news on the George Price shooting, or is Terry Langdon still the headline?'

'The jeweller's job in Rimmington, that's your headline, surely.'

'It was yesterday. Don't you read the papers, Jack?'

'Not yours. Not if I can help it.'

'No skin off my nose. The Rimmington job looks like a London team, the way they set it up with the van.'

'Rimmington's not my patch.'

'You know why I'm here, Jack. Don't you want to be front-page news? A young lad from the estate ODs. That's the headline.'

Frost lost his appetite. He peeled off some napkins from the holder and ran them around his chin and his hands, then scrunched them up and dropped them on his plate. Conversation over.

231

'The nationals are going to be down here, they'll be all over it. Drugs, it's the plague. We'll be like America soon. Tell me what you want to say, Jack, I'll get it out there before you've got Mullett orchestrating one of his press conferences.'

'You want an exclusive, right?'

'I'll take an "anonymous source" from Denton CID.'

'Really?'

'I've got kids too.'

Frost's eyes narrowed on Lane, searching for a glint of sincerity beneath the hack's hardened cynicism. He must have seen something, because he then grabbed another napkin from the dispenser, reached over and plucked a pen from the breast pocket of Sandy's shiny blazer, and began to write on the napkin.

'That's my job, isn't it?'

Frost ignored him and carried on writing. When he stopped, he folded the napkin and stuck it in the blazer breast pocket, like a smart silk square.

'There you go, stick that where the sun don't shine – otherwise known as your front page.' Frost slid out of the booth and exited the café.

Sandy Lane took out the napkin and read it. After a moment or so, the hack smiled – he couldn't have put it better himself. Just the one spelling mistake, a slip of the pen, really. His rheumy eyes then darted about the table as he exclaimed, 'He's nicked my bloody pen!' Just at that moment Angelo's unsmiling wife approached the table and presented the hack with a bill for the detectives' teas and bacon sarnies.

232

Tuesday (4)

Jimmy Drake would be sat at the bar of the Winchester Club, where he could be found most days when he wasn't at the races. It was Jimmy's local, and very accessible, day or night. He just stepped out of the kitchen door, or through the lounge's French windows, and walked down to the bottom of the garden, and he was there.

The Winchester Club was Jimmy's garden shed. His brother-in-law, a local builder, had converted it into a bar. Inside the shed was a polished wooden counter with everything you'd expect to find in a regular pub: a big china ashtray advertising Watneys Red Barrel, a Johnnie Walker water jug, Skol beer mats, bags of KP nuts, and three stools in front of it. Behind the bar were mirrored shelves offering every type of spirit you could want, as long as it was either whisky or gin, and there was a small fridge stocked with beers. The rest of the furnishings were made up of a green baize-covered card table with four foldaway chairs neatly tucked under it, and a portable TV on a shelf in the corner. Almost every inch of wall space was taken up with framed photos of Jimmy and his friends and colleagues at the races over the years. Some dated as far back as the 1940s when Drake was just starting out; it was a photographic history of Jimmy and George Price at the races, taking them from flash young Herberts to grizzled old-timers.

The Winchester Club was strictly members only, and like in the TV series that had inspired the garden-shed transformation, 'her indoors' seldom ventured into it. And as promised, that's where he found Jimmy. At the bar, looking at the paper, with the racing on TV. Jimmy turned round to greet him. But it wasn't much of a greeting. In fact, Drake just looked disappointed. He couldn't blame him for looking at him like that, he was feeling it acutely himself. A sense of shame. But he really didn't need it from Jimmy. A man he'd known for a long time, a man he liked.

But, of course, Jimmy didn't know the full story. Just how far he'd fallen, just how bad things had got. Drake didn't have a clue. If he had, he probably wouldn't have agreed to meet up with him. But he knew it was too late, and Jimmy's opinion of his character didn't really matter now. When you're in this deep, just getting to the other side of it, getting away with it, that's all that matters. And you'll do whatever is necessary. And anyway, he wasn't going to take morality lessons off a bookie's clerk. Sure, he'd take responsibility for his

234

actions, but for all their jocular banter, for all their bonhomie and apparent friendship, in many ways they were the ones who'd got him into this bloody mess in the first place, who kept letting him play. But only he could get himself out of it now.

'What can I get you?'

'I'll have a Scotch, please, Jimmy. Splash of water.'

'Of course you will, a wee dram of Glenfiddich, never a drop of Bushmills, right?'

He nodded. And Drake got up and went behind the bar to pour the drinks. It was never too much trouble for Jimmy to fix people a drink. He enjoyed doing it, enjoyed playing the host, enjoyed playing the role of Dave, the real Winchester Club barman in *Minder*, as much as he enjoyed playing Arthur Daley, its most famous patron.

He'd sat here so many times before with Jimmy and George, watching the racing, having a bet, George being the bookie, and him being the punter, whilst Jimmy served them drinks. Or sat at the card table playing gin rummy, and not for the peanuts on the bar either. It all seemed like harmless fun, even though there was a price to pay – which he did. And then it got out of hand. And then it got dangerous.

Jimmy poured the Scotch and said, 'Inspector Frost, he seems to think there was some significance in you and this "Winston" owing George money. And I have to say, when I saw the amount, I thought there was too. Who's Winston?'

He shook his head, like he didn't have a clue. Of

235

course, he didn't know if Jimmy believed him, but at this stage it didn't really matter. Jimmy's wife was gone for the day. No one knew he was here.

'Oh well, maybe it's best I don't know anyway. It's George's business, not mine. I'm just a humble clerk, a pen-pusher. And I've got faith that he'll be out of hospital soon. Then he'll sort it out.'

'What did you tell Frost?'

'I didn't tell him anything, obviously, or you probably wouldn't be sitting here. And at the time I wasn't sure who Socks was, not really, just guessing. I know now though, don't I?'

'Yes, you do.'

'But like I said, George will sort it out.'

'What if . . .?'

'If he doesn't make it out of hospital?' As he thought about the possibility, Jimmy was no longer the smiling congenial host, he was deadly serious. 'Then I'll tell Frost everything I know.'

'But like you said, Jimmy, you don't know anything.'

'That's true. But by closing time, or when you've had enough to drink, you'll have to tell me something. You understand?'

'I understand.'

Drake handed him the drink. He took a deep swig, followed by two more in quick succession, and then finished it off with a throaty and satisfied 'Ah'. He needed that. He needed the courage, the Dutch courage, as they say, the bottle. He couldn't help but feel the cruel irony of who was providing him with it.

236

'I'll have another, please.'

Drake, like a good, non-judgemental barman, obliged, and turned his back to him to fill his glass from the optic.

From the pocket of his Burberry he pulled out a length of thin orange nylon rope and lunged forward to secure it around Jimmy's neck. The glass fell. Drake tried to say something, some words were formed, but he wasn't listening. He yanked Jimmy back, pulling him down on to the bar, his hands in the leather driving gloves pulling the rope around Jimmy's neck with a powerful force, cutting through the layers of his loose flesh so he could feel the sinew and muscle and, eventually, the bone of Jimmy's neck. It was a sickening feeling, and a sickening sight. So he closed his eyes.

There was nothing Jimmy could do. The man strangling him to death was younger, bigger and stronger. His body just didn't have the speed, agility or energy to put up a fight and remained passive to the end.

There was the sound of breaking glass as the bar shook and spilt its load. He could hear the last gasps leaving Jimmy's body, as you'd hear the air leaving a bicycle tyre with a diminishing hiss. And he could feel it too, his life leaving his body.

He released his grip and heard the muffled thump as Jimmy dropped to the floor.

The man fell backwards and landed on the floor himself, just the other side of the bar from Jimmy's corpse. He sat on the floor and thought about what he'd done. But he'd had no choice. He didn't want to kill him, he'd called him up just to find out what he knew, what Jack

Frost had been asking him. But the minute Drake had called him Socks, sussed out who he was, he knew he had to die.

He carried on sitting there, exhausted, his arms numb, yet he could feel the strain move through them like an electric current. To end another man's life in that way, up close and personal so you could feel his last breath against your face, and hear the croak of the death rattle in his throat, takes something out of you, he thought. Something you'll never get back. He'd heard men talk about such things. For psychopaths it was the very act of killing someone in that fashion that was the point – the thrill, the buzz, the bloodlust, the obsession. To kill someone with a gun, without the physical contact, would seem pointless to such men: where was the fun in that? They needed to feel something. It was the difference between blowing out a candle from a distance, and snuffing it out with your hand and feeling it burn, with the hot liquid wax between your fingers – it felt good.

He got to his feet, raised his arms to the ceiling of the shed and stretched. It was like being reborn. And somehow feeling safer, more secure, content in the knowledge that he was now capable of anything, and that nothing could stand in his way.

'Shouldn't have any problem, not with your curves, Eve.'

'Let's just get it over with, shall we?'

DI Hayward was in her hotel room, standing on the carpet in her bra and panties. Tony Norton was kneeling before her.

238

'It's cold,' she said.

'It'll warm up.'

He was attaching the recording device to her diaphragm area. As potentially awkward as this situation was, Eve wouldn't have wanted anyone else bending down in front of her attaching a wire. Tony Norton was an undercover officer par excellence. He'd worn enough of these devices in some of the most dangerous situations to warrant Hayward's complete trust.

And as Tony had pointed out, getting wired for sound as safely as possible, to avoid detection, was all dependent on body shape. If you were skinny, the recording device was usually secured to the small of your back, or on the thigh. But still this was never a guarantee. Some criminals were adept at checking for devices. This they sometimes did with an over-the-top greeting, in the form of a lingering hug, like you were a long-lost brother or sister, where the undercover cop would feel hands all over them. Or sometimes they didn't trust you from the off, didn't believe you were who you were purporting to be, and they patted you down or asked you to strip off the minute you walked into a room. It was those occasions, rare as they were, that really tested an undercover copper's mettle, called into action their improvisation skills and ability to think on their feet. Working undercover was like being an actor – you took on a character, made it your own, believed it totally. And if you did get asked to strip off, it was because you hadn't rehearsed enough.

Tony Norton was deep cover, which meant only the immediate team and his superiors knew about him. He

239

would never have to reveal himself in a court of law, or stand up in public and give evidence, which allowed him to work more cases, and gave him a longer shelf life as an undercover officer. If evidence needed to be presented, then that's where Eve would come in.

'So, again, how do you know me?' asked Tony.

'We first met four years ago, ticket-touting at the FA Cup final.'

'Who was playing?'

'West Ham against Arsenal. West Ham ran out surprise winners in an otherwise dull match. Trevor Brooking got the only goal in a one–nil victory for the Hammers. Brooking scored with a header, which was an even bigger surprise than the victory.'

'Then?'

'We met up a couple of months later when we were both bringing cigarettes and booze over from France. Then I didn't see you for a year. And then—'

'Why didn't you see me for a year?'

'You were doing nine months at Her Majesty's pleasure.'

'What for?'

'You didn't tell me, and I didn't ask.'

Tony Norton muttered his approval. 'That's all they need to know if they ask. Anything else, tell them to mind their own business. Is it still cold?'

'No, it's warming up nicely.'

John Waters fiddled with the car stereo, trying to find a radio station that wasn't playing Michael Jackson's

'Thriller'. Arthur Hanlon was making short work of a Greggs jumbo sausage roll, and getting crumbs all over the upholstery. They were parked outside Clay House, a block of flats on the Southern Housing Estate, home to Billy 'Bomber' Harris, in a dun-coloured Allegro that Waters had picked up from the station car pool. After his recent handbrake turn that had got kids staring open-mouthed and net curtains twitching, he'd probably never be able to use his car on this patch again . . . Still, it had been worth it.

'Remind me why I'm here again?'

'A hunch.'

Hanlon gave a disapproving sigh.

'You don't believe in hunches?'

'I think as far as scumbag drug dealers go, if we suspect them, we should pull them in. Shake them up, steam in mob-handed, kick down some doors, let them know we're on to them.'

'They know that already, Arthur.' Waters nodded in the direction of the noticeboard at the entrance to Clay House, with its poster showing young Dean Bartlett and a reward for information on his death; it was just one of many that had been plastered around the estate. Uniformed officers had traipsed down every walkway and knocked on every door, handing out leaflets with the same information, and giving assurances that all phone calls would be treated in the strictest confidence. And every Denton panda car had been ordered to patrol the estate at least twice on its round. Even Waters, who was at times critical of where the manpower was directed,

241

and all too aware that the upmarket environs of North Denton were more visibly policed, was pleased with the amount of effort that had been put in, and was sure more was on the way.

Waters was about to explain all this to Hanlon, when his attention was suddenly taken by something deeply unpleasant splattered up the detective constable's trouser leg. 'What's that?'

Hanlon followed Waters' withering look of disgust. 'Bloody hell! It's dried chicken sh—'

'Don't wipe it off in here! What you doing with chickens?'

'Frost worked out that Frank Trafford did in fact have an alibi for the Price shooting. Kelso's farm reported some of their chickens were missing, nicked the afternoon of the shooting, between three and five p.m. Trafford said he was walking back home from the races about then, but there were no witnesses. To get home he had to pass Kelso's farm. Trafford had chickens at his house. I had to take the farmer to Trafford's to identify his hens. They were very excited to see him, they quite literally sh—'

'Thanks, Arthur, I get the picture. So, Trafford's now up on a chicken-rustling charge, and not attempted murder. Good for him, and clever Jack Frost. That's what you call using your egg.'

'Yeah, and now I'm cooped up in here.'

'Oh, mate . . . that's a rotten yolk.'

'Cracked me up.'

The detectives stopped laughing when a white Peugeot 205 screeched up in front of them. Three men

242

got out of the car. One of them was instantly recognizable. It was Tommy Wilkins, this time favouring a lime-green Sergio Tacchini tracksuit and with his arm still in a sling. His two cohorts were dressed in the same 'casual' football-hooligan attire. They looked around them, searching for coppers probably, and then swaggered their way into Clay House.

'Flash bastards!' hissed Hanlon. 'We should nick them just for their dress sense. And those tracksuits don't come cheap, hundred quid a pop. More expensive than a real suit!'

'Yeah, well, we're not the fashion police,' laughed Waters.

Arthur Hanlon rested the remains of the sausage roll on his fat thigh and lifted the binoculars to his eyes. 'Unbelievable. Even the car! It's a casuals car!'

Waters snatched the binoculars from him and took a good look at the white Peugeot. He saw it had green trim and decals, and a green crocodile badge: it was a special edition Lacoste 205. Waters muttered, 'Wankers.'

He handed Hanlon back his binoculars. 'They're flashing their cash.'

'Where's it coming from?'

'Well, let's put it like this, I don't think they're interested in collecting the reward money for information on young Dean.'

Five minutes later and the entrance door to Clay House was flung open, and Bomber Harris and Tommy Wilkins came out with the two other burly-looking thugs.

Arthur Hanlon said, 'Football's on later today, maybe they're joining forces to have a scrap with a rival firm?'

When the four men reached the car, the pecking order of the gang revealed itself in almost comical terms: the doors were opened and the seats pulled forward reverentially for Harris and Wilkins to take their places in the back, like a pair of budget Don Corleones. The designer Peugeot screeched off. John Waters fired up the Allegro and followed.

Tuesday (5)

'From what we've got from Mr Malcolm Crain, the son-in-law, Maureen Drake, Jimmy's wife, found him. They'd just got in, and Mr Crain, his wife and their two kids were waiting in the living room. Then they heard Maureen Drake scream. Mr Crain checked Jimmy, saw the marks around the neck, knew it wasn't natural causes and called us immediately.'

Sue Clarke closed her notebook. She was standing with Frost just inside the Winchester Club, wary of the limited space and mindful not to disturb anything until the Forensics boys had done their work.

The next-door neighbours' kids had already been told to get down from the wall, from where they'd been trying to get a look at what they were sure was a dead body. Shame they weren't so nosy earlier, thought Frost, but they were probably still at school when it happened.

245

PC David Simms and WPC Hanna Davis were already out doing a door-to-door.

Dr Maltby was examining the brass plaque on the shed exterior. 'The Winchester Club – Members Only.' He looked quizzical. 'Isn't that from *The Sweeney*?'

'What are you doing watching the telly, Doc? I thought Radio Four was as far as you dipped your toe into anything as crass as the twentieth century?'

'I keep abreast of these things, Frost.'

'*Minder*,' said Sue Clarke.

'Yes, of course,' said Maltby with a snap of his fingers. 'Alastair Sim's sidekick is in it. Well, it's chucking out time for you lot. We need to get a closer look before they take him away, and then Forensics.'

Frost and Clarke made way for the team to take a fine-tooth comb to the Winchester Club. But before he stepped out, Frost scoped the photos plastered all over the walls, but couldn't see Melody Price in any of them. He'd met Jimmy only once but he'd liked him. At the races he'd profited from Drake's knowledge, both about George Price's secret credit bookmaking operation, and also the horses' form. Frost hadn't been able to keep hold of the money he'd won, but he had held on to the information about Price, and he was determined that it would come good.

It was 7 p.m. when Eve Hayward entered the Bricklayer's public house on the edges of the Southern Housing Estate; even the cover of night couldn't disguise what a dump it was. The pub was attached to a block of flats

246

and a row of shops that included the Codpiece chip shop, a newsagent's for your paper and fags, and an off-licence for when the Bricklayer's was closed. It was the sort of seamless 1960s architecture that was supposed to provide everything the estate's inhabitants could possibly want in one grey concrete slab. Or, less charitably, and as Eve Hayward saw it, it was designed to keep the natives on the reservation.

Hayward looked the part: red puffa jacket, stone-washed spray-on jeans, white boots with a spike heel. She was wearing too much make-up, like she was covering a skin condition. And she was blonde, thanks to a Debbie Harry peroxide-blonde wig that looked convincing enough.

The inside of the pub didn't belie the outside. The walls were covered in a wood-effect laminate that was peeling away from the concrete. The floor was covered in carpet tiles of an indistinct colour that had in turn been soaked in booze and appeared speckled with dried blood. And all the tables and chairs looked like they'd been broken over someone's head at one time or another and put back together with Bostik.

There was an open brick fireplace with a chipped red Calor Gas heater stuck in it; around the hearth there might once have been some brass decorations, in an attempt to make the place look like an olde worlde country inn, but these had been nicked and sold for scrap long ago.

Eve Hayward didn't know if this was the worst pub she had ever been in, but it was certainly up there with the best of the worst of them. In the public bar there were two men playing pool who did actually look like bricklayers in their dusty work clothes. There was a gang of five probably underage girls by the jukebox who glared at her. The music they'd just selected was blisteringly loud and incongruous for the near-empty pub, which seemed moribund to the point of extinction, with Frankie Goes to Hollywood encouraging everyone to 'Relax'.

And sat at the bar was the reason she was in this dump. There were three of them, and the one she was after was instantly recognizable: he was wearing a lime-green track-suit and had his arm in a sling. As she made her way over to the bar she could feel the glares of the girls at the juke-box intensify with each step she made. She was also getting attention from the three men at the bar.

'Can I get you and the lads a drink, Tommy?' she said confidently, pulling a twenty-pound note from her jeans pocket.

This offer threw them. It was bold and businesslike and seemed to put them on the back foot. The three men exchanged quick questioning glances, before Tommy Wilkins, the leader of the pack, said, 'Snake-bite and black.'

The other two lads raised their pint glasses to order the same. Eve Hayward joined suit.

Wilkins clinked glasses with her. 'Cheers . . . ?'

'Rosy.'

Tommy gave a leering grin. '*Rosy*. Mickey said you were a sort, and he wasn't wrong.'

Hayward, now in the guise of Rosy Jennings, laughed, and took a substantial gulp of her snakebite and black.

248

'Mickey' was Detective Inspector Tony Norton's alias, and she could immediately imagine what he'd told them. But he would also have laid the groundwork for her being seen as a major player who should be taken seriously and could be very profitable to them.

'So, what can we do for you, Rosy?'

Hayward's suspicious eyes did a quick sweep of the bar, looking for anyone sitting or standing just that little bit too close who wasn't meant to be. 'I'm looking to fill a Transit van. I'm in the market for lots of clobber with good names, like Armani, Ralph Lauren, Calvin Klein. I need lots of recognizable labels that we can shift quickly. Pirated videos, rebranded and re-boxed TVs and ghetto blasters, you name it. And if it's good merchandise, I can fill maybe two vans a week.'

Tommy Wilkins' narrow gaze honed in on Eve Hayward. He looked impressed. 'Not here.'

'What do you mean, not here?'

'I can't discuss it here.'

Hayward looked around the place and then shrugged. 'I was told this was the place you did business.'

'Things have changed.'

'I'm not really in the mood for messing about, Tommy. I'm looking to fill a Transit van over the next couple of days and take it back to London. I've got customers waiting.'

'Mickey said you was OK, said you was proper people with proper money to spend. But the local Old Bill have got big eyes on us, you see. So if you want to discuss business, you'll have to come with us.'

249

Tommy Wilkins downed his pint with some noisy glugs, wiped his mouth with the back of his hand, the one not in a sling, and burped good and loud.

'Excuse my manners, Rosy, how bleedin' rude of me,' he said with a challenging smirk on his face.

The two others laughed along and also downed their pints, and then repeated what Tommy had just done with various measures of success – or maybe they just thought it good sense not to burp as loudly as their leader, what with the natural Neanderthal pecking order that prevailed in pubs such as these. For Wilkins, propped on a stool at the corner of the bar with a view of everything, including who came through the door, might just as well have been installed on a burnished throne surrounded by the Praetorian Guard.

Tommy got off his throne. 'Follow me, Rosy.'

'Where are we going?'

He grinned, showing a gap where a front tooth used to be. 'For a ride.'

Eve Hayward's undercover rules played back to her in her head: never leave a prearranged location without back-up to follow you. But then again, Eve rationalized, don't come on all brass balls and then not follow through because you've not got the bottle. This was no time to come across as confused, in two minds, torn between different personalities. She was Rosy Jennings. She followed them out of the door and into the dark.

Wednesday (1)

Journalists from the BBC, ITN, LWT, all the national red tops and broadsheets, and Sandy Lane of the *Denton Echo* – who had shouldered his way through the big boys to take his place at the front of the press pack – were all gathered before the steps of Eagle Lane Police Station. At the dais with a microphone in front of him was Superintendent Stanley Mullett. He had just read out a statement that he, under the supervision of Assistant Chief Constable Winslow from County HQ, had prepared the night before. It was factual and to the point.

'Now, I'm sure you have lots of questions, but as I'm sure you will understand, the tragic death of Dean Bartlett is still very much under investigation, so we can't—'

'Sandy Lane, *Denton Echo*!' interrupted the local hack, putting the big boys of the nationals to shame. 'Two points: is Denton, and the Southern Housing Estate in particular, being flooded with cheap heroin; and has Denton police force the ability to get the situation under control, or will the town fall into the hands of gun-wielding drug gangs like the major inner cities?'

'Good old Sandy,' said Frost to Sue Clarke. They were standing away from the media scrum, and out of view from Mullett, ACC Winslow and John Waters, who had been roped in to the 8 a.m. press conference by the top brass. Mainly because Mullett no longer trusted Frost at press conferences, but also because, as Waters suspected, having a black officer in the ranks of white men showed the diversity of the Denton force – which of course it didn't, because it wasn't. It showed that Eagle Lane was on top of things and in tune with the inner-city drug problem that was spreading to the outer boroughs, the suburbs, the market towns and new towns. But whatever the connotations of having John Waters at the press conference, Frost was happy to see him up there for lots of reasons – the most important being that he knew what he was bloody well talking about.

Frost and Clarke had heard enough and left the press pack with its popping cameras and barked questions to get on with work.

'You look gorgeous as ever, Melody. Thanks for coming.'

'When Eamon calls, everyone comes running, right?'

Eamon Hogan smiled. What else can he do, thought Melody. Pointless to deny it, it was the truth and he knew it. And she knew it too. So when Eamon asked her to meet up, she knew she had to go. He'd wanted to pick her up and drive her to the stables that he'd invested

252

in recently, where he was going to keep some of his horses. They could go for a ride – they shared a love of horses, didn't they?

Hogan said he'd be meeting more people there, some jockeys and trainers. Melody knew they were arranging to fix races, and also knew that she didn't want to be privy to that conversation. She would do her part, take the bets that Eamon laid, and work with the information that she had been given, but she didn't want to meet anyone else involved who could later implicate her. And the less she knew about Eamon's business, the safer she was. Her days of taking mad risks for money were over.

So Melody made some excuse, not very convincing, something about having to buy some make-up, and arranged to meet him in the restaurant of Aster's department store in Market Square. She could tell by the tone of his voice that he didn't believe her. But at this point she didn't really care, she wanted to meet in a public place because it was safer. And he was obliging, effusively polite and accommodating. So there they were, like any other couple taking a break from shopping. Eamon had picked the corner booth, which ensured less opportunity for eavesdropping and from where he could see everyone who entered the restaurant. The large dining room was all in pastel colours, and to accompany the blandness of the decor there was piped music that seemed to contain a sax solo every thirty seconds, yet never really disturbed the soft domestic chatter that bubbled away. It was the perfect place not to get shot, garrotted, or have your head caved in.

The waitress came with their orders – a pot of tea for two, eggs Benedict, and the club sandwich for him. It had all arrived in record time: ruthless efficiency or was everything just fast food now?

'I'll be mother,' said Eamon with a wink and another smile as he poured the tea. 'It's a shame you couldn't come to the stables today. I've got a lovely new filly we could have taken out. You used to love horse riding.'

'I haven't done it in years.'

'Has working at the racing jaded your passions, Melody?'

'How's Angie?' she countered.

'She's well. She's in Spain at the moment with little Eamon and Carmen. She sends her love.'

'You're a lucky man. You've got a beautiful wife, two beautiful kids. You've got everything you ever wanted.'

'Not everything. It could have been you, you know that, and God knows I wanted it to be.'

'No, it couldn't, and you knew that.'

Melody picked up her knife and fork and cut into her meal: the poached egg wasn't particularly runny, and the ham that accompanied it curled at the edges where it had dried out. Eamon removed the lethal-looking cocktail stick from his sandwich and took a bite. It was clear that for now, the less-than-fresh food was more palatable than the topic being discussed.

But Melody couldn't let it go. 'You knew that, Eamon, because there was only one person I'd confided in, my best pal, my best friend in the world, and closest . . .

254

companion, shall we say? And, as it turned out, my biggest competition, Angie.'

The secret had been the messy abortion Melody had had in her youth that had left her unable to bear children. Left her feeling like she was in mourning for the lost child, and the children she'd never have.

Eamon said, 'I won't deny I knew. But it was you, you were the only one I really loved.'

'But Angie ran a close second, right? And once she told you my secret, she became the favourite.'

'I wanted children, Melody, what man doesn't?'

'I understand. It's only natural.'

Eamon averted his eyes from her, snapped the cocktail stick he'd been rolling between his thumb and forefinger and tossed it on the table, then laced his hands together in front of his face as if to pray. Only then did he meet her gaze. Melody stayed strong. There were no tears left for him. She'd fallen in love with Eamon practically on sight. She and Angie, both in their twenties, had met him in an exclusive nightclub in Amsterdam, where he bought them champagne all night. The dark looks, the bright blue eyes, and, yes, the power the man possessed served as an aphrodisiac for both women. At first they were prepared to share him – they were young, adventurous, why not?

But it wasn't long before the adventurousness extended beyond the bedroom of the Hotel Prins Hendrik. He introduced her to a world of risk, danger and big money. It seemed that Melody would do anything for him. She

255

even tried to outmatch him, coming up with her own dangerous, wild and profitable schemes. She didn't want to be seen as the gangster's moll, she wanted to be seen as his equal.

But Melody had miscalculated. She was almost too wild, too impulsive, too independent, and in the deeply patriarchal world that Eamon Hogan had grown up and operated in, she was perhaps not the girl you would choose to marry. And once he found out she couldn't bear him children, it was over. But still he had a hold over her, and she him. There was that frisson, still strong enough to set her off into a fantasy that maybe one day things would be different between them.

Deep down she knew it was foolishness to think such things, and she had hoped that George Price would break the spell. And in many ways he had. He was kind, funny, gentle and generous, and had promised to look after her, a promise he'd more than fulfilled by making her a partner in his business. George had understood that she would never be one to sit at home and play the role of the trophy wife. She'd had her own businesses, her ventures. Even though George had given her what she initially wanted, she always wanted more, and she had enough self-awareness to recognize that was her great failing. Like addicted gamblers: they didn't play to win, they played to keep on playing. It was just in her nature to twist rather than stick. And to a degree, George understood that. Maybe he thought he would be the one who could tame her, to finally satisfy her. She knew men, knew their egos, knew that might have

256

been part of the attraction for him. George had married his first wife young, and as worldly as he was in most matters, he was somewhat naive when it came to women. She had worked that out early. And maybe that was part of the attraction for her.

'To be honest, Melody, as lovely as it is to see you, as always, I'm not here to talk about the past, and I certainly don't want to pick at old wounds,' announced Eamon. 'I need you to know something, about George.'

'Yes, of course. I wondered when you were going to get around to that.'

'I just have to say that I had nothing to do with George getting shot.'

Melody raised her teacup to her mouth and took little sips, using the cup as a prop to cover her doubt, her anger, her fear.

'I swear on my children's eyes, I had nothing to do with it,' insisted Hogan. 'Why would I? From a business point of view, we had George right where we wanted him, and he was playing along just fine. He'd do anything for you, you said so yourself. Killing him would just bring unwanted attention. I just thank God he's still alive, and I know he'll pull through. Of that I'm sure. He's a fighter, you told me so yourself and I believe you. Do you believe me when I say I had nothing to do with his shooting?'

Melody blew little short bursts of breath on her tea and took some more bird-like sips as she considered all he'd said. Then she lowered her cup. She'd seen something in his eyes that told her maybe he was telling the truth, and it certainly made sense that Eamon wasn't

257

responsible for the shooting. And, of course, Eamon was right, George would do anything for her, without question. Price was a pragmatist, and if races were indeed going to be fixed, he didn't want to be the bookie who was going to get stung. There was nothing he could do about it, so why not go along with it? It made good business sense.

And the more she thought about it, the more sense it made that Eamon wouldn't try to kill George. She knew Hogan was ruthless: if it was the competition stepping on his turf, or someone ripping him off in a drugs shipment, he'd wipe them out – and whoever was in the room with them – without batting an eyelid. But not a 'civilian' like George, not if he could help it.

Eamon knew that Melody had developed feelings for George beyond her own pragmatism. But there was another reason that trumped all the others as to why she believed Hogan hadn't tried to kill her husband – because he would most definitely be dead if he had.

'I believe you.'

'Good. What have the police said?'

'The officer in charge, Inspector Frost, suspects a bookmaker called Terry Langdon.'

Eamon asked why, and Melody gave a brief history of her extra-marital liaison with the younger bookmaker. She said it was nothing to her, but the silly sod had gone and fallen in love with her. She always thought he was a bit soft in the head. Hogan grinned at this news, and said, 'It doesn't surprise me in the slightest, men fighting over you, doll.'

258

The Irishman then reached into the pocket of his suede blouson, which looked Italian and expensive, pulled out a brown envelope and handed it to Melody. She felt the weight of it and heard the tinkle of something delicate and precious. When she dared to peek inside, there it was, sparkling away, a diamond and emerald necklace, set in platinum.

'Ooh, emeralds, my favourite.'

'Mine too.'

'A gift from the Emerald Isle?'

Eamon shifted in his seat. 'You might not want to wear it around that Frost fella if he comes calling again, if you get my drift.'

Melody had, of course, heard about the jewellery-shop robbery in Rimmington, as it had made the local news. She smiled at Hogan the way you would at an incorrigible schoolboy caught with chocolate sauce around his mouth after licking the bowl. She always thought it would be his downfall: despite all his other wheeling and dealing, he was a thief at heart. Eamon Hogan simply loved thieving. He always said that if you offered him fifty million quid to never steal again, he wouldn't take it. But he would work out a way to steal it from you. The thrill of it, the buzz of it, the adrenalin rush of pulling off an audacious job provided a high like no other. Pulling off 'jobs' appealed to some romantic Robin Hood notion he held on to; dealing heroin was just the new reality of the crime business.

Melody considered the gift. 'There's no strings attached, are there?'

259

'I want you, Melody. You know that, I want you more than any other woman I've ever known. We had real magic between us. And when I think about the time we had together, it makes me feel young again. Makes me feel—'

'Stop, Eamon.'

'OK. Just let me say this: you know how I feel about you, but I want you to feel the same way. Like in the old days. So no, there's no strings attached. It's a way of saying thank you for what you've done. And it's important to me that you believe me, about George.'

'I said I believe you, and I do.'

Eamon gave her a loving smile. He then reached across the table and gently took her hands in his. 'Thank God for that. It would break my heart if you didn't.'

'Why?'

'Because if you didn't believe me, I'd have to kill you.'

His grip tightened around her hands, as he proved once again his ability to go from munificence to malevolence in the blink of a cold-blue sociopathic eye.

Wednesday (2)

Gerald Drysdale, County's chief pathologist, always said he knew more about dead people than living ones. When Frost first heard Drysdale announce this in his deep and sonorous voice, Frost just thought he was being philosophical and rather macabre. But their association over the years had proved his point.

'The great Chekhov said he couldn't understand the character of a man fully until he knew the contents of their stomach. He was a doctor too, you know.'

'Don't you mean Bones?'

'*What?*'

'The doctor in *Star Trek*?'

'No, Frost, I mean the Russian playwright, Anton Chekhov.'

'Oh.'

Frost laughed. Drysdale's long, gaunt and pale face

261

gathered up all its privately educated disdain and dumped it on Frost.

The detective stopped laughing and turned his attention back to the dead man on the slab. The toe tag said 'James Lewis Drake'. It was plain to see there was no need to check the contents of Jimmy's stomach; what had killed him was obvious, a length of orange nylon twine wrapped around his neck with such force that some of the fibres were embedded in the torn flesh.

'Looks simple enough: he was having a drink with the perpetrator, turned away to pour another drink, and the killer sprang at him with the rope. From the angle of the wound, and the sheer force, I would estimate the killer is a man.'

Frost raised an eyebrow at this. 'You only *estimate* he was a man?'

'Never take these things for granted, Frost.'

'If he was poisoned, shot, stabbed, hit over the head with a blunt object in the proverbial library, I wouldn't, but garrotted?'

'The Frinton strangler?'

'Wasn't she an East German circus performer who was built like a brick—'

'Still a gal, though, Frost!'

The DI conceded the point.

Drysdale continued, 'He's at least six feet tall, athletic and powerfully built. Not much from the Forensics chaps, I'm afraid, as far as prints are concerned. I would suggest the killer wasn't an amateur, may well be familiar with this type of murder. He was wearing leather

262

gloves; you would need to when exerting such force on this type of rope, to get the leverage you needed. We may be able to extract some leather fragments, but I doubt they'll tell us much, unless his gloves were made of human skin.'

Drysdale unfurled a smile at the thought. He then held up a board featuring five types of nylon rope of varying thickness, like a sampler you would find in a hardware store. He pointed to the second finest.

'This is the one. Worth finding out who sells it locally, you never know.'

Frost took out his notebook and made a note of the gauge of the nylon rope.

'We'll expect to find lots of variant hairs, fibres, shoe prints, as it was a public place, after all.'

'What was?'

'The Winchester Club.'

'It was a shed.'

'A private members bar.'

'In a shed.'

'No imagination, Frost.'

'You've been watching too much TV, Gerald.'

Frost's pager bleeped into action. John Waters. Urgent.

Angelo wore a permanent five o'clock shadow; he had the kind of face that looked like it needed shaving three times a day. He was a tall but stooped man in his fifties, with a distended belly that was covered by an apron advertising Cinzano Bianco. He delivered the two frothy cappuccinos to the detectives with his usual smiling and

263

incomprehensible bonhomie, something along the lines of: 'Enjoy, long life, be happy, come back again . . .'

John Waters had wanted to meet in private, and as far as Frost was concerned, the Pellerocco Café was becoming his go-to place for privacy. When the sergeant showed Frost the pictures, Frost understood why.

They were photos of Billy 'Bomber' Harris and Tommy Wilkins. They were the result of Waters' impromptu use of his trusty Polaroid. Whilst no substitute for an official surveillance camera with a serious zoom lens – many were grainy and out of focus – the images still did the job of showing the two miscreants advertising their newly acquired wealth.

Waters explained: 'So, as we've established, Harris and Wilkins are not only *not* grassing each other up, but now they're best mates, knocking around with each other in flash cars and expensive clothes. So where are they getting the money? They seem to be doing what they always do, right?'

Frost agreed. Waters laid out pictures of Harris and Wilkins entering the pool hall, the amusement arcade, the burger bar, the video store and various pubs. But he'd saved the best till last.

'And this: look who's going into the Bricklayer's. Recognize this blonde bombshell?'

Frost picked up the snapshot. 'That's not . . . ? It bloody well is!'

It was Eve Hayward, resplendent in a blonde wig and looking every inch the brassy wheeler-dealer barrow girl. Waters produced more pictures of Hayward with

264

Wilkins and two of his 'firm' getting into their white Peugeot 205 and speeding off. Frost had seen enough.

'So what happened?'

'Hayward arrived in a Transit van, parked up and went inside the Bricklayer's.'

'Bold move if you're not from the estate.'

'My point exactly. Ten minutes later she comes out with Tommy and two of his lads and drives off. She comes back an hour later, now with Tommy *and* Bomber Harris, shakes their hands, and drives off in the van.'

Frost considered this and came up with a sly smile. 'She told me she could make a link between the heroin and the counterfeit goods. I said prove it, and she just might well have done.'

'You also said you didn't trust her. Didn't believe she's with counterfeit-goods intelligence . . . ? Whatever it is.'

'They're always coming up with poncey names to call themselves. And anyway, aren't they connected to Customs and Excise?'

'I've still got plenty of contacts in the Met, you want me to make some calls?'

'No, let me think on it.'

Through the steamed-up windows Frost could just about see DC Sue Clarke making her way across the road towards them. Frost scooped up the photos on the table.

'May I?'

Waters gestured *be my guest*, and Frost slipped the snaps into the inside pocket of his leather bomber jacket. Waters looked poised to ask Frost what he was going to do about Eve Hayward when Clarke came in. The DS shifted up in the booth to make room for her.

'How was she?' asked Frost.

Sue had just returned from visiting Jimmy Drake's widow, Maureen, who was staying at her daughter's.

'In shock – she had the doctor with her when I arrived. But once she knew I was there, she wanted to answer whatever she could.'

'And the big question: why wasn't Jimmy at the races yesterday?'

'She was surprised herself. It was marked on the calendar that he'd be at Radleigh Park that day. After forty years, she knew all the race meetings that he worked at. He insisted it was his day off, apparently. Maureen said she didn't think anything of it. But she suspected that he'd had a row with Melody Price. Jimmy didn't like the way she was running the business in George's absence. But one thing was very clear: Maureen didn't like Melody Price either. She said that Jimmy thought Melody was a bad influence on George, and going to get him into trouble one day.'

'How so?'

'That he was taking too many risks. She didn't really know any more. Jimmy seldom talked about work when he got home, but Maureen could tell that he was worried about George.'

'I'm not surprised at that,' Frost said.

John Waters hoisted up his cuff and checked his watch, then finished off his cappuccino. 'I need to go, check if there's any news on Gavin Ross.'

266

Clarke got up to let him out. Before Waters left, Frost said to him, 'That other thing we talked about?'

Waters gave a nod of understanding.

'Leave it with me, John.'

Waters nodded again and then left.

'What was that about?' asked Clarke.

'Nothing. How about our friend, Eve Hayward, have you seen her today?'

'No. Why?'

Frost smiled and shook his head. He then released a Rothmans from the packet on the table and sparked it up. He did a little drum roll with his knuckles on the Formica table and announced: 'I've put in for a warrant to search George and Melody Price's house and business premises, see if there's any other records for Socks and Winston. And I want to reassign a uniform outside George Price's door again, twenty-four/seven.'

'You'd better run that by Mullett first, apparently every available copper is working the Dean Bartlett case.'

'Mullett won't mind, now there's been an actual murder.'

'What about Harry Baskin's man?'

'Bad Manners Bob can stay there too if he likes, the more the merrier. But whoever killed Jimmy Drake, according to our very own Dr Death, is a formidable foe. And anyway, since when have Harry Baskin and his bouncers been working for us? We need a proper police presence on it.'

'David Simms? He's seeing the nurse who saved his bacon, apparently.'

267

'Is he? Definitely not Simms then – when love is in the air it's a distraction. We can talk to Harry Baskin whilst we're at it, too. So far he's been banking on George Price pulling through, so he sees no real reason to talk to us. Now Jimmy's been murdered, he might think again.'

Clarke agreed and they got up to leave.

'I've got a question, Jack. Why didn't you tell John he had cappuccino froth around his gob?'

'Why didn't you?'

She shrugged. 'I thought it looked funny?'

'Me too. Laughs are hard to come by in this job.'

Frost paid the bill, and they headed out into the cold light of a Denton day with Angelo's lilting Italian accent ringing in their ears as he championed the wonders and beauty of life.

Wednesday (3)

The bird swooped round and round as if circling some prey that it was about to dive down on. Then came the terrifying sound of screeching, accompanied by manic laughter that seemed to embolden the bird to squawk some more. It was a sight that filled Jason Kingly with horror and doom.

Terry Langdon was in his Y-fronts, vest and socks, swinging what appeared to be a clothes line above his head like a lasso, with some bread Sellotaped to the end of it.

Jason's head swung violently around to see if anyone else was witnessing this crazy act – no one was. Of course, Paradise, Eden and Utopia were still empty, but Jason's paranoia was justified and he really didn't need a petrol-blue parrot lighting up the skies, with a wanted felon acting as its ringmaster. Was Terry, his cousin and one-time hero, well and truly off his nut?

Jason waved his arms and tried to get his cousin's attention with a cough-inducing stage whisper. When that didn't work, Kingly yelled out his name and told him to get off the fucking roof immediately. Terry responded with a wild-eyed grin and a thumbs-up.

The young estate agent then let himself into the flat. It was even more of a mess today. As well as the empty cans, bottles and takeaway cartons, there were now signs that the parrot had been flying around in the flat and depositing bird shit on the expensive carpet and three-piece suite, and just about everywhere else – including what resembled some early Jackson Pollocks on the walls.

Langdon came through the door with the parrot on his shoulder; all he needed was an eyepatch and a wooden leg to look like a shipwrecked Long John Silver. But the ship he'd wrecked was this showpiece apartment that Jason was responsible for. A cleaning crew would have to be put to work, maybe even a painter and decorator; and Terry would have to pay for it all.

'He came back yesterday. I saw him outside on the wall, so I put some bread on the windowsill and he came straight in.'

'Terry, you can't have him in here, he's shitting all over the place.'

Langdon went over to his trousers, which lay crumpled on the floor, and as he bent down to pick them up, the parrot took off.

'Jesus!' cried out Jason, alarmed at the bird's mad flapping. After some screeching turns around the living room the parrot eventually perched on the open-plan kitchen counter, where there was a saucer of water laid out for him.

Terry stuffed a wad of money into Jason's hand, and fixed him with the wild-eyed stare that he hadn't, as Jason hoped, left up on the roof.

'Listen, Jace, we need to get Simon a—'

'Simon?'

'Yeah, Simon. Simon the parrot.'

'Why Simon?'

'Because it's his name.'

'But it's not.'

'How do you know?'

'Because . . . no one calls a parrot Simon . . . Doesn't make sense.'

'What should I call him?'

'Frost called him Monty.'

'Who's Frost?'

Jason wanted to bury his head in his hands and cry. 'Detective Inspector Jack Frost.'

'Silly bloody name for a copper.'

'Almost as silly as Simon for a parrot.'

'Don't get cocky, doesn't suit you, mate.'

'Jack Frost was the copper who came in here and you almost shot, remember?'

'Course I remember. Though it seems like ages ago now.'

'Right . . . well, it was only two days ago. Anyway, what stopped you shooting him was the parrot. I spotted him outside on the windowsill and Frost went after him.'

'Why?'

271

'Because he knew him, so he was after him.'

'Why, what's he done?'

'Who?'

'Simon.'

'I don't know . . . Flown away, I guess. But Frost called him Monty.'

'Now that *is* a stupid name for a parrot. It's a bloody cliché.'

'The parrot has to go . . . he's a wanted parrot. He's got people out looking for him. And if they find him they'll find—'

'No! I'm not turning him in.' Langdon then looked over at the parrot, its head buried in its wing as it groomed itself. 'We . . . we're birds of a feather, me and Simon, we're both wanted by the law.'

Jason stepped back from Terry to get some perspective and a good look at him, or rather what he had become. Terry didn't notice the way that his cousin was casting a concerned eye over him, because he was now over by the kitchen counter, feeding the bird peanuts and raisins, and cooing and whispering sweet nothings to it. Terry hasn't been here that long, thought Jason, but already he looks like he's going stir crazy. The pressure's getting to him, or maybe it did long ago. Maybe he did pull the trigger and shoot George Price? Jason concluded that Terry looked unhinged enough to have carried out such an act.

Kingly tentatively asked, 'Terry, when . . . when are you going to sort out that passport you were talking about?'

'What passport?'

272

'You said that you were going to ask a mate, or you had a mate that could sort out a passport for you.'

Terry's head shot round to confront him. And Jason saw that his face was full of confusion and vagueness.

'Jesus!' cried Jason, expelling another exasperated breath. 'You said you had a mate who was going to get you a passport, so you could leave the country?'

'Oh yeah, him. And he will, he will.' In two lunging strides he was right next to Jason. He then grabbed his face and held it in his hands. 'First off, we have to get Simon some food, bird food. What do parrots eat in the Amazon?'

Jason didn't know. He'd had little experience of the Amazon, or parrots, for that matter.

'Fruit, get plenty of fruit and . . . seeds! They eat seeds. Nan had a budgie, like a parrot, but smaller, used to eat seeds and a white thing stuck in the bars?'

'Cuttlefish?'

'Now you're thinking. Ask the pet-shop people, they'll know. Get him the best, the best cuttlefish there is, the caviar of cuttlefish – and a cage, we have to get him a cage. The Buckingham Palace of cages.'

'We have to let him go, can't have him in here, there's people looking for him.'

'There's people looking for me, too. We're in this together. Me and Simon. He goes down, I go down, too. It's me and him from here on out . . . *The Defiant Ones* . . . You seen that film?'

Jason shook his head, and took the opportunity to shake it free of Terry's sweaty and manic grip.

273

'He needs a cage, or he'll shit all over the place.'

Jason agreed on this point. It was the most normal and sensible thing Terry had said since he'd got here.

'Bird seed, fruit and a cage. I won't lock him in, mind, he just needs a base, he'll come in and out as he pleases, understand?'

Jason went over to the front door. 'You'll look into getting that passport though, eh? So we can get you out of here.'

Terry pulled another big manic grin. 'Oh yeah, I'll get right on it. Tell you what, though, might see if I can get Simon to teach me to fly,' – he stood on one leg and flapped his arms – 'then I won't need a bloody passport!'

Jason's heart sank as he slipped out of the door.

Wednesday (4)

'How many men?'

'Six.'

'You'll get four. I need a strong presence on the Southern Housing Estate.'

Frost was in Stanley Mullett's office securing search warrants for George Price's home and betting shops. He'd asked for six officers, expecting to get half that amount, so four was a result. Mullett seemed distracted; Frost could tell that the super hadn't enjoyed that morning's press conference the minute he stepped into his office.

'Thank you,' said Frost, rising from his chair to leave.

Mullett signed the warrant, but didn't hand it over. 'Sit down. There's other matters.'

Frost sat back down, and, as if by magic, Mullett produced a copy of that morning's *Denton Echo* from a drawer and slapped it on the satin-finished mahogany desk. Frost

275

eyed the well-thumbed rag. Mullett's red pen had circled a pull-out quote from an anonymous source high up within Denton CID. It was Frost's quote, the one he'd given to Sandy Lane on the Pellerocco Café napkin.

'Recognize this?'

'The *Denton Echo*. It's a publication I have very little to do with, except when it's wrapped around my cod and chips.'

Mullett wasn't smiling. He was in his top-of-the-range executive chair which was adjusted to its maximum height, allowing him the greatest opportunity to look down his nose at anyone sitting opposite him. Frost always felt like he was squashed into a brightly coloured plastic child's chair when sat opposite the super.

'So you don't write for it?'

'I don't know what you're suggesting, sir.'

'These anonymous comments have got your syntactical fingerprints all over them.'

'They *do*?'

'Most of what you're quoted as saying you will do to the culprits when you catch them is illegal.'

'I respectfully ask that you refrain from saying "you" because it isn't me. I've got nothing to do with it. Ask Sandy Lane.'

'I did. He said he doesn't reveal his anonymous sources, not even to his editor.'

'Obviously a principled man, case closed.'

'A gin-soaked hack, and I don't think so. And his recalcitrant stance with his superiors doesn't absolve you of guilt, Frost, it merely puts you in cahoots with him.'

276

'I take offence to that, sir. I don't touch gin.'

'We were up all night working on a carefully crafted press release – and what do we find on the front page?' Mullett picked up the paper and took the opportunity to emphatically slap it down on the desk again. 'The nationals are going with it, too. Let me tell you, and you can relay this to your friend, Sandy Lane—'

'No friend of mine, I can assure you of that. Always keep a healthy distance from the fourth estate.' Frost did his best not to smirk, and failed.

'This cosy little "arrangement" he has with his editor doesn't wash with me, and I will find out who his anonymous source is. And if I find even so much as an outstanding parking ticket for Mr Sandy Lane, he will feel the full weight of the law pressing down on him, do you understand?'

'I do, but like I said, you're talking to the wrong man.' Frost raised his wrist in front of his face to commune theatrically with his watch. He really didn't need this, he wanted to get out there and do his bloody job, not play politics. 'Are we done?'

Mullett seemed to relax and now made full use of the rocking motion of his office chair. His snarl softened and his gaze wandered over to the portrait of Her Majesty up on the dark wood-panelled wall, which always resulted in a reflective smile alighting on his face as he considered his employer.

'I need to ask you something a little more delicate. Between you and me, you understand?'

Frost liked Mullett even less when he was like this,

lurching from giving you a right bollocking to engaging you in false camaraderie. He said he understood.

'Tell me your thoughts on Eve Hayward – what are your impressions?'

Frost's eyebrows shot skywards; was he really asking his opinion? *Out of your league, you dirty git*, was his answer.

What he actually said was: 'May I ask why you ask, sir?'

'I'll be frank, I've heard rumours.'

'About her and Sue Clarke? Totally unfounded. The erotic fantasies of young PCs with too much time on their hands and furtive imaginations—'

'What the hell are you talking about, Frost?'

Frost saw that Mullett genuinely didn't know and hadn't heard the rumours. 'Joking. It was a joke. Or wishful thinking, one of the two.'

'Either way, it's in bad taste, and as far as you're concerned, this is no time for jokes.'

'Sorry, sir, please go on.'

'I've heard that Detective Inspector Eve Hayward has been asking questions about members of our team. About you, in particular.'

'Really? What kind of questions?'

Frost watched as Mullett's magnified eyes behind his glasses narrowed on him, as if weighing up whether he was worthy of what he was about to tell him.

'I don't like people asking questions about my team. Do you know why, Frost?' Mullett didn't wait for an answer.

278

'Because it reflects badly on me. The idea that County has to bring in outside forces to root out bad apples, that suggests that I'm not up to the job. Are you hiding anything from me? Is there any reason Detective Inspector Hayward should be questioning your character?'

'I haven't got a clue, sir.'

Frost said it with such forceful sincerity that Mullett could do nothing but hand the DI his search warrant. However, it came with a warning: 'If you are hiding anything from me, I swear to God, Frost, I will rain down a flood of paperwork on you that will keep you desk-bound for a month.'

Frost met this with a benign indifference that he knew would annoy Mullett, and left the super to contemplate the scenario of Sue Clarke with Eve Hayward, now he'd planted it in his mind.

Melody Price looked genuinely upset. She perched on the edge of the cream-coloured armchair, her bejewelled hands clasped together, her eyes moist with tears. Frost watched her, and was genuinely unmoved. At this stage in the proceedings, Melody was striking him as a supreme performer. She was someone who was able to turn on the waterworks whenever it suited her – and was most profitable. Frost had just delivered the news of Jimmy Drake's murder; and at this point it was definitely profitable for her to shed some tears.

A comforting hand went on to her shoulder. 'Are you OK to continue?'

Melody aimed her big damp blue eyes up at her lawyer and said, 'Yes, I'm fine, thanks, Clive.'

The lawyer then went and stood by the fireplace, as if ready to see Frost out at any moment, and assured Melody that this whole business wouldn't take long. The DI smiled, knowing he had a nice surprise for him.

Clive Felton wasn't known to Frost, and he knew most of the solicitors in the area. But whilst this particular one was new to him, his type was also very familiar, in his dark double-breasted suit, as sharp as his tongue, ready to cut off any lines of questioning that might incriminate his client in any way. Felton had an unpleasant bony face, oiled-back hair and flinty grey eyes that were impossible to read. And in their very brief association, Felton had struck Frost as one of those overly combative lawyers who would rather you arrested his client than talk to them, so he could roll up his sleeves and get stuck into the fight he was itching for. His narrow, unsmiling, hawkish face expressed this perfectly.

'Were you at the races yesterday, Mrs Price?'

'No.'

'May I ask why not?'

'I'd have thought it was obvious. I didn't have a clerk. The job that Jimmy does is very specialized, good clerks are hard to find.'

'So you knew in advance that Jimmy wouldn't be working yesterday?'

She glanced over at her lawyer. The lawyer took up the challenge.

'May I ask why this question is pertinent, Inspector?'

'Because Jimmy Drake was killed in his home yesterday afternoon, and we need to establish his movements and exactly why he was at home on that day, that particular day, a day when he should have been racing. Does this break in routine have anything to do with his murder . . .'

Clive Felton had gestured and made murmurs of agreement that the question was relevant to the case long before Frost had finished. But Frost had hammered home the point to get in *early doors*, to appropriate the sporting parlance, and take the opponent's legs from under him. From now on in, Frost felt assured that the combative brief would be more sparing with his interjections. Clive Felton instructed Melody to answer the question.

'Jimmy decided to retire.'

'*Retire?*' Frost repeated incredulously.

'What's wrong with that? A man of his age, perfectly normal thing to do.'

'When did he inform you of his decision to retire?'

'The other day. Monday. I was visiting George at the hospital and Jimmy was there.'

'Did he give any reasons why?'

Melody shrugged. 'He told me he'd had enough. He was a few years older than George, definitely of retirement age. And I suppose the shock of what happened to George may have spurred him on. He said that he wanted to spend more time with his wife and grandchildren. He's got a few of them, grandkids.'

'He's got four of them, I believe.'

281

'That's right. He was always showing me pictures. Such a tragedy, for them, his whole family.'

Frost had lied, there were seven grandchildren in total. It was an impressive number, and one that Melody Price had obviously taken no interest in, or Jimmy had had no interest in sharing with her. The rest of the discussion at Price's bedside was cast in doubt too. The only witness to the conversation between Melody and Jimmy was George himself. But Frost was sure there were darker matters being discussed than Jimmy spending time with his grandkids, and those may very well have led to his permanent retirement.

'It's cold-blooded murder,' said Frost. 'Jimmy Drake knew his killer, and I strongly suspect that they are already known to us, too. It's just a case of us putting the evidence together, which I'm confident of.'

'How do you mean, they're known to us?'

Clive Felton explained to his client, 'I believe Inspector Frost is implying that it is someone they have already been in contact with, or know to be associated with Mr Drake, so the field is narrowing. Am I correct, Inspector Frost?'

Before Frost could answer the brief's question, the intercom for the front gate buzzed, and he was glad of it. Frost didn't like the idea of answering to Felton and clarifying his position, he wanted to leave it nice and murky and also open to interpretation, to give Melody Price something to think about.

'That'll be for me,' said Frost, standing up, reaching into his jacket pocket and coming out with nothing

282

more than a soft packet of Winston cigarettes that he'd managed to purloin off DC Hanlon's desk. He then went through the routine of patting himself down to locate what he needed.

'It's here somewhere . . .'

'What is, Inspector?' asked Felton, looking contemptuously at the lint-covered packet of Juicy Fruit the detective had just pulled out from his back pocket.

'. . . sure I had it with me . . .'

Felton prompted impatiently, 'What are you looking for?'

'. . . maybe I left it in the car . . .'

The solicitor was now angry. 'What? What did you leave in the car?'

Frost whipped it out from his back pocket and waved it in Felton's face. 'This. You have a good look, I'm sure you'll find it's all in order, and I'll let the lads and lasses in for a good rummage.'

Frost went to answer the door.

Clive Felton had, of course, seen one of these before. 'It's a warrant to search all the premises owned by George. Business and residential.'

'Can they do this?'

'Don't worry, I'll make sure they wipe their feet!' called out Frost from the hallway.

'Don't just stand there, Clive, do something!' Melody Price, with her hands pulling at her perfectly coiffed blonde tresses, began to pace in front of the fireplace. 'I'm not standing for this, they're taking bloody liberties. I've not done anything, I'm an innocent woman!'

283

Felton hushed her and whispered, 'You're hardly that, Melody. Tell me, is there anything in the house that might be of . . . *embarrassment* to you?'

Melody took some sharp intakes of breath as if something ice-cold had just gripped her. She stopped pacing before the hearth and sank down on to the nearest armchair, looking anything but innocent.

John Waters sat on the edge of the sofa, watching the early evening news with great concentration. He was suited and booted in his Sunday best, ready for a night out with Kim. She'd insisted, with all the double shifts they'd been working lately, that they deserved a treat. Even before they'd intoned their wedding vows last year, fully aware of the long hours, conflicting shifts and pressures of their jobs, they'd come up with a credo: when there's never a right time, you make time.

The lead story on the news was about the miners' strike, Arthur Scargill and Maggie Thatcher going head to head, and Waters didn't fancy Maggie's chances of winning that one. This was followed by a report on the protracted eviction of the women peace protestors at Greenham Common, looking as put upon and bedraggled as the inmates in an episode of *Tenko*. Then Sue Lawley said the familiar words, the name of the town and county that had become his home. He thought he'd always be a Hackney boy, and Denton was just a posting before moving on, maybe back to London with some more stripes on his arm. But now he realized that Denton *was* his and Kim's home.

Kim was in the bedroom getting ready, singing and humming along to a mix tape, with Aztec Camera's 'Oblivious' turned up to full volume on the ghetto blaster while she belted out an approximation of the lyrics. She sounded so happy, he didn't have the heart to tell her to turn it down so he could listen to what was being reported. So he got up and went over to the Grundig and turned it down instead – anyway, he knew what was being said. He just had to look at the images flickering on the screen. The BBC reporter on the Southern Housing Estate looked solemn as the kids on BMXs rode behind him, pulling faces and laughing; OAPs stood in their doorways staring at the man they recognized off the telly. There was a shot of the grimy stairwell where Dean Bartlett had taken the lethal dose of heroin, and then it cut to his school photo, smiling and hopeful, the whole wide world ahead of him. Next came a picture of Gavin Ross wearing a black T-shirt with the distinctive radio waves from Joy Division's *Unknown Pleasures* album, and a phone number to call, as he was still missing.

Waters got up again and reached behind his faithful old Grundig to fiddle with the vertical hold until Sue Lawley stopped looking like she was going around on a Ferris wheel.

The soundtrack from the bedroom changed – it was now 'The Reflex' by Duran Duran. Waters winced and closed his eyes, the only reflex it hit him with was his gag one. Kim's lapses in musical taste were forgivable because as far as he was concerned she got everything

285

else right. When he opened his eyes again, he was on the telly, looking like he was singing the song in a very downmarket MTV video. He was, in fact, standing in front of the microphone for the press conference on the steps of Eagle Lane station.

Duran Duran went silent. 'Turn it up, babe!'

John Waters turned round to see Kim in the living-room doorway. She looked gorgeous in a little black ra-ra skirt and boob tube, and a pair of red patent-leather pumps with a high heel that worked her perfectly sculpted calves.

'Oh no, you've gone, just that moody so-and-so now!' she said, attaching a pair of drop earrings.

John Waters looked back to the Grundig and saw the four area superintendents in the background, looking sombre in an obviously posed shot, as the reporter spoke about how the police were preparing to deal with the growing threat of drugs reaching the suburbs and market towns, and who knew where next, the villages?

'Mullett? I almost feel sorry for him.'

'Not your super. Mine. Peter Kelsey.'

'I thought you got on all right with him?'

'Not lately, I haven't. He's been a real pain, driving everyone at work mad, happy one minute, buying every-one drinks, then shouting his head off at us the next. A real moody piece of work, he is.'

'That's bosses the world over, love, one rule for them . . .'

'He keeps flying off the handle at anything, and it's not our fault. The other day we were—'

286

'Let's not talk shop, babe, not tonight. In fact, let's not go out into the big bad world at all,' he said, giving her his lustful attention. 'We can stay in.'

'You're joking?'

'I'd rather just the two of us snuggle on here.' He patted the seat of the sofa.

Kim angled her head to deliver an eviscerating look. 'If you think I've gone to all this effort to snuggle up on the sofa and watch TV, you're crazy. I've booked the table. It's done. And anyway, I have a surprise for you that warrants a bottle of Moët.'

Waters smiled obligingly and calculated the expense. They were going to that new bistro that had opened up recently. Kim disappeared back into the bedroom to put on the finishing touches.

He wondered what the surprise was, but not too much; his mind was still on the Southern Housing Estate, thinking about the plight of the two boys. Heroin use was on the rise. It was 'flooding the streets' – the go-to term used in the press and media when they wanted to lazily sum up what was happening. But floods were indiscriminate, thought Waters – natural disasters that could strike anywhere at any time. Heroin wasn't. Heroin wasn't flooding the streets of Kensington, Knightsbridge or Tunbridge Wells; it was flooding the sink estates. It thrived in poverty, hopelessness, boredom and unemployment.

The room became fragrant with Rive Gauche and Waters snapped out of his indignant reverie, as once again Kim was framed in the doorway. As frames went it was

287

perfectly inadequate – it should have been elaborately carved and covered in gold leaf to hold the work of art that was Mrs Kim Waters. She looked as good as she smelled. Again he felt the pang not to go out, but for different reasons this time.

'I'm not happy about this.'

'So you've said,' murmured Detective Constable Sue Clarke distractedly as she opened the top drawer of a bow-fronted antique chest.

Melody Price and her lawyer had followed the officers from room to room as they searched the house. In George Price's study they had hit what Frost considered to be the real potential treasure trove of evidence, a wall safe hidden behind a painting of Wellington victorious at Waterloo. It was stuffed full of ledgers. There was also a leather-topped banker's desk packed to the gunwales with betting slips and IOUs.

And whilst Frost and the team bagged those items up, Melody had now accompanied Sue Clarke into the inner sanctum of the master bedroom. The bed was a French mahogany four-poster and the walls were adorned with framed nudes, all well-executed copies of masterpieces through the ages, from Botticelli's *The Birth of Venus* to Picasso's *Les Demoiselles d'Avignon*.

Clarke methodically went through all four drawers.

'Told you, nothing,' hissed Melody Price.

The detective then padded over to the first bedside table and went to open the drawer, but discovered it was

288

locked. Clarke turned round to Melody Price, who was stood in the doorway, arms folded, defiant.

'Could you unlock this, please?'

'Key's in my bag.'

Clarke followed the barely discernible gesture Melody made towards the armchair in the corner of the room. It was where clothes got temporarily dumped, rather than somewhere to sit. There was a woman's beige coat draped across the arm and a navy-blue handbag with two big gold interlocking-G clasps on it that told the world it was Gucci, and probably cost more than everything that the DC was wearing. Clarke gave an internal sigh of yearning, and couldn't wait to get her hands on it. She was sure that if Melody Price wasn't watching over her, she'd have catwalked it around the room, checking herself out in the full-length mirror.

As Clarke's hand touched the bag, Melody Price took a sudden and involuntary sharp intake of breath. Sue turned to face her, but Melody was already at her side, and grabbing at the bag. By instinct, Clarke pulled the bag away from her.

'What are you playing at?' asked Clarke.

'It's my bag! I'll give you the bloody key.'

Mrs Price lunged and went to grab it again, and again. As she did so, Clarke, now getting angry, pulled it away from her. This time she leaned too far and as the bag hit the wall, its contents fell out on to the floor.

'You're trying to obstruct me doing my—' Sue Clarke stopped talking as they both looked down at the spillage.

289

Along with a set of keys, a handbag-sized can of extra-hold Elnett hairspray and other sundries, there was a manila envelope whose sides had split due to the weight of the object it was no longer concealing: a diamond and emerald necklace.

Wednesday (5)

Frost arrived at the Shepherd's Crook public house in North Denton at 8.30 p.m. He'd just come from George Price's bookmaking shop near Market Square. Again, there they'd boxed up all the documents and ledgers that might be of interest and had taken them over to Eagle Lane to be pored over. This was nitty-gritty forensic work just as much as dusting for fingerprints or ogling fibres down a microscope. And it demanded concentration, as you soon got snow-blind to the figures and letters in front of you, until you could no longer discern any meaning from them. Frost assured Clarke and the rest of the team that he'd be back later to help them out, but first he had a pressing engagement to attend to.

He made his way through to the private bar. He'd been in this pub before, with its black-waxed beams and low-slung ceiling making you feel like a Tudor squire when you walked in, but it was far from being a local boozer. It had an out-of-town upmarket feel about it. They served food, never showed the football, and it was a safe distance from Eagle Lane, thus making it the perfect place to meet Eve Hayward.

He was early, but she was even earlier. She was sitting at a corner table, a half-quaffed gin and tonic in front of her. Frost got her another G&T and a pint of Hofmeister for himself.

'Thanks for meeting me,' he said, setting the drinks down on the table and taking a seat opposite her. He offered her a Rothmans, which she refused, and he sparked up.

'We had arranged it before.'

'So we had. Although, to be honest, what with everything that's been going on, the heroin overdose and the—'

'The murder of the bookie's clerk, Jimmy Drake?'

'That's right. Interesting you made the distinction of him being a clerk. You know much about racing?'

'I know a bit about gambling – when to take one and when not to.'

'And I bet you always come out on top. Cheers.'

They raised their glasses to each other and took a swig of their drinks. As they did, Frost took the opportunity to assess her at close quarters, and it looked like she was doing the same with him, but he doubted she was enjoying the view half as much. It was hard to tell her age; there were some faint laughter lines around the eyes, but that was about it. She had a flawless quality about her, her skin pegged out tight across high

292

cheekbones and a strong jaw. If he was to assign a number to her, it would be thirty-three, but that arbitrary figure was reached because of the way she held herself – she had the carriage and the confidence of a mature woman.

'So, Inspector Frost—'

'I thought we'd settled on Jack?'

'Jack.'

'Eve. So how was your day, or days, since we last spoke? Been busy?'

'Not as busy as you.'

'Oh, I don't know. I must say, you do look different tonight.'

'Maybe I've made an effort for you.'

Frost let out a crack of laughter. 'You don't know how much I'd like to believe that. But unfortunately, I caught sight of myself in the bar mirror when I was getting the drinks.'

'Don't do yourself down. You should have seen my ex, that little sod would do wonders for your confidence. I can tell, you're what they call an alpha male.'

'Alf who?'

'I saw you giving the briefing, I've seen how the rest of CID treat you. You've got their ear, they respect you, trust you. You may not have all the stripes, but you're the one they take note of for the real cut and thrust of police work.'

'You pick up on these things, do you?'

'I've got a good instinct.'

'Is that why they gave you the job?'

293

'I could ask the same of you.'

'How do you mean?'

'We're the same rank, about the same age—'

'Whoa, easy, love, now I know you're after something. I think I've got a good few years on you, unless you've led a very sheltered life.'

She winked. 'I'm as pure as driven snow, me. But you know what I'm saying, Jack, we didn't make DI by accident.'

'Remind me, how did we edge our way up the greasy pole? Good instinct, ear to the ground, good at picking things up?'

Eve Hayward gave a measured nod of recognition to this. Frost knew he was hitting a nerve as the cocksure smile she was wearing slowly fell away from her red-glossed lips.

'So why are we here, what is it you want to discuss?'

'Sue spoke very highly of you, I thought it would be good to—'

'You're not my type,' he said, cutting her off dead.

'To do what?' she said, laughing in disbelief.

'I said, you're not my type—'

'I heard what you bloody said, and I can't believe that you've got the nerve to repeat it! A bit presumptuous, aren't we?'

Frost gave a nonchalant shrug and then pulled a grin. 'I prefer blondes.'

'Didn't think you could afford to be so picky, mate. Sorry I can't accommodate you.'

Eve Hayward gathered her jacket around her and got ready to leave.

'You're far too modest.' Frost reached into his pocket and pulled out the photos John Waters had taken.

Eve Hayward peered down at them.

'Let's face it, Debbie Harry's got nothing on you. I have to say, I do normally prefer blondes, but in this case, I'm an auburn man all the way.'

'I'll drink to that. Cheers.'

DI Frost put the photo of Eve Hayward back on the little pile, picked up his Hofmeister and joined her in the toast. Hayward had forgone the G&Ts and had joined Frost on pints of strong Bavarian lager.

'You've heard the rumours about you, I suppose?'

'I haven't, but nothing would surprise me. I get to visit lots of areas in my line of work and I usually find the smaller the district, the bigger the rumours. So I'm expecting mid-ranking ones from Denton.'

'That you're running an internal operation, sent here to check on Denton CID's performance. And maybe root out some rotten apples if you find any.'

DI Hayward shrugged. 'You said rumours. What's the other one, then?'

Frost mulled it over as he took another sip of his pint, and decided to save the really juicy gossip about her and Sue Clarke for another time. 'Nothing worth repeating, just inconsequential tittle-tattle, and certainly nothing compared to being on the hunt for bad coppers. Which you've not denied. So who are you after?'

295

'I told you I believe there's a connection between the rash of counterfeit goods that have been hitting Denton—'

'A *rash* that no one in the county had particularly noticed until you brought it to our attention.'

'That's because no one complains about cheap goods even if they suspect they're fakes, because they're cheap and they know they wouldn't be able to afford the real ones.'

'I get the logic. But see it from my point of view: it just makes a good cover story for you to come into Eagle Lane to nose about. Asking questions, about me in particular.'

'Do you want me to tell you what I know, or do you just want to go off on a paranoid rant?'

Frost raised his hands in a gesture of mock surrender, with just a hint of *I'm all yours* thrown in for good measure. He then lit up another king-sized smoke to calm his nerves – she was good, this one, bloody good.

'I'm not after you, Jack. I'm with a special unit that's looking into overseas organized crime that operates in the UK. And if what I think is happening in Denton is happening, then you've really got a big problem on your hands.'

'What do you think is happening?'

'One of the biggest and most dangerous figures in organized crime I know of has just landed on your patch.'

They'd decided to skip the starters. Just go for the main course and dessert, that was the way to enjoy a good meal, insisted John Waters. And no bread either. If you

296

were still hungry after the dessert, well, you could always order another one, or a second helping, as he liked to say. But when the sprightly young waiter turned up and placed the main dishes in front of them, with all the flourish and performance of a magician producing a rabbit out of a hat, and then bowed away from their table uttering, '*Bon appétit*', they both wished they'd ordered starters and a basket of bread each. At La Maison des Délices, they served nouvelle cuisine. Which, as far as Waters could tell, meant the plate looked good, like some minimalist abstract art, with brightly coloured lines and squiggles and dashes and dots that may or may not have been food. It was a feast for the eye, but not necessarily for the belly. There was far too much plate showing for Waters' tastes. And though Kim was beaming with joy at the work of art before her, he was pretty sure she felt the same.

'Wow, I'll never manage all this,' he said, dry as the Sauvignon Blanc the waiter had recommended. 'I hope they have doggy bags.'

Kim burst out laughing and her husband joined her, which turned heads in the polite society they were amongst. North Denton's finest. John Waters gave them the thumbs-up and grabbed the white linen serviette that had been origamied into the design of a swan, gave it a good shake and tucked it into his collar, then went about depleting the dish before him.

'So, tell me, what's the big secret?'

'How's the food, babe?'

'The food is as good as it looks. Come on, Kim, I think

297

I've done very well not asking until now. My patience is second to none. I'm assuming it's good news.'

'If it's good news, surely you can guess what it is.'

'OK, you've got a promotion?'

She rested her knife and fork on the plate, and didn't look too happy with his answer.

'How many guesses do I get?'

'You've got two left.'

'OK, you've wangled some holiday time?'

She shook her head in an unsmiling robotic fashion that made John Waters realize the seriousness of the situation. He should have given it a lot more thought, maybe applied some solid detective work to the problem; but expediency got the better of him, and he just wanted answers, so he blurted out, 'Pay rise?'

She glared at him. He could tell it wasn't what she wanted to hear, and you really didn't have to be a detective to work that one out.

'I'm pregnant.'

Waters' knife and fork fell from his hands, hands that had immediately become weak and clammy on hearing the news, and landed on the china plate with an exclamatory clatter. Again, this drew attention from the other patrons. What followed was a pregnant pause that grew and grew and eventually gave birth to a deep and impenetrable silence. Then, to break the silence, John Waters could feel himself muttering some words, but he almost felt like he had no control over them and certainly hadn't given them much real thought: they were vague platitudes and insincere congratulations that didn't match his

298

alarmed expression. And he could only imagine what his wife saw on his face, because it was enough to make her grab her own serviette and cover her eyes as the tears came.

Frost placed two more pints of Hofmeister on the table. It was their fourth round now. He was impressed with Eve Hayward's staying power, as she matched him pint for pint with the strong gassy Bavarian brew, and showed no signs of flagging. Her voice wasn't remotely booze-slurred and remained crisp, clear and in control. Her glossy red lips never once looked like letting an indiscretion or a tasty nugget of confidential information slip past them. Not that it was ever his intention to let the lubricant of strong lager loosen her tongue, or get her good and drunk so he could dig for dirt and find out exactly who she was, and what she was after. But it would certainly be a fortuitous outcome if all those things happened.

She briefed him thoroughly on Eamon Hogan and his operation. The Dublin-born gangster was nothing if not diverse, believing you needed a broad 'criminal portfolio' to succeed, and that included everything from armed robberies, domestic burglaries, fraud, protection rackets, smuggling, counterfeit goods, and just about every other type of criminal activity you'd care to mention. And amongst these activities there also featured gambling and race fixing.

Hogan loved horse racing, but along with the Irish's natural affinity for the sport, he loved what the betting ring could offer him. All that untraceable cash sloshing about in the bookmakers' satchels: it was the perfect place to launder his money. Whether or not the Dublin gangster had anything to do with the attacks on George Price and Jimmy Drake, Eve Hayward couldn't say, as there was as yet no proof, but like Frost, there had never been a coincidence that she'd been willing to accept when it came to a murder case.

When Eamon Hogan had first got started in the smuggling business, it was to bring untaxed shipments of booze and cigarettes into the Republic of Ireland, and this had led to him dealing in counterfeit goods; it was a profitable sideline that he'd kept in his 'crime portfolio' ever since. But, of course, it was the insidious nature of the drugs trade that had proved the biggest money-spinner for Eamon Hogan. And his adroitness at drug smuggling and distribution had made him one of the top gangsters in the Republic.

There was still the ten-million-dollar question, which Frost dutifully asked: 'Why Denton?'

'A lot of major Irish crime figures have felt the pinch at home with some big arrests. The Garda and the government have been piling on the pressure – seizing their assets, homes and other property, freezing bank accounts – and a lot are moving out of Dublin. Some have gone to Europe, over to Spain, even Marseille and the South of France, running their businesses from afar. But Eamon Hogan seems to be doing it differently: he wants to take over a whole town.'

'For all Denton's charms, we're hardly the Costa del

Sol or the Riviera. Which again begs the question, why sunny Denton?'

'It's up and coming. It has a growing population with a youngish demographic. The property developers have moved in and are expanding with lots of land being made available, and it's just about commutable to London. There's a big council estate in town and others in neighbouring areas that can be infiltrated. But probably the biggest reason is that it's not Glasgow, Liverpool, Birmingham, or London. There's no competition here, no major crime families or gangs to contend with. Plus, and this could be the biggest factor involved, they may well have already corrupted people in positions of power here.'

'Coppers?'

She didn't answer, left it hanging.

Not good enough. Frost wanted answers. 'Sue Clarke told me you were asking questions about me, so you obviously thought I was in the frame?'

'I walk into a station and I think everyone is – potentially.'

'But not now, or you wouldn't be telling me all this. What made you change your mind?'

'Because corrupt coppers on the take are usually the best coppers and really good at their jobs.'

Frost, with all the sarcasm he could muster, said, 'Thanks.'

'What I mean by that is, they blend in and get on with the job, they exploit the system by working seamlessly within it. The last thing a corrupt copper does is challenge the status quo, stick his head above the parapet and kick up merry hell when he thinks it's not working. He doesn't shoot his big mouth off and fight everyone and everything, or come across as a stubborn little arsehole to get the right result.'

'Thanks.'

'You're welcome.'

They laughed. But bent coppers aside, Eamon Hogan's pervasive power made sense of what had been happening. That's why he's been able to recruit Bomber Harris and Tommy Wilkins, two Herberts who hate each other, mused Frost. They had no choice. Plus the fact they're now probably earning more money than they've ever earned in their lives. But just how dark could it get? The DI shuddered and thought back to when Eagle Lane had been badly damaged in an IRA bombing. 'Is there any political angle? IRA?'

'You're asking the right questions, Jack. There's always a certain amount of coexistence between the ODCs and Provos.'

'ODCs?'

'Ordinary Decent Criminals: it's a term used for criminals who have no political allegiances as such, and commit crimes for profit, not to fill the coffers or war chests of any paramilitary outfit. Ordinary Decent Criminals is a term *they* coined, not the Garda, I can assure you.'

Frost gave a heavy sigh as he considered the implications. 'And this has just landed on our doorstep?'

'He plays his cards right, he could end up owning the place.'

'Over my dead body.'

302

'That can be arranged. Like I said, he's ruthless.'

Frost lifted his glass to his lips, took a slow sip of lager and pondered what Eve Hayward had just said – it was the kind of statement that demanded a snappy and ballsy retort. And there were several sharp one-liners that he was sure he could have thrown out that might even have impressed her. But somehow he wasn't in the mood for that.

'Do you have any pictures of Eamon Hogan?'

'Back at my hotel.'

Frost, now impatient, downed most of his drink; he broke his usual rule and actually left some in the glass.

'Can I see them?'

'The pictures?'

'What else?'

Wednesday (6)

'Was everything OK, sir?'

'It was great, just great,' said John Waters distractedly as he collected his Access card off the waiter, a waiter whose French accent seemed to be slipping the more he had to deal with the emotional couple on table number seven. There had been raised voices and Kim had stormed out in floods of tears. So when Waters stuffed a fiver in the waiter's breast pocket just before leaving the restaurant with his head down, he could have sworn he heard 'good luck, mate' in a broad Brummie accent.

Waters found Kim by the Nissan, waiting to be let in. They didn't look at each other as they got into the car. Waters turned the key in the ignition and slipped the car into gear. He took a deep breath and then killed the engine.

'I'm not taking this back home.'

She sat perfectly still, her face not reacting to a single

word or sound he was uttering. To Waters it seemed like she was now locked in her own world of anger.

'Of course I want kids. I wouldn't have married you if I didn't. And I am happy. But I'm scared, Kim, I'm scared, too.'

She let out a heavy sigh, and slowly turned towards him. It felt like she was re-evaluating him, seeing him anew. Big, strong, tough John Waters could look after himself, scared of nothing and of no one. If that's the image he'd projected, he felt himself coming undone – it was false and he felt like a fraud. In this job you were confronted with your worst atavistic fears for your family and loved ones, in crime after crime, day after day. But some hit home harder than others, resonating in your past, threatening your future.

Kim intuited the problem. 'It's the two boys, Dean and Gavin, isn't it?'

'You know I was at that community outreach meeting on the estate, just before it all happened. The mothers asked me what they could do about the problem. And without meaning to, and I certainly didn't plan it, or even want to . . . I ended up telling them about my brother. They now know more about him than you. Because I've never really spoken to you about him, have I?'

'I know his name, Carl, and I know that he was older than you. And I know you miss him, even though you've never said it. But that's about it, because you always shut down when I try to ask you about him.'

'He was three years older than me, but when you're a kid that feels like a lifetime. So I always really looked up to him, he was good at football, funny, smart, always dressed the business and everyone liked him. He started hanging around with the wrong crowd, got into crime, petty stuff at first. But it led to borstal, some prison. Then he got into drugs. Fast forward a few years, and he ended up dead around the back of King's Cross. My mum had done everything she could to help him, she and her friends tried to stop drugs coming into the neighbourhood. But she couldn't stop him. And when he died, that was it, she never spoke about him again from that day on. As I got older I understood, it was like part of her had died too. After a while it was like he never existed. But he did, of course. He got me here. I don't know why I wanted to be a copper, it wasn't a natural thing for me to do, but I think it had something to do with him. Maybe try and stop what my mum couldn't.'

'Then at least something good did come out of it, John. I see the way your mum looks at you, she's proud.'

'Moving here . . . to Denton, I didn't think I was moving to the Lake District or the Cotswolds, but I thought I could outrun it . . . but here it is, on my doorstep.'

'I'm not moving to the Lake District!' she said jokingly. Then, very seriously: 'This is my home and yours too now, for better or worse. And you can't run away from life. You didn't before, you joined the force, and you faced it full on. So don't be scared. You'll be a great father. I wouldn't have chosen you for the job if I didn't think so. There's no manual for this stuff, no rules or guidebook, not like becoming a copper. It just happens.

306

It's my first time, too. I'm scared. But I know it will all be OK – no, it will be better than that, it will be perfect. Trust me.'

'I trust you,' said John Waters with a gratified bobbing of his head, like the world had just been set back on its axis. Whilst he groped around for the right words, she had an unerring knack of coming out with just the right thing at just the right time. She had an innate wisdom that just happened to be wrapped up in a ra-ra skirt and a little black boob tube. I'm a lucky man, he told himself.

'Have you got any pictures of your brother?'

'I do.'

'Let's get home, I'd like to see them.'

He smiled, then reached over, rested his hand on her tummy and kissed her.

'It's a bit early,' said Kim. 'You won't feel any little kicks. Just some rumbling, because I'm bloody starving, can we get a kebab on the way back?'

The strong Bavarian beer had been replaced by French cognac, and the choice of drink complemented their surroundings perfectly. Frost and Eve Hayward were now in the lounge bar of the Prince Albert Hotel, with its country-house grandeur. It was one of the few places in the town where you could drink after hours that hadn't been renovated, modernized and ruined with gaudy neon-blue and -pink tube lighting in the shape of a cocktail glass, desperately trying to convince you that you were in Miami.

307

With the workload Frost had, he didn't dare look at his watch, and, luckily, he couldn't read the dial of the grandfather clock that chimed away in the gloom of the corner, but he knew it was late, too late for a school night. The lounge bar was nice and empty, allowing Frost the illusion that the button-back Chesterfield chairs they were sitting in and the grand marble surround of the flickering fireplace were all theirs. Delusional, maybe, but when you lived above a Chinese takeaway on the High Street, these momentary lapses were allowed. When Frost was starting off on the force, an old copper had once advised him to keep an allotment and go there once a week, and to regularly think about nothing other than complete nonsense. 'You need to empty your mind of the realities of your life and the work you do. It will keep you sane,' he'd said. Frost didn't have an allotment (yet), but he did like to slip into fantasy every now and again. Which seemed to lead seamlessly to his next thought.

'I could tell you that other rumour about you, if you like.'

Eve Hayward was warming her cognac in her hands, staring down at the big balloon glass as if it held the magic and answers of a clairvoyant's crystal ball. As the burnt-orange liquid played perfectly in the light of the fire crackling away in the grate, she smiled a knowing smile, then glanced up at Frost and said, 'I can see you're dying to tell me.'

'Well, you've been so informative, Eve, it'd be rude not to extend you the same courtesy.'

308

'Did anyone ever tell you you've got a very wicked grin?'

'Only our great leader, Superintendent Mullett, and he's a big fan of my dress sense, too.'

She rolled her eyes at the mention of the super's name. 'Why do I feel that with Mullett, there's a scandal involving two dominatrices and him dressed as a schoolboy just waiting to happen?'

Frost laughed and winced at the image and the painful probability of it all.

'Go on then, let's hear it.'

'That you and Sue Clarke spent the night here . . . together.'

Eve Hayward's head slowly rolled back as she let out a peal of laughter. Like the rest of her, Frost enjoyed her laugh. It was husky, raucous, very sexy, and infectious enough for him to join her in it.

Eventually she answered, 'We did spend the night together.'

'I know. Sue said so herself. Quite open about it, she was. I think some of the younger, more imaginative PCs, who mainly still live with their mums, have been indulging in some wish fulfilment.'

Hayward kept smiling, but said nothing more.

Frost kept on digging: 'Maybe they got the wrong end of the stick. They wanted to read more into it than there was, or perhaps not . . .'

'Well, they couldn't have got the wrong end of the stick, because there were no *sticks* involved that night. But they might have got it right on the button.'

'The *button*.'

'*The* button.'

Frost wasn't one to mix his metaphors, but you didn't have to be a poet to work that one out. Eve Hayward laughed some more and dismissed it all with a good-humoured shake of her head.

'Let's keep that rumour going, shall we, Jack? But, seriously, she's a great girl and a really good copper. I think if Sue Clarke is given the right opportunities, she'll go places.' Frost agreed. Hayward added, 'But she's definitely not my type.'

'Then who is? I don't see a wedding ring.'

'You neither.'

'No. My wife passed away eighteen months ago now.'

'I'm sorry.'

Frost paused for thought, a thought he wasn't sure he wanted to have, not here, not now, but it came over him anyway. 'Sounds callous, but we lived very separate lives, seemed like that for most of the time.'

'The work?'

'It always is, but in the end that just becomes the excuse. It's the great default position we have as coppers: we can say we let our work get in the way. It's special pleading, the job ruined my marriage, nothing to do with me, guv, not guilty, it was the job.'

Eve Hayward gave a humourless laugh of recognition, a fellow traveller.

Frost continued, 'But that said, we didn't grow apart either, we were different people right from the off, Mary and me. Funny, I think we had an idea that what made

310

us so different was what made us right for each other. She was from a very well-to-do local family, big house in North Denton. I was from . . . well, the wrong side of the tracks, as they say. Her parents didn't much care for me. Being a copper may have helped for a while, but it's not the same as being a barrister, doctor, banker. I think even they could see I was too mouthy to join the top brass, be like the Mulletts of this world. Still, it held for a while, opposites attract, and all that. That may be true – I suppose if enough people say it for long enough it passes for truth. But it wasn't true for us. We just got more settled in our ways, and never really . . . I don't know.' Frost looked down at his glass and swirled the cognac around the bowl a few times. It made for a good prop, too good to drink. 'How about you, ever been spliced?'

'I got married when I was seventeen. Lasted three years. We met at work, before I became a copper. It was the most boring job in the world, and he was the only reasonably attractive and interesting thing in the place. He was all right, he was just young and stupid, like me. I thought I was destined to work on the factory floor all my life. Luckily the factory shut down, he pissed off, and I was left on my own. It was this or the army.'

'You like uniforms, do you?'

'Believe it or not, I like doing something where I don't know whether I'm going to make it home at night. Does that sound weird?'

Frost shook his head. It didn't sound weird at all. His mind quickly scrolled back to the time he was shot in an

311

attempted bank robbery: he remembered the feeling, not of fear but of exhilaration. He could almost see the hammer hit the bullet in the chamber and pass down the barrel of the revolver, the smell of cordite, the smoke, the searing pain as the bullet tore into his flesh, and at that moment he swore he'd never felt more alive. It was a flesh wound, ugly, but not fatal.

But for all that, there was young DC Derek Simms, PC David Simms' older brother, who hadn't made it home, killed in the line of duty shortly after Mary's funeral. And Frost's old friend and mentor, DI Bert Williams, had suffered a similar fate. His eyes drifted down past his glass to the table and the black file that Eve Hayward had brought down from her room. In there were the pictures he wanted to see. The opposition. The quarry. Eamon 'The Hook' Hogan. And the very reason why you might not make it home alive.

Thursday (1)

Frost was finally pulled from his dream not with a gentle nudge to his shoulder, but with a stiff prod and the words, 'Sleeping Beauty, time to shift!'

When his sleep-gritted eyes had slowly wedged themselves open, he was welcomed with the vision that was Eve Hayward, easing herself into the wide-shouldered jacket of her navy-blue trouser suit. He just caught sight of the silhouette of her majestic chest in the pristine white blouse before she fastened the brass buttons of her jacket. She looked magnificent, fresh and efficient, and ready to go. She had matched him pint for pint, nightcap for nightcap, and *he* felt like death. He just about got himself into an upright position, but the manic circular motion of the room sent him straight back down on to the pillow. He knew that the hangover he was embroiled in was an all-encompassing monster; all the others had just been rehearsals for this one.

As his fogged mind scrolled back, he watched Eve Hayward go through some paperwork on the dressing table and transfer some files into her black attaché case, all the while humming an unrecognizable little tune, and seemingly unaffected by the booze they'd both put away last night.

Did we? Did we actually . . . ?

Frost's bloodshot eyes surveyed the room, trying to piece together how he'd got here. There was only one bed, a double, and it looked like they had shared it. He was in his underpants. His good ones, he'd made sure of that, just in case. Not that he was expecting anything to happen between him and Eve Hayward, but you never know, stranger things happen at sea, and landlocked Denton had been known to throw up a few surprises. And this was his problem right now, he really didn't know. Everything sort of went blank after the third . . . or the fourth, or maybe even the fifth cognac. Is it really possible? he asked himself, with his throbbing head sinking into his hands.

'You'd better get your kit on, Jack, DC Clarke is picking us up in five minutes.'

'Jesus-bloody-Nora,' groaned Frost, his eyes lifting from the carpet just in time to see Eve Hayward slip out of the door with a cheery 'See you downstairs!'

Frost made his way to the hotel lobby feeling as crumpled as the contents of his pocket, the ciggies that, like the booze, he swore he would never touch again. His mouth felt as if it was lined with tar and his tongue

314

furred with shag tobacco. A new, healthier regime was called for.

Before he could ask the receptionist where Ms Eve Hayward was, he spotted her in the dining room with Sue Clarke, enjoying some coffee and chatting away. They looked faintly conspiratorial; maybe they were comparing notes on him. He marched in to face them.

'Morning, Sue.'

She gave a welcoming smile that concealed a mischievous smirk.

'I've just been filling Sue in on what happened last night,' said Eve Hayward.

Frost pulled out a chair and joined them. He was genuinely confused. 'What did happen last night?'

'Eve told me *all* about it,' said Clarke, 'I've even seen the photos.'

Frost felt like his bones had been stripped from his body and he almost slipped off his chair. 'Photos? What bloody photos? You took photos . . . ?'

He then caught sight of a stack of pictures hiding behind the tall silver coffee pot. They were the ones Waters had taken of Hayward undercover in her blonde Debbie Harry wig.

Clarke, barely containing her mirth, teased him: 'What photos were you thinking of, Jack?'

Frost ignored the question and stiffened his back to try to reassert his authority and get on with more pressing matters. 'Has Inspector Hayward filled you in on who she is and what she's doing here?'

'Most of it.'

315

Frost hoicked up the sleeve of his jacket to check the time on his Casio. It made for ungodly reading – it was 7.15 a.m.

'OK, Mullett's briefing is in an hour and a half,' he said, pouring himself a black coffee. 'We better make sure we're all singing from the same hymn sheet.'

'The plan has to be to find a strong enough connection between Bomber Harris and Tommy Wilkins, who are dealing the heroin, and Eamon Hogan. If we pull those two in, and even if they do talk, where's the evidence? There's a good chance they may not even know who Hogan is, and I bet they've not met him, just his two lieutenants, Colm and Shane. He usually likes to send them in first.'

Clarke then asked, 'Who else knows you're undercover?'

'Just you two, and that's how I want it to stay. It has to, or I might as well go home.'

'So there's someone you don't trust in Denton CID, is that it?' wondered Clarke.

Eve Hayward gave a non-committal shrug. 'I know how Eamon Hogan works, he's a corrupter. And if he's moving his operation to this area, he may very well have someone on the force on his payroll already.'

'And you thought it was Jack?'

Eve Hayward threw her a wink. 'I think I've established it isn't.'

'I bet.'

'Oi! Do you mind not talking about me like I'm not in the room?'

'You don't think it's—'

Frost cut her off. 'We don't think it's anyone in particular yet, Sue, we're just playing our cards close to our chest.'

'Not telling even Mullett?'

'Especially not Mullett.'

They drank their coffee in silence as they considered the prospect of a bad apple potentially right under their noses. Frost broke his vow not to indulge in any of his vices and sparked up a crumpled cigarette. As the smoke hit the back of his throat, he really could have done with a stiff drink too, a hair of the dog, a pick-me-up, something alcoholic to cut through the fog.

'The search at George Price's threw up some interesting information and items,' Clarke reminded him.

'I'd almost forgotten about that,' muttered Frost. 'Go on, then.'

Sue Clarke reached down to her handbag and pulled out an A4 photocopy that she handed to him.

'What's this?'

'It's a list of the stock that was stolen in the Rimmington jewellery-shop robbery.' Clarke explained to Eve about the diamond and emerald necklace that she'd discovered in Melody Price's handbag. 'The description matches what I saw perfectly. I bet there's a picture of it somewhere for insurance purposes. Or, even better, we just nick her and—'

'No,' said Frost emphatically.

'Why not?'

Frost gave Eve Hayward the nod to take over.

317

She responded to her cue. 'Because Eamon Hogan isn't just a drug dealer, he's a well-rounded villain who likes robbing jewellery stores, too. And if what you saw is from the Rimmington haul, and I believe you're right, that connects Melody Price to Eamon Hogan. And the George Price shooting, and the Jimmy Drake killing.'

Frost glanced at his watch again: not long now to Mullett's morning briefing. He would have to sit and listen to Hornrim Harry, knowing that the super didn't have a bloody clue what was really going on. And, of course, they couldn't enlighten him – because of their suspicions that Hogan had got his hooks into someone on the County force. They didn't know who it was, or even how high up they were. It could be anyone. It almost didn't bear thinking about, as all their current cases seemed to be growing multiple strands and also turning in on themselves, to become one big toxic heap with Eamon Hogan at the top of it.

A fresh thought hit Frost and he returned his attention to Sue Clarke. 'What else did you find after I left?'

'Still nothing on Socks and Winston yet, but looking through the Prices' business files, we discovered that Melody Price owns Video Stars, the rental shop that Michael Price works at. Which is something neither Michael Price nor Melody bothered to mention.'

'Any coffee left? I'm gasping!'

They turned towards the bulky figure coughing his way towards them – it was DC Arthur Hanlon.

Frost's brow creased at the sight of him. 'How did you know I was here?'

Hanlon winked. 'Clever detective work.'

'I'll repeat the question: how did you know I was here?'

'Me, probably,' said Clarke. 'In case anyone needed to find you I left a message at the station last night that you'd be here.'

When he'd finally picked his jaw up off the carpet, he asked, 'And how the bloody hell did *you* know?'

'Clever detective work?'

Frost's eyes flicked between Clarke and Hayward, feeling like an innocent in some greater female conspiracy.

Hanlon pulled out a chair and joined them at the table, then proceeded to pour himself a coffee in Frost's empty cup, which was met with no resistance from Frost, as Arthur looked like he needed it. Those four or five steps up to the hotel entrance could really take it out of you.

Once refreshed, Arthur Hanlon said, 'I thought I'd tell you in person, guv. We pulled a body out the river last night.'

'Who is it?'

Thursday (2)

Superintendent Stanley Mullett had increased the pressure and the manpower on the Southern Housing Estate. Especially since there now seemed to be a media van representing some TV channel or other almost permanently parked there, just waiting for the latest bad news so a photogenic young hack could spring out of the back of it, microphone in hand. The Assistant Chief Constable's mantra was simple – not only must they resolve the situation, they must be *seen* to resolve the situation, at least until the media and cameras had gone away.

So it was against this backdrop that John Waters and a small army of plainclothes and uniformed officers, armed with warrants, had descended to search the homes of suspects as well as the warren of garages and lock-ups on the estate. Mullett knew that there was nothing that put the public more at ease than news footage showing dozens of coppers dressed like stormtroopers battering down doors, then emerging with some ne'er-do-well in pyjamas and handcuffs and throwing them unceremoniously into the back of a paddy wagon.

The search of the Southern Housing Estate had been planned to start at 7.30 a.m. sharp. Word must have spread fast, because when an hour later Waters and PC David Simms descended on a row of lock-ups to the far east of the sprawling estate, they found one already open, and parked in its entrance was a rusty maroon Reliant Scimitar shooting brake, into the back of which the owner was furiously loading boxes.

He was in his early fifties with a barrel chest and broad shoulders, and he had an impressively fulsome, heavily greased and suspiciously jet-black quiff, to match his black cap-sleeved T-shirt that showed off his muscly and elaborately inked arms. There were lots of tattoos celebrating girlfriends and ex-wives, his love for his old mum, and the various ports he'd visited in his days serving in the Royal Navy, from which he'd been dishonourably discharged. His name was Barry Sutton, but no one called him that.

'How's it going, Sinbad?'

Barry 'Sinbad' Sutton looked up sharply and banged his quiffed head on the hatch of the estate car he was loading, which resulted in him dropping the cardboard box he was holding. This crashed to the ground with the clatter of broken crockery. He winced with pain, seemingly not for the bump on the bonce, but for whatever had got smashed in the box.

'Don't look so worried, it probably doesn't belong to you anyway, right?'

321

Sinbad hunkered down, his quiffed head turning sharply in either direction, obviously looking for an escape route.

'Don't even think about it; as the old saying goes, you're a big man, but you're out of shape.'

Sinbad straightened up and beamed a crooked-toothed smile. 'Mr Waters, fancy seeing you here at this time of morning.'

Waters and Simms made their way to the lock-up down the small grass verge they'd been watching from, and went in to find a veritable treasure trove of stolen goods. Barry Sutton described himself as a trader and a dealer, a hawker and a pitcher. Down at Eagle Lane he was simply known as a receiver.

John Waters approached one of the stacks of cardboard boxes.

'What can I help you with, Officer?'

The detective turned to Sinbad, and it may have been the exertion of lifting the boxes, or it may have been the stress of being up at such an unlikely hour, but his forehead glistened with beads of guilty perspiration.

'Nothing, Sinbad, I think I'll help myself,' said Waters, flipping the lip of one of the boxes, dipping his hand in and pulling out a silver candelabrum.

PC Simms said, 'Looks Georgian to me.'

The DS looked impressed. 'Very good, PC Simms, been watching Arthur Negus on the telly, have we?'

'No, Sarge, been doing my research, hope to make the antiques robbery squad next year. Inspector Frost said it's good to specialize.'

322

Sinbad joined the conversation. 'Well, there's no hallmarks on it so you can't date it, but it's probably Sheffield silver plate, definitely not Georgian, a Victorian copy, of not bad quality. You can read all the books you like, son, but' – he tapped the side of his bulbous red nose with an equally bulbous forefinger – 'you need a nose for these things. I can sniff out a quality antique a mile away.'

Simms grinned. 'Well, when I get back to the station, Sinbad, I'll look it up on the stolen-items database, and then we'll see how good your nose is.'

Waters smiled at the young PC's cheek. 'He's right. Then we'll see if you're Sinbad or Ali Baba.'

Sinbad's face creased in confusion. 'Ali who?'

Waters went over to another box and pulled out a video, *Revenge of the Nerds*, in its cellophane wrapper. 'Any good? I've not seen it yet. Then again, no one has, have they? Not been released in this country yet.' Waters pulled out more of the same. 'You're so nicked, Sinbad, it's not even funny.'

'The bullet is a 9mm. Ring any bells?'

'That's the same calibre as the one in George Price's head,' said Frost with a thread of relief running through his voice – at last things were joining up. And at this juncture, the relief came from not having a completely unrelated murder case to investigate which would stretch their already limited resources.

'And at close range, to the head,' said County's chief pathologist, Gerald Drysdale, lowering a thin metal

323

ruler into another wound on Little Stevie's body: a three-inch puncture just below the sternum.

A slab in the County pathology lab wasn't a destination Frost would have wanted for the diminutive career criminal. They'd locked horns a few times but he had always enjoyed the banter that came with their 'professional' relationship; so DC Hanlon had been correct to deliver the news to him in person, almost a professional courtesy. But Wooder's demise was no great surprise to Frost: men like him seldom died in their own beds. Yet surely he'd have hoped for a better end than this.

There were over a dozen of these punctures all over the thief's torso, and they all needed to be measured and assessed. Gerald Drysdale explained that the after-death stab wounds had probably been made in an attempt to puncture the lungs and get the body to fill with as much water as possible so it would sink to the bottom of the river. The human body, with all its gasses and powerful respiratory system – even when it was dead it was still an effort to keep it underwater. Weights were always a good idea to keep a corpse from bobbing to the surface, but even when weighed down, cadavers had still been known to slip their shackles and reappear.

As he went about his work, Gerald Drysdale managed to hum the notes of something distinctly classical, Wagner perhaps. Frost glanced round at his colleague who was standing by the door, ready to make a quick exit. As big as DC Arthur Hanlon's belly was, he didn't have the stomach for these sights, and was uncomfortably shifting

324

from foot to foot, concentrating on not puking up *again* as the smell of disinfectant clawed at his throat.

'So, you're absolutely sure he was already dead when he was stabbed?' queried Frost.

'Definitely, the bullet killed him outright. The knife wounds aren't the work of a frantic maniac with a blood-lust, if that's what you're getting at.'

'Could have fooled me,' Hanlon called out from the sidelines.

'Wouldn't be the first time, Arthur,' replied Frost without taking his eyes off the butchered corpse of Little Stevie.

Gerald Drysdale continued, 'All these wounds are strategically placed.'

'How about the cuts to the face?'

The little thief's amiable good looks had been decimated with a series of slashes to his cheeks and brow.

'To increase the rate of decomposition, and to attract fish and have them nibble away at him. You'd be surprised how quickly the features of a corpse can disappear out in the wild, in a river – can be almost gone in a couple of days.'

Hanlon made a retching noise in the background.

'Almost done, Arthur,' said Frost with a wicked grin, 'then we can get that breakfast . . . Sausages, sizzling bacon and a stack of black pudding, I reckon . . .'

The DC heaved again and excused himself from the room. Frost thanked Drysdale and went to leave. Before he could, though, he felt Dr Death's grip on him. The

325

pathologist's thin dry lips edged up into an approximation of a smile.

'Not quite, Jack, I've saved the best for last.'

He went over to a desk, retrieved a sealed plastic bag from a tray and handed it to Frost.

'It was used to bind his hands and feet,' said Drysdale. 'I had the Forensics chaps look at it, and they can confirm that it's the same nylon rope that was used to strangle Jimmy Drake. Same thickness, everything. Like I said before, common enough, and yet . . .'

'And yet, coincidences don't exist in murder cases. So Little Stevie now links us to the shooting of George Price *and* the murder of Jimmy Drake. And that gives us one perpetrator.'

The pathologist nodded bleakly.

His body was discovered by an early-morning dog-walker in the next county. He was hanging from the bough of a tree. It looked like suicide. When Ella Ross was given the news, the location confused her at first. What was he doing all the way out there? But as she talked it through, at first with the WPC and the social worker assigned to the case, then finally with Cathy Bartlett, it all made sense to her.

The spot was called Campwood, and it was a wildlife area and camping ground that was used by schools for week-long holidays. Gavin and Dean had been there three summers in a row whilst at primary school, and they had loved the place, coming home with stories of a magic forest and a secret lake they'd discovered. Ella

326

and Cathy concluded it had been a time of innocence for them, and it was the place that Gavin wanted to get back to. It was where he'd decided to end his life.

He'd ridden all the way out there on his racing bike – it was found resting against the tree. It would have been a good hour's cycling. In that hour, what must he have thought about? His guilt, the part he'd played in his best friend's death? Whatever Gavin was thinking, it was enough to fuel his long journey to the place he'd chosen and to take his own life. But there was no note. He just climbed up the tree, a tree by a small pond, a pond that with its lily pads and dragonflies must have looked to an eight-year-old boy from a bleak estate like a magical lake.

John Waters had just finished cuffing Sinbad when he got the news, news he'd somehow been expecting. A bleak thought that he'd not been able to shake since the death of Dean . . . Where one went, the other would follow. When he arrived at St Giles' Church to talk to Ella, he found her with Cathy. It was the first time the women had come face to face since Dean's death. And now the two boys were together again, so were their mothers.

Reverend James Tutt and the social worker were there to oversee the meeting between the two mothers. But whilst it looked like plenty of tears had been shed, there was no animosity, no apportioning of blame, just two friends unified in their tragedy, their hands gripped together, talking and comforting each other.

But the two women weren't alone in their grief. The pews of the church were packed, probably more so than on any given Sunday, and mostly with women, women from the Southern Housing Estate who wanted to show solidarity. Waters recognized many of them from the meeting at the community centre. He suspected that for some, if not most, it was their first time in the church.

Ella Ross and Cathy Bartlett came over to him. Waters stood up. But he could barely meet their gaze, couldn't fathom their grief. He went to say how sorry he was, to offer his sincere condolences, to say that he—

He was cut short by Ella; and in a voice that was unwavering, determined, she said, 'We know what we're going to do. We all do.'

'Just like you told us,' added Cathy, still holding her friend's hand.

Waters looked uncertain. Ella reminded him, 'We're going to show them. Show them who's got the power.'

As Waters glanced down at Ella and Cathy's hands, clasped together, unified, strong, he got it; and he knew there would be more joining them. And as he looked around at the faces of the women in the impromptu congregation, who were now all turned towards him, he didn't doubt their power for a second.

Frost made his way through to Interview Room One; he'd just returned from seeing a distraught Debbie Wooder to extend his condolences and entreat her cooperation with the investigation.

'Afternoon, Sinbad,' greeted Frost, swinging into the room whilst looking down at the printout of the charges

328

against Barry Sutton. 'Santa's Grotto, Aladdin's Cave, Sotheby's of Bond Street and under Fagin's floorboards – they all pale in comparison to what you keep squirrelled away in that lock-up of yours.'

Frost let the charge sheet fall from his hand and drop right in front of the detainee. Sinbad didn't bat an eyelid and remained seemingly unperturbed, his tattooed arms crossed defiantly across his chest, eyes staring straight ahead. Frost ruined his view by sitting down opposite him. The detective then adjusted his head to read a limerick inscribed on Sinbad's forearm. He laughed.

'I've never been to Madras myself, but I'll take your word for it that's what the ladies enjoy. Anyway, getting down to brass tacks,' he said with an emphatic drum roll of his knuckles on the desk, 'we've got enough to nick you and put you away for a good five-year stretch, considering your previous and—'

'I'm not dealing smack! That's why you're turning everyone over, I know that much. I'm against it like you, it's filth and it's sold by scum. I've got kids too, Frost – you think I want them ending up like that lad Dean?'

'Relax, Sinbad, no one's accusing you of selling heroin.'

'Then what you searching my place for?'

'We're searching everywhere. Orders from on high, they just want to shake things up on the estate, make it uncomfortable for whoever is dealing it, and let them know we're not going to let them turn the estate into a no-go zone. There are a lot of good people on that estate. And then there's you.'

329

Sinbad went to say something, but Frost raised his hand for him to stop.

'Little Stevie Wooder was pulled out of the river last night. Shot in the head.'

Frost watched as the solid block of defiance sitting in front of him melted before his eyes. Sutton's tattooed arms dropped to his sides, and the poker face he'd been wearing slipped off and fell to the floor, never to be seen again. Sinbad shook his head, partly in disbelief, but partly not. And that was the part that Frost was interested in.

'Just been to see Debbie. Of course, she's in pieces. Poor cow, whatever Little Stevie put her through with . . . with his *absences* at Her Majesty's pleasure, I know they were very much in love. I'm seeing her again tomorrow. She wants to tell me all she knows. And I know you know something, probably something she doesn't. He was your mate, as well as your business partner. All those years you worked together, he never grassed you up for a lighter sentence. Many villains would have. But he stood staunch, right, Sinbad?'

Sutton gave a slow, thoughtful nod, looking like he was remembering all the years he *didn't* spend in prison thanks to Little Stevie. He cleared his throat and said, 'When he went missing in action, everyone thought he was off with a bird, or casing some big job. I knew different. I knew he was in deep with something. The reason I knew was because he wouldn't tell me all of it. Usually Little Stevie liked to boast, you know, give it large about what he was up to. He was always

330

dropping himself in it. But I knew he was up to something big.'

'Go on.'

Sinbad picked up the charge sheet in front of him, and shook his head again. Like what was written there was all a terrible mistake. Frost grinned, then whipped the charge sheet out of his hand and held it like he was about to tear it in half. But not yet.

Barry Sutton made his opening gambit. 'Drop all charges, I put my gear back in the motor and you'll get whatever—'

'Sod off, Sinbad! We drop the charges, but we keep all your "gear" because it's not yours in the first place – and we attempt to return it to the rightful owners. The rest we sell off at auction and the money goes to the Police Benevolent Fund.'

Sinbad let out a groan like he'd been pummelled in the gut, and not just the wallet. 'Bleedin' hell . . . that's nearly all my stock!'

'It's not *stock*, it's stolen property! Anyway, you can always bid for it at auction. Think of all those poor old coppers you'll be helping.'

Sutton sank back in his chair and steeled himself to do something completely abhorrent to him – help the police with their inquiries. 'Little Stevie was paid top dollar to burgle George Price's properties. Not to steal money, jewellery or anything of intrinsic value. In fact, he was told, if anything *was* taken, he wouldn't get paid. The person paying for the job didn't want George Price to know he was being robbed.'

331

'So what did he want him to rob?'

'Information.'

'A little black book with some names and numbers in it perchance?'

Sinbad answered that question with a smirk. 'How is your head? Nice to see the bandages off.'

'Cheeky sod!' said Frost, scratching the back of his head that had just started to itch where the stitches were pulling. 'That was Little Stevie's handiwork, was it?'

'As I said, Little Stevie loved to boast, especially when he was getting one over on the law. Saw him Saturday evening. We had a pint. He told me he saw you at the races talking to Price's clerk, Jimmy. You had a black notebook in your hand. Little Stevie put two and two together and reckoned it was the black book he was after. He couldn't resist it.' Sinbad grinned. 'Little Stevie said it was like taking candy from a baby, he said you was well drunk, Mr Frost, staggering all over the place. He just followed you out to the car park.'

Frost raised an eyebrow at the WPC by the door who was suppressing giggles.

'Thank you, Hanna, something funny?'

She stopped. 'Not from where I'm sitting, Inspector.'

'Good girl.' Frost then turned his attention back to Sinbad, who was also suppressing a giggle. Frost tapped a forefinger on the charge sheet. 'Careful, you might get me to rethink my generosity as far as your larcenous activities are concerned. You've had a result, son, let's not blow it, eh?'

Sinbad gave a 'fair enough' nod and continued: 'But it

332

wasn't just the little black book, in fact, that was the least of it. Little Stevie was paid top dollar to find some tapes.'

'What kind of tapes?'

Sinbad shrugged.

'Come on, don't go all shy on me now. What kind of tapes? Videotapes, like the ones we found in your lock-up?'

'To be honest, Little Stevie didn't say, and I just took it for granted that it was just cassette tapes. Because I know for a fact that at the races, the bookies have a tape recorder going so they can tape all the bets they take, so if there's any disputes with the punters, they've got it all recorded. And I do know that George Price used to tape-record all his phone calls, so he had proof of the bets that he'd taken.'

'Because gambling debts aren't enforceable by law – it's little more than a gentleman's agreement.'

'Exactly. But there were rumours that Price had tapes of certain people in compromising situations. Real incriminating stuff.'

'Taped conversations?'

Sinbad shrugged. 'If he's taping all his calls, people can get sloppy over the phone, start letting things slip, who knows? George Price, someone else who likes to boast, used to say that he had friends in high places and never had to pay for a parking ticket, could do what he liked.'

Frost nodded. 'I've heard those rumours too. Are we talking bent coppers?'

333

'Little Stevie wouldn't say. But I know one thing: Little Stevie wasn't scared of anyone, but he was scared of whoever it was who was paying him to get hold of the little black book and the tapes. And it looks like he had every right to be.'

There was a knock on the door and Frost beckoned them in. Clarke entered the room, holding up a video-tape. 'I think there's something you need to see, Inspector.'

Sinbad's eyes went to widescreen as he recognized the film she was holding.

'That's from my own private collection.'

'Something we should know, Sinbad?'

'All good clean fun . . . sort of. Just don't tell the wife, she'll kill me.'

Thursday (3)

Stanley Mullett was with Assistant Chief Constable Winslow in his plush suite of offices at County HQ; they were watching the lunchtime news on the large TV set encased in a carved mahogany cabinet that matched the drinks cabinet beside it. Quality throughout, mused Mullett, who fully appreciated that the ACC's office was several steps up from his. Winslow sat behind his teak partners' desk (not unlike the one the President of the United States sat behind in the Oval Office), which put Mullett a good four feet away from him. There was a red leather three-seater couch wedged between two bookcases beneath the mullioned window. The whole office had the feel of a gentleman's club. How Mullett craved a couch in his own office. He had read that productivity is often improved after an afternoon nap, a siesta, if you will. The idea of stretching out on his own couch after a long lunch appealed to him. In fact, Mullett was convinced that if he had this office, with its drinks cabinet, plush seating and seemingly all the necessary comforts, he would seldom leave it. He probably wouldn't ever go home.

'Ah, Mullett, here it is,' said the Assistant Chief Constable, picking up the remote control and aiming it at the TV to turn up the volume.

It was a live report from the Southern Housing Estate. The screen showed a gathering of women outside the community centre. There were about thirty of them carrying banners hastily made out of white sheets, which boldly stated in black paint who they were, what they were, and what they were going to do: 'We're MAAD as hell and we're not going to take it any more!' Some men of the cloth accompanied the group. There was Reverend James Tutt of St Giles', Father Edwards, a local Catholic priest, and a rabbi from Rimmington. The two leaders of the group, Ella Ross and Cathy Bartlett, spoke eloquently about their loss and their determination not to let drugs and the gangsters who sold them take over their community and destroy their children's lives.

The unfortunate acronym, MAAD, stood for Mothers' Alliance Against Drugs, but it also served to sum up exactly how they felt. They spoke of their plans to make their presence felt on the estate, how they weren't going to be cowed by these men. They had a number of events planned, including a march this afternoon through Denton town centre, followed by a town hall meeting, and then regular vigils on the estate to make life for the dealers as hard as possible.

336

The ACC picked up the remote control again and pointed it at the TV until the screen blinked and faded to black, with just a stubborn starburst in the centre. The two men watched it slowly disappear and gathered their thoughts. But it was immediately obvious to Mullett that this was an extremely delicate situation. These kinds of interest groups and protests made Eagle Lane look like they weren't in control of the situation. Mothers up in arms, making their presence felt and effectively policing the area. Whilst no one was yet accusing them of being vigilantes, it was potentially a tinderbox. Drug dealers were dangerous men, and yet the police couldn't outlaw MAAD's presence. The situation called for the utmost sensitivity.

'Your thoughts, Stanley?'

Mullett sighed lavishly, so as to be seen to be giving it some serious thought.

'The reason I ask is because I hear one of your men is behind it.'

'One of mine?'

'Detective Sergeant Waters. Apparently, he suggested the whole thing, or certainly encouraged it once it had been formed. Did you not know this?'

'I . . . I knew he was doing community outreach work.'

'Good idea. Perfect man for the job.'

'Yes. I thought so, that's why I proposed him for it. But as for encouraging . . . MAAD, that's unconscionable. I shall reprimand him, maybe suspend him forthwith until—'

'You'll do no such thing. Not yet, anyway. We don't

337

know how this will play out, which way the wind will blow. But however it does, we need to be on the right side of it. You see?'

Mullett did see. If there was one thing he always did see, it was the importance of being seen on the right side of things.

The ACC played with a snazzy chrome executive toy on the desk and gazed out of the window as if looking for divine inspiration. 'They're mothers . . . mothers with banners and slogans and commanding a veritable army of sympathy; they have the press and the people on their side . . . and they have the church behind them, too. Once you put God into the equation, the game's up. You can't go up against God, you'll lose every time.'

Mullett cleared his throat, as if to draw the ACC back into the room. 'Indeed. How should we proceed, then?'

Winslow stopped his deliberating and gazing out of the window, and turned his attention to Mullett. 'The meeting at the town hall is scheduled for six p.m. this evening. Full press presence, local church leaders, councillors, the mayor, dignitaries – and you, Stanley, and every other county super will be up on the stage with them. We must be seen to be on the right side of this. We must appear to be MAAD, too.'

'*Sir?*'

'Mothers' Alliance Against Drugs.'

Mullett looked enlightened, then nodded in agreement: now they were all MAAD.

*

'Gordon Bennett! Take a look at those beauties!'

'Inspector Frost, let me remind you this is serious police business,' chided DI Eve Hayward.

'I was talking about the palm trees . . . lovely,' said a defensive, yet smiling, Frost.

Hayward, John Waters, Sue Clarke and Frost were gathered in the briefing room around the conference table. The curtain had been drawn across the glass partition that separated it from the main CID incident room. And the sound had been turned down to a minimum. Although it could have been turned off altogether, as there was no meaningful dialogue to be gleaned from the video they were watching on the TV. The 'film' was called *The Pool Boy Gets Wet*. What narrative there was revolved around the plight of the poor pool boy turning up to perform his duties in a villa, somewhere in southern Spain by the looks of it, only to have his endeavours hindered by the owner of the house, a woman in her early twenties attired in the skimpiest of bikinis. In this she was assisted by the housemaid, who was about the same age and wearing the same style bikini, but also armed with a feather duster. Protest as he might, the reluctant pool boy was soon embroiled in an imbroglio not of his own making.

As grainy and amateurishly made as the film was, after only a few minutes one of the female stars was instantly recognizable to the four coppers. It was Melody Price. Maybe ten or so years younger, but it was unmistakably her.

Eve Hayward turned the TV off.

'I think I need to see more, just to make sure it is her!' protested Frost.

'It's her,' said Hayward. 'And I know who the other woman is, too. It's the wife of Eamon "The Hook" Hogan – Angie.'

'He's not in it, is he?' asked John Waters.

'No.'

'Maybe we should check, see if he turns up later,' suggested Frost. 'And I'd like to know how it ends.'

Sue Clarke said, 'We fast-forwarded it, there's another ten minutes, much the same, then the pool boy goes home.'

Frost said, 'How did you find this?'

'All part of the haul we found in Sinbad's lock-up,' said Waters.

Clarke said, 'PC Simms was dutifully going about his work, going through the videos, and the title piqued his interest. He put it on and discovered Melody Price.'

Frost shook his head. 'Mucky little sod, but we'll let him off this time.'

'This is just the proof we needed to connect Eamon Hogan to Melody and George Price,' said Eve Hayward. 'I've made some calls back to Scotland Yard, they're going to run a full intel check on her.'

'I wonder where Sinbad got the video. Shall we ask him?'

Eve Hayward shook her head. 'To be honest, it looks like it's an old film that's been put on to video. It's been in circulation quite a while, no big deal, anybody could have picked it up. Lots of dodgy bookshops sell them and they pass from hand to hand in pubs for a couple of quid.' She tapped her nails on the desk. 'But all roads seem to be leading to Video Stars. Melody Price owns it, Michael Price works in it, and Bomber Harris and Tommy Wilkins have been spotted going in and out of there pretty regularly, right?'

'It was one of the places we'd clocked them going into, all part of their daily routine,' said John Waters, warming to the idea. 'And they always seemed to come out with a video under their arm, and for two unemployed laya-bouts, they never seemed to spend too long in there. In and out pretty sharpish. I don't know about you, but I can stand in there for hours trying to pick a film.'

Eve Hayward agreed. 'Makes you wonder what was really in the box, right?'

'*The French Connection*,' said Clarke absent-mindedly. They all looked quizzically at her until she was forced to give an explanation. 'They had a copy in Video Stars . . . it's about smuggling heroin.'

Frost thrummed his fingers on the table, the noise growing louder as the grin on his face grew bigger. He stopped thrumming, and grinning. 'You know, I don't believe in big sudden eureka moments in our line of work. There are usually lots of little revelations, and they're usually hiding right under your nose in the first place. But this, this is good. You said you could prove a link, Inspector Hayward, and you have.'

Hayward gave an appreciative smile. 'Good work, everyone, I'd say.'

An unsmiling John Waters cut the love-in short.

341

'Then if that's where Harris and Wilkins are picking up the heroin, we have to nick them now and close it down.'

'We do that and we tip off Hogan that we're on to him,' said the London DI. 'Just give me twenty-four hours to get the intel about Melody Price through. Harris and Wilkins are only dealing it, they won't know about Eamon, they're just minnows. Melody Price is our route to Eamon Hogan.'

Waters couldn't disagree more. 'Doesn't sit right with me, leaving Harris and Wilkins out there when we could nick them. And we could always pull them in for something else, selling counterfeit goods, anything – just to get them off the streets.' He turned towards Eve Hayward. 'You've already set up a deal with them, right?'

Hayward ignored Waters and appealed straight to Frost. 'Just twenty-four hours, Jack, that's all we need?'

Frost lit up a cigarette and took some long, slow, thoughtful drags. It was one of those tough decisions the taxpayers paid good money for, and the DI didn't take it lightly. It made sense, but the idea of sitting on the information and not putting the scumbags behind bars – frankly, that grated. Frost was reminded of the old fable about the two bulls standing on the hill watching the heifers grazing below. The younger bull says, let's run down the hill and make hay with one of them. The older bull says, no, let's *walk* down there and make hay with *all* of them. Frost considered Eve Hayward and Sue Clarke: they were unified, determined, and looked

342

like they wouldn't take no for an answer. Frost smirked – now he knew how the pool boy felt.

'So what's this I hear about you and DI Eve Hayward?'

Frost's head popped up from behind his desk. He was on his hands and knees in his office going through his 'filing system', which consisted of piles of papers stacked under his desk. There was no usable space on the desk itself; it was its own San Andreas fault of shifting tectonic plates about to quake at any moment and send the whole heaped mass sliding off. Frost had been working at slowly getting it sorted, ever since Mullett had entered his office two weeks ago and turned apoplectic red at seeing the mounds of paperwork and empty takeaway cartons, with fag butts hidden amongst all the layers. Mullett called it a fire hazard and an assault on all that was decent and true. A bit over the top, but Frost kind of got what he meant when he discovered the ants.

Mullett had just sent through an urgent memo: he wanted a list of all the arrests Frost had made on the Southern Housing Estate over the last six months, to provide some facts and figures he could have to hand for this evening's town hall meeting.

'You what?' asked Frost.

John Waters laughed. He lifted what looked like some tramp's clothing off a chair and sat down. He had brought them both a cup of coffee, and set Frost's down on the only available space on the desk.

343

'Rumour is, you were at her hotel last night. And she was giving you a right sweet smile just now.'

Frost hauled himself to his feet. He scratched his head in a gesture of deep confusion, both at his 'filing system' and at his loss of memory concerning the preceding night with Eve Hayward. He slumped down in his chair and took the mug of instant coffee precariously perched on the corner of his desk. His hangover was fading, but so was his energy, so the caffeine was much appreciated.

'You know, John, I don't comb my hair any more, I use the comb to strategically shift bits of hair around my head to cover the receding hairline, and the growing bald spot at the back.'

'Is that you avoiding the question?'

'No. It's me saying, if that's the rumour flying around about me and the gorgeous Ms Hayward, I'll take it, I'll go with it one hundred per cent, whilst it's still in the realms of possibility.'

'I hope she's not turning your head. Affecting your decision-making.'

'How do you mean?'

'I say we take Harris and Wilkins off the streets now.'

'I say we wait.'

Waters shook his head. His anger mounted with every word he uttered. 'Since when have we listened to her, and what does she know about Denton? Two lads are dead because of those scumbags, and she wants to play the long game with people's lives—'

'Calm down, John—'

'I've sat with those mothers, I knew those lads and—'

Frost shot to his feet and leaned across the desk, his balled fists pressing down on the piles of paper. 'We've all done what you've done, it's part of the job, the worst part! But she's right, it's always the big boys that get away with it and mugs like Harris and Wilkins who end up getting nicked, and the problem doesn't go away, it stays the same. Hogan will just set up shop somewhere else and more kids will get hooked and die, and more mugs like Harris and Wilkins will go to prison, and so it goes on. This is our chance to really do something, to really get the bastards. You know that, John.'

Waters stood up and perched himself on the radiator. Frost sat back down. Both men stayed silent, letting the dust settle.

Frost spoke first: 'So, go on.'

'Go on what?'

'You're an experienced copper. You know the score. I'm sensing something else is bothering you, you wouldn't be here otherwise. You hate coming into my office, scared you'll get rickets, typhoid, bubonic plague . . .'

Waters laughed. 'Between you and me, probably a bit early to say anything, but . . . Kim's expecting.'

'Bun in the oven?'

'To give it its full medical term, yes.'

'Congratulations! So why the long face? Should be over the moon!'

'That's the thing, Jack, Kim's the one having the baby, but I feel like I'm the one going all hormonal.'

Frost grinned and raised his coffee mug, then pulled

345

a face and put it back on the desk. 'Sod this, we need something proper.' He reached down to a drawer and pulled out a quarter-bottle of Teacher's. 'Funny how I can lay my hands on some booze in an instant, but not Mullett's crime figures.'

Frost turned both their instant coffees into Irish coffees.

'You're a lucky man. Never happened with me and the wife. No one's fault, just wasn't to be.'

'It's got me thinking, though. What with this meeting at the town hall, what sort of world is he or she coming into?'

'Ah. So this is what it's all about. You want to lock up all the villains before your kiddie comes kicking and screaming into the world, is that it?'

John Waters laughed again. That was clearly it.

'Let me tell you, we get this Hogan, and I guarantee that will be the best day's work you'll ever do. And your kid will thank you for it, and be bloody proud of you for doing it. Of course, they'll give you a ton of earache, cost you a fortune, drive you crazy, and then they'll leave home just as they're turning into reasonable, normal human beings. But I don't think he or she will have to worry, just as long as you're around.'

'Thanks, Jack.'

'And let's just hope it ends up with Kim's looks and not yours.'

'I'll drink to that.'

Waters took a swig of his coffee, which now kicked the back of his throat like a mule, and was about to say

346

something when the bearded figure of Desk Sergeant Bill Wells darkened the doorway.

'Don't you ever knock, Bill?'

'Sorry, guv, didn't realize you were so *busy*,' he said, eyeing the bottle of Teacher's on the desk. 'Got some good news for you.'

'Hornrim Harry's won the Pools and is emigrating to Canada?'

'No. We've just had a call, and your parrot has been spotted. Guess where?'

Frost arched an eyebrow at John Waters, and both men looked at Wells and asked in unison, 'Where?'

Thursday (4)

'To be honest, I can't remember . . .'

'Surely you'd remember Jack Frost? How could you possibly forget?'

'We'd had quite a bit to drink.'

Clarke, dogged as she was, decided to drop the subject. She was up against a professional. 'Loose lips sink ships' was Eve Hayward's credo, and that obviously applied to her personal life too. They were on surveillance in the red MG, parked a short distance from Video Stars. At this point in time, this seemed to be the location that joined all the dots in the case.

There was a tap on the driver's-side window and a man with thick shoulder-length hair and designer stubble took up the view with his handsome face. Eve Hayward rolled down the window.

'Hello, gorgeous,' said the man, with one of the most winning smiles Sue Clarke had seen in a while.

'Hello, gorgeous yourself,' Clarke muttered, just a little louder than she meant to.

Hayward made the introductions, and DI Tony Norton leaned over her to shake Clarke's hand. He then passed Eve an A4 manila envelope containing the intel on Melody Price.

'Blimey. That was quick,' complimented Hayward. 'Didn't expect anything till tomorrow morning.'

Tony Norton winked. 'You know me. Would have been even quicker, but Melody Price is big on aliases. She's been a Samantha, Roxy, Annabelle, Trudy and Trixie. And she's been married twice before, and those two husbands died of heart attacks.'

'To lose one over a heart attack is unfortunate, but to lose two sounds careless,' said Clarke, rather mangling her O-level Oscar Wilde.

Tony Norton flashed his smile at her again, and she in turn couldn't help but blush. Which didn't go unnoticed by Eve Hayward.

'They were old, though,' said Norton, 'and they were rich. But she's had an interesting career. She's not only been a black widow and a minor porn star and glamour model – she was also an air hostess for three years, flying all over Europe and South America. That's how she met a certain Angie Bexley, who was also an air hostess with that airline at roughly the same time.'

'Angie Bexley, who later marries Eamon Hogan. We've been watching a highly educational film starring our two leading ladies. And it wasn't on what to do if your plane's about to crash,' Hayward told Norton.

349

Clarke was putting the pieces together. 'So, for a girl on the make like Melody, more interested in money than most, and not afraid to take risks, this makes her a perfect target for a drug smuggler like Eamon Hogan, also not averse to taking risks. Was she ever caught smuggling drugs for Hogan in her younger days?'

Norton shook his head. 'She's clean as far as drugs go. But she did quit the airline after three years, somehow with enough money to buy a big house. Started up a modelling agency in Manchester, and, even though her name wasn't ever on the credits, became a player in the porn film business. Not performing this time, but behind the camera, also producing and distributing. Then something happened, she sold the big house, fell off the radar and moved to Spain.'

Sue Clarke chimed in, 'Where she had the good fortune to meet George Price.'

'I've got a feeling if you asked George Price that when he wakes up, he might not see it that way,' said Eve Hayward.

Tony Norton suddenly warned, 'Speak of the Devil, your mark has just turned up. I'll be in touch.' He pulled up the collar of his jacket, then made off down the street and was soon lost in the crowd.

Clarke and Hayward turned their attention back to the video store, and saw a Mercedes 380SL pulling up outside. Melody Price was at the wheel, her long blonde tresses gathered up under a peaked cap, and her face almost completely concealed by a pair of huge diamanté-studded sunglasses. She stepped out of the car; today she was wearing beige jodhpurs, black leather riding boots and a fitted tweed jacket over a red cashmere polo-neck jumper.

'I'll give her one thing, she knows how to dress,' said Sue Clarke on the back of an envious sigh.

'Yeah, it's how she pays for it that's the problem. At least our frocks have a clean conscience.' The DI held up her zoom-lensed Minolta camera and took pictures, like a photographer snapping a model on a fashion shoot, as Melody entered Video Stars.

Five minutes later, the door opened again and Melody emerged from the shop with Michael Price in tow. The hulking son of George Price flipped the red sign to 'CLOSED', locked up and followed Melody into the car.

'He looks rough,' said Clarke. Even at a distance, she could see that his face was glistening with a sheen of sweat. 'Looks like he's got the flu.'

'Or worse,' said Hayward, turning the key in the ignition.

Clarke chided herself for her momentary naivety – of course it wasn't the flu that was ailing Michael Price.

As Frost climbed out of the yellow Metro, his eyes scoured the skies, skies that were clear and blue with just a couple of low-hanging clouds in his field of vision, looking like balls of pulled cotton wool. But no Norwegian Blue. Not that Monty was a Norwegian Blue, if such a thing even existed, but he was blue, and he suspected

351

that all parrots that were even a bit blue were now referred to as Norwegian. Just as they were probably all called Monty, along with every pet python in the country.

Bill Wells had been told over the phone that the parrot was flying around inside a ground-floor flat of Paradise Lodge, where a window had been left open. Frost quizzed Bill, and Wells admitted he'd been suspicious of the caller. As a desk sarge, answering the phone was his stock-in-trade. And as he was often the first point of contact, he prided himself on being able to give a detailed character study of the caller after the most meagre of exchanges. This time Wells thought it was a male in his twenties, and he sounded spooked, like he was in some way transgressing, instead of doing a good turn by reporting a lost pet; he was calling from a phone box, refused to give a name or address and appeared to be in a hurry. Curious, thought Frost.

It didn't take long for Frost to locate Monty. The bird's squawks led him to the very window he had climbed through last time. And again the window was open. Frost peered in and saw the parrot, which appeared to be having a fine old time, hopping around the plush furniture of the flat, seemingly free as a . . .

It looked like the show flat been transformed into one big birdcage – with Trill, fruit, bread and droppings all over the carpet. Along with more wine and beer bottles and cartons of takeaway food. The luxury apartment had been turned into a dump. The jewel in the crown of Paradise Lodge was well and truly Paradise Lost.

And the window wasn't just ajar – it was now wide

352

open! Where the hell was Jason Kingly? Surely this is a sacking offence for the young estate agent? thought the DI as he climbed in. On seeing Frost, Monty flew off the top shelf it was perched on and plunged down towards the detective with a screeching cry that made him cover his head with his hands and duck.

'Bloody hell, Monty! You mad bird-brained little git!' Frost rose up from his crouch and sprang up to grab it, and missed. 'I'm buying this flat, you feathered vandal! Look what you've done to it! I'll have to Shake n' Vac my bloody balls off to get this mess cleared up!'

Monty ignored his pleading, and had perched yet again on the top shelf, king of all it surveyed. Frost, whose favourite reading material was military strategy and history, knew that Monty held all the advantages. It had the higher ground and ruled the skies. And now it was coming in for another sortie. It arched its wings and took off; round and round the ragged detective it went, while Frost again crouched down and drew up his hands over his head. But he moved too late, and he felt the full force of Monty's aerial bombardment on the back of his head. Monty Number Two had lived up to his sobriquet and delivered a number two of H-bomb proportions. Frost could feel it run down the back of his neck, past the collar of his polo shirt. He took more hits to his back, his leather bomber jacket getting splattered. When the aerial assault had finished, all he could hear was laughter.

'Poor Simon. Must have been something he ate, all that fibre. Been letting rip all over the place, he has.'

Frost unfolded himself, wiped his hands on his

353

trousers and faced his mocker. He looked quite different from the depiction of the handsome playboy with the twinkly eyes on his wanted poster. Gone was the Magnum PI moustache; gone was the big blow-dried dark-brown hair that he had apparently taken great pride in. It had been shaved off to a number-one crop. And the fact that he was stark-bollock-naked didn't help matters. But what really marked Terry Langdon out as a complete and utter nut-job was the fact that he had smeared himself in what looked like blue make-up from head to toe. It was patchy at best, but he had still managed a pretty good coverage. Terry Langdon had either genuinely gone mad or he was shrewdly building a defence of diminished responsibility and looking for a reduced sentence.

'Are you the assassin, or a messenger boy sent by a grocery clerk to collect a bill?'

It was a spot-on impression and Frost got it immediately. 'Why are you talking like Marlon Brando . . . Terry?'

Langdon stopped channelling that great actor and now channelled Dennis Hopper doing one of his madder turns, with his wild rolling eyes. It was then that Frost spotted the gun in Terry's hand. The Webley revolver, as seen advertised in the gun magazines at his bungalow. He then caught sight of a video box on the coffee table: it was *Apocalypse Now*, and the tape was probably in the video player. Yep, thought Frost, Terry Langdon has gone all the way upriver without a paddle and it doesn't look like he was coming back.

'Why don't you put the gun down, Terry, and we can have a chat.'

354

'You can't take Simon.'

'Who's Simon?'

'Simon is *all*. Simon is *everything*! Hail, Simon!'

It became apparent to Frost who Simon was when it flew down off the bookcase and landed on Langdon's shoulder.

Frost wasn't about to debate nomenclature with the gun-wielding naked nut-job now: if he wanted to call the parrot Simon, then Simon it was. The detective looked at them both, and wondered whether Terry had painted himself to look like Simon. It seemed that way. And then Frost wondered how exactly *this* absurd comic sketch was going to play out. Would it be a dead parrot, or a dead detective?

As they made their way across the field they realized they weren't dressed for it. It hadn't rained for a couple of days, not bad for early April, but still the fields were damp and muddy, and each footfall sucked at their heels, and splattered sludge up their trouser legs. Sue Clarke and Eve Hayward were aiming for a small stone farmhouse with what could have been a large hay barn next to it.

They had little choice but to go this way; they'd followed Melody and Michael Price at a safe distance, until the urban townscape of Denton and the orbiting villages petered out and turned into dense countryside with tight country lanes. The Mercedes then veered left up what looked like a private road, where they really couldn't afford to be spotted in the rear-view mirror. If you had no business going along that road, then you wouldn't be going along it.

So they parked up, armed themselves with a radio, camera and binoculars and trudged their way across the field towards the farmhouse. Crouched behind a hedgerow, they were able to see two vehicles: the little silver Mercedes and a big black BMW 7 series. Hayward snapped away, hoping to get shots of the BMW's number plate. The farmhouse looked suitably old, but the 'hay barn' looked incongruously new, much more like an aeroplane hangar.

Eve Hayward kept looking through the zoom lens as she spoke. 'We need to get in there.'

'Not without back-up.'

'That's not what I was thinking of. We need someone to break in and take a good look around.'

'Isn't that illegal and won't it compromise the case?'

Hayward kept looking through the lens and didn't answer.

Clarke didn't push it, and asked instead, 'Is that the sort of stuff Tony Norton does?'

'He has his uses.'

'I bet he does.'

'Fancy him, do you?'

'Not bad.'

'He's single, you know.'

'Really? You not interested yourself?'

'I was. And I had my interest satisfied.'

They both expelled filthy laughs which they quickly suppressed, and returned their attention to the farmhouse.

356

'Is that where they're producing the heroin?' asked Clarke.

'No, that's all done abroad, the processing and cutting is done in Holland. The heroin may pass through here, but finding it will be like looking for a needle in a haystack – no pun intended. But pirating videos on a huge scale, and warehousing counterfeit goods, that's a bigger operation altogether, it takes up more space. Don't get me wrong, the heroin is probably in there, but it comes in smaller packages.'

Sue was about to ask something else, when Eve began to click away again on her camera. The fast shutter noise spooked an inquisitive magpie that had settled on the hedgerow they were crouched behind.

Clarke aimed her binoculars and saw Melody Price and two men stepping out of the barn with boxes in their arms. They loaded them on to the back seat of the Mercedes. Michael Price wasn't with them. Clarke focused in on Melody; she seemed to be remonstrating with the two men. Pointing at them, and then pointing towards the open door of the barn. The two men stood impassive, arms folded. Finally the taller one nodded and then raised his hands, palms up, as if to placate her. The other man then went back into the barn, and re-emerged moments later holding Michael by the arm, like an arresting officer. Michael kept his head down, not wanting to look at anyone. The taller man then grabbed him and pinioned his arms behind his back, whilst his shorter and stockier accomplice delivered some powerful blows to Michael's stomach and face,

357

fast punches that travelled up and down his body until he fell to the ground. All the while, Melody Price leaned against the car, her arms folded, almost unmoved by what was happening. Then the two men went back into the barn. Melody helped Michael Price get to his feet and into the car, and she drove off.

Eve Hayward lowered her camera and turned to face Sue Clarke.

'What was that all about?' asked Clarke.

'Those two are Colm Bryant and Shane Riley. They're Eamon Hogan's lieutenants, as ruthless as their boss. My guess is Michael Price has been getting high off the supply, skimming off the top, and he's just been taught a lesson. And from what I could make out, if it wasn't for Melody Price, he might never have made it out of that barn alive.'

Clarke agreed that was how it looked to her, too. Satisfied that was all they were going to see today, they squelched their way back across the field to the car. They walked back in silence, the only sounds being of nature, which was loud enough, with crows cawing in the trees, and some cows mooing in a distant meadow. For Clarke, having seen the violence Eamon Hogan's men were capable of, the walk back seemed a lot longer than the walk there.

When they reached the car, there was an ominous sign. The MG's windscreen wipers had been lifted up. Sue Clarke suggested hopefully, 'Maybe it was kids?'

Both of them knew it wasn't kids. They got in the car and drove off.

Thursday (5)

'You've come to take Simon, right, bang him up, stick him in a cage for the rest of his life, right?'

Frost lowered his hands from the surrender position. 'You don't mind if I smoke, do you, Terry?'

Langdon, who was standing by the living-room doorway, a good fifteen feet away from Frost, said it was OK. Frost took out his cigarettes and offered one to Langdon. He eyed Frost with suspicion and refused it. Frost sighed inwardly – giving him a ciggy would have been an opportunity to get close enough to maybe grab the gun out of his hand. The DI lit his cigarette and took a long slow drag. All the time he did so, he weighed up the scenario. The gun was no longer pointed at him, it now hung limply from Langdon's hand. Monty, or Simon, the parrot was taking up Langdon's attention. Terry was looking lovingly at the bird perched on his shoulder, and the bird was looking suspiciously at Frost.

'I'm not after the parrot, Terry. I've been searching for you. I've come to tell you the good news.'

'What good news?' asked Langdon distractedly, his head still turned towards the parrot on his left shoulder.

Frost began to pad across the carpet towards Terry; now with the distraction of the parrot, maybe he could get close enough to get the gun out of his hand. He got within a few feet, and then the parrot grassed him up with a low warning squawk, and Terry Langdon raised the gun from his side and aimed it squarely and purposefully at Frost.

The little swine, thought Frost, glaring at Monty, who looked like it had a genuine smile carved into its beak.

'Bloody Frost, bloody Frost . . . Pen and ink! Pen and ink!'

Terry Langdon looked dumbfounded, and did a double-take between Frost and the parrot. 'Simon's never spoken before!'

Frost shrugged, knowing Monty must have learned this off the Fongs. 'It wouldn't surprise me if he can say a lot worse about me in Cantonese,' he said, recalling the contempt Old Mrs Fong held him in, especially since the flight of Monty . . .

The detective was then hit with an idea. 'You don't mind if I sit down, do you, Terry? I've been on my feet all day. I'm cream-crackered, as Chas and Dave might say.'

Langdon gave Frost a couldn't-care-less nod, and then carried on whispering in the parrot's ear, trying to teach him his name. 'I'm Terry, Ter-ry, say Ter-ry . . .'

360

A lesser copper would have tried to charge Langdon now, distracted as he was by his Doctor Dolittle routine. But Frost knew that *Bloody Monty* would alert Langdon with another 'Bloody Frost!' He took a seat on the black leather sofa, the sofa that might well become his if he was to buy the flat.

'I'm just going to make myself comfortable, if that's all right with you.'

Langdon didn't answer, and Frost doubted his words had even registered with him. But the parrot, on the other hand, did appear to be paying close attention to Frost. As the detective slowly crossed his right foot over his left knee, the feathers on the back of the parrot's neck rose up. Monty made a low gurgling sound that was familiar to Frost – he used to hear it when he got home from work, but had never been able to work out what the parrot's odd behaviour was provoked by, until Kenny Fong had explained it the other morning. As insulted as he was at the time, right now the information was as good as a loaded weapon, if not in his hand, then certainly on his feet.

As the parrot's head bobbed up and down faster and faster, obviously in distress, Terry Langdon looked concerned and said, 'Is he upsetting you, Simon . . . this Frost . . . this bloody Frost?'

Frost slipped off one shoe to reveal a sock that may have been white at one time, but was now a mucky grey colour.

'Ah, that's better, me plates are killing me . . .'

The parrot let out a deathly screech that made

Terry's head reel back as it screamed in his ear, *'Bloody-Frost.BloodyFrost.Penandink!Penandink!'*

Frost grinned and went for the other foot, yanking the shoe off to reveal another greying sock, but this one came equipped with a handy hole in it so his big toe could poke out.

At this, the parrot screeched like a bat out of hell, flapped its wings and took off. It flew straight out of the window, cursing in Cantonese and cockney, probably. Frost's feet had worked a treat.

Terry dropped the gun and went after the bird, screaming out, 'Don't leave me, Simon!' as he rushed past Frost.

Frost tackled the naked nut-job when he was halfway through the window. As he cuffed and secured Langdon and dragged him back into the flat, he couldn't resist saying, 'It's the flying squad, son, and you're *bloody nicked*!'

'Someone's been in the wars.'

Michael Price glanced up from the copy of *Smash Hits* he had open on the counter to see Eve Hayward and Sue Clarke entering the shop. It was empty of any customers, so Clarke took the opportunity to turn over the 'CLOSED' sign. Michael Price didn't question this move, which didn't go unnoticed by the two detectives.

Considering the beating he'd taken, the visible damage was fairly light, and seemingly not sufficient for him to take the rest of the day off. But Hayward doubted that Michael Price's life was his own now anyway. There

362

was a cut lip, some swelling around his cheekbone, and Hayward suspected bruising around his ribs, as that's where Colm had concentrated his attention.

He closed the magazine, and said apologetically, 'Someone left it in here.'

Eve Hayward saw that his eyes were red-rimmed – it looked like he'd been crying. She smiled, and put on an expression full of sympathy and compassion. The type of face you'd want to sit opposite, talk to, unburden yourself to. 'I read it every chance I get, Michael. Always good to know the lyrics so you can sing along in the car. What happened to you?'

He ran his thumbnail carefully down his cheek and across his fattening top lip, as if assessing what he could get away with. He came up with: 'I fell over. Bit pissed. You know how it is.'

'We know. We know all about it. You didn't tell us that Melody was your boss, did you?'

'How do you mean?'

'She owns the video store. You work here. She's your boss, right?'

'No. I've got shares in it.'

'Is that true? Because we've gone through the deeds we found in your dad's safe, and it's all in her name.'

'No, no, you've got it wrong, she looks after me.'

'It doesn't look like she's looking after you, Michael.'

Eve Hayward reached over and grabbed his left arm, and went to lift the sleeve of his light-blue sweatshirt that had UCLA emblazoned across it. He pulled his arm away and stood back from the counter, startled. He was

363

a big guy, but he looked small and wounded, his right hand now rubbing his left upper forearm.

'How long have you been injecting?'

He bowed his head, his lips twitched and moved, but no sound came out.

'Is that why they hit you? Because you've been stealing from them?' joined in Clarke.

He stood up straight now, trying to look defiant, maybe imposing. But it didn't work, the damage had been done. He just looked pitiful and pliable. And Hayward recognized that look, and knew now was the time to strike.

'You know what happens if you do it again, don't you? It won't just be a beating. These people kill. They kill people who are a threat to them, they kill people they suspect *might* be a threat to them, and they even kill their family. Let me tell you about Colm Bryant. He killed his brother. Colm's brother robbed banks. He was good at it, very successful. But Colm killed him because he became a heroin addict.

'Colm thought, what if he gets arrested for a robbery and gets banged up in a cell, craving heroin? Would he grass on Colm, who was the one the cops were really after, because Colm was part of a gang that was flooding the streets with heroin? That scenario hadn't happened yet. But Colm Bryant wasn't about to take that chance, and neither was his boss. The brother had become a liability. So Colm killed him, and left his body on the streets as a warning: if they could kill their own flesh and blood, they could kill you. Believe me, Melody Price isn't your friend, your family . . . your mother. She isn't helping you, Michael, she's using you.'

Hayward took out a card and placed it on top of the copy of *Smash Hits*, covering Nik Kershaw's pouty little pop-star face. 'Call this number. It's a private number, the person you'll talk to will tell me immediately you've rung, and I promise you, Michael, no one else will know. And we'll make sure that nothing will happen to you, and you'll be safe. I can promise you that.'

Michael Price digested this information with some steady nods of the head. He then reached out and picked up the card to once again reveal the tiny pop star, and put it safely in his pocket.

And for the two detectives, that was good enough, and pretty much as they had planned. They had no intention of dragging him down to Eagle Lane and thus alerting Melody Price and the Hogan gang. A blue-chip lawyer would probably get him out within the hour, and then Michael Price would probably just end up like Colm Bryant's brother. Eve Hayward felt sure that Michael wouldn't say anything to Melody about their visit. She didn't rate his intelligence that highly, but suspected he wasn't that stupid, either.

The two women left the shop and made their way across to the MG, and as they did so, Hayward gave a nod to a man in a battered-looking blue van with 'Top Class Plumbers' stencilled across the side. Sat at the wheel reading a paper was a bloke in a grubby brown

365

boiler suit and an equally grubby-looking blue bobble hat, sporting a full beard, and with a pair of NHS glasses stretched across his face.

'Even in that get-up he looks better than half the blokes in Denton,' muttered Clarke as they got into the MG.

'Yep, he'd have made a great actor.'

As they were sure that Michael Price would be an invaluable witness when the time came, and they suspected that his life might be in danger, a heavily disguised Detective Inspector Tony Norton would watch over him now.

Frost managed to get Terry Langdon dressed and then drove him to Denton General. The inspector figured that Langdon needed medical help more than he needed to be questioned about an attempted murder, an attempted murder that it had become clear over the course of the investigation he hadn't attempted. From being quite literally the case's poster boy (his handsome face plastered all over town), he had drifted into insignificance. Frost was sure that Langdon had not shot George Price, and certainly had not killed Jimmy Drake, or Stevie Wooder. No longer the prime suspect, he was something of an anomaly in the case.

As they drove through town, away from the isolation of Paradise Lodge, Terry's sanity seemed to return, enough for him to stop worrying about the parrot and to address the real pressing issue in his life right now.

'I didn't shoot him. I'm sure I didn't,' he said, sounding rather unsure about the protestation he was making.

'I know you didn't, Terry. But why don't you tell me what happened that day, so I can clear this mess up for you.'

Langdon stared straight ahead of him, his eyes squinting in the low spring sun, like he was deep in concentration and trying to make sense of what had happened, to recall the events precisely.

'I wanted to kill him,' said Langdon. 'I had the gun all ready. Had it planned . . . sort of.'

Frost let out a wry little laugh. 'Yeah, it's the "sort of" part that always goes wrong. Go on.'

'I saw George leave the races early. I thought he was going home. I planned on going to his house . . . have it out with him and tell him the truth.'

'And what was that?'

'That Melody loved *me*, and not him. I knew he wouldn't listen, though. He'd laugh at me. He's looked on me like a piece of dirt ever since I could remember, always thought of me as a kid. But with a gun in my hand, he wouldn't laugh, I'd make sure of that, I'd stick the gun in his big fat mouth!' His voice quaked and he visibly shook. 'He killed my dad. You know that, don't you?'

Not wanting to get sidetracked by the debatable veracity of that statement or to get him any more worked up, Frost agreed with a few noncommittal platitudes that seemed to set Terry at ease.

'He's a bully. He's the type of man who only respects one thing – violence. And I knew that's how he treated Melody. She only stayed with him because she was

367

scared. What else would she be doing with a horrible old bastard like that?'

Frost could think of a few reasons, the most prominent being money. But not wanting to upset Terry, again he agreed.

'I loved her, Mr Frost . . . I really loved her.'

There was something heartbreaking in that statement, even for Frost. It seemed so misguided and out of step with reality, just like Terry Langdon himself.

They reached Denton General and found a parking space near the entrance. Frost was now determined to get as much information as he could before the doctors put Langdon under the chemical cosh, or he just lost his appetite to talk.

He took a pack of Senior Service cigarettes off the dashboard; they must have belonged to Mullett. Frost was in the habit of purloining other people's fags if they left them on their desk, one of the few illicit acts he was good at. He pulled out two cigarettes and gave one to Terry, and the two men sat smoking for a bit, watching an ambulance unload some poor sod who looked like he'd fallen under a bus. Frost pondered the fragility of existence.

'George Price isn't dead, Terry. In fact, he's in that hospital. He's going to be operated on next week, and it looks like he'll pull through. Now, I reckon you're glad to hear that, because you're not like George Price, you're not a cold-hearted bastard.'

Langdon nodded, and Frost saw his eyes moisten as he spoke.

'I couldn't have done it. I probably would have just

waved the gun about in his face a bit. Maybe shot up the tyres of his car, and driven off.' He turned towards the detective. 'Pathetic, aren't I?'

'No, you're not. You're like most of the population. Most people want to shoot someone at sometime or another, but most people can't shoot people. If they could, my job would be impossible, because everyone would be shooting everyone – all the bloody time, probably.' Frost got Terry back on track. 'So, you followed him out of the races . . .'

'Yeah, he was heading toward his home, but I lost him. So I drove along the road I knew he usually took to his house and I spotted his car in a lay-by not far from that pub, the Feathers. The lay-by's only got a narrow entrance where it's all overgrown with bushes, but I just managed to catch sight of his Merc as I drove past. So I stopped, started to reverse, and then I was almost hit by a car coming out – but this car was really motoring, it screeched out of there like it was in a hurry.

'Then I reversed into the lay-by and there he was, George Price, sitting in the Merc with the roof down. I got out of the car. I had the gun in my hand. I called out his name, but of course he didn't answer. His head was tilted to one side, his eyes were closed. I could see he was still breathing. But there was a black mark on the side of his head. When I got closer I saw it was a small circle of blood, with a line of red leading down to his collar. I touched his shoulder, gave him a little nudge, to wake him up, and then he tipped right over to the side. There was blood on my hands . . . Then it all went quiet,

369

no wind in the trees, no bird sounds or traffic rushing past . . . Everything just sort of stopped. Then I looked down at my hands and saw I was holding the gun . . . and with the blood on my hands I thought that I'd done it. I'd never shot anyone before, not even an animal, so I didn't know what it was like to shoot anyone. My head . . . my head got all messed up. I thought I'd had a blackout and it had just happened . . . Does that make any sense?'

'You were confused, Terry, running on adrenalin, fear, you're holding a gun. Who knows what goes through a man's head in those circumstances.'

Langdon nodded, finding succour in Frost's words.

'What happened next?'

'Then all the noises came back, the wind in the trees, the birds, the traffic passing by and a plane overhead, and everything was just incredibly loud. It was like waking up from a bad dream, being back in reality. And the reality was: George Price was dead, and I'd killed him. So I got in my car and got out of there as fast as I could.'

Frost didn't want to put words in his mouth, but he also didn't want him to lose his narrative thread, so he pushed on. 'But it wasn't that easy, was it? Someone was blocking your path, remember?'

'Yeah . . . that's right . . . I remember. As I was pulling out, another car was pulling in. It wasn't their fault. I had to slam on the brakes – would have gone into them otherwise. It was a young couple. They must have got a good look at me. I could see the bloke staring at me, calling me a wanker. He had to reverse to let me out, and I drove off.'

'You drove off fast, like the other car you saw. When you were first reversing, a car sped out of the lay-by. Isn't that what you just said?'

'That's right. I had to brake pretty sharpish that time as well.'

'Whoever was in that first car probably shot George Price. They got to him before you could. Tell me, did you get a look at them at all?'

Langdon dipped his head and looked down at his hands.

'Did you see what make the car was? You must have seen it, in the mirror, perhaps? Think, Terry . . . think . . .'

Langdon raised his hands in front of his face, like he'd never seen them before. Then he started rubbing the blue make-up off his fingers and wrists. 'Why . . . why am I covered in blue?'

'Relax, Terry. I'm covered in parrot shit.' He cringed. 'All down the back of my neck. Supposed to be lucky, but I have my doubts.'

Langdon then looked in the rear-view mirror and saw his face, as if for the first time, lucidly. With his hair and his moustache gone, and streaked with blue eye-shadow, he was clearly a stranger to himself. Terry looked appalled at what he was seeing: the madman in the mirror.

Frost was no shrink, but it was clear to him that Terry's psychotic episode had been gradually abating. But the shock of what he'd done, or thought he'd done, and had now become was driving him nuts all over again. He began to weep uncontrollably. Frost muttered some

371

frustrated four-lettered words. He knew he wasn't going to get any more out of Terry today.

He prised Langdon out of the car, and with the help of two passing nurses got him into the hospital. The on-call psychiatrist promptly stopped Langdon's hysterical crying with a chemical cosh that, judging by the happily zonked-out expression that took over from the one of terror, Frost wouldn't have minded a shot of himself.

He then put a call through to Eagle Lane and got a WPC posted at the ward with strict instructions for her to contact him the minute Terry Langdon became *compos mentis*; Frost wanted a description of who was in that car as quickly as possible.

Heavy on the pedal of the trusty yellow Metro, Frost raced across town to get to the town hall meeting. In the High Street, stuck on a red light, the sight of the office of Denton Premier Estate Agents provoked a thought. His watch told him he had time, not a lot of it, but he would make time for this little bugger.

He found Jason Kingly at his desk, on the blower, talking big about some crummy flat in some crummy area of town. Frost knew it was a crummy area of town when Jason had to reiterate three or four times that it was up-and-coming. Kingly had his feet up on the desk and the phone jammed between his ear and his bony shoulder, leaving his hands free to twist away at a Rubik's Cube. But seeing Frost enter, he turned as red as a post box, dropped both the phone and the Rubik's

Cube, and swung his feet off the desk, knocking over a stack of papers, a coffee cup and an anglepoise lamp in the process.

'Smoothly done,' complimented Frost.

Five minutes later they were in the Metro, both smoking furiously.

'You did the right thing, Jason, calling us. Even if it was only to report the parrot. Why didn't you say Terry was there?'

'I was going to, but when I heard the copper's voice down the phone, I just couldn't do it. It just felt wrong . . . grassing Terry up. So I thought if you found the parrot, you'd find him . . .'

'What's your connection with Terry?'

'He's my cousin.'

Frost expelled a salvo of smoke rings as he gave this some thought. 'He's your cousin, who just happens to have a gun on him, and isn't in the best of mental health. It was lucky it was me who showed up. I could have sent a WPC along there to see what was happening – he could have shot her!'

'I'm sorry, Mr Frost. What's going to happen now?'

'The good news – for you and Terry – is he didn't shoot George Price. He just thought he did.'

'He told me he didn't at first. Then he said he might have . . . Then he was sure he did.'

'Fact is, he didn't have a bloody clue if he did or not. He had what they term a psychotic episode. Went off his trolley over a piece of skirt, that's another term for it.'

373

'Melody Price?'

Frost nodded.

Jason smirked. 'Spends a lot of her time out of a skirt from what I've—'

'All right, son, we've all seen the pictures.'

There was a long pause and the seriousness of the situation settled over them again.

'I knew he was losing it,' said Jason. 'He was scared, only natural, he thought he'd shot someone. But when that parrot turned up, he seemed to go completely off his rocker. Asked me to get him some hair clippers so he could shave his head . . . plumage, as he called it. Then he asked me to get some blue make-up so he could paint himself.' Jason shook his head in disgust. 'He wanted to *be* the parrot.'

'Don't be too hard on him. As you get older, son, you'll find everyone feels like Terry at one time or another – he just wanted to fly away from all his problems.' Frost conceded, 'But usually they go buy a ticket and get on a plane.'

'Is he all right?'

'Looked happy enough to me. But I need you to tell me – did he talk about the shooting at all? Did he say what he saw?'

'No.'

'You said that too quickly, Jason. I need you to think, and think good and hard, take as long as you like. We're not out of the woods yet.'

Kingly made a concerted effort to look like he was thinking, with everything from rubbing his chin to

374

scratching the top of his head. 'He said he was in big trouble . . . "because this goes right to the top", he said.'

'This goes right to the top?'

Jason gave an assured nod. 'That's what he said. I asked him what he meant, but he said he couldn't tell me. He made out that I could be in danger if I knew too much.'

Frost examined the pointed orange tip of his cigarette; it had burnt down to the print. He took one last pull, puffed out another perfect smoke ring and then blew a shard of smoke right through the middle of it. Jason looked impressed and attempted a similar manoeuvre with his cigarette; but he just ended up with a heavy fug in front of his face that left him coughing and spluttering as he stubbed out the butt in the ashtray.

Frost wound the window down further. 'Do you trust me, Jason?'

'Yes, Mr Frost!'

'Good lad. Forget everything that's happened with you and Terry, you won't get nicked, I'll make sure of that.'

Jason let out a noisy sigh of palpable relief. 'Thanks, Mr Frost.'

'But I need to know – when he was talking about this going right to the top, did Terry mention anything about coppers, the police being involved?'

Kingly gave it some serious and again visibly animated thought. 'I remember I said if he's innocent he could go and see you. I said you were a good man. I said you'd give him a fair hearing. He just laughed, said I didn't understand. But he didn't mention any names . . .'

375

Jack Frost sat looking straight ahead of him, his eyes narrowing, deep in speculation as all his hunches fell into place.

'Can I go now, please?'

Frost turned his attention to Kingly, who had one hand on the door.

'Not so fast, we still have some serious matters to discuss.'

'Eh? That's all I know, Inspector. You said . . . I'm not in any trouble, am I?'

'Depends.'

'On what?'

'The deal you can get me on the flat.'

Frost winked, and Jason breathed easy.

Thursday (6)

It was standing room only, except at the front, where they had reserved some seats. Frost had never seen the town hall so packed. The red-brick Victorian civic building had hosted a few concerts over the years, of course: A Flock of Seagulls had played to a packed house a couple of years ago; and The Rolling Stones had allegedly played an early gig here in the sixties, but there was no proof of it, because no one had bothered to cover the event as no one had thought they would make it. Still, at least they had lots of photos of the Flock of Seagulls gig.

But this was different: never had a civic meeting attracted so many Denton citizens. There was a queue to get into the main hall. Frost wasn't one for queuing, and he wasn't in the mood to flash his badge and shoulder his way through the crowd, a crowd that was mostly made up of women and children, from what he could discern. They were supporting the Mothers' Alliance Against Drugs and wearing white T-shirts with big bold Frankie Goes to Hollywood-style slogans on them: MAAD SAYS NO TO DRUGS and MAAD WON'T RELAX – DRUGS OFF OUR STREETS.

He made his way across the black and white tiled floor of the lobby to the noticeboard, lit up a cigarette and waited for the queue to dissolve. It was the local elections next month, so the noticeboard was full of information about the candidates. All the main parties were represented, as well as some local-interest groups, plus the usual array of eccentrics and raving loonies who thought politics was a natural home for them. Frost seldom bothered himself with local politics, he could barely be arsed with national elections, and quietly despised politicians with their self-serving regard for the system. They all made big promises about improving policing and never delivered, and he was pretty clueless as to who was running here in Denton.

But one candidate did catch his eye. The poster showed the incumbent Conservative councillor for the North Denton ward, and a favourite to be re-elected, one Edward Havilland. He was a fat fellow in his late forties, bald-headed with a hem of curly blond running around the sides, and he was sporting a bow tie and a broad smile. But what Frost really noticed was that he had his fingers raised in the victory salute, just like . . . *Winston* Churchill.

Frost took a surreptitious shufti around him, saw no one was looking, pulled out the thumbtacks from the board and pinched the poster, folding it up roughly and jamming it into his jacket pocket. He then dropped his barely smoked cigarette into the fire bucket with a satisfied expression on his face. He often told himself, and anyone who would listen, that detective work was all about luck; and the harder you worked, the further you pushed and the deeper you dug, the luckier you got. He felt like taking some sand out of the fire bucket, scattering it on the floor, and tap-dancing his way into the main hall. He made do with a jaunty tuneless whistle instead.

'There's some room right at the front, Inspector Frost,' whispered a DC from Rimmington whose name he'd forgotten. All the county was present. Frost thanked him and made his way down the aisle. As he did so, he picked out faces in the crowd. Eve Hayward was sitting with Sue Clarke, deep in conversation, probably about him and what a red-hot lover he was – he winced at the thought, still clueless about what had happened the previous night. There were some more Rimmington coppers amongst the serried rows, making conversation with the Denton contingent. They'd probably all end up in the Spread Eagle tonight, drink too much lager and get into a fight. Frost knew how competitive coppers could get. Sandy Lane, Denton's very own and very cut-price Walter Winchell, was with the rest of the press pack near the front. Sandy clocked Frost, and the newspaperman formed his hand around an invisible pint glass which he shook slightly, gesturing for them to have a drink later.

Up on the stage, behind a long trestle table covered

in blue cloth, were Mullett and the three other regional superintendents, as well as the Assistant Chief Constable from County HQ. Frost made sure that Mullett saw him by giving him a thumbs-up, which was ignored with disdain. Still, job done, thought Frost. He'd give it ten minutes then leave in a hurry, looking down urgently at his bleeper. Cathy Bartlett and Ella Ross from MAAD had pride of place; the mayor looked resplendent in his chain, and was flanked by local councillors, including Edward Havilland in his bow tie, who had forgone the jovial look on his poster and was adhering to the solemnity of the occasion. And next to him, looking a little nervous in his Sunday best, was DS John Waters.

Frost edged along the front row and took his seat. It was probably the worst seat in the house. Too close to the elevated stage, he had to crane his neck upwards to see their faces. And because he knew he couldn't spend the next ten minutes doing that, he looked straight ahead, and all he could really see was their footwear, where they'd run out of blue cloth to cover all of the trestle tables. Frost's limited view forced him to examine the feet before him, and he saw some were nervously tapping away whilst others were languidly crossed, seemingly at ease with the situation. All the superintendents' shoes were highly polished, with Mullett's the most effulgent, of course. Their black uniform trousers were spotless, with sharp creases down them that you could cut cheese with. And all had black socks that—

Frost did a cartoon double-take as his eye snagged on a pair of brightly coloured argyle socks in red, green,

380

yellow and blue. His head craned up and he saw that they belonged to Superintendent Peter Kelsey of Rimmington. *Kelsey, Peter Kelsey.* He was an imposing, well-built and strong-looking man in his late forties. Even though he was sitting down, he seemed to dominate his neighbours. With his thick sandy hair and his fair complexion made ruddy through various outdoor pursuits, he could be taken for a typical Scotsman, thought Frost. The DI remembered Kelsey came from somewhere near Fort William, but had moved down south over twenty years ago. But the accent was still solidly there, and he was known to dial it up when it suited him, lending him an authoritative and authentic toughness amongst his southern Sassenach counterparts. Kelsey was also known for being a bit of a flash git: he tooled around in a top-of-the-range German car (a new model every year), took frequent holidays in Bermuda and other locations usually only glimpsed on *Whicker's World*, and there was no grubby copper's mac for him, always a pristine Burberry or black overcoat from Savile Row. His wife was said to have money – good for him, thought Frost. And that's all he really knew about Peter Kelsey. But as the DI was dealing with men like George Price and Harry Baskin, with their love of rhyming slang and nicknames, it was quite enough for right now.

In the end, Frost stayed for the whole meeting, leaving his creaky fold-up chair only once for a cigarette break; for some reason they didn't allow smoking in the grand hall. Frost had seen more and more of these nanny state restrictions creeping in, and wondered where it would all end. The meeting was rambunctious and angry at times, and never less than energetic. Everyone gave a good account of themselves, and Frost had to include Mullett in that; you didn't get to be a super by being a complete clown, no matter how often Frost thought he fell into that category. As far as Denton CID was concerned, it was John Waters' star turn that really captured the audience's imagination, with him talking about his past and growing up in Stoke Newington, the scourge of drugs and the loss of his brother.

But, of course, it was Ella Ross and Cathy Bartlett who gave the most compelling account of themselves and the tragedy that had befallen them, and received the most applause for their efforts. They made it clear that they weren't interested in platitudes and sentimentality – they wanted action. They had already received threats that they would be run off the estate if they didn't disband. But they were going to stand firm.

Frost wasn't really that interested in what was being said at the meeting; he stayed because he was looking for clues, and studying the body language between the two men of interest to him, Peter Kelsey and Edward Havilland. They were at opposite ends of the stage, so they weren't able to interact much. But when the meeting finished, and the members of the panel mingled at length with the general public, what struck Frost was the distance Kelsey and Havilland maintained between themselves: never in the other's orbit, they seemed to be going out of their way to avoid each other.

382

'Where've you been, Jack?'

Frost turned sharply to see Eve Hayward. 'Did we have a date?'

'We were trying to call you, you've been off air. Bill Wells wanted to send out a search party. We've had a real breakthrough.'

'I had to see a man about a parrot. You go first.'

Hayward filled Frost in on the afternoon's work: how she and Clarke had tailed Melody and Michael Price from the video store to the farmhouse; how they'd photographed the beating meted out by Hogan's henchmen; and the intel she'd received on Melody that connected her to Hogan . . .

Eve stopped talking when she realized that Frost wasn't listening.

He was keeping a steady eye on Edward Havilland, but when the councillor got himself entangled in a knot of potential voters, the DI turned his attention back to Peter Kelsey, knowing that these two must soon come together to collude. And when they did, Frost wanted to be there. He knew he might not be able to hear what they said, but with the stakes so desperately high for both men, he was sure their body language would speak volumes.

When they both suddenly disappeared from view, Frost mumbled an apology to Eve and rushed out of the main hall into the foyer, then out into the twilight. He was just in time to see Edward Havilland striding down the road with Peter Kelsey in tow. The fat man seemed surprisingly fleet of foot, or he was just in a hurry to get away from Kelsey. They reached a dark-blue Daimler, from which Havilland's driver sprang out to open the back door for his employer. Frost couldn't lip-read, but at thirty yards and concealed in a shop doorway, he could tell a good brush-off when he saw one. Edward Havilland, looking red-faced and angry, waved his hands in front of Peter Kelsey to draw whatever conversation they were having to a close in no uncertain terms. The rotund politician then lowered himself into the back of the car as quickly as he could, and the Daimler made off in a stately fashion.

Frost studied the man left on the pavement. Kelsey pushed his hands into the pockets of his Burberry, brought out a pair of leather gloves that he pulled on over his large hands, and then punched a powerful fist into his other palm.

On re-entering the town hall, the first person Frost collared was Sandy Lane, who was by the fire bucket, puffing away on one of his thick unfiltered 'gaspers' and sneaking a sip of Bell's whisky from a hip flask.

'Thirsty work this, Jack, listening to do-gooders, politicians and policemen pontificating.'

'Easy, Sandy, someone might accuse you of being a cynical old hack. And a drunk.'

'I'll drink to that. So would you, probably.'

Sandy offered Frost a snifter. Frost took one, but refused one of Sandy's cigarettes and sparked up one of his own less pungent coffin nails. The two men stood smoking and drinking over the fire bucket. To a casual observer, it might have looked like the next thing they

384

were going to do was throw up in it. They were hunched over conspiratorially in a conversation that Frost wanted to keep private.

'It's simple, Sandy.'

'That's my nickname, Simple Sandy.'

'Just get it into the paper, first thing tomorrow, something along the lines of: George Price, whose condition has been steadily improving, is to undergo an operation next week, after which a full recovery is expected.'

'Is any of that true?'

'He is having an operation next week. I don't know what the odds on his recovery are. But it would certainly be doing me a favour if they were thought to be good.'

Sandy Lane weighed this up, his red-lined eyes narrowing on Frost, his booze-blotched face pensive. 'So what's in it for me?'

'If what I think is going to happen *does* happen, it might be in your interests to have a snapper on standby at the hospital. I think someone might try and kill George Price right there in his bed. Of course, it has to be discreet: if you have some bloke standing there with a great big zoom lens and a press pass around his neck, it won't happen.'

The hack pulled a sly grin, exposing a top set of crooked nicotine-stained gnashers. 'Gotcha. Say no more. I know just the snapper. Works a lot of divorce cases for Whispering John.'

'Whispering John?'

'Yeah, Denton's pre-eminent, if not only, Private Dick.'

385

'I thought it was Whispering Dave?'

'Oh yeah. Whatever. Anyway, he's a crafty little bugger, gets in anywhere, very discreet. You won't even know you've been snapped until they serve the divorce papers.'

Good old Sandy. But as much as he admired the hack's old-school press ethics, and had shared a good few boozy lunches with him over the years in the pursuit of their mutual interests, even Frost felt like having a hot bath and a rub-down with the Dettol after one of their meets.

'Here he is, the star of the show,' said Lane, looking past Frost.

Frost turned to see DS Waters loosening his tie like it was a noose around his neck.

'Sandy, I'll see you later, cheers for that!'

'You'll read it first thing in the morning, Jack.'

Frost stalked over to Waters and grabbed him by the arm just as he was about to get entangled in another powwow with some mothers from MAAD.

'Follow me, John.'

Waters looked glad of the rescue: being in the public eye wasn't really his strong point, no matter how photogenic and PR-friendly the top brass thought he was.

'Where we going?' he asked, as Frost, still holding his arm, aimed him towards the sweeping white granite stairs that even after all these years still managed to sparkle. As they made their way up to the third floor of the town hall, Frost filled John Waters in on what he suspected.

*

'What's all this bloody racket?' called a very angry voice.

Frost had been disappointed to find the office locked, but he could see there was still a light on, so he'd been hammering on the door with determination.

The door opened a few inches, to reveal a clerk straight out of Dickens. Frost dipped into his jacket pocket, pulled out his wallet and flashed his warrant card.

'This is most irregular. Our hours are strictly nine thirty to four. I'm only here because our computer keeps crashing, but the good citizens of Denton keep on being born and dying, relentlessly. But I see you leave me no option. Come in.'

Frost and Waters stepped into the town hall's records department. The DI then asked the clerk if he could see the Register of Interests for the local-government officials. Frost knew that all councillors had to declare their business and special interests, and the register of these was made public for voters to peruse; you just had to ask.

His request was met with a conspicuous lack of enthusiasm. The clerk scowled, which didn't improve his appearance. He was rake-thin in his worn grey-tweed jacket and had an Adam's apple that protruded almost as far as his beaky nose, giving him the profile of a wrench.

'Listen, chum, this is a very serious investigation. I don't care what time it is. I need to see those records now, not tomorrow.'

The man tutted and muttered to himself as he disappeared from the counter to get the register.

387

Frost turned to Waters, who still looked in shock from what his boss had told him, especially about the man he'd just shared a stage with.

'Kim always says that Kelsey's a flash sod,' said Waters in a near whisper. 'She calls him Inspector Gadget, he's always got something new to flash – a new watch, expensive pens – he's even got a crocodile-skin Filofax.'

In an equally hushed tone, Frost said, 'We might need to ask Kim some questions about what goes on at the Rimmington nick, see if she's noticed anything off about Kelsey lately.'

'To tell you the truth, it all makes sense. She says that he flies off the handle all the time, especially recently. Has these mood swings.'

'Yeah?'

'Yeah, you know how Mullett is always Mullett. He never changes, he's just . . .'

'Always Mullett, yeah, I get you.'

'Well, Kelsey is up and down like a yo-yo. One minute all happy, mixing with everyone in the pub, buying everyone drinks; next, he's throwing tantrums over the smallest things, not coming out of his office.'

Frost said, 'That figures. When he wins he's happy, when he loses he's not. Typical gambler. And lately he's been losing.' Frost went to put a cigarette in his mouth—

'No smoking!'

The two detectives jumped out of their respective skins as the stealthy jobsworth appeared out of thin air to bark his order.

John Waters laughed. 'Jesus, sneaking up like that, like Kung Fu walking across ricepaper, you are!'

The jobsworth's Adam's apple bobbed up and down. 'Some of these records are over a hundred years old, it's like a tinderbox in here.'

He handed over the file.

'Right,' said Frost, 'we'll have these back tomorrow.'

'No, you won't. They can't leave this room.'

'Can we use your photocopier?'

'No, you can't, it's in the copy room which is now locked. I do not have possession of the key.' He pointed to a small table with two chairs tucked under it at the end of a row of ancient-looking shelving units crammed with dusty storage boxes. 'You've got ten minutes.'

Thursday (7)

Frost drove up the barely lit track to the Coconut Grove. He was alone, having let Waters go home – he deserved something of an early night after his star performance on stage at the town hall. Frost could tell he'd hated every minute of it. And maybe the news of Kim's impending bundle of joy had motivated Frost to let his DS go – after all, soon he wouldn't be getting a wink of sleep, never mind an early night.

But there was another reason for Frost's magnanimity. Harry Baskin didn't like crowds. And in Baskin's book, three constituted a crowd. When there were three people in the room, there was always a material witness; but when it was nice and cosy with just the two of you, there was complicity. And armed with the new information he had, the detective was sure he'd get more out of Baskin with a tête-à-tête than a conference.

'Nice tan you've got there.'

Even in the gloom of Baskin's back-room office, he could see that the club-owner had either been away somewhere sunny or had fallen asleep on Mrs B's sunbed. He sat there looking very pleased with himself, smoking a big cigar, with naked women lying across his desk.

'Looking well, Harry. Put us in it.'

Baskin looked up from the photos of the naked girls and gave him a wink. Then he explained that it was strictly business, as he was auditioning some new strippers; even though it was only April, he was already planning the not-so-traditional Christmas spectacular for the club: this year it was to be 'The Not So Snow White Show'. All the proceeds from the event went to local children's charities. He shuffled the photos together and put them away in a drawer. Frost was grateful, he could do without the distraction.

Harry gestured for Frost to take a seat and explained the tan. 'Been abroad, went off early on Monday and got back this morning, so any crimes committed over the last couple of days in Denton, or the surrounding area, have absolutely nothing to do with me.'

Frost leaned back in his chair, fished his cigarettes out of his jacket pocket and lit one up. 'Let me guess: Tenerife, overseeing your timeshare business whilst your partner George Price is . . . indisposed?'

'Nothing gets past you, does it? That's exactly what I told the concerned parties also involved in the venture. Like I said, anything happens to George, we all stand to lose a good few quid.'

'I suppose you've been keeping abreast of what's been happening back home during your absence?'

'George has his operation next week.' Harry rapped his knuckles on his desk. 'Touch wood, should be on for a full recovery. Again, that's what I told the concerned parties.'

'Jimmy Drake, I was thinking of.'

Harry Baskin stopped grinning, and the big man seemed to slump back in his chair. 'I heard. Terrible business. First George, now Jimmy.'

The club-owner hauled himself out of his seat and went over to his fancy drinks cabinet; once the inlaid walnut doors were opened, it lit up like one of Harry's Christmas shows. He then poured two large measures of Johnnie Walker Blue Label into a pair of crystal tumblers and handed one to Frost.

Without saying a word, they both raised their glasses to Jimmy Drake and took some noisy and appreciative sips of their drinks.

Harry Baskin sat back down at his desk. 'Any news on Terry Langdon, he still the prime suspect?'

'We've found him. And he's not guilty. He's a little bit off his trolley, but not guilty.'

Baskin nodded along in accord to this. 'So, I take it this isn't a social call.'

'Edward Havilland.' Frost said it slowly and steadily so there could be no room for Baskin to say 'Excuse me' or 'I didn't catch that' to mask his reaction. A criminal recidivist like Harry knew how to twist an interrogation in his favour.

392

The burly gangster crinkled his brow in thought. 'Rings a bell.'

'Should ring more than that, Harry. Without Edward Havilland, your strippers wouldn't have a stage to strip off on, and you wouldn't have a leg to stand on.'

'Very good. We're looking for someone to play Happy in the Snow White show – any more gags like that and the part's yours.'

'Councillor Edward Havilland just happens to be head of the licensing committee and pushed through your licence for your club for the next five years. Making *you* Happy.'

'So what? He's liberal for a Tory. I think his stance was that if Denton was to grow as a town and attract investment, it must be seen to be supporting a diverse economy, and that includes a thriving nightclub and entertainment scene to cater for all tastes.'

'Sounds like you've got it off by heart, Harry.'

'It's good to see progressive politics in action.'

'Tell me, is Edward Havilland one of the Denton high-flyers that George Price said he had in his pocket?'

The tip of Harry Baskin's cigar burned bright as the big man's cheeks sucked in the full flavour of his Montecristo. He then picked up his Johnnie Walker and took a slug.

'Because as well as being a member of the local hunt, a keen fisherman and handy with the twelve-bore when it comes to bagging the grouse, Edward Havilland is on the board of Radleigh Park Racecourse, and he was very active in the campaign to get the course reopened

393

after it closed in the seventies. He's even gone on record as supporting the idea of the development of a Las Vegas-style casino in the area.'

'Bring more money in than the poxy garden centre they're planning on building.'

'You probably know more about Edward Havilland than me.'

'It's all a matter of public record, Jack, right?'

'It is indeed. A politician, bon viveur and gambler who bets heavy with George Price. One of George's high-flyers who ensures he never even has to pay for a parking ticket, or so I've been told. And who gets your nightclub licences pushed through. Let's face it, we both know that when it comes to collecting gambling debts for George, he entrusts that to you. A knock on the door from any one of your team of bouncers and they pay up quick, right?'

'If you're suggesting—'

Frost cut him off dead. The banter was over, time for the nitty-gritty. 'Havilland is a big punter of George's, into it for a good few grand. I don't have the exact numbers on me, but we're talking five figures. George has him marked in his book as "Winston", due to his Tory politics, and he's fat, posh, wears bow ties and likes to pose like Churchill. But that's where all similarities to the great man end.'

'George looks like pulling through. And Eddie Havilland wouldn't harm a fly. Why would you say such a thing, Jack?' Baskin smiled indulgently.

'Jimmy Drake's not going to pull through, though, is he?'

Harry stopped smiling. Frost could tell that for all his bravado, he was hurting over the death of Price's clerk. Baskin was a fully paid-up member of the Winchester Club, used to sitting at the card table and bantering away with George and Jimmy. He took another swig of his drink, for some Dutch courage perhaps.

Frost knew he might just have him on the ropes. 'Listen, Harry, this is murder. And it's one of your own. Jimmy Drake was a good man. But he knew too much and someone killed him. There were two names in that book, both of interest to me: Winston and Socks. I also don't think Winston is capable of killing anyone, but Socks is a different matter.'

'So tell me who Socks is.'

'I was hoping you'd tell me.'

Harry Baskin shifted in his seat, supremely uncomfortable at the idea of telling Frost anything. Nothing personal, just business.

Frost understood. So he eased Harry along: 'That's OK, Harry, I'll tell you who I think Socks is. It could just be someone who likes wearing brightly coloured socks. Someone a bit flash. Or, knowing your and George's Stepney roots, how about a little bit of cockney rhyming slang: sweaty sock – Jock. So, a Scotsman with a penchant for wearing coloured socks is just crying out to be nicknamed Socks.' Frost watched as Harry Baskin just sat there, saying nothing, but denying even less. His silence spoke volumes. 'But cockney rhyming slang and a man's choice of socks aren't going to get me anywhere; I bring that before the CPS and they'd laugh

395

at me. I need some hard proof. I need to make the connection. Jimmy Drake would have provided it, if it looked like George wasn't going to make it. Until Socks got to him. Then there's Little Stevie Wooder – you know Little Stevie?'

Harry shrugged. 'He's been in the club.'

'He was pulled out of the river last night. Shot with the same calibre of bullet that's in George's head. Feet and hands bound with the same rope that Jimmy was strangled with. Stabbed all over multiple times so the body would sink.'

Harry shifted in his seat again, sat up straight and put his glass on the desk. 'Go have a look round Jimmy's bar. Have a drink in the Winchester Club. You'll find your connection.'

Frost stood up. He didn't say another word as he left Harry's office. Like Baskin had never spoken.

John Waters rubbed a knuckle over a tired pouchy eye as he tried to focus on the road. He was in his car driving as fast as he could to the Southern Housing Estate.

Ten minutes earlier he'd been asleep on the sofa with Kim. He hadn't even had time to change out of his suit; as soon as he'd got home he'd collapsed on to the sofa, where Kim joined him for a cuddle. They'd planned on getting a takeaway. Kim, who tried to encourage healthy eating, said he could have whatever he wanted as a reward for his performance at the town hall. But they ended up just dozing off in each other's arms, perfectly content and ignoring their growling stomachs. Quite

396

some time later the phone went, and they let the answer-phone pick up. But then Waters heard the panicked voice of Cathy Bartlett, and he quickly got off the couch and took the call.

When Ella Ross and Cathy Bartlett got back to the estate from the meeting, Ella found that superglue had been squeezed through her front-door lock. So she was staying the night at Cathy's place, which was a ground-floor flat. About half an hour earlier, they'd heard voices outside and when they sneaked a look through the window, they spotted two men hanging around. They were wearing baseball caps with the peaks pulled down low, so the women couldn't make out their faces. But they looked like trouble, like they were working out how they could break in. John Waters said he'd be there as quickly as possible. He said sorry to Kim and kissed her goodbye.

When he arrived on the SHE it was around eleven. But even at this late hour there were usually still some kids about, teenagers gathered in knots, drinking cider and smoking fags by the playground. Usually, there was also someone telling them to keep it down or threatening to nick them. It was just the way of the estate. But not tonight: the streets, courtyards, all the communal areas seemed deserted.

Waters parked up and got out of the car. As he turned the corner of Grafton Way towards Cathy's block, he heard glass breaking. But Waters could tell the difference between a dropped pint glass and a window being smashed. And then came the screams, women's voices

397

raised in terror. Waters ran towards the block, and as he rounded the corner of the building, he saw that Cathy's flat was ablaze. In the same field of vision he saw two men in baseball caps making their escape.

Waters was sprinting now. He knew that only one thing causes an explosion of fire like that: a Molotov cocktail. He hammered on the front door, but got no response. He rammed his shoulder into it a couple of times, but it didn't budge. The next quickest way in was through a window, but not the one that the firebomb had been thrown through, as the curtains there had ignited and were now a sheet of flame. He took off his jacket, wrapped it around his fist and punched in the only other available window. He felt the heat being drawn towards him and fresh oxygen being sucked into the flat like fuel, feeding the fire's voracious appetite. He could also feel his stomach getting ripped on the broken glass left in the frame as he crawled through.

He'd come in through the kitchen window and ended up with his hands in the sink. As he rushed into the hallway, he saw them, Cathy and Ella, huddled there, choking on smoke. He threw his jacket over to them so they could cover their mouths with it, and headed to the front door. They gestured wildly at him that it was jammed, that they'd already tried to open it, but in vain. Waters retraced his steps, grabbed the jacket they were cowering under and yelled, 'Get up, move, come on!' as he pushed them into the kitchen, just in the nick of time to avoid a sudden surge of fire devouring the hallway carpet.

398

Smoke filled the flat completely now, black acrid fumes clawing at their throats, searing their lungs. There was no door to the kitchen and the fire was relentlessly making its way towards them.

Waters laid the jacket over the jagged window frame and grabbed the woman nearest to him; he couldn't see which one it was, and as every second now could make the difference between life or death, he didn't need to know. 'Through here!' he gasped in desperation, knowing he wouldn't be able to give them any more instructions. The smoke and heat were sapping his strength. But with whatever resolve he had left, he lifted her up and pushed her head-first through the window. Someone must have been on the other side of the window by now, because she seemed to get pulled through it to safety.

Waters spun round to grab the other woman, who had collapsed on the floor. He felt a new blast of heat and his hair being singed, his skin being scorched. He lifted her off the floor – she felt smaller, lighter and also more lifeless, as though the smoke had already got the better of her. Waters let out a roar as he tried to summon the last of his strength to lift her out of danger. The cry was also one of agonizing pain, as the burning lash of the fire attacked his back. He raised her limp body over the sink, started to push her through the window and saw her being yanked free.

He thought he heard sirens and panicked voices, saw flashing blue lights . . . the smoke forced his eyes to close . . . he wondered if he'd kissed Kim before he left the house . . . he was so tired when he left . . . but he was sure that he had . . . he was sure he'd kissed her goodbye.

Frost stole up the path like a thief in the night. There were no lights on in the modest 1930s semi, so when he came to the side gate, Frost felt it safe to switch on his pocket torch to light his way down to the bottom of the garden and the Winchester Club. He was sure the house was empty; Maureen, Jimmy's widow, was staying with her daughter, at least until the murderer had been found. In Frost's experience, the victims of a crime such as the one Maureen had endured often moved home for good. Murder is quick, but for those it leaves behind it lasts a lifetime.

But even with the certainty that the house was empty, Frost moved stealthily down the garden path, not wanting to disturb nosy, if well-meaning, neighbours. He unwound the length of police tape that was barring his way, and then found that the padlock was off the shed door. He went in and turned on the light. Spread out across the walls of the Winchester Club was a photographic record of Jimmy Drake's life in racing. Frost always suspected that the murderer would be somewhere up on the walls; most killers were well known to their victims. But now Frost knew who he was looking for.

As well as the photos, Frost's eyes were immediately drawn to the optics behind the bar, and particularly to the bottle of whisky with his name on it – if your name happened to be Johnnie Walker. The detective, never one to take liberties when it came to the etiquette of drinking, and always careful to buy his round, put a quid in the bookmaker's satchel that served as the Winchester's till. He also helped himself to one of Jimmy's Hamlets. Lighting up his cigar, he started to have second thoughts about Paradise Lodge: was it too posh and designer for him? Plus the fact that it didn't have a garden. The more he thought about it, the more he thought that every man should have a shed at the bottom of the garden, and every shed should be like the Winchester.

Frost got to work. He started at the top left-hand corner of each wall and worked his way along, examining each photo. It was three fingers into his second tumbler of Johnnie Walker that Frost belted out a victorious 'Yes!' like his horse had just won the Grand National. He was crouched down, looking at a series of three photos featuring George Price and Jimmy Drake at the Epsom Derby. They were wearing custodian helmets, and they were surrounded by coppers, with their arms around a young, but unmistakable, Peter Kelsey, probably in his mid-twenties. There were two other photos, more recent and even more pertinent to the case – these had been taken at Ascot. Peter Kelsey and Edward Havilland stood with George Price, probably about ten years ago, judging from the fashions, big teardrop collars and flares. They all looked happy, prosperous and very chummy. George Price with his late first wife, an elegant-looking woman in a wide-brimmed summer hat for Ladies Day. When did it all go sour for Kelsey and

George Price? Frost had noticed that there were no photos of Melody up on the walls.

The detective was then hit by a more compelling thought – it was clear that Kelsey had forgotten about the photos. They weren't in the most prominent of places in the shed, but surely he would remember them. Wouldn't he . . . ?

Frost eased himself up from his crouch with an accompanying creak – but even his joints weren't that bad. It was the shed door opening. Frost was almost upright, and about to turn to see who was behind him, his hand on the aluminium pocket torch (wishing it was something more substantial, like a cosh or a good old-fashioned copper's truncheon), when he felt the air split with the force of the blow and the nauseating sound of wood against skull. The light faded, and it was game over for Frost as he slid down the wall.

Friday (1)

It was on the second page of the *Denton Echo*, a small column of copy from Sandy Lane, chief crime correspondent, reporting some good news for a change: 'George Price, 62, a local bookmaker who was the victim of a shooting last Friday, is expected to make a full recovery, according to the prognosis from a respected neurosurgeon who is to operate on Price early next week.'

The front pages of the paper were taken up with the arson attack on the Southern Housing Estate. Two men had been arrested, notorious local thugs Billy 'Bomber' Harris and Tommy Wilkins. Three people were in hospital. Ella Ross and Cathy Bartlett were suffering from smoke inhalation but were expected to make a full recovery. However, Detective Sergeant John Waters was in a critical condition with third-degree burns covering his back and legs.

Patricia Kelsey entered the kitchen dressed in a smart

blue skirt and a cream-coloured blazer with padded shoulders and some kind of gold brocade running down the front of it. She looked, to Peter Kelsey's eyes, like a million dollars, as they say. Her heels clicked on the expensive slate floor as she fussed around, filling her bag with keys and money. She was going up to town to have lunch with some friends.

Kelsey sat at the table, the paper in his hands, but no longer reading it. And he wasn't really listening to his wife, either. He knew that 'up to town' meant London, not Denton. He expected that his wife would pay for lunch on her credit card, and probably go around the shops afterwards, spending freely on it. Kelsey wondered at what point it would be refused, maybe even cut up in front of her. Oh, the shame and humiliation she would feel, in front of her little cluck of pampered hens.

He almost laughed at the thought. She didn't deal with the finances, all that was left to him. She didn't have a clue. All the bank and credit card statements went straight to him. And now they came in the form of final demands stamped in red.

But she certainly knew how to spend it. And he didn't blame her; he'd encouraged it, he'd always wanted his wife to look good, to have the best of everything. She deserved it. She had that innate breeding about her, like a true thoroughbred. The type he backed all the way. And when he was winning, she spent freely. The trouble was, when he lost, she still spent freely. He won a lot, or used to. But he couldn't stop. He never could. He'd even seen a shrink who'd told him that gambling to him was

404

what heroin was to a junkie, and he would end up the same way. Of course he'd dismissed the warning; I'm no lowlife addict, he told himself. But still he couldn't stop, extending his line of credit until it had run out.

She kissed the top of his head, and looking at the front page said, 'What a terrible story. Anyone hurt?'

'Yes. One of ours, a DS from Denton.'

'How awful.'

'Yes. I must . . . I must go to the hospital. Go and see him.'

'Are you OK, darling?'

Kelsey didn't turn round to answer her question. Of course, she'd been asking him that a lot these last two or three months. He'd blamed his moods on work, said he had a lot on. He'd not cried in front of her, he always managed to excuse himself from the room just in time. So he was happy that she'd left it at that, and hadn't demanded an answer from him; today he wouldn't have been able to control the quake in his voice. Maybe he could have blamed it on the fact that he knew John Waters, had shared a platform with him at the town hall only the day before – a nice lad. And at that moment, he meant it. He worked with Waters' wife, Kim. She was a good copper and so was her husband, by all accounts. And so was Kelsey, at one time.

After the gentle thud of the front door shutting behind his wife, Peter Kelsey finally gave vent to his feelings. He threw the kitchen table over, sending the crockery, the pint of milk, the toast and everything else on it crashing to the floor. This was the day, he was sure of it, this was the day when it would all go.

He dried his eyes and stood up. He had some business to attend to. He had some things to finish off.

Frost's eyes ratcheted open like . . . déjà vu. The pain in his head was also horribly familiar. And so was the location. It was the same room he'd woken up in on Sunday morning, after the last time he'd been 'coshed over the canister', as Waters had termed it. Frost was aware that his head had been bandaged yet again, but made a point of not dwelling on it. Knowing what to expect this time, he just sat up straight, swung his legs around and got out of bed. His clothes were hanging just where they'd been put last time. He got dressed and made his way along the hospital corridor.

But something was very different this time: the corridor was packed with faces he knew, all coppers. He was groggy. He thought he was seeing things, hallucinating. The scenario didn't seem real. There was Sue Clarke with David Simms, Arthur Hanlon and Bill Wells; there was no banter, and they all looked grave.

Cheer up, he thought, it's only a crack on the head – another one. They should be used to it by now. Or maybe they knew something he didn't. The doctors might have discovered something, a brain haemorrhage, maybe this was it, maybe this was the end—

'You might as well forget our photo op, not a chance of him making an appearance now,' a voice whispered in his ear.

Frost turned to see an equally grave-looking Sandy

406

Lane. Of course, he got it immediately. There was no chance of Kelsey trying to finish off George Price now; with all these coppers milling around, it looked like Eagle Lane on a bad day. Frost cursed, then caught sight of a weeping Kim Waters, with her hands grasped before her almost in prayer, being comforted by some colleagues from Rimmington.

'What's going on?' he asked Sandy.

'What happened to you? Weren't you at the fire too?'

'What fire?'

Clarke came over. She too had been crying, her eyes still brimming with tears. She sat Frost down and explained what had happened. John Waters was in intensive care, and there was a good chance he wasn't going to make it. No one could see him.

Frost sat there listening to the information, but not really absorbing it. Sue then told him that he'd been hit over the head with a cricket bat by Jimmy Drake's son-in-law, Malcolm. He'd been staying in the house for the last couple of days, as Maureen Drake was worried about it being empty. He thought Frost was just an intruder. Frost barely acknowledged these facts. But the description felt apt, because that's exactly what he felt like right now – an intruder. At this moment in time he felt completely and utterly bloody useless. Unable to help his friend, unable to even string a sentence together to offer words of comfort to his colleagues, and to Kim, his friend's wife.

Frost knew one thing: he had to get out of there, leave John Waters to the experts, leave Kim in the hands of

407

people who wouldn't say something stupid. He needed to get on with his job.

'Peter Kelsey tried to kill George Price, and he *did* kill Jimmy Drake and Little Stevie Wooder. And I have the proof—'

Stanley Mullett raised his hand for Frost to stop. 'I don't doubt you do. After your recent conduct, Frost, I doubt that even you would be so suicidal as to come in here and accuse a fellow superintendent of . . . murder, if you hadn't good reason.'

'Thank you, sir. I think,' said Frost with an uncertain wobble of his bandaged head.

Mullett was sitting behind his desk, looking at Frost and DI Eve Hayward. There were, of course, other members of the team missing, and one in particular. And if, as Frost and Hayward had explained, the George Price shooting, the Jimmy Drake murder and the heroin death were connected, Mullett was more than prepared to let Frost act as they thought best, and damn what the Assistant Chief Constable thought.

'From what you've told me,' said Mullett, 'and I hope you're not holding any more back—' The detectives gave a resounding 'no'. 'Then we need to interview Edward Havilland and Melody Price. First of all, what about Harris and Wilkins, are they protesting their innocence?'

'They have a rock-solid alibi,' said Frost. 'At the time of the arson attack they were in the Blind Blacksmith pub doing a deal . . .'

Frost turned towards Eve Hayward to ask her to explain.

'That's right, sir, I purchased a Transit van's worth of counterfeit goods from them – videos, clothing, electrical goods. We have it all on film. It was to get them off the streets.'

Mullett gave a cautionary nod to this. 'Of course, we need to find Kelsey first. Put in all the usual measures.'

Frost said, 'I have officers at his home now. No one appears to be in. We were wondering, sir, if you had any ideas where—'

'I know he has a house near Fort William, or more of a croft, I believe. Other than that, Peter Kelsey has remained something of an enigma to me, and to the other superintendents in the district. A man who seemed to live well beyond his means and always had money to spend, expensive clothes and the like. His behaviour hadn't gone totally without comment, there were rumours of low-level corruption, but never any proof. Many dismissed the rumours as jealousy, from people envious of his lifestyle. He was ... charming, likeable. And to be honest, despite the nagging doubts, no one really looked too hard. And I hold myself partly responsible for that. If I had doubts, it was remiss of me not to register my concerns, to act upon them. I'm telling you this because whatever else happens, that will go in the report.'

A deep silence fell over the room, heads were bowed in thought.

Frost spoke first: 'I think we are all to blame when it comes to one of our own, sir. None of us want to believe it, because we all want to believe we're all in this job for the same reason.'

The super took a deep breath. The moment of reflection passed and he seemed to be the Mullett of old again, as he asked: 'Do we know the whereabouts of this Eamon Hogan?'

Eve Hayward said, 'No, Superintendent, but we believe he's in the county.'

Frost added, 'On our patch, sir.'

'Then let's get him off it and put him where he belongs, Frost! I shall be at Denton General today. So you'll know where to find me.'

Frost couldn't help but smile. He knew that Mullett would feel as redundant as him hanging around Denton General. But he understood his reasons for wanting to be there – a man of theirs had fallen, and sometimes just being there was enough. Frost concluded that John Waters was right: Mullett was always Mullett, except when he wasn't, and on those rare occasions he was almost bearable.

Friday (2)

Edward Havilland was in his office on the second floor of the town hall. It was a small office with an anteroom where his secretary sat. He was at his desk going through his drawers, and emptying them of anything that he might need for the next four weeks. As the incumbent councillor for Denton North, he had to vacate his office until after the election. This was his second term in office – for the last election, such had been his confidence in being re-elected that he didn't take a thing. This time, even though the opinion polls were good, he was filling a box.

If he had a sense of impending doom about the election, it was only compounded by his secretary knocking on his door and informing him there were two police officers to see him. Havilland gave a resigned smile at this, and looked down at one of the open drawers.

'Councillor Havilland?' prompted his worried secretary.

411

'Yes, thank you, let them in.'

Detective Inspector Jack Frost and PC David Simms entered the cramped office and introduced themselves. Havilland, still maintaining the smiling and affable façade of the public servant, offered them coffee, which they refused, then invited them to sit down, which they did.

'How can I help you, gentlemen?'

'You look like you're going somewhere, Councillor Havilland,' said Frost.

Havilland explained the formalities of the elections. Frost's expression didn't change throughout, even though Havilland peppered his explanation with self-deprecating anecdotes and jokes. Frost eventually cut him off by reaching into his jacket pocket and taking out the photos that had been on the wall of Jimmy Drake's shed. All the players: George Price, Peter Kelsey, and Havilland.

The councillor's eyes were fixed on the three photographs now laid out before him on the desk. The forced joviality instantly slipped away. Game up, he thought. And then he seemed to relax back into his chair. The strain of the last few weeks or more – he couldn't even remember how long the hellish spiral had been going on for – had taken its toll.

'What . . . what do you know?'

'We wouldn't be here if we didn't know everything, Winston,' said Frost. 'But we need you to tell us where Socks is. Peter Kelsey. Before he kills anyone else.'

Havilland slumped down further into his chair; his spirit depleted, all hope gone. 'When my secretary told

412

me you were at the door, I thought I would find a gun in my drawer, to do the decent thing. A glass of brandy, a prayer, the end.'

'Is that the decent thing?'

'Inspector Frost, I lost sight of that some years ago. I always said that if it came to this, I would . . . do the decent thing. It was my coward's way out, but it just made me carry the madness on, saying yes to Peter . . . when I should have said no. And I should really have done the decent thing and come to you, to put a stop to it.' He shook his head, as if a new thought had just struck him, or maybe just the banality of the obvious. 'It's insidious, once it has you in its grip.'

'Indeed. George Price got shot, and Jimmy Drake and Little Stevie Wooder ended up dead.'

'That was Peter, not me,' said Edward Havilland, making an emphatic gesture with his hands as if stressing a point in the council chamber.

'But you knew about the murders, you knew what he was going to do.'

'Peter told me that he was arranging a meeting with George Price to try and settle the debt once and for all. I didn't really pay much attention to him, by then he was pretty unhinged with it all. He was still gambling, but now he was losing, more and more. I think even George Price had cut him off. He was desperate. I don't know much about the shooting – I didn't want to know. I wanted to wash my hands of it.'

'But you didn't. To wash your hands of it would have meant coming to us and informing us about Peter

Kelsey killing two men, and admitting to your being privy to it. But you didn't, you're a gambler, you waited to see how the cards would fall. If George Price died, all well and good, no need to talk . . .'

Havilland raised his hands to his face, to cover his shame perhaps, or to shield himself from the reality of what he had become, and what was happening to him. The unrelenting presence of the two policemen, staring down at him, wanting facts, answers, the truth, made his situation inescapable.

He lowered his hands, his fat face flushed as he fought back the tears. He then took a key from the pocket of his yellow silk waistcoat and unlocked the bottom drawer of his desk. 'This is what I really came to get today . . .' He reached in and—

Frost leaned across his desk and grabbed him – his hand barely fitting around the fat man's arm in the sleeve of his brass-buttoned blazer. Havilland looked shocked by the move, then quickly attempted to make light of the situation and laugh it off.

'Good Lord, Frost, you think I have a gun in here?'

'I'm not a gambler, Mr Havilland, and I'm really not prepared to take that chance. But it's more for your own protection than ours, considering the conversation we've just had.'

'Suicide is best committed without an audience, otherwise it's just a cry for help.'

Frost let go of his arm and Havilland retrieved a video-tape from the drawer and handed it to the detective.

'I suppose you could describe this as the smoking gun.

414

Everything you need is on there. That's what Peter was really after, not the little book or any other tapes that George Price had about how much we owed him. You see . . . and I doubt it makes much difference . . . but it wasn't all about the money. If we'd just admitted to getting into debt with a bookmaker, then not being able to pay, well, it's not the worst thing in the world. I think the public can forgive certain financial improprieties, no matter how they occur. Indeed, falling victim to a bookmaker like George Price could have even elicited some sympathy.' Edward Havilland's gaze fell reluctantly towards the tape now secured in PC Simms' hand. 'But this was a different matter altogether. Our behaviour, I'll admit, was . . . unconscionable, considering our positions.'

PC Simms glanced down at the video he was holding like it could bite.

Havilland continued: 'Our reputations would have been in tatters, had that come out. For Peter not to have a job, not to have the income to continue the lifestyle he'd enjoyed, would have been anathema to him. And, of course, with blackmailers you always keep paying. It never stops. I didn't doubt for a second I'd have ended up paying for copies of the tapes for years – or until I'd run out of money. But Peter, he couldn't stand it. It was driving him mad. Maybe it was the policeman in him, but he felt he had to do something. Try and solve the problem. So he acted. He arranged to meet Price to have it out with him once and for all, demand the tapes. I don't know what happened for certain . . . You'll have to ask Peter that. But it's pretty clear to me what

415

probably happened: George Price refused, and Peter . . . Well, like I say, you'll have to ask him, I wasn't there.

'But I blame Melody Price more than anyone. It was all her doing. Big tough George Price, my God, she really had him under her thumb. The female of the species being deadlier than the male, that could have been written about her.'

There was a knock on the door and another plain-clothes officer entered the room. He went straight over to Frost and whispered in his ear. Havilland watched as Frost gave him the nod, and the other detective then went and stood by the door.

Havilland knew now that it was all over. It had hit him in stages, and there would no doubt be greater depths he would plummet to, he knew that now. It was finally over. It seemed as if his office was no longer his; the other detective wasn't introduced to him, didn't even look at him.

'Where's Peter Kelsey?'

The councillor broke out of his reverie, and Frost repeated the question. Edward Havilland shrugged, then shook his head. 'I suppose you've been to his house. I don't know where else he'd . . .'

Havilland's gaze drifted over to the wall behind Frost. The DI turned his head to see a calendar; it was familiar to him, it was the same one he'd seen in George Price's house, and Jimmy Drake's, too. It was a Radleigh Park Racecourse calendar.

416

Friday (3)

It was the last day of the Spring Festival of Racing at Radleigh Park. It was bright and crisp, and the going on the Polytrack was as good as if the horses were running on a big green carpet – which they almost were.

Frost ground out his second Gitane on the grass outside the Champagne & Oyster Marquee. He must have pinched the pack off Edward Havilland's desk when the councillor was read his rights and taken away. He made a note to himself to stop nicking other people's cigarettes. These gaspers were awful, they were French and strong. But after seeing what was on the videotape, it was clear that Havilland's tastes ran to the unpalatable and the strong.

'Sorry I took so long, bloody traffic,' said Sue Clarke, approaching him. 'It's the last day, it's always like this, apparently.'

'Got any more news on John?'

417

'Last I heard he was stable.'

The way she said it didn't fill him with relief. And he didn't want to press for more information, not now. There was work to do.

'What are we actually doing here, then?' Clarke queried.

'Peter Kelsey, he may turn up here.'

Sue Clarke screwed up her face. 'You're joking! We've heard he's headed for Portugal. That's what his wife told us. She was caught stealing a handbag in Selfridges, and not Miss Selfridge on the High Street, but Oxford Street, London.'

'Now you're joking?'

'No. She had her credit card declined and threw a hissy fit, said it was all a mistake, and was asked to leave. She came back an hour later and was caught with the bag up her jacket. West End Central turned up and told her the bag was the least of her worries, and once the hysterics had stopped, she told them about the house in Portugal, in the Algarve.'

'Right, let's go.'

'But what *are* we doing here? I mean, Jack . . . this is the last place he'll be.'

'Edward Havilland thought he might turn up here. He said it was just a hunch. But it was his first thought, and no one knows Kelsey better than Havilland.'

'Not even his wife?'

'*Especially* his wife. Because Havilland and Kelsey are hooked on the same drug.'

Frost and Clarke made their way into the packed

betting ring where the bookies were shouting the odds for the next race, trying to attract the punters, and where the tic-tac men stood high on their boxes waving their arms about in the coded semaphore used to shift money around the ring. At the height of the betting, it really was as fraught and fast-paced as the trading floor of the London or New York Stock Exchange. Frost could see how men like Kelsey could get caught up in the excitement and buzz of it, and lose their soul in the pursuit of the big, easy money. Or maybe it was just the times they were in. Greed, if not quite good yet, was certainly acceptable. Everyone was hooked. It was the new high. And for men like Kelsey and Havilland, it was proving a lethal drug.

'She's on the move,' said Clarke, as Melody Price, in her head-to-toe furs like a predatory animal, slinked off her box and was soon lost in the crowd.

The two detectives picked their way through the throng of punters to George Price's pitch. It was now manned by two new employees, and not out of the George Price and Jimmy Drake old school of grizzled cigar-chomping, Crombie-coated, trilby-topped book-ies. They were young and sleek in sharp suits and striped shirts, and they wore their hair slicked back with gel.

'Where's Melody gone?' asked Frost.

'Who wants to know?' countered the one now doing Jimmy Drake's job.

Frost pulled out his warrant card. 'I do, sunshine.'

'Powdering her nose.'

'Where's her *bodyguard*?'

419

'Keith? He's at home, we look after Melody at the races.'

'Is that right?' Frost wiped the smirks off their faces by snapping shut the bookie's satchel and tearing the list of runners off the board. 'I suggest you two boys go home, because today she's going to need a bit more muscle than Wham!'

Frost commandeered the Walkman-sized cassette player used for recording the bets and told Clarke to wait there, in case he missed Melody, then made his way up to the grandstand concourse.

It didn't take long – Frost spotted Melody right by the ladies' loo. But even so, he spotted her too late. She was pressed against the wall, and it was Peter Kelsey who was doing the pressing. He didn't actually have a hand on her, but his six-foot-three presence loomed intimidatingly over her, and she was justifiably terrified. Kelsey was wearing a peaked cap with the rim pulled down as low as it would go, and a pair of silver-framed aviator sunglasses – he was doing a good job of covering as much of his face as possible. But it was unmistakably him. Kelsey's hands were pressing down in the pockets of a black trench coat, not his signature Burberry, and Frost could only imagine what he was holding – a gun, a knife, an orange-twine garrotte; any one would be sufficient for the *ex*-Rimmington superintendent, and killer.

What had started as a wild hunch was now a stark reality. And Frost realized that he had little more on

420

him than a sharp pencil to tackle Peter Kelsey with. And it was too late. Kelsey had gripped Melody by the arm and was marching her towards the exit.

'Jack! Over here—' started to yell Melody Price, who had spied him through the shifting wall of the crowd.

Kelsey hissed at her to be quiet as, alerted by her cry, he spotted Frost, too.

That was the last thing Frost needed. He wanted to put out a call to all officers in the area, summon a fire-arms unit, secure the place. Do the right thing. Do what Superintendent Peter Kelsey would have done before he turned rotten.

On the teeming concourse, a corridor seemed to open up like the Red Sea, or that's how it felt for Frost, and maybe for Kelsey, too. What happened next unfolded almost in slow motion; just how it had played out the last time Frost had taken a bullet. Kelsey's grip tight-ened around Melody's arm, and his other hand pulled the gun from his coat pocket, a Beretta 92 semi-automatic, then quickly pocketed it again. He'd stopped by the entrance to the bar, to make sure that the detect-ive clocked the pistol.

They both stood looking at each other for what seemed like an interminable amount of time, at least for Frost. It wasn't even a Mexican stand-off, because the sharp pencil he had in his pocket was no match for a loaded gun. So he moved first, and he gestured to a table that had become available near the counter. Kelsey nod-ded, and practically dragged Melody over to the table and dumped her in a chair. Frost joined them.

'Jesus, Jack, what the hell—'

In unison, Frost and Kelsey both told her to shut up, or words to that effect. Melody got the message. It took a moment for the two men to adjust to their new circumstances.

Peter Kelsey spoke first: 'This is a bloody mess.'

'It is. And it needs resolving as quickly and as peaceably as possible . . . sir.'

'*Sir?*' Kelsey laughed.

'Do you gentlemen really need me here, if you're going to resolve it? Give you a bit of privacy?'

They both gave her looks that again shut her up.

'I called you "sir" because you're still my superior officer, and I'm sure I don't need to tell you what to do. Even now, with all that's happened, I think you know what the right thing to do is. But you need to act fast, surrender. I've called this in and armed officers will be here soon, if they're not already—'

'Forget it, Jack. I don't think you've done anything of the sort. I saw your face, you've been caught with your trousers down.'

Frost tried to resolutely laugh off the suggestion, but of course, Kelsey was right. 'Mind if I smoke? Don't worry, all I've got in my pocket is a pencil.'

Kelsey gave him a nod. Frost reached into his jacket pocket to retrieve the French ciggies – and whilst he was in there, he took the trouble to turn on the tape recorder. He offered the Gitanes to Kelsey, who refused with a sour laugh.

'I see you've been talking to Eddie Havilland. He

422

lives over in France half the year, which makes another reason he's unfit for his job.'

'Yes, me and Winston did chat.'

'That's right, Frost, *Winston*. Very clever, you worked it out. How about me?'

'Socks. As in, sweaty sock – Jock. Put that together with your liking for colourful argyle socks.'

'George and Harry, a pair of flash cockney bastards, got a stupid name for everyone. What did Eddie tell you?'

'He gave me a tape. I saw you on it, in a hotel room, with a couple of girls, neither of whom looked like your wife. Snorting cocaine. All pretty tame, sort of thing that makes the headlines seemingly every day; but career-ending for a copper nonetheless. And as for Havilland, his proclivities did run to the—'

'Disgusting?'

'There's no accounting for tastes. Right, Melody?'

'I'm not saying a word until I can speak to my lawyer.'

Kelsey whipped out the gun and shoved it in her ribs. She went to scream, but Kelsey, with his free hand, grabbed at the back of her neck and squeezed it. 'You'll tell Detective Inspector Frost everything, or I'll blow you away right here, right now!'

'OK . . . OK . . .'

Melody Price regained her composure and told her tale. George Price had been running high-stakes card games at some hotels in the Denton area, and in other locations where he regularly worked the races. To liven

423

things up, and keep the punters happy, there was plenty of food and booze, and Harry Baskin spiced it up further when he started to provide 'hostesses' in the form of girls from his club. Then Melody came on to the scene, and she turned up the heat even more with drugs, cocaine. The devil's dandruff, the marching powder, was making its presence felt and was thought of as a harmless party drug, almost socially acceptable in certain circles. Its price made it the drug of choice for the moneyed elite. Of course, it was Eamon Hogan who supplied the drugs.

Once Melody had married George Price, the Dublin gangster, who already fixed races in Ireland and had his hooks into some Irish bookies, sensed a real opportunity with George. And once Hogan found out who attended some of the big-money private games, namely Kelsey and Havilland, he saw even more opportunities. He could blackmail a councillor and a top copper and have them in his back pocket. It was perfect for his future plans to relocate to the British mainland.

And this is where Melody really excelled; the ex-porn star, who'd worked both in front of the camera and behind it, knew all about hidden cameras and how to secrete them in hotel rooms. Soon they had the *Citizen Kane* of blackmail footage: Kelsey snorting cocaine and enjoying three-in-a-bed romps; and Havilland, well, Havilland splashing around in the bathroom with two very well-paid girls who were willing to test the waters of his depravity for the right money. Either way, now the two public servants were not only under the cosh

424

with their gambling debts, but well and truly on the hook with Eamon Hogan.

Click!

Melody stopped talking and Kelsey turned towards Frost as the tape came to an end.

Kelsey shook his head and tutted, 'You'd make a lousy undercover copper, not like your little friend Eve Hayward.'

Frost reached into his bomber jacket and put the tape recorder on the table.

Kelsey considered the device. Then, with his free hand, he adroitly turned over the C60 cassette and pressed record. 'Good idea, Frost, get it all down. I need . . . I need to tell you everything so . . . so it's on the record in my own words. First off, just a small thing in the greater scheme of things: I gave Eamon Hogan the details of the jewellery job in Rimmington. I hid vital evidence that would have pointed directly to his gang. Then George, George Price . . .' He started to laugh.

Melody Price glared at him. Before she could say anything, Frost asked, 'What's so funny?'

The brittle laughter quickly stopped. 'I'm sorry. I just thought, you probably think I took his day's takings to make it look like robbery. Being a copper, throwing you off the scent. And I suppose I did, or at least that's what I told myself. But in reality, I took the money because I genuinely needed it. By then I was just a common, desperate thief, really.'

'I never thought it was a robbery. Or if it was, it was

425

carried out by a rank amateur. George Price had on him a watch and gold money clip that were worth more than what was in his bag. Also, how fortuitous for the robbers for George to happen to park up in that spot.'

'I arranged to meet him there, but I didn't plan on shooting him. I just wanted to reason with him. I wanted the tapes. I told him to hand them over, or burn them, just get rid of them. I was practically begging him. He just sat there in his car . . . smirking . . . like I was dirt on his shoes. We used to be friends, or at least that's what I thought. But I was just an easy mark for him, a gambling addict, a money tap that he wasn't prepared to turn off. Not once did he try and stop me getting in deeper and deeper. He owned me lock, stock—'

'I take it he refused to give you them.'

'He said he'd think about it. But Eddie was right, he knew it was useless trying to reason with them. They would always keep a copy, just in case. It was a sword of Damocles hanging over our heads . . .' Kelsey's free hand again gripped the back of Melody's neck, and she expelled a whimper of fear. 'This bitch would make sure of that!'

'Jack! Do something!' she gasped, her terrified eyes bulging.

'Easy, Superintendent Kelsey, easy. So when George Price refused, you shot him?'

'Good work, Frost – remind me of my rank, keep me talking? Right?'

'Not for me, for you. Like you said, your wife, your family, you want to tell them.'

426

Melody breathed a sigh of relief as Kelsey took the pressure off her neck.

'I thought I'd killed him. If I had, maybe I wouldn't have killed the others . . . Jimmy Drake and Little Stevie. I caused pain . . . I know that. I killed two men . . . two people. For that I'm truly, truly sorry.'

'Two?'

'Yes . . . that's all.'

'Young Dean Bartlett and Gavin Ross? How about them?'

Frost watched as Kelsey swallowed hard. His mirrored lenses reflected the detective's face, and he couldn't hide his contempt. Whatever decency, whatever copper there was left in him, Kelsey was feeling it now, feeling it finally die. He didn't have the answers for the madness, for what he'd unleashed, and Frost suspected there wasn't enough tape to capture how he'd withered into the hollow man he had become.

Kelsey made a gasping sound, like he was trying to catch his breath. 'I need a drink. My throat's dry. A wee dram. That will get me talking, a nice glass of Scotch.'

Frost glanced over to the bar; the latest race had started so it wasn't too busy. He stood up.

Melody looked alarmed. 'You're not leaving me, Jack?'

Kelsey urged him on. 'She'll be fine. No more, it's over.'

'Then why don't you give me the gun?'

'Don't push it. What difference would one more make, right here at the races? Poetic justice, this is

427

where I lost most of it. Now, are you going to get me that bloody drink?'

Frost raised his hands in a placating gesture, then went to the bar and ordered three whiskies. He wanted a Hamlet cigar, but realized that would be pushing his luck. The drinks came. A thought struck him: what Havilland had said about a genuine suicide needing privacy, otherwise it's just a cry for help . . . Kelsey had spent an age looking at that tape recorder before he turned it on . . . Is that when he'd decided to kill . . . *Christ* . . .

He left the drinks on the counter and ran back over to the empty table. There was a commotion outside the bar, and he heard from some way off Melody Price scream, 'Get off me!'

On the concourse, there was a scrum of people now returning to the bar, and as he forced his way through the crowd, he saw Melody Price sprawled on the floor with Sue Clarke astride her, putting on the handcuffs.

'I came up to see what was taking you so long, and saw Lady Muck here running off, so I grabbed her, and she whacked me and tried to get away—'

Frost took a fistful of Melody's hair, pulled it hard and barked, 'Where's Kelsey?'

'The men's!'

Frost ran towards the toilet, and he saw two, three, four men running out of it, scared, just like if a madman with a gun had rushed in and emptied the place. Frost went in.

Peter Kelsey, with his aviator sunglasses and peaked

428

cap now discarded on the floor, was standing in front of the mirror. Tears streamed down his red mottled cheeks. His face was distorted with torment, guilt, self-loathing, and it was tearing him apart. On seeing Frost he turned sharply towards him and raised the gun.

Clarke handed Melody over to uniform, and made her way towards the panicked crowd on the concourse who were gathered near the men's toilet. Two more uniformed coppers who were on duty at the races joined her. Clarke told the crowd to move away, it was police business. She stopped dead when she heard the sharp crack of the gun being fired.

Three Days Later

Frost was at Denton General. He'd just parked up the Metro when he saw PC David Simms, in his civvies, walking out of the hospital with a pretty blonde. Frost recognized her as the nurse who'd come to the young PC's aid with the bedpan and seen off Bad Manners Bob. Good for Simms, thought Frost.

He collected his tin of Quality Street off the passenger seat and made his way into the hospital. He'd been spending too much time in this place of late, he thought, but there was only one person he wanted to visit today – DS John Waters. His friend and colleague was now officially off the critical list and stable. The other patient of note, George Price, had had his operation earlier in the day and was expected to make a full recovery – just as Sandy Lane had fictitiously reported. But what a changed world George Price would wake up to. His best friend, Jimmy Drake, was dead and his wife, Melody,

430

was now at an undisclosed location being paid for by the government and about to start a new life without him, under a new identity.

Melody Price, her survival instincts fully functioning and ready to spring into action the minute she felt the net closing in, had cut a deal with Eve Hayward and the serious crime team in London. The minute she was nicked she told them she could give them Eamon Hogan.

To achieve this, they had to work fast. She was to be a honey trap, a role she was perfectly suited to. Melody called Hogan that very day, before the end of the last race at Radleigh Park, and informed him of what had happened to Peter Kelsey. The story she told was: Jack Frost had confronted Peter Kelsey at the races. Kelsey had admitted he'd shot George, and killed Jimmy and a thief called Little Stevie. Melody said she reckoned that Kelsey had gone there to confront her, probably kill her for her part in the blackmail. Kelsey, obviously unhinged, managed to get away from Jack Frost and run into the men's toilets, where he then shot himself in the head.

Of course, that bit was true. But what she neglected to tell the Irish gangster was her part in it, and the fact that Frost had her full confession on tape, a confession that now put the powerful puppet master, Hogan, at the very centre of the whole criminal conspiracy.

Melody cooed down the phone to Hogan about how upset she was – what if Kelsey had managed to get to her? The shock of his violence and how close she'd come to getting killed by that maniac copper had spooked her; it had made her realize how short life was and how precious each moment was, and she didn't want to be alone tonight. And with George expected to make a full recovery and be home soon, this was their only window of opportunity, and she was desperate to see him, for old times' sake. With her tearful quivering voice still managing to sound coquettish and sexy, it was an award-winning performance from her. Eamon Hogan said he had been waiting for this call for years. They arranged to meet at an anonymous-looking motel off a main road some twenty miles from Denton.

And it was there that a masked firearms unit arrested him, with some twenty officers being involved. Eamon Hogan was carrying a gun equipped with a silencer; a large carving knife and a roll of tarpaulin were found in the boot of his car. It wasn't clear if the ruthless and suspicious gangster had gone there to make love to Melody Price or to kill her. Or maybe both.

This is what Frost was pondering as he made his way down the hospital corridor. Then he spied a figure at the other end of it, outside John Waters' ward.

'Hello, Jack.'

'How are you, Eve?'

'Tired.'

They went over and sat down on the orange plastic chairs. Frost opened the tin of Quality Street and offered them to her. She selected a blue one. Frost raised an eyebrow at this choice, and mulled over whether this was a good thing or a bad thing. Good, because it would leave the pink and orange ones to him, or bad, because

432

it suggested that her taste was suspect. He erred on the side of caution, and decided it was a good thing – after all, he told himself, who the hell am I to be so picky?

'I went by Eagle Lane to say goodbye to Sue, drop off an Action Man for her little boy.'

'It's not one of those cheap knock-offs, I hope?'

She laughed. 'No, he's a proper one. Got a beard to cover the little scar on his cheek. And to see Superintendent Mullett and the rest of your team, thank them for all their hard work and help. They said you were at home, but the dragon lady at the Jade Rabbit said you'd moved out?'

'I did, yesterday. I'm now living in paradise with a bird.' Jason Kingly had handed over the keys to the flat on a gentleman's agreement that Frost would proceed with its purchase pronto.

Eve Hayward's eyes widened, and Frost swore he could detect a little tremble in her bottom lip, which she quelled by forcing out a smile and muttering something along the lines of, 'Oh, that's nice.'

Jack Frost smiled right back at her. 'I never told you about my bird. He's blue, a Norwegian Blue. But they say that about all blue parrots. I suspect he was actually born within the sound of Bow bells, what with all the cockney rhyming slang he comes out with.'

'I'm intrigued.'

'I was rather hoping you would be.'

Acknowledgements

Thanks to: Frankie Gray, Natasha Barsby, Elisabeth Merriman, Phil Patterson, and Emlyn Rees for the tip.

Read the previous books in the series . . .

FIRST FROST
by James Henry

A *Sunday Times* Top 10 Bestseller

Denton, 1981. Britain is in recession, the
IRA is becoming increasingly active and the
country's on alert for an outbreak of rabies.

Detective Jack Frost is working under his mentor and
inspiration DI Bert Williams, and coping badly
with his increasingly strained marriage.

But DI Williams is nowhere to be seen.
So when a 12-year-old girl goes missing from a
department store changing room, DS Frost is
put in charge of the investigation . . .

'*Not only a gripping mystery, but an exclusive look
at Jack Frost's early years*'
David Jason

'*The success of* First Frost *is incontestable. This is a
palpable hit . . . [a] dark, but glittering pearl*'
Barry Forshaw, *Independent*

FATAL FROST
by James Henry

May, 1982. Britain celebrates the sinking of the *Belgrano*, Princess Diana welcomes the birth of her first child and Denton Police Division welcomes its first black policeman, DC Waters – recently relocated from Bethnal Green.

While the force is busy dealing with a spate of local burglaries, the body of fifteen-year-old Samantha Evans is discovered in woodland next to the nearby railway track. Then a fifteen-year-old boy is found dead on Denton's golf course, his organs removed.

Detective Sergeant Jack Frost is sent to investigate – a welcome distraction from troubles at home. And when the murdered boy's sister goes missing, Frost and Waters must work together to find her . . . before it's too late.

'*I can't recommend it highly enough*'
Martina Cole

'*A palpable hit*'
Independent

FROST AT MIDNIGHT

By James Henry

August, 1983. Denton is preparing for a wedding, with less than a week to go until Detective Sergeant Waters marries Kim Myles. But the Sunday before the big day, the body of a young woman is found in the churchyard. Their idyllic wedding venue has become a crime scene.

As best man to Waters, **Detective Inspector Jack Frost** has a responsibility to solve the mystery before the wedding. But with nowhere to live since his wife's family sold the matrimonial home, Frost's got other things on his mind.

Can he put his own troubles aside and step up to be the detective they need him to be?

'One of the most successful ventriloquial acts in crime writing'
Financial Times